My ot

My short stories are:

The Tall Boy (story no.1) is part of a trilogy. The other stories being:

2. The box, the ring and le calmar.
3. Just the ticket

These stories range from WW2 to modern day.

My stand alone short story is:

Fools Gold - A bullion heist story

My other book is:

As luck would have it - A story of one man's journey from riches to rags and then what happens next

All of the above short stories are what I like to call 'commuting stories', as they are short enough to be read whilst on a journey. The book will take a little longer. It's probably about one week's worth of commuting.

The trilogy can be read by any age group, while from 'Fools Gold' onwards these are primarily aimed at an adult audience.

All are available on Amazon.

Dedication

This book is dedicated to all those who,
not of their own choosing, are alone.

Prologue

He stepped through the front door of the Belgravia mews house and straight into the sunlight of a beautiful spring morning. It was a little chilly, but otherwise perfect.

Considering this was the centre of London, the UK's largest sprawling metropolis, it was blissfully quiet, almost. Just the sweet sound of birds singing in the gardens opposite, the gentle woosh of a passing aircraft and the distant hum of traffic.

He tripped lightly down the three steps and toward the gate. He was in the peak of physical and mental health and generally felt good, for the first time in a long time. After all, although he was already extremely physically fit, he had just completed the most intensive mental training of his life. Had he not, he probably wouldn't have been quite so immediately aware of an out of place noise that pierced the silence and was approaching fast from his right. It was a motorbike and it had mounted the pavement just a few metres away from him. It headed straight for him as he was about to walk through the gateway and on to the pavement.

With catlike agility he leapt back, grabbed the tops of the two gate posts and swung his legs up, all within a split second. His legs thrust forward and came into contact with the motorcyclist, at thigh level. The impact was enough to force the rider and bike off course and straight into the rear of a parked car. The impact between the bike and car was enough to cause the rider to be thrown over the roof and onto the bonnet.

As soon as his feet came back into contact with the ground the phone in his inner breast pocket rang. His instincts were now pulling him in two directions. Grab the motorbike rider or grab the phone. Decision made, he quickly crossed the road to distance himself from the scene of the crime and answered the phone. After all, the rider didn't look like he would be going anywhere soon.

"K." He answered as instructed.

"Well done. First test passed. Loss.Scope.Left."

The phone went dead.

He moved rapidly away from the mews, checking that all was clear. Then, prior to disposing of the burner phone, he checked the destination of the replacement, which would always be one hundred squares west and one hundred squares south of the what3words code given. The code was also reversed for good measure. It was calculated that this should keep any would be eaves droppers at bay, for long enough to evade discovery anyway.

'K' had an app. on his phone that would work all of this out, so that all he had to do was go to the what3words square that actually appeared on his screen.

Before carrying on with his morning, he took one last quick look back toward the carnage and briefly mused at the fact that the whole stunt had been set up to test him.

A few moments later the rider slid off the bonnet, dusted himself off and collected the bike, which he rested on its side stand before walking away. The stuntman's departure from the bike had been choreographed perfectly. A recovery truck was already on its way to collect the car and bike.

A small crowd had gathered and one person asked the rider if he wanted any of the emergency services. He declined the offer gracefully and proceeded to walk away. The crowd dissipated in a collective daze. The whole scene had been surreal. No one had noticed K as he melted into the foliage on the far side of the street.

'I'm famished.' K thought to himself, so he headed for his favourite cafe. He would collect his new phone on the way.

Ages 7-15

Chapter 1

"**K**evin!" Miss Thompson's voice floated through the ether and fluttered gently into Kevins consciousness. In reality, she had just shouted at him, as yet again he was daydreaming.

"Yes Miss?" Enquired Kevin, in all innocence.

"Kevin, this really won't do. You must pay attention or you won't learn anything".

"I was paying attention to most of it, Miss."

"Really, then repeat any of what you've heard."

"What do you mean Miss?"

"I mean, tell me what I've just said. Anything at

all would be good."

There was a general titter around the classroom.

Although life at home was grim, Kevin generally enjoyed his time at the very nineteen sixties, utilitarian style, East End junior school. It had good friends, wholesome food, which sometimes even tasted alright, a playground and a field. It allowed him to escape from all that lay in wait at home. Unfortunately escapism for Kevin quite often meant drifting off during classroom time, as well.

"I can't Miss. I can't remember what you said. I'm sorry
Miss."

Miss Thompson was well aware of Kevin's home life. It wasn't pleasant. He had it very tough and for that reason she always tried to be reasonable, whilst showing no favouritism with him while he was in class. The problem, as ever, was trying to strike that balance in front of the rest of the children.

"Could you please come and see me after class?"
"Yes Miss." Kevin knew that he was in for another 'good talking to.' After all, it happened at least twice a week. He could take it. He was made of sterner stuff.

Kevin was a scrawny lad with dark wavy and usually unkempt, hair. He had intense brown eyes that always felt to anyone on the receiving end of a stare, as if they were penetrating them. He was naturally inquisitive and wasn't shy about asking questions, but unfortunately that kind of enthusiasm wasn't reflected in his school work.

Something of Kevin's school uniform was always ill fitting, whether it be his shoes, his shirt or his blazer and none of it was particularly clean, yet through all of this he was generally of an upbeat disposition, that was until something or someone, upset him.

Even though Kevin was only seven, he had become very adept at looking after himself. He had to in all reality.

Chapter 2

The terraces of small grey brick houses stood in endless rows, each identical to the neighbour. Most still had the outside privy at the end of the garden, although they also now had an indoor toilet with the privies long since being used as garden sheds. Everybody knew each other by name and everyone knew everyone elses business.

Alfies backyard overlooked Kevins, but that's where the similarities ended both between the two boys and their respective homes. Alfie's home, although identical in size and shape, to Kevins, was immaculate. Kevins was a tip. Alfie was what was known as a swat and on bad days at school, he was known and ridiculed as the teacher's pet. Kevin on the other hand was smart but lazy and ill disciplined. There were few words that could accurately describe Kevin, his home or more amazingly, why Alfie was drawn to him.

Alfie lived with his Mum. His Dad had died when he was only three and therefore Alfie had no real recollection of him. He only remembered what his mother had told him, which was that his father was a decent man who always did the best that he could for the family. She also made it quite clear that because his father never aspired to much academically and therefore never earnt a great deal, they would never have the chance to move away 'from this hell hole', as she always described it.

For this reason alone, Alfie's Mum wanted much better for him and his little sister. Education came above all else, therefore hanging around with boys 'like that Kevin from over the back', was very much discouraged. Regardless of his Mum's feelings, Alfie always felt sorry for Kevin because even at their tender young age, he was well aware of Kevin's home life. This was mainly due to the fact that it could generally be heard, above all the other noise, coming from over the garden fence.

Alfie did study as his mother requested, but he also befriended Kevin and that wasn't easy. He had to earn Kevins trust and the way that he found to do this was through humour. He knew that Kevin had little to laugh about, so he found what would make him laugh and then capitalised on that. It eventually worked, but Alfie still felt a little as though Kevin was tolerating him rather than actually liking him, although he did now at least stand up for Alfie, whenever the need arose. Alfie was no fighter.

There could never be any visits to Kevin's house because his own mother would find out and that would be the end of their friendship. This was no real loss as he never particularly wanted to meet Kevin's parents. The pair would meet at the nearest park instead, where once the jocularity was out of the way, Alfie would generally try to help Kevin with any school work that he might not have understood, didn't listen to or just didn't want to ask the teacher about.

These clandestine meetings continued until they went to the senior school.

Chapter 3

In a street not too far from Kevins there lived a little girl who thought that he was the best thing since sliced bread. She shared a similar home life, but because she never got involved in fights and arguments and was generally well behaved at school, she was one of the many children who live their lives under the social radar. The school had no idea what was going on behind her front door.

Daisy Wilcox was nine when she was first sexually assaulted by her stepfather. This was something that continued until Daisy left home. It also went on with her mother knowing, but powerless or rather, too weak to intervene. She would reconcile her behaviour with the fact that it was better to be with the man you know than with no man at all. Unlike

Alfies mother, she wasn't willing to go it alone. Her new husband had, as a matter of priority, knocked whatever confidence she had, out of her.

It wasn't as if she was unattractive either, far from it. In fact Daisy had heard it said that her real dad looked like Elivis Presley. Of course she had to find pictures of the real Elvis to establish why this would be a good thing. It was just a shame that he didn't hang around once he knew that Mrs Wilcox was pregnant.

Daisy completely understood Kevin and his plight and for that reason she initially admired him from afar, as she had no idea how to approach him. Fortunately, at her age of innocence she never made any connection between what was going on at home with the fact that Kevin was a boy and therefore possibly trouble.

Eventually even Kevin could not fail to notice that he had an admirer, although he couldn't understand why this little strip of a girl would want anything to do with him. As she was very persistent he gradually let his guard down and in fact was very grateful for the friendship and the attention. After all he didn't receive either at home and if it weren't for Daisy and on occasion Alfie and also to a degree, Miss Thompson, he would have had no compassion in his life at all.

It was nice to have someone else his own age, to talk to, even if she was a girl.

On one rare occasion when Daisy had Kevin all to herself, she decided to have a proper, ten year old version of a heart to heart, talk with him.

"So Kevin, what are you going to do when you grow up?"

"I'm going to join the army, like my dad." He said with absolutely no hesitation.

"Well, if you're going to join the army, then I am too."

"Daisy, you mustn't do as I do. You must choose what to do for yourself."

"I am and I want to join the army. Someones got to look out for you." Daisy didn't mind what she did as long as it was within sight of Kevin.

"I can look out for myself thank you Daisy. I've had to do that for all of my life so far."

"I know, but we are so alike and we get on well together and we understand each other. I don't have anyone else Kevin."

Kevin's heart melted, just a tiny bit.

"Listen Daisy, if you want to join the army, that's fine by me, but I won't always be there for you. Please remember that."

"And I won't always be there for you either, but I guess we'll be somewhere near each other."

Kevin thought that Daisy was very sweet, but that she didn't understand what she was saying. There was no way that she would join the army. She was too girly.

They generally walked home together until Daisy turned into her road. She always subconsciously slowed her pace once there. Kevin always had to wait until she had turned into her front path because she would spend most of the walk going backwards and waving to him.

Once she'd gone, Kevin would walk on and then he would do exactly the same when he reached his road. There was definitely no reason to rush.

As soon as he walked through his front door, his mum started.

"You're late. Anyway go and fetch my fags, there's a love."
"Okay mum."
"Your fathers been on a bender again, so don't disturb him, right?"

Kevin didn't need telling twice. His Dad

would knock nine bells out of him if he were disturbed, while he was 'resting his eyes.'

"Yes Mum." Then after a second or two. "I can't find your fags mum. Where are they?"

"Use your fucking eyeballs son. That's what God gave them to you for."

Kevin didn't reply. He knew better. He just carried on looking for his mum's fags. Luckily he found them in her handbag and because he managed to do it quickly, he managed to avoid a beating.

"I'm hungry mum." Kevin knew what the answer was going to be, but he had to ask. If he helped himself, he would be wrong and if he asked he was wrong. Either way it made no difference to the outcome.

"So?"
"What can I eat?"
"I dunno. What's in the cupboard?"

Kevin looked. He also looked in the fridge where the only thing that they had in abundance was mould and filth. The little light had long since given up the ghost.

"There's some beans. Can I have the beans?"
"Yes of course you can. As long as you replace them." Even this was said in a

condescending way, but it was as close to being pleasant as Kevin's mum could get.

"Yes mum."

The routine was always the same. Kevin would have to steal a few bob from his mum's purse and then go to the corner shop, where he could purchase the replacement beans. For some reason, this system appeared to work.

His mum never questioned where he had got the money from. It was almost as if she condoned the theft and that she felt that she was teaching him some kind of life skill. Where this scheme fell foul was when Kevin tried to spend more than the cost of a can of beans. He had tried this once and paid the price.

Those bruises like all the others, had healed, like they always did and his ribs no longer hurt. Not that anyone else was any the wiser. Both of his parents were very adept at hitting him where it wouldn't be seen and Kevin would be punished further if he were to wince in front of anyone.

Chapter 4

"Thank you for staying behind Kevin."

"That's alright Miss. I'm in no hurry to go home."

'I bet you're not. You poor little darling'. Miss Thompson thought to herself. "Well young Kevin, what have you got to say for yourself?"

"I dunno Miss."

"Kevin, you really must pay attention, you know. I am trying to educate you and without education you will go nowhere."

"Where would I want to go, Miss? I don't know what you mean."

"I mean you won't know how to read or write or do sums and you will need to know all of those when you leave school and get a job."

"Why willI I need a job?"

"To earn money to pay for things."

"I don't need money to pay for things. I take Mum's money and if she hasn't got enough she says that I can take what I need."

"What do you mean, take what you need?"

"Well, if Mum sends me to the shop, she tells me what she needs, then I pay for what I can and just take the rest."

"Oh Kevin. That is stealing and you can get into a lot of trouble if you steal."

"I'll get into trouble if I go home without the shopping. Which one is the worst trouble, Miss?"

That last statement almost broke Miss Thompsons heart and she couldn't honestly answer Kevin's question, so she tried a different tack.

"Kevin. I'm well aware of your home life. We all are."

It was as if Miss Thompson had lit a blue touch paper and Kevin was the firework.

"What are you talking about? You know nothing. There's nothing wrong with my home life. Just leave me alone." Kevin shrieked. He then turned and ran through the classroom door.

'Well that worked a treat.' Miss Thompson

mused. 'I honestly don't know what to do.' She resolved to approach the headmistress and at least obtain the view of another person.

Chapter 5

Alfie was never going to join the army. The fact was that he didn't really know what he wanted to do, but whatever it was it definitely wasn't going to involve fighting. He'd witnessed enough of Kevin's scrapes to know that was not the path for him. His Mum wanted him to go to university and then go on to be some kind of academic.

At the grand old age of nine, none of the decisions being made on his behalf meant a thing. He didn't really even understand what an academic was. He just thought that it was some kind of teacher and he definitely didn't want to be one of them either.

Whilst over the park one evening, when they were both a year or so older, Kevin said something to Alfie that, although he couldn't appreciate it at the time, would stay with him and eventually help to set him off on his own path of destiny.

"Don't waste your life brawling like I do Alfie. Be a good person and you won't ever need to fight."

"But you're a good person Kev. You're not the one who usually starts fights. You just seem to attract them."

"That's exactly what I mean Alf. I attract trouble and there's no need for you to. You're smart, so use your brains not your fists. Do good and use your brain." This was as profound as a ten year could be and it certainly struck home with Alfie. After all, if Kevin said it, it must be right.

Alfie lost contact with his old friend when he went off to grammar school, but he never forgot the serious conversation that they'd had and the wise words proffered.

Chapter 6

As Kevin got older his temper worsened and generally he needed little excuse to get involved in a fight. He had no idea that his temperament was being nurtured, promoted and even condoned, by his father. He just thought that he was doing the right thing and therefore his dad would be proud of him.

"You're just a bully, you are and I'm telling my dad." Screamed another of Kevin's many classmates, who had succumbed to his mood swings.

"Yep, that's me and I'm not bothered who you tell." said Kevin with an air of gravitas.

Kevin had smacked the other boy in the eye. Not for any particular reason, but just because he was angry about something and therefore someone had to suffer. His dad had told him that he would feel better if he hit someone whenever he felt stressed or angry and because of his age, Kevin never thought to question yet another one of his dad's pearls of wisdom. Not that he would ever feel brave enough to question his dad anyway.

Later that day there was a knock at Kevin's front door.

"Your little brute did this to my boy." An angered parent stated, while pointing to a very distinctive black eye.

"Wow, that's what I call a bullseye. Well done Kev."

Kevin stood just behind his dad and said nothing. He didn't want to upset his father, but he also didn't feel good about what he'd done. He thought this a little odd, as situations like this had never bothered him before.

"What do you mean, well done Kev? You're supposed to be a responsible parent and teach your kids right from wrong. What your kid has done is wrong."

"Really. How could he have done it better then?" Kevin's father was enjoying this. He always did and if the conversation didn't go his way, he would just do the same to the parent as his son had to the boy.

The other boy's father grabbed his son's hand and dragged him back down the path. He didn't look back.

"You mustn't have anything to do with that boy. Do you understand?"

"Yes Dad."

"I'm going to have a word with your headmistress about him."

The pair got into their car and drove away.

Kevin's Dad just laughed and slammed the front door. He cuffed Kevin 'affectionately' around the back of the head.

As he grew older, Kevin did have to admit to himself that sometimes he couldn't understand his fathers logic. It just didn't feel right. Also, the other boys didn't seem to react in the same way whenever they were angry.

Chapter 7

7 500 miles away in the city of Ussuriysk, which is just north of Vladivostok, two young boys aged nine and ten, were sitting on a wall, in a small run down park and squabbling over a game of chess. Little did they know that when they were older their lives would be turned upside down. After all, at their age they had no idea what they'd be doing next week, let alone when they were older.

"So, Andreiv, you think that you have me do you?"

"Of course. You've already made two big mistakes and I can see that you're about to make another."

The first remark was said to make the younger player feel as if his game plan was going wrong. Mikhail knew that his sparring partner was the superior player, so sometimes he had to resort to slightly underhand tactics.

"No I haven't. It's all part of my game plan." This was said with a little uncertainty.

Andreiv was still young enough to be almost convinced when anyone older than him, even when it was only by six months and even when it was only Mikhail, said anything in an authoritative way to him.

"Andreiv, how dare you. Just remember who the senior player is here, will you?"

"Only by six months and I also know that you cheat."

Mikhail suddenly got up and knocked the chess board that had been perched on the wall between them, onto the floor. He wasn't going to be judged by a child, especially not a child who looked like he was going to win, anyway.

He stormed off, left Andreiv to pick up the pieces, rebox them and then chase after him.

The following day they were both in school and it was as if nothing had happened. They often argued, but the ill feeling never lasted longer than an hour or so.

They were both very intelligent and both excelled at science and mathematics, therefore they both tended to be in the same class for these. Even though there was a six month age difference, it just so happened that they fell into the same year at school.

Their mothers were also best friends and they used to work in the same factory. This meant that the boys even walked to school together and were dropped off at the school gates, so that their mum's could continue to the factory.

Mikhail's father worked as a road builder for the local council and Andreiv's was an office supervisor. This was sometimes seen as a bone of contention between the boys as Andreiv's dad was obviously far superior to Mikhails, after all he went to work in a collar and tie and he was a supervisor. The fact that as a road builder Mr. Kuryakin could earn overtime and bonuses and therefore far outstrip Mr. Artemyev's meagre pay was totally lost on two young boys.

They all lived in the same nineteen sixties built, extremely utilitarian looking and now run down, block of flats, albeit one floor apart.

Chapter 8

On another occasion, when Kevin was around nine years old, he waltzed into the house after school, threw what was his version of a school satchell on the stairs. It was in fact an old second world war gas mask bag that his dad had found somewhere. He then proclaimed that two paki's at school had just planted a tree for the environment. His dad handed him an ex army machete and just said: "You know what to do with that don't you son?"

Kevin innocently replied: "I know they're paki's dad, but I can't kill them."

Once his dad had stopped laughing, he just roared: "Chop the fucking tree down, you dope."

"Oh, right. I'll do it after dark."

There was never any point in questioning his father's dictats, after all he was a war hero and knew exactly how to deal with the enemy. The enemy in this case being anyone who didn't appear to be English sounding or worse still, looking.

As soon as it was dark, Kevin trotted off down the road, blissfully unaware of just how guilty he looked carrying a totally undisguised weapon. He arrived at the school perimeter fence and proceeded to climb, after throwing the machete over first.

He landed deftly on the grass, collected his weapon and proceeded toward the tree. Once he had made sure that he was at the correct tree he proceeded to unsheath the machete and it was just then that a flood light came on, shortly followed by a booming voice.

"Oy Keenan. What the 'ell do you think you're doing?" It was the school caretaker Mr Sheen, otherwise known as 'sheen the clean' or 'spick and span'.

"Nothin'." Replied Kevin. Trying lamely to hide a machete that was nearly as tall as him, behind his back.

"Come 'ere boy."

Kevin was in trouble again and as usual,

he shouldered the blame. Any punishment that the school gave him would be far more lenient than that he would receive at home. He confessed to stealing the machete from his father's bedroom and said that he just thought that it would be a laugh to chop a tree down.

Of course the headteacher didn't buy any of Kevin's story, but couldn't prove otherwise, so she just put Kevin in detention. It would be pointless to send a letter to Kevin's parents as they would never respond. They probably wouldn't even read the letter once they had seen that it was from the school.

Kevin was tasked with writing an essay on the wrongs of racism and the destruction of other people's property. He never completed the essay, but there was absolutely no point in putting him back into detention again. Not for the same misdemeanour anyway.

Punishment of any kind was a fruitless exercise as far as the school was concerned, as their powers were limited.

Chapter 9

When Kevin was eleven he left his junior school and was relocated to a different senior school. This was after a unanimous recommendation was reached by the junior school staff. The decision was based on the fact that whilst they all felt deeply sorry for the little lad, they would be glad to see the back of him. They acknowledged that whilst he would be with different teachers in the senior department, he would still be at the same school. Moving him to another school would give both them and him a fresh start. The fact that no preference had been put forward by Kevin's parents made the school's recommendation that much easier to implement.

Although once he moved to the new

school he lost contact with his old friend Alfie, Daisy did remain glued to his side, as she moved to the same school. She just bent her mother's ear until she capitulated and because Daisy's family lived in the same catchment area as Kevin's, the move was agreed.

At around the same time as Kevin changed his school he was also taken into care. He had no idea that this was even being considered. It all happened very quickly and started with another knock at the front door of his home.

It hadn't escaped the notice of the visitors, that the front garden was a tip, with a mixture of refuse, uncut grass and the remnants of a scrapped car, all present. What remained of the front fence was hanging out toward the pavement and when they approached the front door, there were two wires sticking out through the door frame where they assumed that a door bell was once affixed. As there was no knocker, they rapped on the dirty glass.

"Ah, good morning. Mrs Keenan I presume."

"Who's asking?"

"My name is Gordon Smythe and this is Miss Strachan. We're from Social Services. May we come in?"

"No, you may not come in. What do you want?"

"Well, we can discuss this on the doorstep, if you wish. We're here to discuss Kevin."

"What's that little shit done now?"

"It's not so much what he's done, although he has done some nasty things, by all accounts. It's more to do with you really."

"What about me? Kevin's mum removed the remains of her cigarette from her mouth, flicked it past the two visitors and turned to face the other way. "Doug, come here. I'm being questioned by some busybodies from the council." She thought it was time to call for backup.

Kevin's dad straightened his crumpled and dirty vest and approached the front door in as straight a line as he could muster.

"How can we help?" He said, with his attempt at a polite voice. Unfortunately it came out very slurred, so both of the Social Workers were immediately aware of his current state.

"We're here to discuss Kevin."

"What about him?" The false politeness had now been replaced by plain slurred speech.

"I'd much rather we discussed this inside, but as that clearly can't happen, I will just tell you that we have a court order and the relevant paperwork that empowers us to take Kevin into care. Do you understand?"

"'Course I do. I thought you'd never ask. I'll get his coat." With a certain amount of glee in his voice he then shouted up the stairs. "Kev, grab a bag, you're moving out."

The Social Workers weren't quite expecting it to be that easy and hadn't even had the chance to establish a potential foster family yet. However they couldn't refuse Kevin the opportunity to escape the nightmare that was his home, so they left with both him, one tatty old suitcase and what appeared to be a gas mask bag.

Kevin's last memory of home was the sound of the front door slamming behind him and the faint sound of raised voices from behind it.

If he'd have heard what the row was about it would have only served to help him know that wherever he was going was going to be better. His mother was berating his father for losing her little fag stealer, food runner and general dogsbody.

What she also knew but didn't dare mention was that any drunken beatings, as handed out by her old man, would all be coming her way from now on.

Chapter 10

N ow that Kevin was in 'big' school, fighting with other boys didn't always go to plan, especially as he now found himself at the bottom of the new school hierarchy. It didn't stop him from standing his ground however and he didn't care how big or old his adversaries were. Of course even Kevin couldn't hope to win all the time especially when put up against a much larger foe and sometimes more than one. Win or lose the very fact that he never backed down earned him a level of respect from his peers.

There was one boy in particular who always tried to make Kevins life even more miserable than it was already. He carried out all sorts of subversive stunts, from hiding Kevins PE kit to stealing his homework, not that

Kevin often submitted any. Subversive or not, Kevin knew who the perpetrator was, as his adversary wasn't blessed with a huge amount of intelligence and generally managed to leave some kind of calling card, his personal odour being chief among them.

The lad's name was Trevor Edwards and he was two years Kevin's senior. He was very overweight for his age and he was a couple of inches taller than Kevin. He had a terrible acne problem and an unhealthy sheen that made him look like he'd been waxed. Like Kevin, he also had a father who didn't take kindly to being told that his little Trevor had lost a fight.

The main reason for Trevor's dislike of Kevin, other than the fact that he could earn some brownie points with his dad, if he beat Kevin up, was the fact that he had a soft spot for Daisy and he very much didn't appreciate the fact that she clearly favoured Kevin.

Kevin was well aware of Trevors feelings for Daisy and also of his dislike for him. He wasn't particularly phased by either, but in the main he did not try to exacerbate the situation. After all in Kevin's mind Trevor was just an irritant, albeit a rather large one.

Typically, on the rare occasion when Kevin felt like teasing his slow and built more for comfort than speed adversary, the scenario would be something similar to this:

"Oy Keenan."

Kevin would keep walking and ignore Trevor. He knew that Trevor wouldn't give up his pursuit, whilst it remained at this speed. In fact he knew that it would only serve to wind Trevor up more, so he'd just carry on.

"Come 'ere you twat."

Kevin would slow down just enough to make Trevor think that he was getting within touching distance and then he would break into a trot. Trevor would break into a sweat.

"I'm going to get you Keenan and when I do ……….."

"Up yours." Kevin would shout while showing a single digit. He would then disappear around the nearest corner and head for his newest home. He would then be on his guard for a few days to await his fate.

Trevor could never catch Kevin, so he would then try and think up some subversive way to punish Kevin. One that didn't involve physical effort, hence the homework stealing etc.

Chapter 11

Daisy and Alfie both sailed through senior school or in Alfies case, Grammar school, without too much trauma. They both did very well with their final exams and they were both confident that they could do well at whatever they chose when they left school.

Alfie would be going on to University of course because it was his mother's wish. Daisy had no intention of going to university, but in her own way she did believe in her abilities. She was still intent on joining the army, if that was what Kevin was going to do. Unlike Alfie she didn't need to worry about her decision not to go to university as she didn't get any kind of academic support from her mother and she couldn't care less what her step dad thought.

The only real problem that Daisy had while at senior school was that of fending off unwanted admirers, but she could be fairly ruthless in this regard as she had a step father at home who warranted this kind of behaviour, but never got it because she was afraid of him. She took out some of her frustration on ugly, spotty boys instead.

Alfie continued to be a swat, although he did accumulate a small but exclusive circle of friends, unlike when he was in the infants school. He found that most children who attended the grammar school either naturally wanted to aspire to greatness or were being driven to this by their parents. This meant that he fitted in with most, rather than being on the outside looking in as he had before.

Chapter 12

Kevin spent from the ages of eleven to sixteen in care. He was moved from family to family, with the same report from each. They couldn't really handle him and his reaction to any form of punishment was to just 'suck it up' and then carry on as if nothing had happened. He was becoming a feral child and no amount of discipline was altering that course. He was prone to bouts of temper, swearing and a general lack of respect for his elders.

The only redeeming characteristics that Kevin appeared to demonstrate were that he did appear to know right from wrong with regard to moral behaviour, even though this had never been taught at home. He also appeared to be fiercely patriotic for someone so young, but this could sometimes lead to problems of its own.

The patriotism stemmed from the tall stories told to him by his father, who had served in the army himself, prior to being dishonourably discharged for violence toward a commanding officer, among other things. Of course, Kevin was never told about the dishonourable discharge and always thought that his dad was some kind of hero. He naturally thought that he had just left when his term was complete.

He was also told by his mum, that his fathers drink problem had started because of the stress caused by seeing action in the army. A few years later he was to find that this was a million miles from the truth also.

While he was still a young teenager, one of his early sets of foster parents suggested that he might like to take up boxing, so they took him along to a club for an initial assessment. He said that he loved the look of it and that he'd give it a go.

After six weeks, a call came through from the boxing coach. He said that Kevin was very confident and totally unphased by the size of his opponent, but that he would be better placed if he channelled his particular skill set through martial arts. Evidently Kevin felt the need to involve his feet and any other peripheral part of his body that could be used as a weapon. He did understand that he should only use his fists when boxing, but felt compelled to defend himself in any way that he could.

Fortunately there was a Kung Fu class that was held in the local community centre each week, so Kevin was enrolled. He loved this even more than boxing. After all, he could now use his whole body for fighting without fear of breaking any rules or so he thought. At least he was no longer limited to only using his fists.

Initially everything was going to plan and for once in his life Kevin appeared to be listening and learning. He absorbed all that was taught and put what he'd learned into practice. This was until one poor lad took an extra beating for what seemed to be, no apparent reason. The lad's name was Hamish and Kevin took an immediate dislike to him because he had a funny accent and definitely wasn't English.

The Kung Fu master separated the boys and took Kevin to one side.

"Kevin, you must control your anger. Anger and violence do not achieve anything because they are uncontrolled emotions. In fact they take control of you, right at the very time when you must remain in control."

"But he's a foreigner and we don't want foreigners here." Kevin said proudly.

"What makes Hamish a foreigner, Kevin?"

"He's not British, is he." Said in a self righteous manner and as a statement, not a question. "He's got a foreign name and he has a dodgy accent."

The master explained that where someone comes from doesn't make them a bad person. He also said that in fact Hamish was Scottish and that Scotland was indeed a part of the British Isles. Once the explanation was over he made Kevin apologise to Hamish and shake his hand.

For once, this was all explained in such a way that Kevin actually paid attention and understood. He couldn't understand why, but the master commanded respect and Kevin gave him the respect that was due. This was a special power that, so far throughout Kevin's short life, only the martial arts master and one other person, had been shown to have. The former owner of this power being his old teacher Miss Thompson.

Of course he didn't really know what the

definition of respect was, he just knew that he was happy to be in the presence of these two people and when he was happy he listened. Where Miss Thompson fell short was merely by virtue of the fact that she couldn't knock seven bells out of Kevin, should she want to.

When this particular session was over the master held Kevin back and as well as imparting some more of his own wisdom, he took the time and trouble to listen to Kevin's story. Kevin likewise decided that the master would understand and so he told his story. The master was visibly shocked and he still didn't know half of it. He believed that the best way forward was to give Kevin something positive to hang on to.

"You have a rare talent Kevin. You are a natural born fighter and if you keep this up, one day you could become a master."

Kevin couldn't really believe what he was hearing and thought that the master was just trying to make him feel better after what had obviously been a disastrous evening. However the master hadn't finished.

"Fighting should always be a last resort, so what you need to do is channel your skill and only use it either in self defence or in the defence of an innocent bystander. At the moment, you are letting your ability control you."

"I do understand, I think."

"Together we can work on turning that around, if you desire that."

These words and others that followed from the master, resonated with Kevin as young as he was. This was the first time in his life that someone had bothered to educate him in a way that meant something, something tangible, something that he understood and therefore in a way that he would try and live up to. This was something that continued throughout Kevins time at Kung Fu.

Without being told as much, Kevin began to understand that his father was a racist and that he wasn't quite the man that he had always led him to believe. This discovery shook him initially, as he felt that he was losing a hero. However this emotion was soon replaced by a feeling of loathing for his dad and a feeling of great admiration for his martial arts teacher.

This was the closest Kevin had ever got to the feeling of parental love.

Chapter 13

Daisy didn't have the advantage of being taken into care. She had to continue with her dreadful homelife, in the same way she always had done. For her there was no way out.

The only two small concessions that she had were the that as she grew older she became very adept at avoiding her home and especially her step dad. She learnt very early on that she couldn't confide in her mother. The other concession was that she had managed to stay in contact with Kevin and they had become like brother and sister, even as Kevin was continually on the move. He found that he needed her as much as she needed him.

Consequently as soon as Kevin joined

the boxing club, Daisy joined and much to everyone's surprise, not least of which Kevin's, Daisy was good, very good. What Kevin couldn't know was that every time Daisy stepped into the ring, she only had to picture her step father as her opponent and she would be on fire.

Daisy also followed Kevin to Kung Fu. He never encouraged her or in all honesty, wanted her to join these clubs, but he was glad she was there, especially as she seemed to enjoy them and she was good.

They travelled together and went home together. That was until the journey meant that they had to part in order to reach their respective destinations.

In all this time they had never even held hands. That was the last thing on Kevins mind, but the first on Daisy's.

Chapter 14

Alfie did extremely well at school and while he didn't aspire to become an academic he did find most of his lessons easy, especially mathematics and english. His little sister also did well, but this was really because she had to, as she was following in his footsteps and everyone kept reminding her about how well he was doing.

Every now and then Alfie would think of Kevin and wonder how he was doing. Not only had they each gone to different schools, but Alfie had heard that Kevin had been fostered and therefore had no idea where his old friend now lived.

He never saw Daisy either, but that didn't come as any surprise as he knew that wherever his old friend was, she wouldn't be too far away. He did know where Daisy lived but didn't feel good about going round there and asking her where Kevin was. He didn't want her to think that he was missing his mate. That would make him look weak. Not only that but because Kevin was continually on the move, Alfie would be forever popping round to ask where his friend was now. 'Kevin's probably got a new bunch of mates.' Alfie would think, when he needed to make himself feel better about his inability to put the effort in.

He had no idea that they would meet again later in life and that Kevin would once again have a need of Alfie's excellent brain.

Chapter 15

Kevin climbed the ranks of Kung fu in record time. No one from his centre had ever achieved the black belt status in the same time scales. He lived and breathed Kung fu and spent whatever time he could at the centre, either learning or helping to teach the novices.

What Kevin was learning, along with the physical aspects of his chosen martial art, was the theological and therefore for him, the calming and thought provoking side. He learnt to control his temper and he learnt other values such as leadership, commitment and loyalty. He even began to understand the power of communication over fighting, when the opportunity arose.

Kevin's young life was turning around slowly, but only because of the effort that he and his mentor were putting in.

Needless to say, his shadow followed him through the ranks and whilst Daisy never quite had that killer instinct, she was still by far the best girl fighter that the club had.

One night, when they were both fifteen and on the way home from the weekly Kung Fu lesson, Daisy decided to confide in Kevin with regard to her homelife. She spared no detail and Kevin just sat totally mesmerised. At least that was his initial state. Once the total horror of what Daisy had to go home to had sunk in, Kevin just wanted to go back with her, drag the low life scum of a stepfather outside and make sure that he couldn't have the capacity to rape anyone ever again.

Fortunately his training kicked in and this stopped him from following through with those initial thoughts. Instead, he just promised that at some stage the peasant would be made to pay, but not yet.

"You be careful Kevin. I don't want you getting into trouble. Certainly not on my account."

"I can take care of myself thank you Daisy. I'm certainly not scared of that bastard."

They ended the conversation there, primarily because neither knew how to take it any further forward.

Kevin knew that he could take care of himself when it came to any kind of physical contact with other boys or even men, however he wasn't sure how to comfort Daisy, so he just clumsily pulled her to him. That was the closest they'd ever been and Daisy just melted into his arms. Although this honestly hadn't been planned by her, she felt completely resigned to his affection. It was as though she was being wrapped in a warm quilt and she had to resist the temptation to close her eyes and daydream.

Unfortunately she had slightly misread the situation and as she turned to kiss Kevin, he just recoiled and held her at arms length.

"What do you think you're doing?"
"I'm sorry Kevin, I just thought…"
"You thought what Daisy Wilcox. What exactly were you thinking?"
"Surely, even you must realise, you oaf."
"Realise what? All I know is that we've never been that way with each other. I do hate hearing about what happens to you and if there were anything I could do to stop it I would, but that doesn't mean I want the same thing your

step dad does."

"Well, I'm glad about that because he only wants my body. I just thought that you might like me for all of me. Why do you think I've stuck around all this time? I love you Kevin, you stupid idiot. Surely you must know that."

"I had no idea Daisy, honest. I just thought that we had similar shit home lives and that we understood each other. A bit like brother and sister really."

"I suppose to be honest, that was how I felt in the beginning, but as we've grown older, my feelings have changed. I thought yours might have as well."

"I don't know what to say Daisy. I think we both need to go home and think about it all."

Once at home Kevin thought long and hard for about a minute. He couldn't reach any conclusion, so just dropped the subject. It seemed like the best course of action.

When he finally fell asleep he did have a smile on his face though.

Ages 16 to 23

Chapter 1

T revor left school as soon as he could. He was never going to stay long enough to take exams that he knew he would fail. He never received any educational encouragement from his father. In fact the latter had other plans for his offspring and this meant that Trevor had a job to fall straight into.

The pharmaceutical industry beckoned as this was what Trevor's dad had an involvement in. In fact he owned a string of Pharmacy's, however this business was just a front to his real money maker, illegal drug distribution or to put it more bluntly, the running of a county line organisation.

Until Trevor started working for him, he knew nothing about this side of his dad's business. In fact Trevor was so naive and gullible that initially he thought that he was learning the tricks of the pharmaceutical trade. It didn't take too long before even the gormless Trevor discovered that his father, along with running a 'legal' company, was dealing with illicit drugs.

This made Trevor love his job all the more. He loved anything that was on the wrong side of the law. It made him feel powerful and he felt untouchable, after all his dad had his back. He could earn good money too.

Luckily he didn't suffer from any kind of guilty conscience, so had no problem relieving other youngsters of their hard earned cash in order to boost his coffers. He never hung around long enough to witness the after effects, not that this would have made him feel bad. If they were dumb enough to want what he was selling, he was only too happy to oblige.

He lost touch with both Daisy and Kevin and found that he didn't miss either, although he would have still liked to meet Kevin down a dark alley so that they could get reacquainted. Thinking about it he would have liked to meet Daisy down a dark alley to get reacquainted as well.

Trevor consoled himself by thinking that he was going on to bigger and better things. After all, with money came power. That was not necessarily how his father saw it, but then he didn't really care what his useless son thought. He was never going to pose a threat.

Chapter 2

Unlike in the west, there would be no choice of school as Andreiv and Mikhail progressed, so they stayed together throughout. They both passed their exams with flying colours, although as with their chess, Andreiv always attained the slightly higher pass marks. Something that he was far too diplomatic about with regard to rubbing his friend's nose in it. He did appreciate that had the tables been turned Mikhail would have been only too happy to brag about it.

They both went on to university, where they majored in science and both in chemistry as their preferred science. Their lives were inextricably linked, but they were not gay and both enjoyed the company of several girlfriends, when time permitted. The only major difference was that Andreiv always treated any girlfriend at the time with the utmost respect and did his best to make her feel like a princess. Probably too much so, he later realised.

Mikhail on the other hand, had a much more rudimentary approach. If he couldn't get what he was after, he moved on quickly and without suffering from any guilty conscience. He never treated his girlfriends badly, he just wasn't going to waste too much time on them and certainly not much of any hard earned cash.

Because of their consistently high pass marks and their ability to understand and question whatever was being taught to them, they were already being monitored by a certain state department, as all young proteges were. The state would not let potential talent go to waste, if it could help it. Also where it could be monitored it could be controlled and unbeknown to either, they were already being controlled.

There was a certain department within the political hierarchy, which had a plan and that plan needed a couple of young, extremely bright chemists. A couple of young scientists who, if all went terribly wrong, wouldn't be missed by anyone other than their parents and parents never posed a threat to the state. It was all very neat as there couldn't possibly be any loose ends.

A couple of elderly gentlemen were rubbing their hands together with expectant glee. They just hoped that they both lived long enough to see the plan through.

Chapter 3

Kevin was now sixteen and as far as he was concerned there was only ever going to be one choice of career. He was going to join the army. He wanted an adrenaline filled life and this was the only way that he felt someone of his background was ever going to achieve it.

At this age he was already nearly six foot tall and still growing. He was well built and generally a good looking lad. He'd learnt to control his anger and he no longer felt the need to argue with his fists. With regard to this aspect of his life his reputation preceded him anyway, so most other local young lads didn't bother to argue with him. In fact it made him popular as he was seen as a kind of protector or bodyguard, by some. He never felt comfortable with that kind of attention because at heart he was still a loner and much preferred his own company or failing that, the company of one other person.

kevin had no contact with any of his past foster parents and certainly none with his actual parents. He did still kind of hold a candle to his father and his army career, although other aspects of his fathers behaviour had even diluted this feeling of late. With regard to his relationship with Daisy, he'd very subtly distanced himself after that night, two years earlier. He didn't want to put either of them through a similar situation again. He did keep in touch, more by phone than through any other means and he did often think of her plight. He hadn't forgotten the promise that he'd made, with regard to the fate of her step dad.

The one thing that he could console himself with was the fact that whatever Daisy would decide to do, she would do well. He felt that she was far more intelligent than he ever would be.

The army beckoned and Kevin had little trouble joining. When asked what he wanted to achieve, he just stated that he wanted to go wherever the action was, so for that reason he was put straight into the infantry. They soon found that they had a natural soldier in their midst. He obeyed his orders without question, had no problem with any kind of hardship and carried out whatever tasks as instructed, diligently. They also saw how fit he was. He was by far the fittest new recruit in the current intake and he found the basic training a breeze. A few of his peers, as well as the officers even found out about Kevin's martial arts prowess.

After six months of basic training Kevin was approached by his drill sergeant, who took him to one side and suggested that he take himself off to the officers quarters immediately. Kevin just wondered what he had done wrong, but headed straight there anyway.

"Ah Keenan, come in." The Lieutenant greeted him at the door. It was almost as if he were expecting him. "Go through to the Captains office please. It's right through there."

'Well he didn't appear miffed with me anyway.' Kevin thought as he walked toward the office door.

From the Lieutenants demeanour, it didn't appear to Kevin that he was in trouble, but he couldn't think what a Captain would want with him.

He knocked lightly on the old wooden, but newly painted door.

"Come." Was all that was barked from the other side.

Kevin removed his cap and entered.

"Private Keenan sir." Kevin said as he saluted the Captain.

"Take a seat Keenan. I want to have a word with you."

"Yes sir. Here sir?"

"Of course there, man. Where else are you going to sit?"

Kevin sat.

"I've been told that you are a bit special. Do you think you're a bit special?"

"No sir."

"Why don't you. You're in the army. Doesn't that make you special?" The captain knew all about Kevin's general background and obviously about his progress within the army. He thought that keeping Kevin on his toes was the best way to handle him. He was also well aware of Kevin's fathers disgraceful army record and therefore he needed to work out for himself whether this young man would be just as troublesome.

"Yes sir. It does sir, but no more special than anyone else here."

"Good answer Keenan, however that's not the kind of special that your peers are referring to. They seem to think you have something about you and that you stand out from the crowd. Do you know what they mean?"

"No sir." Kevin genuinely didn't know. He did know that he was super fit compared to the rest of his unit and he obviously knew that he held a black belt in a martial art, but did that make him special?

"Listen Keenan, you have the potential to make a great soldier, but we have to make sure that you aren't from exactly the same mould as your father first. Do you understand that at least?"

"Well not exactly sir. I thought that I was trying to live up to my dad's high standard. I know he's fallen off the rails since leaving, but he was a very good soldier."

The Captain took some time before answering. It was now blatantly obvious that this soldier had been led a merry dance by his father. He decided not to beat about the bush and just tell it as it was.

"I'm afraid your father was dishonourably discharged for beating up an officer and for continually being found drunk whilst on duty. It would appear that he has not been totally honest with you. I'm sorry Keenan. I know how it is to find that your father is not the hero that you think he is or at least as he's painted himself to be."

There was never going to be any easy way to tell this young man the truth about his father, especially as he had obviously never been told the real story.

Kevin took a few seconds to compose himself and then it was as if he'd never heard the story. He immediately compartmentalised that part of his life just like he had to with so many other parts of it. It was the only way he could continue to move his own life forward.

"I promise you sir, that I'm not like my father. I don't even drink. If you know anything about my background you will know that no sane person would want to live their life in any way shape or form, like either of my two parents. I don't even know where they are."

"Excellent, excellent." 'This boy is like a sponge' The Captain thought. 'We can make of him what we want, if we get this right.' He went on to say. "In that case the first thing that I intend to do is promote you to corporal and the second is to move you."

"Thank you sir."

Even the promotion was accepted in a very understated way. The Captain liked this.

"You haven't heard where I'm moving you to yet."

"No sir, but I'm sure you have my best interests at heart."

"Oh I do, but I have our country's best interests at heart before yours".

The Captain explained where Kevin would be going and when he was to go. He was vague about why though. Kevin knew very little about his destination and thought it best not to ask. He was excited anyway.

Chapter 4

Alfies younger sister had moved into a flat with her long term boyfriend and his mum hadn't been happy about that, however she was soon distracted from worrying about that particular situation, as for a very different reason she was not best pleased with her only son. He was still living at home and was still very much under her influence, so she couldn't understand how such a thing could happen.

"You've done what?"

"I'm sorry Mum."

"How could you? After all that I've done for you."

"It wasn't planned, believe me."

Alfie was eighteen and should have been

preparing to venture off to university, but instead he was about to become a father and therefore was going nowhere as far as higher education was concerned.

The only girlfriend that he'd ever had was pregnant. He wouldn't have minded so much, if they had been at it like rabbits, but he'd only slept with her twice and being a virgin on the first occasion, he had put his dick everywhere but where it should have gone, so all he achieved on that occasion was to make a nasty mess of the sheets. It must have happened on the second attempt, where as far as they were both aware, he had managed to hit the bullseye.

"I'm going to do the right thing and marry Mary."

"You young fool. How are you going to support her?"

"I'm going to go to police college and take up a career in the force. I'll still make you proud of me yet, you see if I don't."

His mother had broken down at this point and pulled him close. After her sobbing subsided and she'd had a small chance to get her head around the issue, she just said that he did make her proud and that everyone is entitled to at least one mistake, even if it was a humongous one.

"Would you like me to go round and speak to Mary's parents?"

"No, it's okay Mum. I've already spoken with them and they have taken pretty much the same stance as you really. They were very upset initially and then Mary's Mum asked her if she wanted to keep the baby."

"What did Mary say?"

"She said that she did and that she wanted to stay with me. I never knew that either, but I am pleased."

Alfie did get into police college as he had promised his mother. This gave him the opportunity to keep his other promise too. The one that he'd made to a friend a long time ago.

After a while his mother had become secretly pleased about the turn of events, as it meant that at least one of her offspring would still be around the house for a while longer. She would never let on though, as she had to continue to portray the strict mother figure. She felt that this compensated in some way for Alfies lack of a father. She was also quietly pleased about the fact that she was going to become a grandmother.

Mary and Alfie had a quiet wedding. It was arranged so that it would take place before the baby was due and also before college was due to start. It took place at the local registry office and both sets of parents attended, along with a couple of close friends.

Alfie would have dearly liked his old friend Kevin to attend his special day, making the assumption that Daisy Wilcox would have attended too, as she was always glued to Kevin's side. As it was, he had no idea where either of them were. He had heard that Kevin had joined up, but with which service, he wasn't sure. He hadn't seen his old pal since school, but he'd never forgotten him and something told him that they would meet again. A thought that he dismissed as a pipe dream.

Regardless of his old friend's absence, the day went very well. The weather was kind to them and the ceremony ended with a small reception at the back of a local pub. Mary looked gorgeous as always, even though her belly was slightly more rounded than it had been a month earlier. His mother cried all day on and off. He wasn't sure where she was getting all the water for her tears from or the constant supply of tissues. This made him smile.

Alfie was a very happy and contented young man and his new bride Mary, adored him. Between them they would soon have a small bundle that they would both adore to. He didn't let on to his mum, but he was already considering the possibility of the happy family being together under their own roof. He'd leave that thorny subject to a different day.

Chapter 5

Afghanistan was never going to be a bed of roses, but Kevin got stuck into whatever came his way. He didn't mind where he was as long as he was where the action was taking place. His enthusiasm was almost infectious.

He was serving in the dreaded Helmand province and was about to go out on night time reconnaissance. It was a bright moonlit night and even Kevin felt nervous on such nights. To a sniper he could be easy pickings, if he so much as put his head up in the wrong place.

He had just left his billet to reconnoitre the surrounding area. He dropped into a curved trench and was just about to progress stealthily along it when someone to his left and just out of sight said: "Keenan!" in a whisper that could only be described as sounding slightly effeminate but authoritative.

"Who's there?" Kevin replied, while hesitantly raising his M249 automatic rifle towards the direction that the voice had come from. 'Whoever it is, knows me, but I should be the only person patrolling this section at this time of night', he thought to himself.

Just then, there was the sound of a single gunshot. It sounded as if it were coming from a hundred yards or so away, but it was hard to tell in the pitch black. It was shortly followed by a ricochet just a few yards from where Kevin and the unknown voice were standing.

Luckily, Kevin had seen the nozzle flash and as his firearm was already raised, he immediately managed to squeeze off a shot of his own, straight toward the flash. There was the sound of another shot, but this time the flash appeared to be aiming at the sky. It then went silent, until a few seconds later:

"It's Sargeant Wilcox. Please lower your weapon."

This time Kevin could clearly hear that this was a female voice.

"Come here Keenan." Whoever she was,

she sounded like she meant business, so Kevin collected his ammo and made his way along the trench as instructed. He and whoever she was, were the only two in this stretch of the trench.

"Hello Kevin. Have you missed me? By the way, I think you hit that sniper, well done."

Indignantly Kevin replied. "No. Who are you? Is this some kind of wind up? Then the penny dropped, like a stone. "Daisy, is that you?"

"Sergeant Daisy to you soldier." This time said with warmth.

She reached forward and grabbed Kevin by the lapels, pulled him forward and said "This is the kiss that you wouldn't let me have a few years ago, okay?"

They kissed for what to Kevin at least, seemed an eternity. Kevin felt a little unsure that what he was doing or feeling was right, but this time he wasn't going to push her away. He felt different somehow and the kiss felt right, so he allowed himself to get lost in its perfection, just for a second.

"Daisy, wow. It's great to see you. What the hell are you doing here?"

"Same as you, you numpty. Eliminating

the bad guys, before they eliminate us."

"Where are you based then? I haven't seen you around before."

"Only just posted. It looks lovely, but I wouldn't holiday here."

Daisy avoided the question about where she was based, but Kevin didn't press.

"So, Sergeant ay?"

"Yes and I see that you're a lowly corporal."

"Ah, but not for long." Was all that Kevin could think of. He didn't mind being out ranked by Daisy. He felt sure that she would have worked hard for her promotion and he certainly remembered just how smart she was.

"I want to move to the special forces." Kevin had said with pride.

He wasn't bothered about the stripes on his arm. He just wanted to do something really daring. This didn't come as any surprise to Daisy.

"As in the SAS?"
"Maybe."

Daisy's story was that once she had discovered Kevin was serving in Afghanistan, she'd pulled a few strings in order to try and find out where he was based. It took a while, but finally she had found him. He was actually quite close to where her unit was, so as she didn't have long to get to him, she made for his base as soon as she could. She just wanted to surprise him, hopefully in a good way. That part had worked at least.

Daisy's radio crackled and a voice started to ramble on in a foreign tongue. Kevin just thought that they'd managed to pick up someone elses transmission, that was until Daisy answered in the same language and in a very obviously irritated way. Once the conversation had finished Kevin just sat and waited for Daisy to explain. She was reticent at first, but finally stated that she'd picked up the native tongue and that was all part of her training.

"It was an agent that we're using to gather information." Then before Kevin could say anything, she continued. "Listen Kevin, I've got to go. I really shouldn't have been here in the first place." She said no more and made to leave. "It was lovely meeting you again Kevin. Don't let it be so long next time." She said with a cheeky grin.

"Where are you going? We've only just met. When will I see you again?" Kevin felt like a schoolboy again, except that this time Daisy was no school girl. She was looking and sounding a lot more like someone that Kevin would like to get to know again. It didn't seem fair that his old friend could waltz into his life and then just swan off again, within minutes.

"Oh, so now you decide that you have missed me, do you Kevin Keenan?" With that, she turned and walked away.

"Daisy!" Kevin hissed as loudly as a whisper would let him.

She continued around the corner and was gone.

Kevin sat in the bottom of the trench and wondered what that was all about. There was something a little odd about the whole affair. 'Why was she so evasive.' He thought. 'Was it purely a coincidence that she had just shown up? Who was she talking to and why did she sound irritated?' He consoled himself with his last thought. 'She did appear to be working on intelligence gathering, so I suppose she could easily find me.' He let himself smile. After all it was lovely to see her, whatever the circumstances.

He finished his patrol and made his way back to the billet, where he headed straight for the kettle to make a brew. His head was still awash with several different and conflicting thoughts. He asked if anyone else would like a mug of tea. He then chatted with the guys for a while and casually enquired whether any of them had seen a rather dishy looking woman sergeant around. Once the laughter had died down, Kevin had already received his answer. However one of them did finally reply, albeit in a condescending way.

"Dream on soldier. You need to get some shut eye."

Kevin never did see Daisy again during the conflict and he never heard her name mentioned, until much later.

Chapter 6

Nothing had changed. The streets looked the same. The weather was the same and the people looked the same. Even the smell of the place was all very similar.

He was home on leave and just for old times sake Kevin walked back to his parents house. This was not the same. It had been completely spruced up and now a car was parked on a herringbone brick driveway, where once a broken down fence and yards of overgrown 'lawn' once stood. It was evident that his parents no longer lived there and that was fine as far as Kevin was concerned. He certainly wasn't going to try and find out where, or even if, they lived now.

There was another reason for going back

to his roots however and that was because he had made a promise to both himself and someone else, many years ago and he was going to keep that promise if it was the last thing that he did. He was going to try and control his emotion, although with regard to what this bastard had done to Daisy, this was difficult to control. He was going to serve justice, albeit not the kind of justice that would be recognised in a British court.

Kevin turned into Daisy's old road and immediately set about reconnoitring the property. He hoped that her parents hadn't done the same as his own and moved elsewhere.

Once ensconced in a safe and discreet place, he kept a secretive eye on the house. This kind of observation was second nature to Kevin now. It was one of the many means of survival that he'd learned in Afghanistan. He found it easy to watch without being noticed. This allowed him to gain all of the information that he needed in order to carry out a successful mission. The difference with this particular operation was that it wouldn't take place in a foreign land and wouldn't be carried out against enemy soldiers or terrorists. It would be carried out in his home country where he should have been bound by British law. He wasn't going to let that stop him.

A night time raid was planned and Kevin was ready. He had witnessed the comings and goings of Daisy's parents over a few days, making sure that he recognised both and he was as sure as he could be that they would be safely tucked up in bed when he struck.

A stroke of good fortune came when, on the day of the planned visit, Daisy's mother drove away from the house and didn't return that night. He assumed that she must be staying with her parents or a friend, but either way, he now didn't have to deal with her prior to dealing with her husband, Daisy's step father.

The only slightly odd thing that he noticed while spying on the property, was the fact that a foreign looking neighbour seemed to be spending an inordinate amount of time in his front garden, but he didn't appear to be paying attention to Kevin, so this was dismissed as inconsequential.

What Kevin couldn't possibly know was that the property did have a 'Sold' sign until a couple of days earlier and was therefore currently empty. The 'gardener' had removed the sign and placed it behind the wall. Kevin also didn't know that the white Toyota Avensis that was parked a little further up the road belonged to said 'gardener' and one other accomplice, who spent most of his time in the car, reconnoitring the ame part of the road as Kevin. Up to this point they were both blissfully unaware of each other, however one was about to be spotted by the other.

He waited until around two a.m. the following morning, knowing that this was generally when people were in their deepest sleep. He then easily entered through the french windows, at the rear of the house, after cutting a semi circular piece out of the glass adjacent to the lock. Fortunately they were still of the old wooden type, so only had the one central lock on the main door.

He crept up the carpeted stairs and as he did so he made his gag ready. About half way up, one stair creaked, so Kevin instinctively stopped, stood back against the wall and listened. He let a few seconds pass and there was no sound, so he continued.

The gag was specially prepared so as to prevent the victim from emitting any noise. This was going to be necessary, very necessary. He didn't make any more sound during his ascent and once he was on the landing there wasn't any sound coming from either of the two bedrooms.

The only thing that he couldn't possibly know prior to breaking in, was which one of the two bedrooms Daisy's step father would be sleeping in. He tried the first and bingo, there was a big fat lump in the bed. This had to be his target as the only other occupant was away. He approached stealthily and just as he was about to strike he noticed, in the moonlit room, that there was a huge stain on both the pillow and the sheet adjacent to the head of the recumbent body.

Knowing instinctively what had happened, Kevin thought it safe to switch his torch on. As soon as he did so, he could clearly see that Daisy's step father had a slit across his throat and it was evident that he had been killed very recently as the blood was still flowing freely from the open gash.

He wasted no more time at the crime scene, so he retraced his steps, while checking that he'd left no incriminating evidence, en route. Once outside the building he quietly closed the french door and then clung to the wall as he approached the front of the house.

Checking that the street was empty, he then walked swiftly away. While walking it dawned on him that there was absolutely no good reason to close the door, except maybe to make him feel better. The hole that he cut in the glass, would be noticed as soon as the authorities arrived on the scene. It also dawned on him that the murderer may well have still been in the house. 'How did he or she get in?'

Kevin made sure that he was at least a couple of streets away before hailing a cab. This way there would be no witness to the fact that he had been seen in Daisy's road. Fortunately because he had been in London, even at around three o'clock in the morning, he didn't have to wait long. He made his way back to the London District barracks, which were his temporary home, as he had nowhere else to go while he was back in the UK.

By getting the cabby to drop him off before reaching his goal, he had tried to make sure that he couldn't be traced to his destination. This was just in case the cabby was questioned about his late night customers, on that particular night.

Once back inside, he kicked off his boots and laid back on his bunk. He ran through the possibilities in his head. He quickly dismissed the fact that it could have been Daisy, as throat slitting just wasn't her style. Far too messy and unsophisticated. Also, as far as he knew, she was still in Afghanistan. There was only one real possibility that he kept coming back to. 'After all these years, it must have been Mrs Wilcox. She was the only plausible candidate. After all that would explain why she was conveniently absent the very weekend that he was murdered.' He paused for a second, letting his mind play catch up. 'She must have come back, let herself in, done the job, then let herself back out. Her alibi would be that she'd never left wherever she'd gone for the weekend. Very clever.'

It never dawned on him at the time that he would have witnessed her approaching the house. He was so preoccupied with the who, he wasn't considering the how. His emotions were also pulling him in two directions. There was the frustration of not being able to carry out his promise to Daisy and the relief of not having to carry out cold blooded murder. It was all very confusing.

After staring at the clinically white ceiling for what seemed like hours, he did eventually fall asleep. Still fully clothed and mentally exhausted. His last thought was. 'At least that filthy bastard was dead, whoever did it.'

As soon as he woke the following morning, he lay still for a while and found himself still possessed by thoughts of the recent activities. Something didn't stack up. He was well aware that he was not as intelligent as Daisy, but he was no fool. Something odd had been occurring lately and he didn't believe in coincidences. First the odd visit by Daisy who wouldn't give anything away, then the irritated conversation with a mystery foreigner and finally the very timely murder of her step dad.

'Mind you it was lovely to see her and if ever a person deserved what he got, he did. Should I be worrying about any of this really?' Kevin parked those thoughts for now and stood up to make his way to the washroom, which was clean but very basic. He needed a distraction so he paid particular attention to his surroundings. The room had tiled walls and floors, white basins, each with a mirror in front, a row of toilet cubicles and a couple of showers, complete with curtains and most importantly it had no heating and a constant dripping noise that was coming from inside one of the cubicles. As always, it was braising, even on what would turn out to be a lovely day. The place could definitely have done with a woman's touch and a plumber of either sex.

He'd never paid so much attention to a washroom before, but it didn't take long for his mind to wander again. 'Regardless of who actually carried out the murder, the most important thing is that hopefully no one saw me leaving the crime scene last night'.

He finally put last night to bed for a while and thought about breakfast instead. He finished his ablutions and headed straight for the mess hall. At least he hadn't lost his appetite.

Chapter 7

U niversity had gone pretty much as both boys expected and like most Russian children who were blessed with the privilege of going into higher education, they kept their heads down and studied. It didn't pay to be disobedient and in a small way that helped because it definitely focussed them both with regard to being studious. It also helped that they found their chosen subjects easy and therefore excellent pass marks continued to be achieved. Of course, without either being aware, they were still being closely monitored.

They were in their final year and both were looking forward to whatever lay ahead.

"I received a letter today." Stated Mikhail, with some trepidation. Official looking letters rarely bought good news.

"So did I." Chipped in Andreiv. "Have you opened yours yet?"

"No."

"Shall we open them together. One of us might have got something good."

"I doubt that very much, but I suppose it won't hurt to see what they're both about."

During their lunch break they walked to a nearby public garden and entered, making for the nearest available bench. The garden was a typical municipal affair with flower borders around the edge and a fountain in the middle. Lawns being between the two. The fountain didn't work of course. There was a path that ran round between the flower border and the grass. The whole area was surrounded by railings, which were always surmounted by the neighbourhood children at night, once the gates were locked at sunset.

The pair decided to eat their food first and then open the letters.

"You go first." Mikhail still tried to play the 'I'm older than you card' even after all these years, but Andreiv didn't mind really.

Andreiv tore open his letter and the first thing that he noticed was where it had come from. His heart sank.

"What is it Andreiv?"

"Open yours before I say. Let's at least see if they're from the same place."

Mikhail opened his very tentatively, as if a bomb might detonate when the flap was lifted. He read the contents to himself and whilst doing so he showed absolutely no emotion.

Andreiv couldn't read his friend's face at all. "Well?"

"Well by the look on your face I think I can confirm that it's from the same place, but read yours out loud, then I'll confirm whether the contents are the same."

Andeiv removed his letter, unfolded it slowly and began to read. He'd only read the first line when Mikhail confirmed that the contents were identical.

"Well I wasn't expecting that."

"Me neither. Why would they want us?"

"Because we're the next big thing obviously." Mikhail wasn't very emotionally mature and never quite knew when funny remarks were called for and when they were better left unsaid. He hadn't really processed the gravity of what was being intoned in the letter.

"How can you be funny at a time like this?"

"Because I'm not sure how else to react. What do you think we should do?"

"I think that we should report to the central laboratory. That's what I think."

"Yes, of course. It says that they want us to work on a new medication. I wonder why they want us two rookies?"

"We'll find out soon enough. At least we're doing this together."

That evening both young men arrived at their respective homes, which were still with their parents and still in the same block of unprepossessing flats. Once they had each removed their coats and hats and gone through their other respective returning from work routines, they both explained the situation to their parents.

Both mothers cried because their boys were going to be sent many hundreds of miles from home and because according to the nature of their work, there could be no communication.

When both mothers met the following morning they agreed that their sons might as well have been sent to prison. They both sobbed again.

Ages 24 to 26

Chapter 1

During her term in Afghanistan, Daisy had become disillusioned. She had put a lot of effort into her military career and felt that she'd gone above and beyond with regard to both working hard and studying in order to gain promotion. Along with learning Russian she'd even taken the trouble to learn basic dari, which was the most commonly used Afghan language, so that she could help with any necessary information gathering.

Intelligence was where Daisy now felt her

particular skill sets lie and for the last couple of years she had developed a yearning to join one of the UK's secret services. She'd kept this ambition to herself initially however, as no opportunity had arisen, so she just utilised both languages when the opportunities allowed and when it suited her. She saw her use of the Russian language especially, as being a tool by which she could maximise her chance of gaining entrance into MI6, at a later date.

During a lull in the information gathering one night, Daisy had confided in her contact, as he was about the only person who seemed to want to listen and because they both spoke dari no one could interfere as they would just assume that more information was being discussed. Daisy didn't know at this time that he also spoke fluent Russian, but then he didn't know that she did either.

A couple of weeks after their 'off the record' chat, Daisy was approached by the Afghan contact, who said that he may be able to help with regard to her progression through the ranks and maybe even help to give her a foothold into the secret service, especially as he was already there. He told her that all she had to do in return for this help, was give some harmless information of her own.

"I thought that you operated

independently. I didn't appreciate that you were affiliated to the British secret service."

"I have to be seen to be operating independently. It's for my own safety."

"I suppose so. Anyway, what possible reason could you have for wanting information from me?" Daisy remained quite polite, but couldn't quite fathom what was occurring.

"All I can tell you is that there are certain parties who are interested in keeping tabs on what is going on at ground level." He wasn't lying of course, so didn't feel bad about giving this particular answer. Not that he would have felt bad anyway. It was a real bonus that she believed that he worked for the British secret service.

Daisy got quite excited, as initially she thought that maybe this meant that the British secret service was playing one of its covert games and that this might just be the opportunity that she'd been waiting for.

"So what does harmless mean exactly?"
"I can't go into detail now, you'll find out soon enough."
"Will it be just you and I that know of this arrangement?"
"At ground level certainly. Obviously I have people above me. They will know of you, but

that is to your benefit."

She decided that if it were to help her gain the promotion as promised or better still, a move into a secret service, then it might be worth it. She also decided that if her contact was feeding information to her, he must either be legitimate or a very smart enemy agent. Either way, she decided to play along. She did appreciate that she could be playing a dangerous game, but she felt up to the task and also felt that she would be a match for any man intellectually. 'This could be quite an exciting challenge either way.' She mused.

Daisy had no idea that she was actually being groomed by the GU who are one of the new arms of what used to be known as the Russian KGB, although she did know that something dubious was going on. It didn't help that the Afghan agent was tall, dark skinned and extremely handsome. She had been warned that the Russians were renowned for using sexual advances as a way to get whatever it is that they need, but there was no tangible proof that Ahmed was working for the other side.

It was during the time of her initial liaison with Ahmed that Daisy had bumped into Kevin, but it was not until much later that she wondered if that visit had been engineered. After all she didn't really know who it was that knew where Kevin was. She just accepted the information graciously and then headed straight for him.

For a while she thought that maybe the reason for the liaison with Kevin was purely to test her ability to keep her mouth shut. 'If they did arrange for my visit then it would probably mean that they had been spying all the while Kevin and I was chatting and kissing. I hope this hasn't put Kevin in any kind of danger.' She thought worriedly.

Although Daisy always suspected that there was something odd about this passing of two way information, she allowed the promise of promotion to cloud her judgement. She was being inducted into the GU without really knowing.

It was only once her contact felt that she had given enough information to hang herself, that he finally let her know who he worked for and therefore now, who she worked for. She was devastated. Part of her couldn't believe that she'd been taken in like this. The other part could however. She had known that there was something not quite right about what had been going on and yet she'd allowed herself to let her guard down because of false promises.

What made all of this worse was that it dawned on her that she'd betrayed her country and that she had always felt that she was far too smart to be led into a situation such as this.

"What do you really want from me?"

"Just more of the same really. The more that you give the more you'll be repaid."

"In what way will I be repaid?"

"In what way do you want to be paid?"

Daisy couldn't really believe what she was about to say, but she was already aware that any other answer would be futile. Although it was late in the day, she needed to think smart.

"Well, now that I've pretty much burnt my bridges with my own country, I'd like a promotion please. My plan always was to gain promotion within the British military, so I'd like to do the same within the Russian military or maybe one of your secret services." Daisy thought for a second, then added. "I actually don't feel as bad about this as I thought I would. I don't feel any great loyalty to England. It's not like it ever treated me well."

"Good, then we have an agreement. I'm sure you can appreciate what might happen if you decide to renege on it?"

The full gravity of what Daisy had just agreed to, now hit home. 'What have I done?'

She was visibly shaking, but didn't dare let the Afghan or Russian or whatever he was, see this. She still didn't let on that she was fluent in Russian. This might still be of some assistance when necessary. It was the only ace that Daisy had remaining up her sleeve.

Chapter 2

Kevin was back in Afghanistan and blissfully unaware that he had been spotted by the GU, whilst on his sojourn to Daisy's parents house. They were still reconnoitring the area from within the Toyota, which was parked down the road from Daisy's house, when they spotted him approaching and then entering the property. They had literally left the property a few minutes prior to his arrival. At some time in the future this information could prove very handy to the GU. It could help to deflect blame for instance.

Fortunately for Kevin, the agents who had been sent to carry out the 'mission' weren't aware that he was the man who Daisy had met in the trench and the photos that they had taken of him leaving her parents house, weren't of sufficiently high definition to identify him. They had to rush the shots because they weren't expecting to have to take any and it was dark. Although the road was street lit the Wilcox house was midway between lamp posts. It could have been a very different story had it not been for the poor lighting conditions.

Kevin had by now reached his full height of six foot four and was built like the proverbial brick outhouse. He had a reputation for being a loaner, but was perfectly well behaved when in company. He was known for being fair, but equally, he was tough. He could certainly handle himself.

He continued to serve on the front line and sometimes behind enemy lines and whilst there he earnt a couple of commendations. He was also promoted to sergeant and had earned the complete respect and trust of his men.

One evening, just after returning from a sortie into enemy territory, to gather intelligence, he was summoned to the CO's office.

"Come in Keenan." His CO growled.

Kevin strode in confidently, stood to

attention and saluted.

"I'm afraid I'm going to have to let you go lad."

"Really sir. Why?"

"Well, it's come to my attention that you've been doing some outstanding work out there." Said while wagging a finger in the general direction of Kevin's chest.

"Thank you sir. I think." Kevin had no idea where this conversation was going.

"Well, anyway, off you go."

"Where to sir?" This was becoming more mysterious by the second.

"You'll soon find out. Go and pack your kit immediately. There is a car waiting. The lieutenant will take care of you."

Kevin stood to attention. "Thank you sir."

"Dismissed Keenan. Oh and good luck."

Kevin turned and marched out of the office. This was the closest to feeling on cloud nine that Kevin had ever felt, but he still had no idea why. He just knew that something good or at least exciting, was about to happen.

He ran back to his billet, packed and was on his way to the car within fifteen minutes. On arrival he couldn't help but ask the waiting lieutenant where they were going. He received no answer.

The drive took about twenty minutes and during that time the officer in charge of the wheel said nothing. Kevin had absolutely no idea where they were or where they were heading, but couldn't help feeling that he was on the brink of a new adventure. Either that or the Colonel was playing the part of a smiling assassin and he was going to be taken somewhere for a disciplinary or worse. 'What could be worse and why drive me somewhere else for it?' He mused. 'No, it must be good, whatever it is.' He was back to smiling again.

Even though he had lived through a lot of cruelty and general negativity in his life, he was still very much a 'cup half full' kind of person, so he firmly believed that it would not be the latter. He knew that he hadn't done anything that warranted that sort of behaviour.

Finally the car slid to a halt in a cloud of dust and Kevin could just make out a doorway that appeared to be built into a hillside. He jumped out of the car and grabbed his bag from the boot. As soon as he closed the lid the car sped away.

"Thanks for the ride. The conversation was scintillating." Kevin shouted at the rapidly disappearing dust cloud. He laughed out loud and then remembered where he was.

After taking a good look around, in order to acquaint himself with his surroundings, he discovered that other than the slight mound in front of him, there were no redeeming features. He walked, not quite so confidently towards the door

and just as he got to within a couple of feet, it opened before he could knock.

"Get in here now. Do you want your bloody head shot off?"

That was Kevin's introduction to the SAS.

Chapter 3

It was sometime after Daisy had come to terms with her new arrangement that her contact finally confided in her, that he'd had her stepfather 'dealt with'. On the one hand she was extremely grateful and happy, but on the other, she felt that such a decision should have only been made after consultation with her. 'How much more of my life will be taken from my control?' She thought.

"It was you who told me that he was a worthless piece of shit and that he should die for what he'd done."

"I didn't expect you to act on it though. Thank you all the same."

"We did it to demonstrate that the GU can do whatever it wants to whoever it wants, really. If it did you a favour in the process, then

I'm glad." This was said with just a suggestion of threat. "A man was seen loitering near the house and then he came back shortly after my men had left. We were lucky to have seen him the second time. He broke in through the rear door. Do you have any idea who he might have been?"

It took a few seconds for Daisy to digest this information and then realise exactly who it could have been, but as soon as she did she decided that this was one piece of information that she wasn't willing to impart to her new ally. Of course this also meant that the GU possibly weren't aware of her meeting with Kevin either, otherwise they should have known who the shady character seen at her old address was.

"No, I have no idea. What do you think he wanted?"

"Well, that's the strange thing because no sooner had he broken in, when he left. He took nothing."

"How odd. Although, if he were breaking in with a view to stealing something and then came across the body, he would definitely have left quickly. Would you not have done the same?"

Daisy was doing her best to try and shorten this particular conversation, so she deflected the question with one of her own. She couldn't risk giving anything away.

"I suppose I would, yes." Ahmed said unconvincingly. "Anyway, let's hope that whoever it was, left their prints or some other piece of evidence. It would certainly help us. We managed to get a couple of photos of him anyway, so we'll forward those onto the police."

The conversation did indeed finish there, but it immediately left Daisy with a new dilemma. 'Do I try and get word to Kevin and let him know that he was seen and photographed?' She decided against it for now, although this bothered her greatly. If she hadn't been in such a precarious position herself she would have taken the risk. 'I will get word to him as soon as I can though. I just hope that it will be in time. At least it doesn't sound as though they know who he is, at the moment.'

She was right about that at least. They didn't know exactly who he was, as the photos weren't of good enough quality. Also, unbeknown to her, it wasn't the GU who set up her meeting with Kevin. Fortunately the information that she'd gained in order to facilitate her request, had come via a legitimate source. The problem was that she didn't know that.

Daisy wasn't accustomed to the feeling of real stress, but she now understood what that particular emotion felt like and she had it in spades. She was on the wrong side of loyalty to both her country and her best friend. ' Things can't get any worse can they? What a fool I've been.'

Chapter 4

Trevor was loving life. He was born to be a crook and besides, he wasn't smart enough to get a proper job. He didn't necessarily want to be a drug dealer, as any kind of dodgy dealings would do, but beggars couldn't be choosers. He just wasn't born to abide by the rule of law and this gave him a feeling of power.

His dad had taught him well, but he could never quite bring himself to say how proud he was of Trevor's prowess as a runner. This was because he wasn't proud at all of course. He thought that his son and heir was a complete arse. Besides he wouldn't have known or cared less, what being proud of a son truly was. He just needed the stupid little boy to do his bidding and Trevor was quite happy to do so.

He misguidedly thought that it was doing his fathers bidding and doing it well, that would make his old man proud.

It wasn't just Trevor's father who thought of him as an arse as those others who knew him, thought of him more as a lowlife tosser, than a crook.

According to Trevor however, the only part of his life that sucked, well the two parts actually, were that he still shared a flat with his dad and that he didn't have a girlfriend. He could pay for sex and he often did, but it wasn't the same as owning someone. Being in total control of someone was Trevor's idea of a perfect relationship. He needed someone that he fancied of course, but he also needed someone who would do what he wanted them to do and not just in bed.

The second part of this dilemma was about to change however, as while he was out delivering some 'goods' one day, he was walking past an alley in a particularly poor and run down neighbourhood, when he heard a noise coming from underneath a filthy tarpaulin.

He tiptoed tentatively toward the plastic sheet and stopped just short of being able to reach out and grab the material, when something made him think about the possibilities. 'It could be a cat or some other animal. It could be a fox. I don't know that I'd like to come face to face with a fox.' All these connotations and some others crossed his mind, but driven in the end by simple inquisitiveness he leapt forward and yanked at the tarpaulin with one swift movement.

Underneath was a girl, huddled in the foetal position. A filthy, skinny and wretched looking teenager. It was hard to tell, but if Trevor was to hazard a guess he would say that she was about sixteen or seventeen. He thought that she had blond hair, but it was hard to tell because of the greasy matted state of it and the fact that she had an equally filthy baseball cap on. She was wearing a dirty pair of trainers with no laces and a pair of torn jeans and a t-shirt that looked like they hadn't seen the inside of a washing machine for several months, if ever.

While he stood looking down at this frightened and frankly disgusting looking strip of a girl he heard a small voice:

"Don't hit me." Was all that she said.
"I'm not going to hit you." It wasn't like Trevor to feel benevolent to anyone, but there was something utterly defenceless and innocent about this wretched girl. Even he, for a very short period, couldn't

help but feel sorry for her.

"What are you doing in there?" Was the best that he could come up with.

"I'm living here, what does it look like? Do you think I lost my earring or something?"

"Alright, I was only asking. What else am I supposed to say?"

"You could offer to give me some money."

"To do what with, exactly?" Trevor knew exactly what she'd do with the money. He could clearly see the puncture wounds on her arm. "I'll get you some food, how about that?"

"Well that would do for now, I suppose."

"Will you stay there while I get some?"

"Will you come back with some food?"

"I will if you will."

"Then I will."

Trevor left for the shops. Initially, he couldn't believe he was doing this, but then he started to consider how he could turn this predicament to his advantage. It was almost as if his brain was thinking on his behalf, without him knowing what was occurring. Once he had regained some level of control, he got back to thinking what he wanted to think. 'This is what our business does to people.' Was his first thought. His second was: 'I wonder if she does a turn?'

Trevor was not about to soften for

anyone. He was on a mission to become rich and nothing or no one was going to stop him. Some food was a very cheap price to pay for what may be on the agenda later.

He walked down the street and as soon as he turned the corner he came across a small grocery store that was on the opposite side of the road. He waited impatiently at the lights and decided to cross anyway. One car had to swerve around him and the driver leaned on his horn. As the car passed, Trevor just gave him the middle digit while looking straight at the driver in his rear view mirror.

He strode into the store feeling jubilant about his win over the innocent driver. Purchases made, he left the store and a few minutes later he was back at the tarpaulin. He lifted it, only to find there was no one there.

"Fuck it. Stupid little bitch." Trevor was incensed that he'd been taken for a mug. He'd been taken for a mug, once too often. Someone would have to pay. 'If only that driver would come back this way.' He thought to himself.

"Charming. Your command of the English language leaves a little to be desired. Anyway, sorry about that, I just had to go for a wizz." The small voice came from behind a skip that was itself situated behind the tarpaulin. She stepped out while still doing up her flies.

"I thought you'd done a bunk. What else was I supposed to think? I hope you washed your hands?" Trevor chuckled and thought that his stupid remark was extremely funny. This made him feel better and he no longer felt quite so much like he needed to kick someone.

"Here's your food. What's your name by the way?"

Katy sat before accepting the handout.

"Thanks and why do you need to know?"

"I don't, I'm just making conversation. A little gratitude wouldn't go amiss."

"I gave you a little gratitude by saying thanks. Are you going to hand that food over or what?"

Trevor grudgingly handed over the pre-packed sandwich and the bag of crisps. He even purchased a latte for each of them.

"It's Katy, Catherine. Is that enough or do you want my surname as well?"

"No, just Katy is fine."

Trevor stopped asking questions and just sat and watched Katy eat. The sandwich and crisps were both gone in a few seconds and she wiped her mouth on the back of her hand.

Katy was already of the opinion that Trevor was a tosser, but thought 'where needs must and all that.'

"Would you like a bath and a bed? No strings?" Of course this wasn't what Trevor was thinking at all, but he was doing his best to sound genuine.

"Why?" Katy was extremely wily for someone so young. She knew that men didn't make offers like that without wanting something in return. "Why would you offer me a bed and bath with no strings attached? You don't look like a saint."

Trevor wasn't sure what to say. He knew that he'd been rumbled, but he didn't like the fact that someone could see through him that easily.

"Look, I'm offering you a wash, a place to lay your head and I'm not a murderer, so you can sleep sound in that knowledge. The rest, you'll just have to take a chance on."
"Okay. I guess I can live with that amount of honesty, for now."

She threw out a dirty hand for Trevor to take in order to help her up. He just looked at the outstretched limb and decided against touching it. He turned away, just to make sure that Katy understood.

"I haven't got germs you know."

"Oh yes you have. You just can't see them."

"Charming."

"Just get up."

Katy got up, threw her sandwich box and cup under the tarp, picked up her shoulder bag and a carrier that had seen better days and then proceeded to walk just behind Trevor. There was plenty about him that she still wasn't sure about, but a bath and a bed were both sorely missed and too tempting to turn down. 'I might get some more food as well.' She smiled awkwardly to herself.

While walking, Katy started to open up and told Trevor at least some of her story. It involved a boyfriend who got her into drugs and then ditched her.

She then went on to explain that by the time he'd finished with her, her mother didn't want her back and said that she couldn't handle her any more, so she threw her out. Her father had left when she was young and she had no idea where he was or even if he was still alive. Even her old friends had gradually fallen by the wayside once they knew that she was heavily into drugs. In fact they'd started to distance themselves once she'd hooked up her ex, as no one liked him.

That was all three months ago, so the streets were, for now, her only option and she made ends meet by doing whatever was necessary. She told Trevor that she had turned sixteen three weeks ago.

They approached Trevors car where, once Katy's bags had been slung into the boot, they both got in and sat. Trevor put the key in the ignition, but didn't start the car. He too decided that confession was good for the soul so he opened up, but he did it in such a way as to make what he now did for a living sound almost decent. It didn't work, but Katy thought that at least he was being kind of honest with her. This didn't stop her from taking the piss out of him.

"So, you are a drug runner for your dad because you enjoy being on the wrong side of the law and you don't want a proper job, but eventually you want to go it alone and do something else dishonest. Does that, about sum it up?" Katy couldn't help smirking when she noticed Trevor squirm slightly, at her accurate summary.

He hadn't realised that she was being sarcastic, but he didn't appreciate her smirking anyway. 'This girl could be trouble.' Trevor thought. 'She's far too lippy. I'm going to have to be careful with what I tell her and I'm going to have to keep an eye on her movements while she's with me. Especially who she may be talking to.'

He responded flatly. "I suppose it does, yes."

He started the old Ford Fiesta that his dad had bought for him, shoved it into first gear, dumped the clutch and promptly stalled. So, much like a tennis player who is forced to make a second serve, he had to move away much more sedately on his second try.

He still managed to clip the car that was parked directly in front of him.

Katy giggled.

"Oh shut up you silly little slut."

Even at her tender young age, Katy had been called worse, so she just let that hurtful comment pass. Technically, he was correct anyway.

"You do know that you hit that car, don't you?"

"I said shut up. I can always leave you right here."

Katy was beginning to think that might have been the better option.

Chapter 5

L ife in the SAS was tough, even for Kevin. As soon as his initial training was over he was sent on several extremely dangerous missions. These were to gather intelligence and also to take out snipers and anti tank outposts. Any of these sorties could have cost him his life, but he found that he lapped up this kind of action. Until now, like most of the public, he'd had no idea what goes on behind the scenes, in order to keep the free world safe. He was only now beginning to understand.

It was even tougher in the SAS for Daisy, especially as she was now tussling with her conscience on a daily basis. She was trying to remain loyal whilst having to pass information to her contact.

As the law had changed in 2018, with regard to females joining, Daisy applied straight away and based on her exemplary record to date and her language skill, was accepted. She didn't let her interviewer know that she was fluent in Russian either because she thought that somehow this could end up compromising her in some way. She had no idea how, but thought that it was better safe than sorry.

The move to the SAS had been prompted by the GU, as she could be far more useful to them if she was a member of one of Britain's special forces. She found that serving in what was basically a secret service, was a lonely affair, which under normal circumstances wouldn't have bothered her too much but because of her predicament, it was lonelier still. The GU still thought that she only spoke dari. Like the SAS,

they weren't aware of her Russian, however Daisy was now only too aware that Ahmend spoke Russian.

She found that the best way to stay safe was to stay distant. That was not just from the enemy the British
were fighting, but also from the foe she was now working for. She kept the information

brief but relevant and she certainly didn't make any personal advances on her contact. She didn't want him to get the wrong idea. It was for this reason that she couldn't even begin to comprehend what happened next.

"We need you back in Russia and the only realistic way to get you out soon is for you to marry me. Sorry about that." This was said with a huge smirk on his face. He was obviously already looking forward to the wedding night.

"Why do I need to go to Russia when I'm serving a purpose here?"

"You are needed to serve more of a purpose back there."

"What do they want me for?"

"I have no idea. I've just been told to extract you and I need to do it without causing a fuss."

"Is getting married the only way?"

"No. I could always get you pregnant." The smile remained as broad as it was at the outset of the conversation.

"You could try. I'll settle for a fake wedding thanks."

Daisy now felt that she was in way over her head and worse still she couldn't see any way out. Luckily she wasn't the nervous type, at least outwardly, so she was just going to have to go along with this plan until she could make one of her own.

She needed to try and get out of this wedding, she definitely needed to try and stay out of Russia and she also needed to get that message to Kevin, urgently.

Chapter 6

A text message came through: 'They've got photos but they don't know that it's you. I know it wasn't you. I've gone rogue for now. Bear with me. X'

Kevin knew immediately who had sent the message and therefore it only took a couple of minutes to figure out what the first part referred to. He knew this in part because the message was signed with a kiss and as far as he knew none of his close male friends were gay or worse still, fancied him. He also knew who it was because there were only a precious few people who had his number. Kevin never handed this out until he had personally vetted whoever the lucky recipient was to be.

He had no idea what the second part

meant, but he felt that it wouldn't be long until he found out. He also knew instinctively that he shouldn't reply to the message.

'Who did kill Mr W? And how does Daisy know about it? This must have something to do with her being coy at the trench visit as well. She's in trouble, but I've no idea why or how. What the hell does 'gone rogue' mean?'

Although Kevin was enjoying life in general, every now and again the stress of his particular line of work got to him, so like anyone else he needed to let off a bit of steam. It didn't help when he received messages like the one that he'd recently read. He decided to head off to the mess, which in the evening doubled as a bar, albeit a restricted one. He wasn't intending to get drunk, but for once he just needed the company of other people and a pint or two.

Just as he was heading across the compound and toward the entrance to the mess, four young middle eastern looking men appeared from behind a building. Each was holding some kind of weapon, one held a curved sword, another a baseball bat, the third a chain and the fourth a long knife. They were dressed in military garb, but not of a type that Kevin recognised. Their clothing appeared to be a hotchpotch of different uniforms.

He took all of this information in, digested it and weighed up his options, all within a couple of seconds.

"We don't want you foreigners here." The man with the curved sword said with an English accent. That at least would explain why his command of the English language was excellent.

'He must have been educated in the UK. I wonder if they all were?' Kevin was processing any information that he could. It all helped with regard to waying up the situation and with intelligence gathering.

"Well I'm sorry about that, but there's not a lot I can do about it." Kevin replied coolly.

"I think we need to show you just how much we don't want you here." The sword man said whilst looking straight at Kevin with an unblinking stare. He looked like he was on some kind of drug. A couple of the other lads giggled. 'So, they must all speak English.'

"I don't want any trouble." Kevin knew exactly where this conversation was going, but tried diplomacy anyway.

The guy with the chain ran straight at Kevin, while wildly spinning his chain above his head. This took the others by surprise, so initially they all just stood and let him approach on his own. This obviously played into Kevin's hands, so as soon as the chain got within grabbing distance, Kevin grabbed the end and in one swift move, stopped the chain and wrapped it around his adversaries neck. He manoeuvred himself into such a position as to be behind his assailant, but able to see the other three, who were all now approaching. He had to disable the first attacker quickly, so he broke his neck by yanking back on the chain, with one massive jerk. He dropped the still writhing body and prepared for the other three.

They approached from three different directions at once, so Kevin quickly assessed in which order to take them on. He went for the sword man, assessing that he posed the greatest threat. Without even looking in the direction of this would-be assailant, Kevin swung his leg up and caught the man straight between his legs. The sword man folded and as his head came forward, Kevin swung his other leg up and crashed his foot into the forward leaning face. The sword dropped to the ground and Kevin grabbed it before the other two had time to get any closer. He swung the sword and let it go, propelling it straight toward the third assailant. It entered his chest and took him off his feet. He was dead before he hit the ground.

The fourth and what looked like the youngest man, dropped his weapon and ran.

This was all over in a matter of a couple of minutes, but Kevin hadn't finished just yet. He grabbed the second man, who was still alive, by the hair and pulled him toward the mess. Before entering he asked the now conscious assailant where he'd learnt his English. He just said, "School." They went inside.

Two terrorists dead, one now held captive by the SAS and one who ran away without his weapon or dignity. 'Not a bad night's work.' Kevin smiled to himself.

Chapter 7

Alfie had been quietly and conscientiously making his way through the ranks of the metropolitan police force. He was now an inspector and he was hoping to attain the rank of chief inspector in the not too distant future. He was a smart cookie and whilst he was softly spoken and sometimes taken for a soft touch, he invariably got his man or woman. He had a knack for taking on and solving the more complicated and intricate cases.

He was now based at New Scotland Yard and felt that this was the epicentre of British policing. He was currently working on an interesting drugs case. It appeared that someone was smuggling in small quantities of cocaine and it didn't appear to be coming in through the normal channels. It had only come to Scotland Yard's notice because a drug addict who had collapsed and been picked up by the police, was tested and found to be using a variant of cocaine that wasn't currently known about.

Inspector Edwards was given the job of tracing the source and he relished the prospect. He and his small team had received a briefing and he had only just collected the case notes. He had only just started to read through them when a constable on his team came rushing into his office without stopping to knock. Something that drove Alfie up the wall as he was as a stickler for protocol, no matter how petty.

"The addict has died sir."

"Which addict? Addicts are dying every day and could you please remember to stop and knock before entering?"

"The addict who was using the drug that we're trying to chase down. Sorry about the door sir. I just thought it important that you hear this straight away."

"I thought that they were fine when they left here. Man or woman, by the way?"

Alfie hadn't been given any details during his briefing and because he'd only just picked up his notes he was none the wiser with regard to such things as the sex of the drug user.

"She was alive then, but she only made it literally to the end of the street before she collapsed. She was dead before she got to the hospital. Young woman, by the way. Well girl really."

Alfie smiled at the Constables total naivety. He was oblivious to the fact that he'd spent the whole of the last statement saying 'she', before adding that she was a woman.

"Right, that puts a whole new slant on this investigation. I better tell the old man. We need more resources. This has become an urgent inquiry now. We could be looking at murder." Alfie stopped to think for a second and then continued. "Can you bring me the identity of the victim and get the lab. to rerun tests on that coke. There may have been something in it that we haven't found."

"On it sir." With that the young officer left and Alfie sprung into action. 'This is what proper policing is all about.' He mused. 'Do good and use your brain.' A friend had once said and it had never left him. It had become his mantra.

Chapter 8

"**M**ake yourself at home. I'll get us a couple of drinks."

Katy thought for a second, then decided to dive straight in. "I take it, you can get my stuff as well?"

"I can get any stuff, but I can't get it for free, if that's what you mean?"

"I don't have any cash."

"Then you'll just have to go without, won't you."

Another couple of seconds thought was given and then Katy decided that she'd try and play the long game. After all this could be a veritable honey hole, if she played her cards right.

"How about, if I scrub up nice and you

approve, I could become your girlfriend. I'd look good on your arm don't you think?"

Trevor couldn't really look this gift horse in the mouth, although he still felt that he was being played. As long as it worked out to be a win-win situation he'd have to grin and bear it, for now.

"You'd better go and scrub up then and I'll see what I think."

"Where's the bathroom? I'll need a couple of towels and a flannel. I'm not using what you use."

It suddenly dawned on Trevor that his dad knew nothing about this cosy little arrangement and he wasn't likely to take too kindly to it. 'What to do?'

"Go and jump in and I'll bring the towels."

"You perve. You just want to watch me shower."

"Maybe, but do it anyway."

Katy got up and left the room. Trevor followed with his eyes.

'I've got to find a way of convincing dad that Katy staying here is a good thing.'

Chapter 9

The decision to get out of Afghanistan was eventually taken out of Daisy's hands. A rumour was being passed around that she was a spy. Fortunately for Daisy the rumour was passed on to her by someone who didn't know her.

Initially she had no idea how that particular rumour could have started, but it didn't take long for it to dawn on her who it must have been. 'Why though?' she quizzed herself. 'He didn't need to do that and it will just forever besmirch my name.' She gave it some more thought. 'Of course, that's why he did it. It virtually guarantees that he gets his way.'

Needless to say, when Daisy tried to

contact Ahmed to quiz him, he wasn't available for comment. In fact he stayed well out of the way until shortly before Daisy left the service.

She found the whole affair extremely awkward and embarrassing and it left her feeling that there was only one possible way out. Exactly as he'd planned. She had thought long and hard but there was no other way. She would have to go along with the wedding plan.

When she finally plucked up the courage to speak to her commanding officer, she felt that she sounded very unconvincing.

"I do know the real reason why you are leaving, you know?"

"I'm sorry sir, I don't understand." Daisy was dumbstruck. 'Surely he hadn't heard the rumours and worse still believed them?'

"Oh, I'm sure you do, young lady. You don't have to go, you know. You could have some time off to get married and then return to duty." The CO wasn't going to press his point, but he couldn't help being intrigued by the suddenness of the loss of one of his best personnel. If he could hold on to her he had to give it a try.

Daisy hadn't heard the CO mention the marriage as she was too busy thinking that she'd been rumbled as a spy and she was considering her response. It was only while she was thinking that it suddenly dawned on her that the marriage was the reason that the CO thought she was leaving. She couldn't believe her luck, although she now had to respond to the fact that he was trying to accommodate her and she had to give a sound reason turning the offer down.

The relief on her face must have been visible. "It's complicated because we are of different religions and no he isn't a soldier." Daisy knew that this was an unconvincing answer, but she felt uncomfortable about telling an outright lie, especially on top of everything else that she'd done. "I'm afraid it does mean that I have to leave."

"Very well. I wish you all the very best in that case. You may leave when you are ready."

He had heard the other rumour, but he had instantly dismissed it. 'The spy stuff has obviously been started by someone who has seen her with her foreign chappy.' He just wanted to hear the reason for Daisy's departure from her. What he was fairly sure of was that she was still lying, but he couldn't work out why. 'Maybe she's got herself up the duff.'

The quizzical look faded from his face and he spent no more time thinking about Daisy's situation. He just picked up the next sheet of paper from his inbox.

Daisy resigned her post from the SAS and she felt that she'd lost any remaining dignity. She certainly wasn't looking forward to the next stage in her life.

She had finally made contact with Ahmed but as soon as she started to talk, he cut across her and insisted on only discussing the wedding. This was all that he was interested in, however before any marriage was to take place she needed to make her view known. Irrespective of any other subject she needed to let him know exactly where his marital responsibilities were to start and finish.

"We'll see." Was all that he said in his irritatingly jocular manner.

"You'll be wearing your testicles as earrings, if you so much as try to kiss me." Was Daisy's response. "Oh and what was the point of starting a rumour about me being a spy? Before you deny it, please do not insult my intelligence." She wasn't going to give up trying to get this point across either.

Daisy knew exactly why he had done what he'd done, but she just needed to let him know that she knew it was him. As soon as she had asked however, she regretted it as it now sounded childish. It didn't sound that bad in her head.

"I won't deny it. I thought it would help you make your mind up about leaving. Call it a gentle persuader, if you will." He said this while smiling.

She couldn't believe that once upon a time she had found this creep charming. Now he made her skin crawl. Daisy just glared at Ahmed and left the room before anything else was said. She knew that she could put herself on a very perilous footing.

Another text was sent to Kevin, although Daisy had no idea what good it would do her: 'Have to go to Russia. X'

Daisy threw her phone away before Ahmed could get his greasy paws on it and also just in case Kevin were to reply.

Although he initially had appeared indifferent about Daisy's wish to leave and the reason given, the CO had given the situation further thought and decided to make some very discreet enquiries about who it was that his star soldier was marrying.

Chapter 10

T revor wasn't sure how to approach the thorny subject, that was Katy, with his dad. The only practical solution to this dilemma was to try and sell the idea that she could somehow be useful. That way she may be able to stay for a while.

"Hi dad, when are you going to be home?" Trevor never liked calling his dad, but as he never knew where he was, it was the only way he could prepare himself.

"What have you done now, you little prat."

"Nothing. I just need to know when you're going to be here. I've got a proposition to put to you."

"You've got a proposition? You can't even spell the word."

Sometimes Trevor hated his father. Well, most of the time actually, but he needed him for now, unfortunately.

"I have, so can you just tell me when you're going to be here?"

With that the front door opened and slammed back against the wall. His dad wasn't in a good mood. This wasn't unnatural of course, but this looked like a particularly foul one.

"Are you alright dad?"
"Do I look alright?"
"No."
"Daft bitch only went and died, didn't she. Now the old bill are crawling all over the place, asking questions."
"Who died?"

"One of my clients. She was a reliable punter and up for trying anything. She used to put the word around as well. You just can't find people like that. Sometimes she even run as well. She's left me right in the lurch." He went on. "This has really inconvenienced me. What I can't understand is why she snuffed it. I was told that this was top notch stuff."

He produced a small plastic bag with a white powder in it. It looked exactly the same as all the other white powder that Trevor had seen. "She always seemed to be in control. Well, as in control as you can be of course." This statement brought about the first smile that Trevor had seen on his father, for a while. It was more of a smirk really.

Trevor decided that now wasn't a good time to broach the subject of Katy, so instead he just collected her from the bedroom, where she'd been waiting patiently and introduced her as one of his usual floozies. This at least would be accepted by his father.

"This is Katy."

"So? What was this proposition that you were going to put to me?"

"It can wait. I think you just need to come in and put your feet up for now. You need to wind down."

"Don't tell me what I fucking need to do. You're up to something. What is it?"

"It's nothing bad dad and it can wait."

Luckily both Trevor and Katy had manoeuvred themselves so that they were between the front door and his dad, so their escape route was open. They made their excuses and left. The subject of Katy moving in would have to go on hold for a while.

"Anyway, that's him." Was all that Trevor said as they headed out.

"He looks like a real charmer." Katy replied and then thought, 'I see where you get it from now.' She smiled, but Trevor wasn't looking anyway.

"He's okay actually. Just had a bad day." Trevor couldn't even convince himself that what he was saying was true and that definitely came across in the way that he'd said it.

Chapter 11

"Russia? Are you sure?" Alfie had never heard of cocaine being produced anywhere in the eastern block before.

"We're as sure as we can be sir and that's not all, it's completely synthetic." The Sergeant was holding a piece of paper in his hand. It was a report from the laboratory.

"How can we know it's Russian?"

"Evidently the chemical makeup. There are traces of substances that either come from there or are manufactured in a certain way and only in Russia, as far as we know."

"As long as the boffins are sure." Alfie knew that there would be a hell of a furore if they got their information wrong. He went on: "How come the lab hadn't already picked up on this?"

"They had. They just couldn't believe it, so they were waiting for verification before releasing their findings."

"What about the young lady?"

"We're still trying to identify her, sir. She had no possessions with her and no real distinguishing marks. All I can say with any certainty is that she didn't have a criminal record. We have no prints or DNA on our files."

"Okay, thanks. Of course that really poses a problem now doesn't it?"

"What, not knowing who the young lady was? I suppose so, but we will find out soon enough."

"I didn't mean her. I mean the fact that the cocaine was produced in Russia. How the hell do we progress that part of the investigation?"

"Well we could start by approaching the Russian Embassy, couldn't we?"

"We could, but that sort of thing is way above my pay grade. I'll have to speak with the old man."

Alfie made arrangments to have a confidential chat with his governor. It was usually next to impossible to get to speak to him urgently, but the old man seemed intrigued by this particular story, so he granted Alfie and audience immediately.

"Russia? Are you sure? We could get into

all sorts of trouble if you're wrong."

Alfie had to smile at the irony of his boss saying exactly what he'd said only an hour before.

"The lab has double checked sir and they are certain that the chemicals are of Russian origin."

"Shit. That's all we need. I suppose I better put a call into Whitehall."

"Yes sir. Good luck sir."

"Okay Inspector. Leave it with me. I'll get back to you."

"Sir." Alfie left the old man's office, not sure what he was going to do until he heard.

As soon as he arrived back at his office, he found that he did have another pressing question. He approached the Sergeant who was sitting at his computer.

"Sergeant, can you come with me for a second please?"

They stepped into the Inspectors office.

"Do we know who is running these drugs? Who's getting them off the Russians and distributing them around here? Are they anywhere else?"

"We have no idea currently, sir."

"About which question?"

"Any of them."

"Why not?"

"I don't think anyone's asked." The Sergeant always felt compelled to tell Alfie the truth, even when it may be to his cost. It was as if his boss had some kind of spell on him.

"In that case, I'm asking. Can you put the word around and speak to whoever you think needs asking. We should know all the local lowlife at least, so start with them. Let them know that someone has died and that this drug could be poisonous and the same outcome could befall their customers. Also, let them know that the coke is synthetic. Don't mention Russia. We don't want them to know that we're on to them. Not yet anyway."

"What's your thinking then sir?"

"I think that information should start to cause a panic and then they'll want answers, so start to keep tabs on some of them. They should lead us to whoever it is that is supplying them."

"Yes sir." The Sargeant left thinking that he had just got off extremely lightly this time. He also left with a daunting task ahead of him.

Chapter 12

It transpired that all four of Kevin's attackers were from England, but their families originated in Afghanistan. They had travelled back to aid the Taliban. They had no real idea what they were fighting for or what they were going to be asked to do, once there. They had all started to lose heart, as the fighting wasn't as romantic in real life as they'd been led to believe. It was ugly and dirty and they soon realised that they could very much end up dead, without really understanding why.

Lashing out at Kevin was really just a way for the four young men, who had lost their way politically and patriotically, to try and get rid of their frustrations and also to try and get back on side with the Taliban. The plan had failed, big time.

The captive terrorist did mention one thing that grabbed Kevin's attention and that was that he believed that there was a female agent who was feeding information to the Taliban. He couldn't say who she was or where she was working. He'd just heard a rumour. He didn't mention whether he knew that the agent was British and Kevin didn't want to ask.

Kevin now knew what the second part of Daisy's first message referred to. She'd become a spy. 'But why and why tell me?' Kevin had no idea what was going on. The second message hadn't helped either. 'Why was she on her way to Russia when it was the Taliban that she was helping?'

'What the hell was going on?' Kevin was going to try and find Daisy. He knew that at the bottom of all this, Daisy was in trouble. Why else would she be messaging him?

He eventually found out where she had been based, but by the time he located that, she'd left. He put in a request to talk to her CO. He knew that he was going way out on a limb, but as far as he was concerned it was the only way that he could make any progress.

He was granted an audience on the proviso that he got his own CO to contact

Daisy's first. Now, he just had to convince his own CO to make the call.

"Why Keenan?" Kevin's CO was a man of few words.

"Because I think we have a British individual who is in trouble sir and she is ex-service."

"What do you mean by trouble?"

"I think she's been abducted to Russia under the guise of being an agent. It's quite a long story sir, but if I can visit her old CO, I may be able to join some of the dots."

While Kevin was still present his CO put in a call to Daisy's ex CO.

"I can vouch for this young man and I think that this might be in both of our interests if you talk to him."

A few more pleasantries were exchanged between the two commanding officers and then the phone went down.

"Right lad, you better get yourself over there. He's expecting you and for what it's worth he already shares your concerns. Oh and Keenan, please report straight back to me."

"Yes sir, of course sir."

Kevin left the Commanding Officers office and immediately requisitioned a vehicle for the following morning at 08:00 sharp. He made sure that he was up and waiting for his chariot. It arrived at exactly 07:59.

"You're early." He said while smiling at the young driver.

"Can you take it round the block and be back here at 08:00?"

"Of course sarge." The private said while giving Kevin a strange look.

"I'm joking you plonker."

"Oh. Anyway the keys are in the ignition, sarge." The private still wasn't quite sure how to take this rather large and burly looking sergeant.

After the initial checks had been carried out and witnessed by both, the four by four was released to Kevin and just like when hiring any vehicle, photos were taken of its current condition. This wasn't actually needed, but Kevin felt better for doing it. Of course any bullet holes would be discounted as they weren't seen as being the drivers fault. Still, he didn't want any unwarranted reprisals afterwards. The one thing that he didn't need to worry about, unlike when hiring a car in civvy street, was replacing any used fuel.

He jumped in and drove like a thing possessed and not so much because of the need to try and help Daisy, but because of the need to keep his head on his shoulders.

Twenty minutes later he arrived at Daisy's old base, which looked remarkably like the one that he'd just left. He pulled into the compound, turned off the engine and ran to the nearest building.

"Excuse me soldier, where's the CO's office?"

"Just through there Sargeant. He'll be having breakfast at the moment."

"Right, thanks." Kevin thought it wise to let the commanding officer finish his breakfast. He needed him on side, so with that in mind he decided to go and get some himself. While he was sitting in the mess his insignia hadn't gone unnoticed and there was a general buzz around the tent. Someone decided to be brave and approach Kevin just as he was about to tuck into his un-runny egg and bacon.

"You SAS Sarge?" Said in all innocence and with a certain amount of awe.

"I couldn't possibly comment, son."

"No, I suppose not, but your badge does kind of give it away."

"If you breathe a word of that to anyone, I will sneak back one night and dismember you." Kevin said with a beaming smile on his face.

The soldier wasn't quite sure whether he was being serious or not, so decided that now was a good time to beat a hasty retreat and let the Sargeant get on with his breakfast. He backed away, not taking his eyes from Kevin until he fell over the end of a bench. There was a roar of laughter.

Half an hour had passed since Kevin finished his breakfast, so he decided that the CO had had plenty of time to finish his. He took the last mouthful of tea, banged his mug down on the table and set off for the CO's office.

As usual there was an Adjutant parked outside the CO's office, so Kevin had to negotiate with him first. Once he was convinced that Kevins appointment was genuine and had ticked the corresponding form accordingly, he knocked on the office door and announced Kevins arrival.

"Come." Boomed from within.

Kevin marched in confidently and saluted the officer. He stood to attention whilst introducing himself.

"Take a seat Keenan and then tell me what you know."

Kevin relayed the whole story, including details of the spurious text messages and exactly what he thought they meant.

The CO sat and listened attentively,

taking in all of the detail. He didn't respond immediately after Kevin finished speaking, but eventually he said. "That explains why she came out with that cock and bull story about getting married. I knew she was lying."

"She told you that she was getting married. Who to?"

"I've no idea. She just said that he was foreign. Well she actually said something about his religious beliefs or something like that. I knew that was rubbish."

"So you don't believe that she was getting married?" Kevin knew that he was beginning to sound paranoid, but he couldn't help himself."

"No I don't and based on what you've told me, I believe that she's been told to say that in order to quickly and legitimately absolve herself of her responsibilities here. She's in some kind of trouble. That's what I believe."

"I believe she is sir. Can you please tell me whatever else it is that you know?"

The CO chose to be just as open with what he'd gleaned about Daisy's case and between them they now believed that she had been coerced into cooperating with the enemy and that they now held her. What neither of them could understand was whether Daisy had initially volunteered her services, though neither could believe that, or what the

Russians could possibly want with her now, especially back in Russia.

"Do you think they've taken her back to torture her sir?"

"She means alot to you son, doesn't she?"

"I didn't realise just how much sir. We grew up together and she was just like my kid sister really. It's down to me that she joined up, in the first place."

"Well, for what it's worth, I don't believe that theyv'e taken her back to torture her. That's not their style. They generally use their agents in the field and then once they've extracted all that they can they either recall them for further assignment, retire them or kill them, if they believe that they are going to prove to be a nuisance."

"So they could be re-assigning her?"

"It looks like they might yes, but hopefully by the sound of her message, she is going along with them just to act as a double agent. Very dangerous."

"What can we do?"

"Nothing lad. We just have to sit back and wait to see if she resurfaces."

"I suppose so sir. Anyway thank you for listening to me and at least there are two of us that now know the whole story. Of course I've got to repeat the story back to my CO as soon as I return."

"Good luck Keenan and we'll keep each other posted should either of us learn anymore."

"Yes sir." Kevin saluted and returned to his ride. It was now lunchtime, but he wanted to get back and brief his own CO before any detail was forgotten,

Chapter 13

Reception at the Russian Embassy was cool, very cool. Alfie had attended with his superior and an official from Whitehall.

Initially the Russian Ambassador didn't even want to entertain the idea of the British police entering his sovereign property, but he finally relented or was directed to and so he reluctantly allowed the three an audience. 'It could be amusing, I suppose.' The official convinced himself. 'After all they have no idea what I look like.'

They were ushered into a side room. It was still very austere, but definitely not one of the finer rooms.

'This is their way of demonstrating just

what they think of us. One up from a broom cupboard.' Alfie thought. He guessed the other two were thinking the same, by the way they were looking around.

A rather pompous and overweight, middle aged gentleman walked in and without any introduction, plonked himself behind the large desk.

"Please sit gentlemen." There were only two chairs.

'Oh, they do like their silly little games. I have a feeling that this interview is going to go nowhere.' Alfie was proved correct, but not until the ridiculous political game had been played out.

"How can I help gentlemen?" No apology, for the lack of seating, was proffered by the Russian official.

Alfie had obligingly stood to one side, allowing the two more elderly and senior gentlemen to take the two seats. He wasn't convinced that they were even in the presence of the Ambassador, as he felt sure that he'd seen him once while on diplomatic duty. He wasn't going to mention this though as he felt that the Civil Servant would know.

Alfies boss took the lead. "This is rather

a delicate matter and I'm not sure how best to approach it, so please forgive me but I'll just tell it as it is."

"Please continue."

"Thank you." There was a short pause. "A young lady died of a drug overdose the other day and we have reason to believe that the drug that she had taken was manufactured in Russia."

"What do you mean manufactured?"

'That was a quaint response.' Alfie thought. 'He didn't immediately dismiss the concept of a drug coming from Russia. He wasn't even concerned about the death. He just asked what we meant by manufactured. It's almost as if he is aware of the drug and he can't believe that we know.'

"I mean that we have examined a sample of the drug and we can clearly see that it is completely synthetic and that it would appear that its constituent parts come from Russia."

"That is preposterous and just another example of the west trying to besmirch the good name of Russia."

Alfie let out a little snigger, which he immediately regretted as the other two stared at him with synchronised disdain.

"We can of course prove where the

chemicals come from, but I'm sure, from your response, that you don't want to progress this discussion any further?" This was said by the White Hall representative.

"No, I don't. Good day to you gentlemen. I'm sure you can find your own way out."

"Of course." Stated the White Hall representative.

They walked away together and made for the two large doors at the end of the room. Just before leaving however, the Civil Servant stated, in a less than quiet voice: "Of course that wasn't even the Ambassador you know."

Alfie couldn't help sniggering for the second time. 'I knew it.'

"Edwards, you must stop that immature sniggering."

"Yes sir. Sorry sir."

"At least until it's as effective as that last outburst." He laughed and patted Alfie on the back. "What a fiasco. Who was that guy anyway?" He said while addressing the White Hall suit.

"I've no idea, but I will find out and when I do I'll be sending a formal letter of complaint to the real Ambassador."

"And you think he'll get to read it do you? Don't snigger Edwards."

"Wasn't going to sir." Alfie lied.

"Probably not, but at least they'll know that we know who it was that we spoke to. They hate it when our intelligence actually works."

"I'm not sure how we will progress this investigation now." Said as a statement rather than a question.

Alfie wasn't sure whether he should respond, so didn't.

Once it was known that the three British officials had left the building a call was immediately put through to an office in Moscow, but the recipient wasn't overly bothered by the news.

"So, they know. What can they do with the information?"

No more was said.

Chapter 14

"Dad, I really must speak to you."

"I'll be there in five minutes. Just let me get in and take my shoes off before you start."

That was as close to a civil remark that Trevor's dad ever made. He was in a good mood for once.

The apartment door opened and this time it didn't try and make its way through the party wall. His dad was home and Trevor immediately felt his stomach cramp. 'Katy better be worth this.' Is all that he could think. As usual Katy herself was in Trevors bedroom, staying well out of the way.

"Hi dad. Can I get you a drink?"

"Oh for fuck sake, come on then tell me

what you've done this time?"

"Nothing. Do you want a drink or not?" Trevor felt indignant now, but he checked himself before it ended in another full blown row.

"Go on then, I'll have a beer, but tell me about the trouble that you're in while you pour it. The suspense is killing me."

Trevor went to the fridge and fetched a can of lager. He then grabbed a glass from the wall cabinet. He waited until his dad had sat down and then handed him the tin and glass.

"You better pour this. My hands are shaking." Trevor hated feeling like this in front of his dad. It was just another show of weakness as far as either of them was concerned.

"Anyway, you know Katy?"

"No. Katy who? Is it that the hooker that I saw sneaking out of your room the other day?"

"She's not a hooker. Not yet anyway."

Katy heard that last statement and it confirmed what she'd always thought about Trevor. It also confirmed that she needed to get out as soon as she had the means to do so. She knew that she'd have to be careful though, as she only had this one chance and she had no intention of going back to sleeping under a tarpaulin.

"Oh right. What is she then?"

"She's my girlfriend, that's who she is."

"If she's your girlfriend, why did you say that she's not a hooker yet?"

"Well, she's a druggy so she's unpredictable."

"So you want one of our customers as a girlfriend. Is that really the best that you can do? Is that even wise?"

"It is for now, yes. Anyway, can she stay here please?"

Trevor's dad thought for a few seconds and then a strange grin formed on his lips.

"She can as long as she's useful."

"What do you mean, by useful, dad?"

"Well for now I just mean cooking and cleaning, that sort of thing. Later, who knows?"

This was exactly the response that Trevor was both hoping for and expecting, although he wasn't quite sure about the later bit. For now he'd have to settle for this minor victory.

"Thanks dad."

Trevor left the living room and headed straight for the bedroom.

"I heard." Katy said, as soon as he entered. She parked her emotions for now.

Luckily it never dawned on Trevor that the words 'I heard' also meant that she'd heard about her not being a hooker yet. He was just chuffed that his dad had bought into the idea of Katy staying, at least for now.

"Oy, Katy. Fetch me another beer would you? There's a love."

"He didn't waste any time did he?" Katy said to no one really, as Trevor clearly wasn't listening.

She made her way downstairs and went to the fridge to fetch another can. 'My time will come and so will yours. The pair of you.' She allowed herself a small grin.

Chapter 15

"I have grave doubts about the legitimacy of what we're being asked to produce. What do you think, Mikhail?"

"I've had grave doubts for a long time, but here isn't the place to discuss this."

"I'm not sure we should discuss this anywhere."

"We must. It's becoming too important to brush under the carpet."

"Okay, but we do it after work and we do it a long way from here."

That evening the pair of them made prearranged excuses to their respective parents, left their block of flats and walked to the gardens that they used to play in as children. For once the weather had stayed fine all day and it was a lovely evening. This time the visit to the gardens would be for a much less wholesome reason.

After having a good look all around, they both decided the coast was clear and that it was as safe as it would ever be, to discuss they're misgivings.

"So, you go first Mikhail. You said that you've had doubts about the legitimacy of what we are doing, for a long time. When did you start doubting and why and also why didn't you tell me?"

"Well my young friend, all I can say is that I thought it strange from the moment we were drafted in. Why hire a couple of green behind the gills youngsters, stick them in a small but brilliantly equipped laboratory and then give them specific targets to achieve, which they don't appear to want anyone else to know about. It all seems a bit cloak and dagger to me, even for Russia." Mikhail stopped to draw breath, before continuing. "Why couldn't we do what we have done in a large well resourced lab, where we could have picked the brains of far more experienced scientists? In fact why didn't they just get more experienced scientists to do this anyway?" He went on. "To answer your final question. I didn't tell you because there was nothing to tell. I just had doubts and you know as well as I do, where gossip can lead."

"I must admit that none of that had really ever occurred to me. I just assumed that they had picked a couple of talented youngsters, knowing that we stood as good a chance as anyone in achieving what they wanted."

"I'm sure that's exactly what they wanted us to think."

"What else have you doubted then?"

"The output, that's what. That, my dear friend, is where you come in."

"How?"

"Isn't that where you have your doubts? Isn't that why we're meeting here this evening?"

"I suppose so, yes. I don't like what we're being instructed to produce. It doesn't matter what they call it or what they say that they intend to use it for, I believe it has the capacity to be dangerous and God forbid it should fall into the wrong hands."

"That's exactly what I think. What do you think we should do about it?"

"I think that we should do nothing and just continue to do as we're told. Anything else could have dire consequences."

"I suppose so, although that doesn't sit well with me." Andreiv had decided that he couldn't do as his friend suggested because it wasn't right. However, he would continue for now and look for the right time to make their creation known to someone.

They both stood and then followed the path back toward the park gates, where they exited and turned right to head home. They still appeared to be the only ones in the park, which was a little odd, as it was a lovely evening.

Mikhail didn't arrive at work the following day, but there was a note pinned to the back of the lab door. It was where Andreiv hung his coat, so whoever had pinned it there knew exactly what they were doing.

The note was printed and just said: Mikhail won't be available for work anymore and if you don't want to go on long term 'sick' leave, I suggest that you continue with your work and don't talk to anyone.

It was signed: Sincerely GU

Andeiv read the note in total disbelief. He just slumped to the floor where he had been standing and cried. He cried for most of that morning. He didn't have anything for lunch and in the afternoon he just sat at his desk and stared out of the window.

His friend had obviously been murdered by the Russian secret service and for what? Just because of an overheard discussion in a park?

'If that were the case, then I'm just as guilty, but of course their precious project would grind to a halt if I were taken out as well.'

No work was done that day or the next, but at the end of the first day Andreiv thought it only right that he go and give the grave news to Mikhail's parents. He had no idea what he was going to say.

By the time he reached their flat he had decided that he was going to say that his friend had met with an accident at work. He didn't know exactly what the accident was as he wasn't in the lab at the time. Because of the secret nature of what they were being asked to produce, the body was taken straight to the morgue.

Andreiv knocked on the front door and waited. After a short delay it was answered by a very upset woman. It was Mikhail's mother and she just waved Andreiv inside, without saying a word.

Andreiv walked through to the living room and stood until Mikhail's mother came in. She pointed to a chair, so Andreiv sat. He was just about to start his speech, not stopping to realise that the lady of the house had obviously already received the bad news, when she started to speak.

"I know about it Andreiv."

"Really?" Andreiv just waited for what may be coming next.

"I know that my little boy is dead."

"I came to tell you."

"Bless you Andreiv. Although why you felt that you should be responsible for telling me, I don't know. After all, unless you were driving the car that hit him, why would you?"

Andreiv was completely taken aback by this comment. Someone had already invented a story and relayed it to Mikhail's mother. 'Well that means I don't have to
lie at least.' Was the first thought that sprung into his mind. He immediately felt guilty for thinking this.

"I just can't understand why I can't see him. They say that he must stay at the morgue until the investigations are complete."

"Well I suppose they do need to check on his injuries and if the driver is denying that he or she killed Mikhail, they will need to to decide what it was that actually killed him."

This comment just made Mikhail's mother sob even more. Andeiv tried to hand her a handkerchief, but she just pushed his hand away. The word 'killed' had just re-emphasised the finality of the situation.

The front door opened and Mikhail's father walked in. He'd had his usual hard day at work and knew nothing of his son's fate.

"You go Andreiv. Leave this to me please."

"What are you two up to?" was his fathers opening gambit.

"Young Andreiv was just leaving. See you later lad."

"Yes, good evening to you both." Andreiv left swiftly, but even before he'd reached the ground floor he could hear Mikhail's father shouting in a distressed manner. He quickly shut the street door behind him.

What neither Andreiv or his old friend had known was that their new drug had already started to be distributed in small doses and to a chosen couple of dealers. One of whom was based in Paris and that one had sold some on to a dealer in London.

The London dealer and the Russian Embassy in London had both just found out that a young lady had died from some sort of cocaine poisoning. One of those two knew exactly where the drug had come from and the other neither knew nor cared.

Chapter 16

The fake wedding took place in a small village just outside Samarkand in Uzbekistan. It was carried out purely for the photos, so that Daisy had something to send back to her friends at her old base. This was Daisy's attempt at making the ceremony look legitimate. Ahmed couldn't care one way or the other about the ceremony. His thoughts had already moved elsewhere.

He was determined to hold her to the promise of a wedding night that involved pressing some flesh. This couldn't have been further from what Daisy had on her mind, but for her own safety's sake she went along with it to a point.

The wedding night went pretty much

as she knew it would, with one exception. However it didn't go as Ahmed had planned at all. He had showered and shaved, obviously still firmly committed to his version of what was to take place. He dressed in his most exotic and alluring suit and once ready he made a grand entrance into the living room. Daisy was sitting at the small writing desk that was situated in the corner. She briefly looked up and then continued to look at the map that lay sprawled out in front of her. She was dressed exactly as she had been, just after the wedding ceremony i.e. jeans and a tea shirt.

To Ahmed it didn't look like she had made any effort to get ready for the night time activities. He had no idea that Daisy wasn't joking when she'd said that he wasn't to touch her.

"When are you going to prepare?"

"Prepare what? You've already eaten."

He put that statement down to good old British humour. The truth was that she was going to get out of this farce of a marriage as soon as she could. She had absolutely no intention of letting him anywhere near her.

"I made how I felt and what wouldn't happen, perfectly clear to you. You're the one who insisted on the marriage. I am not interested in you."

"I will make you interested, you silly woman." This was seen as totally unacceptable behaviour, from a woman and besides it hurt an eastern gentleman's pride, to be spoken to in this way. "I can overpower you and make you do my bidding."

"You can try Ahmed, but I definitely wouldn't recommend it."

Ahmed wasn't aware of Daisy's martial arts background. He was aware that she was fit and that she'd been trained by the British special services. 'She is still only a woman.' He thought with a little less conviction than he would have liked.

Ahmed made his move, but as soon as he lunged forward to grab Daisy by the arms, she swung round with one leg outstretched and took his feet out from under him. He quickly recovered however and sprung up towards Daisy's throat, with his arms outstretched. She was ready for him, so she just parted both of his arms and at the same time swung her foot up and connected with his genitals. She then

grabbed his collar with one hand and struck an upward blow with the palm of her hand, to the base of his nose. He immediately froze, as his nose bone had pierced his brain. He then went limp, so Daisy let go of his collar.

Ahmed's lifeless body dropped to the floor. She felt nothing. She just looked at him laying there and wondered how she was going to get rid of the body. An hour later she was fast asleep. Ahmed was still laying where he fell. She had decided to sort out the problem in the morning.

Chapter 17

Katy was extremely grateful to have a roof over her head, but it wasn't easy going, especially as she had to satisfy a guy who she wouldn't normally have given a second look at. Still, she counted her lucky stars that his father hadn't made any advances so far. She also counted her blessings that Trevor was as thick as the proverbial and better still he was out at the moment.

"Katy, have you got a minute?" Trevor's dad called from the living room.

'Maybe I spoke too soon.' She thought. "Sure, what's up?" She always trod carefully around the pair of them, but particularly around Trevor's father.

"Come in and sit down please. I have a

favour to ask."

Katy put down her tea towel and trotted into the living room. She sat on the edge of the sofa and waited for whatever bombshell Mr King was going to drop.

"First of all, call me Martin please. You've been here long enough now I think."

"Okay Mr. err, Martin."

"I'll get straight to the point. How do you fancy working for me?"

"Well, I don't really know. What would it involve?"

"It would involve you doing more of what you do anyway, really. With regard to drugs that is."

"You want me to push?"

"No, I want you to run."

"You mean collect them and deliver?"

"Precisely."

"So what exactly would be expected?"

"Well before we get to the nitty gritty, let me tell you that it's well paid and the more you run the more you make. You could easily make enough to afford your own place. I do know that your first choice wouldn't be to be shacked up with that dipstick son of mine."

"He's alright and he's been good to me."

"That's only because you've been good to him, so please don't start feeling any kind of loyalty toward him."

"Okay, so my question still stands. What's involved exactly?"

"I will tell you where to go and cover any expenses. You will just go, collect and return with my goods. My only rules are that you remain clean while you're on the job and you tell absolutely no one, including Trevor, what you're doing. Finally, should you be arrested, you don't mention my name."

"Wow, you really know how to sell a job don't you."

"I'm just telling it the way it is. No job that pays well comes without risk. What do you think?"

"Can I have a day to think about it, please?"

"Of course, but I will want an answer by this time tomorrow."

Katy turned to walk away, but just before she did so she turned back and said that she'd do it.

"Fuck me that twenty four hours flew by." He chuckled.

"What choice do I really have? I didn't need a day to weigh up my options."

"Good girl. You can start in the morning."

Chapter 18

No further headway had been made with regard to the Russian cocaine investigation. It was almost as if whoever was supplying this variant was aware that the police were on to them. It also looked like any users, who were fortunate enough to have survived, were under pain of death not to speak about their dealers. They weren't likely to cut off the hands that fed them anyway.

There was only one slim lead and that was the pharmacist. Someone just happened to mention to one of Alfies constables 'the pharmacist', as if he or she were some kind of DC comics villain. No more was know, except that he or she was local to the investigation.

The girl who died was just an average girl.

She was a college student from a middle class family and she lived in suburbia. Although Alfie now knew her identity, she had no police record, in fact no record of any kind, that would help.

The Russians had been as helpful as everyone knew they would be, so Alfie was going to have to rethink his strategy. Whatever else happened, he had to find the source of the drug somehow, especially as it now looked like a second victim had succumbed. He was just awaiting confirmation of this. He didn't have to wait long as the following morning there was a gentle knock on his office door.

"Morning sir. I remembered to knock."

"Well done son. What have you got for me?"

"The lab has confirmed that the cocaine was from the same source."

"Right, so do we know anything about this person?"

"We do sir." The constable went on to explain the drug addicts details and the only real conclusion that they could deduce was that the dealer must be the same person who supplied the young lady. This was based purely on the physical locations of both victims.

"We need to start checking local pharmacies and in particular, who owns them."

Chapter 19

Kevin was having as much luck with regard to finding Daisy as Alfie was of finding the source of the drugs. All he had managed to find out, along with the fact that she had indeed served in Afghanistan, was where she was based and that she had been gathering intelligence. The one fact that he truly didn't want to believe and couldn't understand was that she had left to get married. After this, it then appeared that she had left for Russia, either on her own terms, because she was coerced or because she'd been abducted. Confusion reigned.

'She must have been groomed.' He thought. 'But I still don't understand why or how. She was rock solid. There must be a very good reason why she turned, if she's turned.'

Finding out that she'd got married particularly felt like a body blow and initially he couldn't really understand why. It took a while to fully digest and it left him feeling very odd. It finally dawned on him that it must be the feeling of love that he was dealing with. He'd never felt this way before and he didn't like the power it had over him.

A few days later and with his head a little clearer, the other conclusion that was drawn, finally struck home. 'It could be that she is indeed a double agent and if so, she's playing an extremely dangerous game. That's obviously what she'd meant when she said that she'd gone rogue.'

Of course this didn't explain the other details, but all Kevin could do now was play the waiting game. He would just have to see if any more messages came in and then be on his 'A' game with regard to decoding any hidden meaning in them. He needed to know exactly where she was so that he could formulate a plan of extraction.

As dangerous as it might have been, he decided to risk sending a short message to Daisy. It just read: 'Are you okay. X' This at least would suggest to her that he had seen her messages to him.

Nothing came back. He immediately regretted sending the message. 'What have I done? What if Daisy wasn't the recipient of my message? What if they now decide that keeping her alive is too risky? What if it leads them back to me? I know I can look after myself, but we're talking about the Russian secret service here.'

It felt like his oldest friend and now the love of his life, had just vanished. He was deeply concerned, especially as it appeared that he was powerless to help and he could have been the reason for her disappearance.

Kevin went back to soldiering to the best of his ability, but he couldn't shake off his worry. He knew in his heart of hearts that Daisy was in trouble. He also knew that outside of his duties as a soldier, Daisy had become his number one priority.

He was totally unaware that Daisy, for just the kind of reason that he had considered, had disposed of her phone.

Chapter 20

A phone rang somewhere in the apartment and it woke Daisy from her already very disturbed slumber. It sounded slightly muffled, but was clearly coming from the living room. Daisy slid out of bed and just for a second she'd forgotten about the silent visitor who was still lying spread eagled on the floor in the next room.

She opened the bedroom door and was immediately confronted by the reminder. She followed the ringing phone to its source, but it stopped as she got to the middle of the room. It was obviously Ahmed's phone, but where was it? She hated the thought of poking around his cold dead body. The phone rang again and fortunately she realised that it was coming from somewhere within his jacket.

"Shit. What am I going to do with you, you arsehole." She said out loud as she stepped over the corpse.

One side of the jacket was already laying open on the floor. The phone clearly wasn't there, so Daisy pulled the other side back carefully, as if the body could suddenly spring into life and attack her. She removed the still ringing phone and looked at the number. It meant nothing to her, but then she didn't expect it to. For some completely random reason, she pressed the green phone and waited.

"Who is this?" Spoken in English, but with a heavy Russian accent.

"It's not Ahmed." She didn't really know what to say, but felt that she had nothing to lose by talking to whoever it might be. In fact she might just be able to turn this conversation to her advantage.

"Hello Daisy." The caller said very matter of factly. "Where's Ahmed?"

Daisy was a little taken aback by the fact that the caller knew who she was, but soon recovered as she realised that information such as this would be readily available to whoever Ahmed dealt with. It might even be the

Russian who had requested her departure from Afghanistan.

"He's dead and he's currently laying on the living room floor."

"How did that happen?"

"I killed him."

"I warned him that you were smarter and stronger than he thought. What did he do or do I not need to know?"

"Oh you can know alright. He tried it on with me, when I'd already warned him to lay off."

"You'll have to excuse my lack of understanding of your English idiosyncrasies, but I think I understand."

"Can you help me get rid of the body?"

"Well that rather depends, doesn't it Daisy?"

"On what?"

"On what you will do in return."

"What do you want me to do?"

"I'll come over and we can discuss that. I'll bring some help with me. Don't worry it's not that kind of help. It's the kind of help that can make bodies disappear."

"When will you come? I've no idea when I might get thrown out of this room."

"Don't worry, I'll come now. I'll be about half an hour."

"Okay thanks."

Daisy returned the phone to Ahmed's breast pocket. For a moment she considered texting Kevin from it, but then decided that the people who were about to visit would surely go through Ahmed's messages.

Forty five minutes later there was a soft tap on the hotel room door. In fact had Daisy not been passing, she wouldn't have heard it. She peered through the spy hole and saw that three gentlemen were waiting patiently on the other side. She guessed that this was her new phone contact and his two accomplices, so she opened the door.

"Please come in."

The three men walked past Daisy without saying a word. The man who entered first was short and stocky with a short black beard. He wore a dark blue suit and Daisy assumed that he was the man who she had spoken with. The other two were both huge and each looked like he had been hewn from granite. These were not men to mess with. They carried a large rug between them.

The two rock men just rolled the body that was still precisely where she'd left it, into the rug, lifted it and its contents onto their shoulders and left the room. The thick set man took a seat and invited Daisy to do the same.

"We know all about you Daisy."

"Really. Is that good or bad?"

"We are indifferent about your past. We just needed to know whether you were of any use to us."

"Am I?"

"I believe you are, yes. Especially as your Russian is excellent."

"Thank you." Daisy was completely taken aback. "How do you know that I speak Russian? Even my boss didn't know."

"We just do." He wasn't going to elaborate.

"What do I call you by the way?"

"You call me sir."

"Yes sir." This wasn't going to be a walk in the park, Daisy decided.

"We need you back in the homeland so that we can brief you on your next mission. I will arrange transport. Please be ready."

He handed Daisy a phone.

"I will need your old phone please."

"I don't have it, I'm afraid."

"Why not?"

"I thought it prudent to ditch all of my old contacts and start again. I certainly didn't want to receive any unwelcome calls."

The man with no name didn't look entirely convinced.

"How did you dispose of it?"

"I burnt it. I was passing a building site where an incinerator was burning, so I threw my phone in. I wasn't seen, so don't worry."

"Oh, I won't." He said almost threateningly. "Your new phone is to be used for official calls only. Any numbers that you may need are already on it. All calls will be monitored."

"Of course." Daisy was inwardly petrified, but at least she'd managed to lie albeit unconvincingly about the reason for disposing of her old phone. Hopefully she'd managed to keep Kevin out of trouble so far.

"I'll be in touch." He left the room without another word, closed the apartment door behind him and walked to the lift. Daisy went to the window to see if she could see him exit the building. She wasn't too sure what use that would be, but she
didn't see him anyway. She did see a dark blue, unmarked van come out of the hotel car park and just wondered if her ex husband was taking his last ride in the back.

'Well at least that little mess has been cleared up. I've just got the rest of my life to sort out now, starting with checking out of here, minus one husband.'

Daisy decided that the best way to deal with that little problem was to not check out at all. She boldly walked through reception with her one bag and just kept walking.

Chapter 21

Trevor wasn't happy, again. He needed to do something different. Something for himself. Both Katy and his father appeared to be having a ball and it wasn't fair.

Katy was now earning more money than she'd ever dreamed of. She was very good at what she did, which was collecting and paying for the goods and then distributing them where necessary. Soon she'd be able to afford to move out, but she would have to broach that subject with Trevor first. She felt that this would only be fair, as without him she wouldn't be where she was now. Also, she didn't want him coming after her. She'd even managed to cut right back on her own need for the drugs. She only had to look at the state of most of her punters to know that wasn't a look that she aspired to. Luckily for her it hadn't quite got to a real addiction stage, but even so she felt proud of the fact that she was coping without it, nearly.

Trevor's dad could see how well she was doing and put it down to the fact that she was delivering the goods, literally and that she was just squirrelling her money away. He had no idea that she was filtering some of his customers away from him and starting her own supply network. Unwittingly she'd certainly risen in his esteem. In fact Trevor suspected that Katy had even shared his fathers bed, as he wouldn't have a thing said against her. That was a sure sign.

The other sure sign was the fact that his dad had paid for Katy to learn to drive and then bought her a car and that wasn't a tatty old Ford Fiesta either.

There were therefore two options left open to Trevor. One was to permanently remove Katy and the other was to start a business in his own name. He decided on the second as whilst he'd be quite happy for the silly little bitch to be pushed under a bus, he didn't want to suffer any repercussions from his father. Whether he'd dispatched her personally or arranged for a third party to do it, his dad would know that he was somehow responsible.

Trevor took himself off to the nearest pub where he could sit with a pint and start to make plans. He'd never made a plan before, so the first problem he faced was how to go about making one. On the way he popped into WH Smiths and purchased a notepad and a pen. 'You need to make notes.' He thought smuggly. 'Any great planner makes notes.' He felt better for his purchase, so continued his journey fortified by this thought.

He arrived at the pub, parked his Fiesta across two bays and promptly walked in and ordered a lager. The waitress asked him for some id., which fortunately he had by means of his driving licence. He took an immediate dislike to this particular member of the bar staff and made a mental note to make her life a little more stressful. He then remembered that he'd left the all important note pad and pen in the car, so went back to retrieve them.

Finally, ensconced at a quiet table with pad, pen and lager to hand he set about coming up with his master plan. This didn't include doing anything about Katy for the very reasons that he'd already considered. Maybe he would deal with her at a later date, but for now the plan would be based purely on business.

He started writing and before long he had a rather less than extensive plan of action:

1. New supplier
2. New clients
3. New car
4. New flat
5. MONEY!

Happy with his plan, his priority was certainly going to be to find a new supplier or suppliers.

He sat back and drank his lager. A small amount found its way onto his shirt, but of course he wasn't aware of this.

Chapter 23

Although Andreiv missed his old friend greatly he had pressed on with his work and had now produced what he'd been asked to. As far as he knew, he was the first person in the world to do so. He had produced completely synthetic cocaine. This had been carried out on the premise that it would be used for purely medicinal reasons. This he thought rather dubious, but he had no idea what the real reason was.

Clinical trials had been started but what the people that were in the know didn't inform Andreiv, was that there had already been a few fatalities, a couple of which had occurred in the UK and that was most embarrassing, but no reason to stop production. The authorities weren't overly bothered about these deaths because the people being used as guinea pigs were either addicts, prisoners or other lowlife scum. That was according to those who administered or sold the drug. Also, the planned market for the product was huge and that meant that a few deaths now were of no concern. The drug would surely be refined over time.

Andreiv's work didn't stop there however, because as soon as his cocaine was released for testing he was summoned to a meeting. A few days later there was a car waiting outside his home. There had been no mention of a driver being sent, so he was completely taken aback when on leaving for the meeting a man approached him and requested that he get into the back of the car.

"I'm sorry but I have to get to a meeting." Andreiv said in all innocence.

"I'm here to take you to the meeting."

"But no one told me that you would be here." The problem was that no one trusted anyone else and this sometimes led to total confusion.

"You sound surprised." The driver said while raising his eyes to the heavens.

"I suppose I am yes, but I do know what you are saying." Even Andreiv knew the way that his home country operated. After what had happened to Mikhail, very little surprised him.

"So please get in. We mustn't be late otherwise it won't just be you who gets into trouble."

Andreiv still had no real idea what was going on, but he could see that the driver was genuinely concerned for his own welfare.

They spent the next hour traversing busy rush hour roads and traffic, but they did manage to arrive before the allotted time. As usual, no words were spoken and the car left as soon as Andreiv had alighted. He entered the building not having any idea where he was supposed to go, but within a couple of seconds another man appeared from nowhere and ushered him toward a lift. The pair of them exited the lift on the third floor and Andreiv just trailed along one step behind his guide.

A door opened and the guide walked straight in and pointed to a seat. Andreiv took this to mean that he was to sit there. The pair of them waited for five minutes before a door at the far end of the room opened and two men and a very attractive woman entered.

Andreiv was directed to stand, so he jumped up. There were no pleasantries and no introductions. He was told to sit once the others had.

"We want you to do the same with cannabis. You have six months." This statement was made by the nameless gentleman who sat opposite Andreiv. He appeared to be the spokesperson as the other couple just sat motionless and listened to the entire conversation.

"I have no idea how long it will take to synthesise cannabis and I'm sure you don't."

"You will do it within six months because I am telling you to. Don't give me smart answers otherwise you will go the same way as your friend. You are not the only protege you know. You just happened to be handy."

"Yes sir. Sorry sir." Andreiv could feel himself dying inside while he was conceding to these animals.

During the meeting the spokesperson decided it would be prudent to remind Andreiv of his friend's fate. Like Andreiv needed reminding.

"You never did ask what became of your friend by the
way. I'd be only too happy to go through the details."

A shiver went right through Andreiv. This was exactly why he didn't ask what had happened to his friend. He knew well enough what the outcome was. He didn't need the details and he definitely didn't want to go the same way.

"No thank you." Andreiv didn't want to sound arrogant, so the

best that he could manage was to sound deflated. "Do I get any additional resources? After all, you took the best partner that I could have."

"I will see what I can do, but you get on with it in the meantime. I will call in from time to time, to check on progress."

"You didn't do that before."

"I trusted you before. By the way, you're getting a pay rise in recognition of what you've accomplished so far. There, its not all bad is it?" This was said with the expected irony.

Andreiv knew that he'd be watched wherever he went, from now on. Of course he probably had been anyway.

A short while later he received the promised reward for his efforts so far and in fact his family were moved to a much more extravagant flat. All this was aimed at securing his continued silence of course, whilst emphasising that the powers that be, could do anything they liked with his family. None of this altered the way that he felt about what he was being asked to produce.

He made a mental note to string out the project as long as he possibly could without looking obvious. He was determined to make someone aware of what was going on, but he needed time to work out who he could trust, if anyone.

Chapter 24

Katy had finally managed to amass enough money to be able to put a deposit down on a flat. She was on her way up. She was working very hard and she felt that she deserved it. It did mean that she had to sleep with Martin (Trevor's dad), on more than one occasion, but that was a small price to pay. He was marginally more pleasant than his son and he was loaded, therefore it was a no brainer as far as Katy was concerned.

The only time that Katy had been insistent about anything was when Martin had offered to purchase the flat for her. She didn't want to be beholden to anyone. Whilst she was fairly happy with their arrangement, she wanted to maintain a certain amount of independence and a home of her own was top of that particular requirement.

Finding potential new clients was one of Katy's particular strengths, but she'd also managed to find a couple of new suppliers. She tried to sell this as being proactive, however Martin didn't take too kindly to her interference in what he saw as very much his side of the business. He needed to be in total control of all purchases and he needed to be able to mask his nefarious activities through his legal business. He still had no idea that Katy was actually weaning clients away from him.

Selling the concept of the two additional dealers to Martin was all part of her plan and although he was annoyed, he did accept that the additional dealers could help. Her main aim was to use them to supply her own embryonic business. This meant that as he was aware of their existence she could utilise the pair without fear of being rumbled.

She still worked for him and she tried her hardest not to let him down. She just utilised the other two suppliers to feed any additional requirements. This arrangement seemed to be working well so far. She ran two different books and made sure that she kept most of her clientele totally separate from Martins. All except those that she'd pilfered that was.

The long term plan was to build her own business empire and she was going to use the Kings to help her do it. After all, they had both used her.

26 – present

Chapter 1

The two elderly gentlemen who were seated outside the cafe in a Moscow side street were each sipping their traditional tea. None of this new fangled western coffee for them. They were making childish and derisory comments about passers by and the traitorous coffee drinkers who were sitting nearby. It was harmless fun as far as they were both concerned. Of course this was all just a sideshow.

Once the jocularity had been dispensed

with they reflected on what had happened over the last couple of years. Even now they could barely believe that the purely speculative and strictly off the record conversation of two years ago, had led to this project being the success that it had become.

"Well, what have we done Grigori?"

"We've unleashed the tiger, that's what we've done." Grigori let out an indiscreet titter at his own comment.

"If this project works as planned, we will control all of the drug traffic in nearly all of the capitals of europe."

"We will control all of the drug traffic in all of the capitals in europe. We will then control europe. Just not in a way that is currently obvious to them and by the time it does become obvious the damage will have been done."

"Of course."

"Almost as importantly, we will make millions for our country, while doing it."

"We must be patient and we must plan impeccably. If we get this wrong we will not be around to make the same mistake a second time."

"You don't think that we've gone a tad too far?"

"Well we have the full backing of those who know far more than we, so no I don't."

They both took another sip of their tea, sat back and for the next few minutes returned to absorbing all that was occurring around them. It was a very pleasant morning, after all.

Grigori and Bogdan were both staunch old guard politicians and they shared a hatred for the west. They particularly didn't appreciate the dissolution of the USSR, the loss of their precious empire or even the Berlin wall coming down. Such a symbol. In their minds the west was going to pay for this and now they had a plan that would make this happen or at least would start the process.

They had been given an unofficial blessing to proceed on the proviso that the Russian Government wouldn't be implicated in any way. They had given their assurances.

Although they were both officially retired they did like to keep their hands in. Another way of putting that would be to say that they liked to meddle and if it were at all possible to cause trouble in the west, then they were always completely on board.

"We need someone to project manage this whole affair now. Someone intelligent, someone with a military background I would suggest, someone who wouldn't crack under interrogation."

"I thought that was us?" Said with a certain amount of irony.

"It has been until now, but now that we are in a position to go live and therefore international, we run far too much risk of getting found out and neither of us want that."

"So we also want someone who we can afford to throw to the wolves."

"Exactly, but not until they've served their purpose. We must offer them all the support that we can until then, otherwise the entire plan will fall apart."

"Of course. Do you have anyone in mind?"

"Well yes, as it happens I do and she has already been introduced to our boy in the lab."

"A female. I never thought I'd live to see the day."

"Not only a female, but a female from the west. She has all the right credentials, including fluent Russian and she is totally disposable."

"Excellent. When can she start?"

"She has."

"When were you going to tell me?"

"When I was sure and to be quite honest she only recently came to our notice."

"Can she be trusted?"

"I shouldn't think so."

"She sounds perfect."

"I knew you'd like her. That's why I started

her straight away."

"That's that particular problem solved then. What will be the next I wonder?"

"They are challenges my friend, not problems."

"Yes of course. Our next problem is a challenge."

"You are an oaf."

"Thank you old friend. I'll take that as the criticism that was meant."

"It's a good job you humour me you old buffoon." Grigori gave a slightly demented laugh.

In all the years that they had known each other Bogdan never quite knew when to take Grigori seriously and that was just how Grigori liked it. Although it bothered Bogdan sometimes, he didn't dare ask if Grigori was joking, as he might not like the answer. Grigori just couldn't help playing mind games, even with his old friend.

They both rose from the table and Grigori checked inside the cafe to make sure that the staff were otherwise occupied. "Go." He hissed. They left swiftly without paying.

As old and as wealthy as they both were, they still got a kick out of these minor pranks.

They had purposely chosen a cafe

that was away from their normal haunts. Somewhere they didn't have to worry about returning to, for a while anyway. When they were far enough away, they slowed and both agreed that It had been a very good day so far. They also agreed that they would soon have to come up with another type of prank as their hearts wouldn't be able to cope with the fast walking any more.

Neither of them were bothered about the stress caused by ripping a small business owner off, just the swift getaway afterwards.

"Oh Grigori. We are pure evil aren't we?"
"I suspect we are Bogdan. I suspect we are."

'I don't know Bogdan. Sometimes I think that your heart's not in the total destruction of the west anymore.' Grigori thought to himself. 'Maybe I'm going to have to find a way to pension you off, old friend.'

Chapter 2

Kevin had now served Queen and country for ten years and had an exemplary record. He could see no reason for that to change in the foreseeable future.

At his base somewhere in deepest Helmand province:

"Send for Keenan would you. This is one discussion that I'm not relishing."

"No sir. I completely understand. I still can't believe it."

"We must keep this under wraps, you understand?"

"Yes sir. I'll go and fetch him."

The adjutant didn't have to look far. Generally, if Kevin wasn't on his bunk he was in the mess. There was little else to get up to when someone was quite willing to take your head off. He found Kevin on his bunk and luckily he was alone.

"Ah Keenan, you are here. The old man wants to see you pronto."

"Right lieutenant. Any idea what for?"

"He'll explain when you get there."

Kevin ran across the small camp and entered the CO's outer office. This in itself was just a small tent which was attached to a larger one. As the adjutant was still behind him, Kevin went straight toward the inner office door. A voice from the other side of the doorway shouted for him to enter before he'd quite reached it.

Kevin entered, saluted and went to stand in front of the only available chair.

"Don't sit Keenan. This won't take long."

The adjutant stood in the doorway, but was promptly ushered away by the CO.

"Can you leave us please lieutenant. I'd like a private word with this man."

"But what if you need a witness sir?"

"I'm sure I won't, but thank you anyway."

The adjutant left with his tail between his legs. He was going to miss out on a juicy conversation officially. Of course he was only ever going to be just the other side of a strip of canvas, so unofficially he would hear everything. He sat with ears pricked.

Kevin sensed that all was not well.

The CO got straight to the point. "We have reason to suspect that you may have been involved in a murder. What have you got to say for yourself?"

As usual Kevin only needed a split second to digest what had just been thrown at him, before coming back with his statement.

"If you're referring to the young lads who jumped me sir, that was a while ago and I thought that I'd been totally honest and up front with my report."

"It's not about that affair I'm afraid. It's about one that took place while you were on leave last year. Ring any bells."

"Yes sir. It does sir, but I can categorically say that I didn't do it. The guy was already dead before I got there."

"Was he indeed? Then what, may I ask, were you doing there?"

"I'd gone there to kill him sir."

"Why?"

"Long story short. I made a promise to a friend a long time ago and I keep my promises."

"Rather a grand gesture Keenan. Why did this man deserve to die, especially twice it would appear."

"He was a rapist. A child rapist. He was my friend's stepfather."

"And I suppose your friend was too scared to mention this to anyone."

"Yes sir. Her mother knew, but turned a blind eye."

"Did she? Right, well anyway you were seen leaving that property and we have photo's." The CO produced the photograph's and briefly showed them to Kevin.

"How do they know that's me? It looks like it could be anyone."

"Nice try Keenan. We checked where you were at the time these were taken and funnily enough, you were in the area. I'm sure your adversaries will have done the same." The CO was on a roll, so continued. "Obviously whoever sent these also has copies and this leaves me and the service with a rather difficult situation to deal with."

"There is a slight upside to this scenario, if you don't mind me making an observation sir?"

"How can there be any possible upside to the fact that you have been captured on film or whatever they use these days, at the scene of a murder?"

"Well sir, as I see it, I've been grassed up by someone who was also at the scene of the crime. They couldn't have photographed me otherwise and also in order to know about my whereabouts whilst on active duty they must either be spying for us or against us, which makes them military adversaries either way. It also places them at a murder scene at the time of murder. I'd say that they were at least equally potentially guilty as me. Do we really need to worry about them?"

"I've got to say Keenan, I hadn't considered any of that, however that still leaves us with a predicament. We don't want any negative press, especially while we are on active duty."

"I understand sir. What do you intend to do with me?"

"Well first of all, I can say that I believe your story. Of any man that serves under me, I would suggest that
you are the most honest. That said, I do have to be seen as doing something about your case. You do understand, don't you Keenan."

"Certainly sir. Would it make it any easier if I were to just disappear?"

"How so?"

"Well, if I go without you knowing, then you can't be blamed for not cooperating with the authorities or whoever comes knocking."

"Good man Keenan. I must admit I had no idea how to handle this blessed case. I'm a military man through and through. These personnel issues never sit well with me. Give me a battle plan to sort out and I'm your man."

"You certainly are sir." Kevin knew that this sounded sycophantic, but it was true.

"I'll give you forty eight hours and an aircraft, that I know nothing about and then I'll come looking for you. Does that sound fair?"

"Yes sir, thank you. It sounds more than fair. Then all I have to do is somehow prove my innocence. I don't suppose you know the source of the photo's?"

"Funnily enough I do yes. It was one of our ex agents. Well he was the one who handed them over anyway. I say ex because he appears to have gone missing. His name was Ahmed and that's all I know about him. He used to liaise with us via a female member of staff, but she's also now absent. Rumour has it that they'd got married. I assume that this is your Daisy don't you?"

Kevin didn't quite know how to react to the last part of the CO's information. Daisy was indeed either playing a very dangerous game or she had genuinely married a spy and they'd eloped. Although he couldn't believe it, it looked like it was the latter, but there was nothing he could do about that now.

Kevin instinctively knew why the photo's had been sent. 'He's grassed me up to keep me away. She must have told him about me, but I can't believe that she knows what he's done.'

"I've got no idea sir, but I will find out. I'll leave now sir and can I just say that I've loved every minute of serving under you and even more so, serving in the SAS."

"Just go Keenan. I'll let you know when to rendezvous with your aircraft." A small tear formed in just one of the old man's eyes. Luckily Keenan hadn't seen it and after a fleeting second it had been eradicated. The last time he had shed a tear for anyone or anything was when his old dog Sam, had been put down.

It was dark outside now, so Kevin slipped back to his billet. He waited until everyone was either asleep or out on a recce., then packed one small bag and left immediately, to wait in the shadows until word came through.

'So, they do know it was me. I hope Daisy wasn't privy to this information.'

Chapter 3

In a small but quite well equipped part of the rundown factory, which was situated on the outskirts of Rostov-on-don, Andreiv continued to produce his synthetic cocaine and where he could he refined it. The one thing that he couldn't guarantee was how safe to use it was however, as the authorities had stopped supplying him with 'volunteers'. The number had been dwindling and even in a country the size of Russia, questions would inevitably be asked, if too many people started disappearing.

If and when he required assistance in the lab, he would have to apply for it, stating exactly what it was that he hoped to achieve. If it was given it was on a very temporary basis. This was to protect the secrecy of the project.

Only Andreiv knew exactly what went into the entire process and indeed what the end product was.

Unbeknown to him, the project was only sponsored by a small department within the government, which meant that a large contingent officially had no idea what was going on and if it were to ever go wrong or information about it were to leak out, heads would roll.

Because the cocaine synthesis had been a resounding success, if you didn't count the handful of people who had died from it, Andreiv had been commanded to produce a fully synthetic version of another drug. If he could do this, Russia would corner the European market on the two most prevalent social drugs, whilst as an aside gather intelligence.

They would do this by utilising two methods. One by using bully boy tactics. Something that they were not averse to doing and the other by making their versions of the drugs, more cheaply than anyone else. After all they didn't have to worry about the costs associated with growing or those of risking reliance on smugglers for shipping. Also, the various salaries that had to be paid to planters etc. were avoided. All costs were internal and therefore could be controlled.

On a more sinister note they could also control what went into the drugs, so if for instance, they decided to reduce the population of the western world somewhat, they could just add a little something to the spliff or crack. This sounded like a particularly excellent idea to the two elderly gentlemen who had initiated this project.

As far as could be ascertained the one weak link in all of this was a young man by the name of Andreiv, for although they had got him to document every part of the process, there was no way of knowing if all that he had written was accurate. They were concerned. If they had the time and the official government backing they would have duplicated the process, based on Andreiv's notes, but they had neither.

Also, as the project manager was a westerner herself, they couldn't rely on her to keep a watchful eye on Andreiv and they didn't have the resources to keep an eye on her either. This was all part of the price to pay when the project was not an officially backed scheme and when the project manager was expected to be expendable.

As for Andreiv himself, he now knew

beyond any reasonable doubt that what he was being expected to produce was not going to be used for medicinal purposes. He was going to keep a promise that he'd made himself and on behalf of his old friend. He was going to let someone know what was going on. He just didn't know who.

Chapter 4

There was a short helicopter ride to an airstrip somewhere else in the province. Kevin had no idea where he was, but then he had no need to know. The pilot just said. "You'll have to run, lad. See that Hercules over there with its engines running? Well it's waiting for you. You must have friends in high places."

"Right, thanks." Kevin grabbed his bag, slid the door back and jumped down, not bothering to use the short ladder. He ran straight toward the waiting aircraft, being careful not to run through the area where the giant propellers were rotating.

Of course Kevin wasn't the only passenger on board. There were about twenty injured personnel, their support staff and equipment and some other military equipment, presumably broken. All heading for home.

Thankfully the flight, other than some turbulence, was long but otherwise uneventful. He had a couple of conversations with the other passengers, but managed to avoid any detailed reason for going home or where he had been based. He even kept his insignia hidden. When asked, the reason given was that there was a family emergency and that he'd been released for short term home leave.

The Hercules touched down at Brize Norton in the early hours of a November morning. It was dark and freezing, but no more so than Kevin was used to in Afghanistan, where it could be boiling during the day then drop to below freezing at night. It did serve to remind him that he needed some clothes, fast.

At least he was now back in the United Kingdom, but he was about to become homeless. He had no plan. He had nowhere to go and the only saving grace was that he did have some money. The one good thing about serving abroad, especially in a theatre of war, meant that he couldn't really spend his earnings. As he'd been abroad for the better part of his ten years in the army, he had managed to squirrel away a few thousand pounds. Not enough to purchase a home, but enough to keep him from starving, for the foreseeable future anyway.

He did have a bed for the night because as far as the base was concerned he was just a soldier returning from Afghanistan. His CO had called in a favour to make sure that he wouldn't be impeded when he exited the base. The reason given was that he was on a secret mission, which in a way he was, as he was on a mission to find the people who set him up. He was also on a mission to find Daisy. He felt that if he found one, he would find the other.

First thing in the morning he had breakfast and then bummed a lift into London. Luckily a truck was taking supplies to the London base and there was room for a passenger up front. He chatted amiably enough with the driver and just kept the conversation away from anything that was likely to identify him or his destination. He convinced the driver that he was going home for personal reasons, but he didn't expand. At least that part of his story was consistent with the one that he'd told the other passengers on the plane. He had removed his SAS insignia permanently before leaving the compound.

During the many gaps in the conversation, he had plenty of time to think. 'I need a job fast. That'll help stop my savings from disappearing.' Even with Kevin's rudimentary education he was savvy enough to realise that he needed to keep topping up his savings at least at the same rate that they were being used to keep him alive. 'I also need some clothes and some other necessities. I need to change my ID. I know I'll become Dan because I'm desperate and it's nice and simple. Even I'm not likely to forget. Dan who though? It's got to be Smith hasn't it? Dan Smith, that's me from now on.'

"Right, here's your stop. I've got to go on down to the stores."

"Thanks mate. I appreciate it."

"No worries. I hope everything goes alright. We've all been there you know."

"Is it that obvious?"

"Well when someone spends as much time as you did, saying very little. It obviously meant that you had something or someone else on your mind."

"Well, thanks again anyway." The name's Dan by the way. Kevin thought that he'd try it out and see what it sounded like.

The driver jovially said. "Of course it is. See you later Dan."

Kevin disappeared around the back of the truck and retrieved his bag. He banged on the side and then waved to the driver whose reflection he could see in one of the door mirrors. He then proceeded to leave the barracks and head back towards his old stomping ground. He had no real reason to go that way. He just had no other way to go.

Chapter 5

This particular October it was already cold in Moscow, even by their standards. The Russian winter had made an early appearance this year. Daisy was going to have to change her wardrobe. She had been given one week to acclimatise herself to her new home.

She now had a small apartment that overlooked some gardens, a regular salary and a pass. She had no idea what the pass was for, but she felt sure that it wouldn't be long before she found out. All that she had been able to establish so far was that she was going to manage a project on behalf of the Russian Government or a part thereof. For now, she was going to make the most of her down time.

The week passed quite quickly and Daisy found that it gave her the opportunity to brush up on her colloquial Russian. She had shopped for food and clothes and spent some of her time in a couple of cafés. All of which helped in that regard.

Exactly one week later and as she had been informed, her new phone rang. It sounded like her friend with no name.

"Someone will be waiting outside your apartment at 08:00 tomorrow morning. Please be ready and sit in the rear of the vehicle. Do not talk to the driver. Oh and bring your pass. You won't get in without it." The phone went dead.

"Charming. Good old fashioned Russian hospitality, I suppose." Daisy said out loud. She then thought. 'I suppose I will have to get used to that.'

Sure enough, at exactly 08:00 the following morning Daisy looked out of the rear of her building and saw a small Lada that was occupied by an oversized driver. 'That has to be him.' She grabbed her bag and coat, locked the front door behind her and left. She got as far as the lift door before realising that she didn't have her pass, so she quickly ran back to collect it. 'That would have made a great first impression.' She thought as the lift door opened.

Half an hour after her departure someone let themselves into her flat and searched it thoroughly. They found nothing of interest, luckily for Daisy, but they did stay long enough to install the usual listening devices. There would be no privacy for her, not even in the bathroom.

Fifteen minutes after she left, she arrived at a huge grey office block. Whilst on the journey she did just happen to notice a black Lada Vesta with two almost identical looking gentlemen, heading in the opposite direction. There was something odd about that car and its occupants, but Daisy didn't have the luxury of time to ponder the issue before she arrived at her destination.

In his best English the driver just pointed to a door and said. "In there."

Daisy didn't answer, as instructed. 'Even that could have been a test.' She wondered.

It didn't take long for Daisy to start to think that her every move was observed. 'I wonder if they'll even bug my flat? Was that where those two jokers in the black car were going?'

She entered the door, which nearly

yanked her shoulder from its socket when pulled and then nearly took her off her feet when it closed behind her. For some obtuse reason this reminded her of the till in the TV program 'Open all hours'. At least that put a smile on her face. This was gone as quickly as it had arrived however, when a voice from upstairs harshly said in Russian.

"Up here."

Daisy only just had time to look up and register where the voice had come from, when the figure disappeared. She had to show her pass to the uniform at the front desk before climbing to the floor that she believed was correct. When she arrived at the top of the stairs, all she could do was stand and wait. She had no idea where to go now and there were at least ten doors leading off of this shabby but once opulent corridor.

A door creaked open slightly.

"Come." Was the next order barked and at least she had definitely heard where it came from this time.

She walked toward the corresponding door and entered tentatively. She wondered if it was going to fight back, like the last one, but it yielded without putting up a fight. Yet again the figure who had opened the door had already disappeared inside, but this time only as far as the room in which Daisy now found herself.

There were three men all sitting at the far end of a huge oval table. They each had a large file in front of them.

"Please sit Miss Wilcox or would you rather be known as Mrs Sidorov." There was a less than discrete chuckle, but at least that meant that the gentlemen had a sense of humour and the speaker had so far been moderately polite.

'Maybe they're not all the same.' She mused. "Miss Wilcox is fine thank you." Daisy sat at the far end of the table.

"We're curious as to why you chose to defect?"

'Wow. They get right to the point.' Daisy was completely wrong footed by this comment, especially as there was no lead time. 'Think Daisy, think.'

The interrogation or interview, as it was preferred to be known, was being carried out by experts who knew exactly how to get what they wanted from an interviewee. Every part of the morning so far had been conducted in such a way as to put Daisy on edge, both physically and mentally. She liked to think that she was up to the challenge, however she had thought this before and that didn't go too well for her.

"Well, Miss Wilcox? It was not a difficult question. They come later." Another snigger from the other two.

'Honesty, to a point, is the best policy here.' "I became very disgruntled with the way that the army was treating me. I felt that I'd gone above and beyond for them and my country and I'd received very little reward." Hardly stopping to draw breath and aiming to halt any oncoming barrage of questions, at least for a few minutes, Daisy went on. "I'm very ambitious and I'm intelligent and I see myself as an asset to whoever I work for, as long as the remuneration is there. I also speak fluent Russian, as I hope you can see."

"This is not a job interview Miss Wilcox, so please desist from the sales pitch. It doesn't impress us. Having said that, what does impress us is your obvious talent. Not least of which is your ability to take on a trained espionage agent in your living room and dispatch him. Very impressive. You also have the ability to get on with whatever task is given to you and more importantly, to get that particular job done. The one thing that does concern me, is that you appear to have no sense of loyalty. You will go with whoever pays or promotes you the most."

"That's not entirely correct, if I may say so. I will go with whoever sets me the greatest challenge and then remunerates me correctly for it, should I complete that challenge. As far as national loyalty goes, why should I have that? My country didn't look after me as an asset."

Another one of the three now took up the questioning. He was bald and heavy and he wore a pinstripe suit of the type that would have gone out of fashion in the west, at least fifty years ago. There was also something very disconcerting about the way that this particular gentleman held himself and the way he stared straight through Daisy. He had the look of an old school Nazi and he made Daisy squirm very slightly, in her seat.

"How do we know we can trust you?"

Daisy thought. 'I'll fight fire with fire'. "You don't, but if I do let you down in any way, I'm sure you'll be letting me know."

"Oh, we will Miss Wilcox." Mr pinstripe just smiled a deathly smile and Daisy felt sure that under his suit was the garb of the grim reaper. She consoled herself slightly by thinking that the Russians wouldn't have gone to all the trouble that they had so far, if they weren't interested in her.

"In that case Miss Wilcox." It was the turn of the third musketeer, who was younger and slimmer than either of his two peers. "We have a mission for you and just to spice things up a little you are going to be flying solo. In other words, whilst we may be supplying you with your orders, equipment, travel permits etc. you will not be granted any access to the Russian government and we for our part will deny any knowledge of your activities. Do you understand Miss Wilcox?"

Daisy wanted to say, 'What's not to understand? You want me to take on something extremely risky and you don't want any comebacks,' but she didn't, instead she said. "Yes, but can I please ask you gentlemen, why me. Surely you have fellow Russians who could do what you are asking of me?"

"Well Miss Wilcox, you have one and possibly two obvious advantages. The first is that you are a westerner and therefore can move around in Europe with relative impunity. The second, well, we'll leave you to ponder." Another small titter.

'Jesus. The universal language of men never gets any more mature.' Daisy smiled lamely at the three men. As far as she was concerned, they'd lost their right to call themselves gentlemen. They were all peasants in suits.

"We will convene another meeting here tomorrow. Be ready to be collected at 08:00. We will discuss the project details then."

"Sounds good." Said Daisy, as brightly as she could, but just to put a damper on that fleeting feeling:

"Oh, it won't be Miss Wilcox. You may go."

Daisy left the building feeling bewildered and a little scared. Once she was outside she found the gorilla in the small car was waiting just where she'd left him.
She assumed that he was going to give her a lift back to her apartment, so she got in.

They drove back to her apartment in total silence. Daisy paid no attention at all to the passing scenery as she was deep in thought. She entered the door to the flats and rode up in the lift on autopilot. She was still trying to deal with all of the thoughts that were flying through her mind. What she did know instinctively was that as soon as she was inside her flat she needed to look for bugs. Her instinct had served her well because she found three relatively easily and luckily they were all just listening devices, so she very carefully removed the one from her bathroom and relocated it to the kitchen.

She had to make doubly sure that there wasn't one already there as it would be obvious to the listeners that two devices were in one room and therefore that someone had been tampering with their equipment. Hopefully that room would sound very like the bathroom, especially as the kitchen was nearly as sparsely furnished as the bathroom.

She had no idea whether she had located all of the devices that were planted, but for now at least, she felt that she not only had some privacy in her bathroom with regard to the normal bathroom activities, but that she also had one room she was relatively sure she wouldn't be overheard in, should she need to speak to someone privately. She could always run water as a background noise, just to make sure.

Chapter 6

As the drugs case had ground to a halt for now, although still ongoing, Inspector Edwards was reassigned to a case that was more urgent. It was a murder case that they were having some difficulty solving.

Someone had been stabbed in their bed, for no apparent reason. Nothing was stolen, not even moved and there appeared to be no motive. All that the police had to go on was the fact that the perpetrator supposedly served in one of the forces and that they had let themselves in through the french doors, which were situated to the rear of the property.

The reason for this suspicion was based purely on the fact that a photo, which had been anonymously handed in, appeared to show a uniformed person on the property at the time of the murder.

Alfie diligently read through all of the case notes and immediately suspected the wife. Whether she had used a third party to actually carry out the murder was another story. He needed to arrange an interview with her straight away. He also needed to gain permission to view the body, which was still in the mortuary and would remain there for the foreseeable future, even though the wife was pressing for her husband to be released for burial. 'That may be another reason to suspect her.' He thought.

Alfie made a note of his initial tasks and assigned them accordingly:

1. Interview wife. - DI Edwards/ Constable Bylett

2. Get photo enhanced (if possible). - DI Edwards

3. Try to find source of said photo. - DI Edwards

4. Check over body and speak to pathologist. - DI Edwards

5. Re-visit crime scene. - DI Edwards/ Constable Bylett

"Right lad. Can you get hold of Mrs Wilcox and arrange a meeting? Please don't mention the word 'interview'. For some strange reason this tends to put people on edge. Just tell her that we'd like a chat." He grinned while saying this.

Alfie always spoke to his junior staff as if he were a father figure even though he was still only in his late twenties himself. He felt that this was friendly but without demonstrating that he wanted to be a friend. There was a distinct difference. The idea was that they would always know where they stood and therefore hopefully, they would respect him for it.

"Yes sir."

"Also, can you please arrange for a visit to the path lab. That will be for me only?"

"Will do." The officer stood and waited for the next order. There wasn't one.

"Well, what are you waiting for lad?" The officer turned on his tail and left for his own desk where he could start to make some calls.

Alfie pulled up the donated photo on his PC. Unfortunately the picture had been taken in near darkness. There was only the street lighting as background illumination. 'I wonder if I can get this picture enhanced in such a way as to make that figure stand out?' He made a couple of calls.

"Hello young Alfie. What can I do you for?" It was an old friend of Alfies mother who got back to him first. Photography had been his business for many years, although this had mainly been during the analogue era.

"Oh, hi Mr Staples. Long time no speak."

"Yes indeed, so I'm guessing that you're after something. Especially with you being a high flying officer of the law and all that."

Alfie did wish that his mother didn't keep telling everyone about him. There would never be any point in him working under cover because the rest of the world would know before he stepped out of the office.

"I am actually, but before I do ask it would be very remiss of me not to ask how you and Mrs Staples are?"

"Well actually Alfie, the Mrs passed away last year. It was the cancer that got her in the end. I'm fine anyway thanks, barring the odd creak here and there."

"I'm very sorry to here about your wife. She was a lovely lady, as I recall."

"She was indeed lad, anyway don't get me started. How can I help?"

"How's your digital photography?"

"With regard to taking pictures the principal's the same, so I should be okay. What is it that you want?"

"I need a photograph to be enhanced. There is a person in it who has been snapped in the dark and the picture is a bit grainy."

"Send it over lad and I'll see what I can do."

Okay. Are you alright with emails and attachments and things like that?"

"Cheeky young scoundrel. I'll have you know that I keep myself up to date with all the latest techno whatever."

"Right, sorry. I'll send it straight away. What's your email address?"

Chapter 7

F or the first few nights he slept rough. Sleeping rough was of no consequence to Kevin, but trying to find somewhere that was conducive to a good night's sleep and away from other humans was proving to be an issue. He was in the east end of London after all. On the upside he was never going to be far from the necessities of life. He eventually found an alley that appeared to be suitable, so once he'd hidden his bag he scouted the remainder of the neighbourhood to see what other amenities were available.

The following morning and after a surprisingly good night's sleep there was a short walk to the nearest toilet facilities, where he could at least freshen up for the day ahead. While there he considered his immediate predicament and decided that a medium sized van would be best as his short term base. It would serve as bed, storage and transport.

With a new sense of purpose and a new day ahead, Kevin felt good. He set off to find the nearest newsagent with a view to purchasing whatever papers were available that might contain local vehicle ads. He was going to locate and then hopefully purchase a set of wheels.

After several non-starters: one with too much rust, another with a ropey sounding engine and then one that clearly had its mileage wound back, going by the wear on the pedals and drivers seat, he finally settled on an old Ford Transit, which had six months MOT on it. It was older than he was envisaging and it cost more than he really wanted to spend, but at least it appeared to be reliable. It was solid and it even came with half a tank of fuel.

The old boy selling it said that he was retiring and had no further use of his trusty old van. That was the story given anyway and Kevin liked the old fellow. He thought that he sounded genuine.

He registered the van under the name of Daniel Smith and he used an address that was nearby. He made sure that the address had an external post box. This way he could keep an eye out for the postman and hopefully get to the post before the rightful owners did. He didn't worry about insuring it. His logic being that the van wasn't worth much and he wouldn't be travelling far in it, so he shouldn't be having any major accidents. Anything minor could be dealt with on a cash only basis.

After a week of his new way of living, Kevin had already developed a routine. He would park his van one street behind the main road and then walk to the local shops in order to make a note of any jobs that were being advertised in the newsagent's window. He would also buy the local papers, for the same reason.

While walking he would also call into a few of the other shops to inquire as to whether they might require any casual workers. He was now a man with a van, but unfortunately there were no takers. All of the store owners were either fully staffed or they were struggling to pay themselves let alone another member of staff.

By preference he would have liked a job where he was working on his own, but he was aware that beggars couldn't be choosers. He needed an income, any income, as long as it was legal.

History had taught him long ago that he wasn't at his best in company, although he was polite and amiable enough. Since leaving the forces and getting back to civvy street, this had all been reaffirmed. Everything that he'd seen about civilian life so far, appeared frenetic. He just felt that he would be safer on his own.

He noted a couple of numbers that had been posted in the newsagents window and circled a few that were in the papers. He then made his way back to the van in order to call any prospective employers.

He'd only had his trusty steed a couple of weeks when on this particular day, he turned the final corner that led into the road where he'd parked it and had to look twice as there was a car parked where he'd left the van. He walked past the spot and looked all around just in case he'd forgotten exactly where he'd left it. On returning to the spot where he knew that he'd parked, he noticed glass in the curb. The car was parked on top of it. His heart sank.

While he had been away looking for work, it was obvious that someone had come along and smashed the side window. As it was an old van it wouldn't have been difficult to hot wire. Luckily there had been no money in the van and his phone was with him. All of his other worldly goods however, had disappeared along with the van. Not that he'd had time to accumulate much so far.

He couldn't report the crime to the police, for obvious reasons, so he resolved to just start all over again. Once again this would begin with trying to source a cheap but reliable van, but this time with even less money in his pot.

After one uncomfortable night with no bedding or warm clothes he struck lucky, if lucky is the right way to describe what happened next. He actually found his van. It was dumped just a few streets away from where it was stolen and it was up on bricks. The wheels were missing, the driver's side door window had been smashed out, as he had already guessed and there was no sign of his belongings, but even with all of that damage he was so pleased to have found his old van. At least he knew its condition and he now wouldn't have the expense of purchasing another van.

All he had to do now was find a set of wheels and probably a whole door. He still had the keys, so starting it wouldn't be an issue once he'd sorted the wiring out. The ignition switch was still in situ but the wiring had been pulled out of it when it was hotwired.

It only took a couple of days to source some tools, the wheels and a door, which of course was the wrong colour, but did have a working window. During that time he slept in the van again, even though it was missing a window. This was to make sure that it wasn't vandalised further.

Once all of the requisite parts were together he set about changing the door lock for his original and then reconnecting the wiring. Luckily he'd received some rudimentary mechanical training while he was serving. It was enough to get him through his current predicament. The door and wheels took no time at all to fit, although the door was incredibly heavy for one man to install. He found that the bricks that had been conveniently left under the van came in handy as door jacks.

He then installed a tracker in the van and also did his best to make it look like it wasn't worth stealing. The newly acquired door helped greatly with this. The remainder of his most necessary belongings would have to be purchased either as and when the need arose or when an opportunity came up. He'd start with a proper sleeping bag.

His phone enquiries about work bore

no fruit. 'Still tomorrow's another day.' Kevin would think to himself. He always remained upbeat and only had to visualise how a lot of the Afghans were currently living, to count his blessings.

Chapter 8

This time Daisy was waiting for the driver and it clearly took him by surprise, as he accelerated toward her as soon as he realised that it was she who was standing by the curb. He slid to a standstill and she got straight in. They set off at a slightly more sedate pace than that demonstrated a few minutes earlier.

Once at the same building that she'd visited twenty four hours earlier, she made straight for the same office. As she approached the door a voice from behind her shouted "come". The meeting was clearly going to take place in a different room. 'Are they really going to this much trouble to keep me on my toes?' She thought. She would never find out of course. She entered the office, which just like the other, looked very much like an ex-state room, complete with a dusty chandelier.

"Sit there." The gentleman who had mentioned the assignment yesterday said, while pointing to a chair.

Daisy sat and then listened to the plan. She couldn't believe what she was hearing, especially the part where he mentioned that she was going to be solely responsible for delivery of the requirement and that failure was not an option. 'What have I done? Was this some kind of nightmare that I will wake up from? Is there any way out?' All very relevant, but next to useless thoughts. Daisy had to dig deep.

Anyway, the answer to the last thought was a simple no, so this made the thought of grappling with the remainder that much easier. Still totally bonkers, but easier.

What the Russian government or a part thereof, were asking her to do was to coordinate the removal of non cooperative criminals from the west, specifically the drug barons from Paris, Milan and Madrid initially. The idea being that Russia was going to control the flow and sale of their own home manufactured cocaine and marijuana and also install their own people, thus giving them a personnel and financial foothold in each country. She then had to organise and oversee the distribution of the Russian synthetic drugs, via a network of homegrown criminals.

She was to become a drug baroness, but only if she could dislodge the existing incumbents.

"You have one month to come up with a plan. You can have whatever resources that you require and that we agree are required. You will even have access to representatives from our own underworld and they will show you the way. Don't let them get the better of you because they will try, I'm afraid. Treat this as you would any other project, but do not fail. By the way, you have been promoted to Colonel and you are now a fully fledged member of the GU. This will give you all the clout that you need in order to get things done. The GU headquarters is based in the Khoroshevskoye Shosse, although you will only report to this office."

A few seconds were taken in contemplation before continuing. "I would just ask that you do not go throwing your weight around and that any requests or questions come through me. You have to remember that there are certain factions within our own government who aren't totally on board with this scheme. They certainly wouldn't respond well to a woman's demands."

What he really meant was that most of the Russian government weren't even aware of this scheme officially and that the government was still very much a male chauvinist regime. Also, whilst she was a Colonel in the Russian Secret Service, this amounted to nothing as she had to carry out all communication through 'the office.' Her hands and mouth, were tied and gagged respectively.

"Remember, we will reconvene here in one month's time."

Daisy was actually quietly excited and she was looking forward to this challenge, however she had to remind herself that although she portrayed the image of a non loyalist entrepreneur, she was most definitely not a defector or a traitor. She would do all that she could to satisfy the Russian demands, whilst trying to make sure that the west were kept informed of all that she could safely divulge. She was about to play her deadliest game to date.

What no one had bothered telling Daisy was that they had let a small quantity of their cocaine onto the market already. This was to test both the distribution methods and the take up potential. They were also doing the same with the marijuana that had now been synthesised successfully, almost. They also hadn't mentioned the deaths.

Chapter 9

Trevor was desperate to prove to his father that he could do just as well as Katy, if not better, so he took himself off to France in order to locate new suppliers. He had a couple of contacts in Paris and was sure that one of them would come up with the goods.

He was aware that he wouldn't be able to use the cover of his dad's pharmaceutical company but felt that if he could procure the right stuff at the right price, his dad would forgive him his inadequacies and congratulate him on his forward thinking.

After a fairly uneventful ferry crossing, except for the continual arguing and bickering with various ferry staff and border guards, he made his way bad temperedly to Paris, where he managed to get lost in the back streets several times, even though he was using a satnav. This was eventually ejected out of the window of his Fiesta. Just staying on the right hand side of the road was using all of his mental capacity.

Finally and just as the sun was setting, he checked into a small three star hotel in the Rue Cortambert, which was just to the west of France's capital and quite close to the Eiffel Tower. He waited for the concierge to carry his case upstairs to the room, so when that didn't happen he tried to complain to a member of the reception staff, who decided that the best way to deal with him was to speak exclusively in French.

Kevin finally gave up and swore at the two of them before taking his own case upstairs. He wasn't happy, but then what was new?

The reception staff member laughed out loud and just said "English pah."

He was still fuming when he reached his door, so he dropped the key twice before finally gaining entry to the small but otherwise adequate room. As soon as he'd unpacked he made a couple of calls.

"Trevor, mon ami. To what do we owe this

pleasure?"

"Hi Pierre. Can we meet?"

"Sure. Shall I come to you?"

"No, non. We need to meet somewhere neutral." Trevor thought that his one word of French would somehow impress his French colleague. He was wrong of course.

'What an English plonker.' Was exactly what Pierre was thinking. "I'm sorry. I didn't catch that. Can you speak more slowly?"

"When you say more slowly, do you mean more slowly in English?"

"Yes please."

'This guy is struggling with his own language, let alone mine.' Pierre grinned to himself. "Okay, where and when?"

"How about at the foot of the tower at eight tonight?" It was the only place that Trevor knew and it was big enough not to miss.

"That's fine. I'll see you there."

Eight o'clock came and went and there was no sign of Pierre.

'I gave specific enough instructions and he's a local. What could have happened to him?' It was now eight fifteen.

Trevor's phone rang. He saw that it was Pierre. 'Here comes the excuse.' He thought.

"Where are you Trevor? I've been here for nearly half an hour."

"Well I've been here for fifteen minutes and I can't see you."

"Have you tried looking?"

"I'm looking now, but you're still not here. If you're running late just admit it and I'll.........."

Pierre stepped out from behind the foot of the Eiffel Tower that was diagonally opposite the one that Trevor was standing behind. They saw each other at exactly the same moment.

Still on his phone, Pierre said. "You didn't say exactly where to meet by the tower did you?"

"No, 'spose not. You know this place better than me. Why didn't you suggest which leg to stand by?"

"Would you have known which one I meant if I did?"

Ignoring the last question Trevor just irritatedly said.

"Anyway, you can put your phone down now as you're only a hundred yards away."

"Yards. What are yards?"

"Yards, metres. We can talk without phones now." Trevor hung up.

Pierre burst out laughing. It was too easy

to wind this English chump up.

Trevor looked all around to make sure that they weren't overheard. He'd suddenly lost what little sense of humour that he had.

"Can you please take me seriously Pierre. I'm here to put some business your way."

"Of course Trevor. Please forgive me."

"I need a new supplier. Obviously he or she needs to be cheap but above all else they need to be reliable."

"I think I can manage that. What are you after?"

"Nothing exotic. Just the usual. I can take pretty much all you can get."

"What has brought this about?"

"I need to prove to my father that I can be trusted with bringing business in. I also want to do something for myself."

"Will you be taking some stuff back with you?"

"I didn't think so, but I suppose I could."

"Okay. Come and see me tomorrow morning and I'll set you up. Don't forget to bring cash."

"I won't. Where shall we meet?"

"I'll come to your hotel."

"What time?"

"Ten."

"Is that ten in the morning or evening?"

'My God, do I really have to deal with

pillock?' "In the morning Trevor."

Trevor was never good at being dictated to, but he did appreciate that he wasn't in the driving seat with regard to this deal. He just needed the business to work.

"See you tomorrow."

He didn't sleep much that night. He'd never carried drugs across the channel before. He wasn't even sure how to carry them. 'Why did I agree to this? If I back out now though, I'll look like a pussy. Shit.' He had no idea what or how much he would be carrying.

Pierre turned up the following morning, at ten o'clock sharp. He was carrying a large backpack crammed with crack, which was only thinly disguised by being pushed into the sleeves and legs of the clothes within. 'Hopefully he'll get caught and then I can get on with my life.'

"Come in, come in. For Christ's sake do you expect me to just carry that bag on my back and walk straight through customs?"
"Well you don't expect me to do it do you? However you carry this load you are exposed. Now just give me the cash and I'll be on my way. I'll get in touch once you are back at home, if you make it home of course." He laughed.

Trevor was way out of his depth, but he'd come too far to back out now. He went to his case and withdrew the cash. 'I carried this lot over, I suppose. Surely, I can carry the goods back.'

He handed over the agreed sum and took the bag.

"Good luck friend. Please let me know that you've arrived home safely." He left a couple of seconds for effect. "Otherwise I won't be able to do any more business with you."

Pierre was gone and Trevor was left sitting on his bed alongside a large bag of highly illegal drugs. He needed to try and get back home right away. There was no point in just sitting and dwelling. Delaying his departure only gave him time to worry more.

He checked out of his hotel, without leaving any tip. That made him feel a little better. He then headed for the ferry terminal with the bag in his boot and absolutely no idea how he was going to deal with it once he arrived. He decided that he would just try to act as natural as he could and blag the rest. 'Everyone has a holdall in the boot, don't they?'

He arrived at the terminal and managed to get waved through. It was a good job that no one looked closely at him as he was sweating profusely and it would have been obvious that he had something to hide. Of course he wasted no time congratulating himself on his great achievement. However this only lasted until he realised that he was going to have to go through it all again once he reached Dover.

Chapter 10

Life in the van wasn't good, but it was better than life on the streets. Kevin had found a part time job washing dishes at the back of a fast food restaurant. His one concession was free food, which was just as well because the money was a pittance and only covered his basic running costs, like fuel for the van and the food that he needed when he wasn't happy to eat deep fried whatever.

After a few weeks of this mind numbing and wallet draining work, Kevin decided that the only way that he was going to make any real money was to work for himself, so he decided that he was going to invest in some gardening equipment. He knew absolutely nothing about gardening but he could cut grass and he knew what most weeds looked like.

He invested a couple of hundred pounds in some second hand equipment and two hundred fliers. 'Hopefully the phone will ring before I'm completely broke'. He thought to himself while he was reclining in the back of his van and listening to the radio.

On that particular day, the local news came on and for once he was listening. "The police are still asking that any member of the public who may have been within the vicinity of Pemberton Street at around two a.m. on the night of the twenty sixth of September last, to come forward and speak to them regardless of whether they believe they saw anything. A man who is either serving or ex-military personnel was seen in the area and they would like to identify this person in order to eliminate him from their enquiries".

Kevin sat up and banged his head on the racking. "Shit that hurts". He said aloud. 'I hope no one was passing the van and heard me. So the police have the dreaded photo. I suppose it was only a matter of time.'

It hadn't dawned on him at the time that he would have been better off being dressed in civvies. He wasn't even carrying any with him and he wrongly assumed that because his little sojourn was carried out after dark, it wouldn't matter how he was dressed. 'How was I to know that there would be someone taking happy snaps? Anway, they have no idea who they are looking for, so I mustn't panic. What I must do is invent a much more detailed back story, just in case I do get questioned by someone.'

That evening Kevin put pen to paper and invented a past life for himself. He was careful enough to base it around the areas that he knew, but he was also careful enough not to include any characters that he might have known or schools that he attended. He would say that he was in foster care because that could remain vague and at least it wouldn't point anyone toward actual parents, especially as he was now Dan Smith. He knew that he'd never remember what he'd written, all in one go, so he rehearsed whenever he could. Eventually, even he was convinced that he was Dan Smith.

Fortunately Kevin was able to prepare his alias before any gardening work came in, so he would be Dan to all of his new customers, who hopefully would never find out that he wasn't who he said he was. This would help to strengthen his story.

After a couple of weeks the news

story appeared to have died down. It wasn't mentioned anymore and it had disappeared entirely off the local papers. Kevin had also managed to pick up a few gardening jobs. It looked like word was starting to get around. One customer had even recommended Kevin to her friend, saying that she very much appreciated that he was a grafter, but that he didn't know a dandelion from a daffodil. When Kevin heard this it did make him smile, but he wasn't sure whether it was a compliment or not. Of course it was absolutely true.

Life was finally on the up, although he was a long way from putting a proper roof over his head. At least he had some money in his back pocket and his savings had stopped their downward slide.

Chapter 11

The photograph wasn't brilliant, but you could just make out the insignia on the uniform. Whoever he was, he was a member of the SAS. It was also clear that the soldier was male, clean shaven, tall and slim and most probably white, although this was where the enhancement didn't help much. The low light played havoc with the skin tone.

Alfie had been to see Mrs Wilcox and was now fairly sure that she wasn't a suspect. She was just too jittery and didn't seem at all like a person who could kill someone in cold blood. She also had a cast iron alibi for her whereabouts over the relevant weekend. The one thing that he did pick up on, however, was the fact that she definitely wasn't sorry to see the 'old bastard' gone.

During his visit to see Mrs Wilcox, Alfie took the time to check around the crime scene. He noticed the broken but boarded window in the french doors. Whoever did that made a very neat job of it. They'd used a glass cutter, thus avoiding the making of any noise and also making the edge of the hole in the glass as smooth as possible. Obviously the intruder knew exactly what they were doing.

While he was looking around, Mrs Wilcox followed him and chatted away remorselessly. It would have been very easy to miss one of her throw away comments, but luckily Alfie picked up on it immediately.

"So anyway, I just thought it a little odd that my key had moved."

"Sorry, Mrs Wilcox. You say that your key had been moved?"

"Oh yes. I just meant that when I came back home the day after the murder I had to let myself in by using the spare key. I often do that, it just saves me carrying my usual bunch. Anyway, as I lifted the pot and bent to collect the key, I noticed that it was in a different spot. I know it sounds daft, but I always leave it in just the same place and it wasn't. In fact there was even a dry patch where my key had been laying until it had been moved."

"You didn't mention this before?"

"Well no. To be quite honest I never really thought about it. I certainly never thought that it would have any relevance to the case."

Alfie didn't want to upset her by chastising her, so he just thanked her very much for being so accommodating and made his excuses to leave.

As soon as he arrived back at the office, he called a meeting. He needed to make some progress urgently and so now would be a good time to assess all that had been learned since he took over the investigation.

"I've checked with the morgue sir and the only relevant information that I've been able to gleen, is that the murder took place sometime in the early hours and that the murderer was left handed."

"Can they be certain about the left handed part?"

"Yes. As far as the wound goes, it could only have been carried out either by someone who is left handed or someone who took the trouble to swap hands in order to carry out the murder. Possible I suppose, but highly unlikely."

"Okay thanks lad."

"How did your meeting with Mrs W. go?"

"Well, I can be fairly sure that she wasn't the murderer. One interesting fact did come to light though."

"Go on."

"Well she seemed sure that someone had moved her spare door key from under a pot that stands on the step and to the left of the front door."

"So?"

"It could only have been moved during the time of her absence, which of course runs right across the time of the murder, so the murderer may have come in through the front door."

"But the glass was cut at the rear. Why go to that trouble?"

"I don't know. It may have been done to throw us off the scent." Alfie sat down at his desk and put his head in his hands. He had assumed his 'deep in thought' stance. His constable left quietly, closing the door behind him. He'd seen it all before.

Alfie continued with his deep thought. 'Unless the real murderer went in through the front door and the would-be thief, who just happened to get himself caught on camera, went in through the back door. This would at least explain how it was that someone just happened to be there to take a photo of the suspected murderer. Alfie had the photo now, but he was no closer to knowing who the possible intruder was.

'I must find out who sent in that photo?'

Chapter 12

In order to make her project work, Daisy decided that she was going to have to fight fire with fire. She would make it her priority to utilise the knowledge of the Russian underworld in order to help her understand how to gain control of the European underworld.

She couldn't really comprehend just how exhilarating she was finding this work. Living life on the extreme edge was what she craved and this was definitely just that. She was about to set up a meeting with the type of people that you wouldn't want to meet at any time in your life, let alone down a dark alley.

"My name is just Dimitri, as far as you're concerned. What's yours?"

"It's Daisy and that's as far as anyone is concerned."

That one statement appeared to take the edge off the initial introduction. Fortunately Dimitri smiled. He liked a woman with balls.

"Who are the others?" Daisy asked as politely as she could. It felt like she was in the presence of cut throat pirates dressed in twenty first century suits or the Russian equivalent thereof. At least that was the mental image she had as they all filtered into the dingy room and sat, not waiting to be asked.

They came in all shapes and sizes and in total there were half a dozen of Russia's lowest, sitting around the table.

Before Dimitri could answer, Daisy noticed a couple of them were smoking and that had to stop immediately. If there was one thing that she wasn't going to put up with, it was that filthy habit.

"Please extinguish those filthy cigarettes and don't smoke while attending these meetings. The rest of us don't want cancer, even if you two do."

There was laughter from around the table and some odd looks were exchanged.

Neither of the two who were implicated,

knew quite what to do. They certainly weren't used to being spoken to in this manner and had she been anyone else, she would have been taken down a peg or two. As she was being backed by the powers that be however, they both extinguished their cigarettes by throwing them on the carpet and treading on them.

They had all been briefed prior to the meeting. They were told to be on their best behaviour and to listen to what Daisy had to say. The carrot dangled before them was that this project could work very much to their advantage financially. Daisy was also instructed to sell it to them on that basis.

"Dimitri." This cut right through the general gossip and brought him up short. "Tell me what you know of this project." Daisy continued to assert her authority. If she was to stand any chance of gaining any respect at all, she would have to continue in this vein.

Daisy already sensed that this was going to be akin to trying to keep the attention of school children. She decided that for now at least, this would be the best way to treat them. She was extremely aware that she would have to limit this behaviour if she wished to remain alive once the project was over.

"I only know what we all know and that

is that you have a project to complete within one month and that you need our help in order to accomplish this task. I do also know that it could benefit us all if this project were to succeed."

'Well at least it would appear that Dimitri wasn't brain dead. He, at least, could prove to be useful.' She decided there and then that she would try and cultivate Dimitri to become the criminal spokesperson. She had a hunch that she could deal with him and then hopefully leave him to communicate with the others.

"Excellent, then I'll outline the aim of the project and hopefully with your cumulative expertise, we shall succeed."

Daisy performed her sales pitch. The problem was that the more she talked, the less convinced she was about a successful outcome. She just hoped that this negativity wouldn't show.

"What we've got to do is obvious to me. Not easy, but obvious." The archetypically scarred gentleman sitting directly opposite Daisy outlined his plan. There was a titter from a couple of the assembly, but those who had more than a smidgen of grey matter were silent.

Dimitri just said. "It could work." No one laughed this time.

Daisy noticed this and made a mental note of the fact that he seemed to have the respect of the others. 'I was right about my choice of spokesperson. Now I just have to convince him to take on the mantle.'

Chapter 13

The rumour mill was in full swing and Katy, like everyone else, had heard about this cheaper cocaine that was coming from Europe, but she was sceptical.

Trevor on the other hand wasn't. He'd managed to get through customs with his haul. Fortunately, none of the staff that he'd upset on the way out, were on shift for the return journey and he was now reaping the rewards.

As he was managing to sell the stuff at a higher price even though it was costing less, his dad was quids in and although he never mentioned anything, he was quietly proud of his offspring, for the first time in his life. After all, his boy had not only managed to strike up a new lucrative deal, he'd done it all off his own back. He'd even carried the stuff back himself. That took a certain amount of courage and that was something that he'd certainly never seen the little scrote show any of before. Of course it could have been down to sheer stupidity and that would fit his MO much more closely. 'Still impressive.' He thought.

As far as Trevor was concerned there was only one very large fly in his ointment and that fly was called Katy. She'd stolen a lot of his trade and she could be stealing his dads as well, not that he had any proof. Worse still she was still way more popular than him. Although she was pushing the stuff, the crack heads would come to her for advice and she'd give it, along with selling them more of course.

Katy had moved into her own flat now and she didn't have anything to do with either Trevor or his old man, except for stealing their clientele. She even ran her own team and they were spreading like a fungus. She had been savvy enough to select runners who could look after themselves too, so no matter how much pressure Trevor and his crew had tried to apply, no one was budging. In fact he'd lost a couple of his best heavy weights for the foreseeable future, as they had run into a few of Katy's own and now they were residing in a local NHS establishment. Something had to be done about her.

Trevor had never even thought about actually killing someone before and as much as he didn't really want to do it now, he could see no other option. 'She's bought this on herself.' He would think to himself, whenever he felt that justification was needed. This would be the second time he'd had to plan something, so like last time he headed for the pub. This method of planning had worked before and this time he already had his notebook and pen ready.

After a couple of pints, all that he'd managed to write on his notepad was:

1.   Where
2.   When
3.   How
4.   Plan B

He left the pub feeling disgruntled. It bothered him greatly that he was going to have to put a lot more work into this plan. What made it worse was the fact that he couldn't ask anybody else for some help. Certainly not his father. If he were to try and convince his dad that she was fleecing him, he would just dismiss it as jealousy and he would probably strike Trevor and that would hurt.

The one decision he had made was the fact that she had to go. It was the only way he could get his business back.

While sitting at home and sipping a straight whiskey, Martin King was thinking the same thing. He now knew what Katy was up to but he wasn't about to discuss this with his dipstick son.

Chapter 14

There was a knock on the door of an office, which was located in a large grey building, somewhere in south London. To anyone passing it looked the same as all the other large grey buildings in and around the capital.

"Come."

"Oh, good morning. My name is Inspector Edwards."

"Please sit and let me know how I can help?"

"Thank you and thank you for seeing me at short notice."

There was no answer proffered, so Alfie continued.

"I have a picture here that I believe shows

a person dressed in the uniform of the British SAS. Can you please confirm that for me?"

"Certainly. Please let me look."

Alfie passed the copy over and the Colonel took no time at all to confirm that it was indeed one of his men or at least someone dressed as one of his men.

"Why do you need this information verified, may I ask?"

"We have an ongoing murder investigation and we just need to eliminate this person from our investigation."

"Do you know when it was taken and by who?"

"I can tell you exactly when it was taken but unfortunately I can't tell you who took it or even why they felt it necessary to take it. It was handed in to the police anonymously."

"Can you leave the picture with me? I'll make some enquiries of my own, if that's alright with you?"

"Certainly. I'll leave you my card. Please feel free to call at any time." Alfie reached inside his coat and retrieved a business card. He handed it over. He then thanked the Colonel again and left.

As soon as he'd gone, a phone call was made and the voice on the other end spoke from a base somewhere in Helmand.

"So, they're onto Kevin are they?"

"Well they are on to someone in the SAS. They've asked if I can help identify the person. They've also asked if I have any idea who took the picture."

"Right. I think it's time don't you?"

"Certainly."

Chapter 15

Gardening was hard work, even for someone who was really fit. Now that the work had started to become more regular it also became more relentless. Kevin tried to give himself regular breaks but it wasn't always easy. He didn't want to let any customer down, but his diary was starting to dictate otherwise.

"I'm sorry I'm late Mrs Keller. My last job overran slightly."

"That's alright love. I know how it is. I can see by the look on your face that you're having a rough day. Shall I put the kettle on?"

"That would be lovely, thanks. I'm just going to pop to Saino's to grab a sandwich, if that's okay?"

"Of course. Tea'll be ready when you get

back."

Sainsbury's was just round the corner. Had it not have been Kevin wouldn't have dared ask a customer if it was okay to leave just before starting. He grabbed a sandwich and an apple and was just leaving the store, when someone shouted.

"Oy Keenan."

Kevin had become so used to being known as Dan Smith that for a second he thought someone else was being called, but once he realised it was him that the less than friendly outcry was aimed at, he turned. He immediately regretted doing so as it was Trevor King. There was no mistaking that podgy, greasy and smug looking face, even after all this time.

"Keenan. Haven't seen you in years. What are you up to?"
Kevin shouted. "Trevor, why don't you cross the road." 'And get run over while doing so'. He thought, but then carried on. "And talk instead of shouting across it."
"Right then. Hold on."

Trevor had to wait for what seemed an eternity before he could cross and a passing bus obscured his path for a split second. He finally reached the other side and stood right on the spot that Kevin had occupied less than thirty seconds ago. He'd vanished.

"You twat Keenan. I'll find you, then you'll wish you'd stayed put."

A couple of passers by stopped to look at the lone pedestrian who appeared to be having a conversation with himself.

"What are you looking at?" He yelled at them. Before storming off.

Kevin arrived back at Mrs Kellers, who although a little put out by his delay was soon back on side. If there was one trick that Kevin had learned in his short and illustrious career, it was how to butter up his clients. By the time that he left, he was back to being the best gardener that she'd ever had, even though he had inadvertently pulled up a couple of her plants.

Trevor was going to make it his mission to hunt down Kevin, as soon as he'd dealt with Katy. He didn't need to convene another solo meeting in order to make a plan. He was just going to punch the twat.

He had no idea that Kevin was not only ex SAS and therefore trained in unarmed combat and all the other physical training that being a member involved, but was also a black belt in Kung Fu.

Chapter 16

I t wasn't easy working with high calibre criminals, especially those who thought that a woman's place was at home, preferably dressed only in a pinny with high heels and with hot food always waiting on the table.

'Neanderthals.' Is exactly what Daisy thought, each time they met.

"So, gentlemen." Even that word caught in her throat. "I believe we've reached a consensus with regard to our plan and I hope that I can count on your full support."

"You can Miss Wilcox." Dimitri now appeared to be the spokesperson for the group and that suited Daisy down to the ground. "On your say so, we will put into action exactly what we've agreed."

"You can put it into action as soon as you are ready Dimitri and might I suggest that you and I oversee the project jointly as you will be much more suited to observing exactly what's going on than I." Daisy thought that a bit of buttering up now would do a power of good and also Dimitri would be far less lightly to say no, while still in the presence of his peers.

There was the usual snigger at Daisy's proposal. "Jesus Christ must you always behave like school children?"

"Sure. Why not?" Was the answer given by one of the more vocal representatives.

"Of course Daisy. That's not a problem and shut up you lot. Come on, we've got work to do." He said that with a smile on his face and everyone seemed to take the comment as it was meant.

What Daisy hadn't realised was that gaining agreement from that bunch of cut throats was the easy part of her new role. She now had to sell it to the federal ministers and they were a far tougher crowd.

She needn't have worried, as the federal ministers had no idea how to achieve their goal and they were only too happy to see that Daisy had taken the challenge seriously and on face value appeared to have come up with a sound plan. She'd also managed to do it with the full cooperation of the underworld. They found this amazing, but were not about to congratulate her as that would have appeared soft,

"It sounds as though this is going to take some time."

"It will, but if we wish to virtually guarantee that we succeed, it is the best way. This was agreed by everyone at the meetings." Daisy was sounding and feeling more confident now. After all, she had the very worst that Russia had to offer, on her side.

"Is everything in place?"

"I just need to get some key people in place and then we are ready."

"So, dear girl, when do we expect this project to go live?"

"Tomorrow, with your blessing."

"Excellent. That is good news."

"Yes sir. I thought that there would be no point in any delay."

"Please keep us appraised of progress and if you do run into any issues try to bring us the solutions rather than the problems."

"Certainly. If you will excuse me I have much to arrange in the next twenty four hours."

"You may go and Daisy?"

"Sir."

"Good luck. You'll need it."

"Thank you sir."

Everyone was ready and the project went live the very next day, as Daisy promised. Things were looking up.

'I might make General yet.' Daisy only half heartedly mused. She desperately wanted to be seen by the west as a double agent, but there was a fine line between that and traitor.

Chapter 17

The light was on and there was someone at home. She'd entered the flats about half an hour earlier. This had been observed from a vehicle that was parked on the far side of the road. The occupant of the vehicle was sweating profusely, so much so that the lenses of his binoculars were steaming up.

'I need to wait until later. I need her asleep and I need the street to be deserted.'

Trevor made himself as comfortable as he could. He had loaded the car with food and drink. The only thing that he hadn't considered was where the nearest toilet might be, so on a couple of occasions he had to relieve himself in an alley, without being seen. 'Why did I arrive so early? I could have driven here much later.'

As usual Trevor was getting angry. This was generally aimed at other people, but he was just as adept at being annoyed with himself.

At least he'd had the forethought to find out exactly which of the flats was Katy's. He had done this by hanging around and watching, but also by getting one of his runners to pester her neighbours, until he was sure that he knew exactly where she lived. He couldn't afford to be seen personally. 'I'm not so stupid after all.' He thought with the usual smug grin on his face. 'And she's going to find out that it's best not to mess with me.'

The lights in the corresponding flat were finally extinguished at around eleven o'clock, so just to be on the safe side Trevor waited another hour. The street was now quiet and with a bit of luck, Katy should be asleep.

'It's now or never.' Trevor was doing his best to bolster his courage. The one thought that was driving him was that he knew that Katy would forever be a thorn in his side, if things were to continue as they had so far. Even his dad had said so, with rather too much glee in his voice. She had to go.

'When I think about what I did for that silly little bitch. She wouldn't be where she is now if it wasn't for me. She deserves what she's got coming to her.' He jumped out of the car and although the night was cold, he was still sweating profusely. He was about to cross the road when a police patrol car drove past and as it did so it slowed. For a second Trevor's heart was in his mouth, until it turned a corner and disappeared. He retreated back to his car for a few seconds, wondering whether it was going to turn around and come back, but it didn't.

Living nine tenths of his life on the wrong side of the law brought about its problems, not least of which was high blood pressure, but luckily for Trevor he was too stupid to recognise or acknowledge the symptoms. He continued on his way.

Fortunately the lock on the security door at the foot of Katy's stairs was broken. He hadn't even considered the fact that he might not be able to get as far as her front door. What he had done though was gain a spare flat door key. He had obtained it from his dad and he didn't dare ask how come he had one or why. He was dead chuffed that he'd thought to do that. After all that was the kind of thing that a real criminal would have done.

He tiptoed up the stairs and then stopped at Katy's front door. He groped for the key in his pocket and once he'd found it, he retrieved it and reached for the lock. He froze.

He'd suddenly lost his courage. He turned and walked hurriedly back down and crossed back over the road to the safety of his car. He climbed in and sat staring at the window of Katy's flat. 'Come on, it's simple, let yourself in, enter the bedroom, walk up to the bed, blow her brains out, leave.' It was the second to last part that gave him the most trouble.

After a fairly lengthy self pep talk Trevor repeated the exercise. This time he made it into the flat. There was
a light coming from under the bathroom door, so he hid behind the living room curtain. He heard the toilet flush and then the door open. 'She still doesn't wash her hands.' Stupid thought. 'Like it matters now.'

He stayed very still and then heard what he assumed was the bedroom door closing. He didn't want to have to face her while she was awake. There was no way that he could pull the trigger while those doe eyes were staring down the barrel of his silenced gun. Of course she could scream as well and that wasn't part of the plan.

He crept out from behind the curtain and made himself at home by laying behind the sofa for a while. He waited and within five minutes was sound asleep. He awoke with a start and for a few seconds couldn't remember where he was. 'Shit, I've been asleep for an hour. I hope I didn't snore.'

He couldn't believe that he hadn't been discovered, but it looked like he'd got away with his minor indiscretion. He pulled himself up, checked around and then proceeded toward what, by a process of elimination, had to be the bedroom door. He entered and could immediately see the form of someone sleeping in the bed. He had to act straight away, as he didn't want to bottle it again. He took aim at the head, closed his eyes and pulled the trigger. There was a thud like noise and the gun jumped in his hand. He nearly let go. Then there was silence. He looked down and blood started to show as a growing patch on the quilt.

He ran out of the flat and into the hallway, not even stopping to close the front door and then he threw up as soon as he got to the top of the stairs. He ran down the two flights, hardly knowing how he'd got to the bottom safely and as soon as he reached the outside, he threw up again.

He ran blindly across the road, waving the gun around, so that any passing pedestrian could have clearly seen it and he continued past his car until some form of reasoning kicked in and he realised it was parked just a few yards behind him. He turned back and slowed to a walk. He was mentally and physically exhausted. He lowered the gun and got into his car. He threw the gun onto the passenger seat, started the car and headed for home.

As soon as he arrived he headed for the shower, but stopped to throw up once more while passing the toilet. He finally climbed into bed at around three a.m. and went straight to sleep, until four, when he awoke in another sweat. This time a cold one. His head was full of demons, some dreamt and some thought. 'Oh fuck. What have I done? It takes a real villain to get a kick out of killing someone. I never want to have to do that again.' He finally drifted back off to sleep and didn't wake until around eleven the following morning.

He hadn't even noticed the parking ticket that was stuck to his windscreen.

He also hadn't stopped to question why his father had been so co-operative with regard to loaning him the flat key or why he had made the remark about the fact that Katy needed to go.

Chapter 18

The rain was coming down so hard on the streets of London that it was bouncing back up again, giving the opportunity of getting anyone soaked from below as well as above. Unfortunately for Alfie he had to go out. 'What a rotten day.' Alfie thought to himself. 'It's days like this that a nice quiet desk job would be lovely.' His mobile rang and broke into his thoughts.

"Hello, Detective Inspector Edwards here." Alfie had now gained promotion and had finally shaken off his uniform for good. He was a full time detective and he'd already decided that he was never going to answer the phone by using the term DI Edwards. He thought that was reserved for the telly.

"Ah DI Edwards. Can you talk? It's Colonel

Wyatt here."

"Of course Colonel. Fire away."

"Well. I think we may have found the chap you're looking for."

"Excellent. Who is he?"

"I need to talk to you in person if I may and there may be a third party attending, by video."

"That's fine. You just tell me when and where and I'll be there."

"Can you come to my office at say noon tomorrow. That will make it three thirty p.m. local time."

"Local where?"

"You'll find out tomorrow. Bye for now."

"Goodbye sir."

Alfies mind was awash with possibilities. The first and most pronounced thought was, why do we need to speak to someone who is obviously abroad? Secondly, could it be that our boy is now serving overseas?

He put the phone to his ear again. This time to make a call. After a couple of rings it was picked up at the other end, but before the recipient could answer, Alfie started:

"Constable Nixon. Clear your diary for tomorrow. We've got an important meeting."

"Yes sir."

"I'll see you at the office at oh eight

hundred and dress smart, we're visiting the army and you don't want them to think we don't know how to dress."

"Yes sir."

"And get plenty of sleep."

"Yes sir." Constable Nixon wondered what was going on. Even the old man had never spoken in this manner before.

"See you tomorrow sir."

"Got to go." The phone line dropped.

The following day Alfie was in the office early. He needed to make sure that he was fully appraised of all the latest evidence before they met with the Colonel. He also needed to make sure that he had prepared for any possible questions. He did not want to appear amateurish in front of a senior member of the forces, after all he was representing Her Majesty's Metropolitan Police Force.

At eight o'clock sharp Nixon arrived. He came in carrying two cups of coffee.

"Thank you lad. Please sit."

Nixon did as he was told and Alfie took him through the details. Although Constable Nixon was almost fully appraised of the current situation, minus the phone call from the day before, Alfie wanted to make sure that they were both singing from the same hymn sheet.

At around eleven they left for their rendezvous. They arrived early and found an empty space in the visitors' car park. They then entered the very Victorian Gothic and very military looking building, where they were met by a desk sergeant who asked them who it was that they were meeting. He then asked them to take a seat.

While they were waiting they discussed the various paintings that were hanging on the walls, trying to guess which campaigns each might be depicting.

"No, no lad. That one's definitely the Boer War.

"Ah, but is it the first or second?"

"I didn't know there were two."

"Oh yes. We lost the first. It was in 1880, I believe."

"Well Nixon, I'm impressed."

"You shouldn't be sir. I read the plaque on the bottom as we came in. Ask me another and I'll get it wrong."

"Well, full marks for observation anyway."

They both chuckled, but just as they did so they were called to the Colonel's office.

"Come in gentlemen." The Colonel

blustered in a friendly but very old guard sort of way. "Would you like tea or coffee?"

"Thank you sir, I'll have…" Said Constable Nixon, but before he could continue, Alfie cut across him.

"Err no thank you sir. We really must press on."

"Right then, please bear with me and I'll raise the other party."

The Colonel turned his laptop to an angle such that all three of them could see the screen. He tapped a couple of keys and a face appeared.

"Good afternoon old boy, it's Colonel Wyatt here, along with Detective Inspector Edwards and I'm sorry I didn't catch your name son?"

"It's Constable Nixon sir."

"And Constable Nixon."

From the other end the voice said "Good afternoon all. Of course I'm three and a half hours ahead of you here."

They all knew that he was, but there was only one person in the room who had any idea where the other Colonel was. Alfie didn't want to ask as he wasn't sure if he was supposed to know, so he just let the other Colonel go on with his introductory speech. He finally got to the point.

"Well gentlemen, I can tell you exactly who the photo is of, but before I do I want to tell a story about that person." The Colonel was trying his best to build some suspense. He knew that he only had one shot at telling this story and he wanted that one shot to be his best. The person in the photo warranted this at least.

The full story of the veteran involved was told and by the end Alfie and Constable Nixon were both transfixed, so much so that they both nearly forgot that they actually needed a name.

"Anyway, the person that you're looking for is sergeant Kevin Keenan. I'll leave it to you now and hopefully you will take all that I've told you on board whilst you are casting judgement."

It didn't sink in initially, but slowly it dawned on Alfie that it was 'his' Kevin Keenan. 'Kevin. I know it wasn't you.' Was Alfie's official assessment once he'd let all of the evidence sink in. He couldn't let on that he knew Kevin. He didn't want anyone to think that he'd be prejudiced in his assessment.

"So, we've got him sir. We've got the bastard."

"Don't be too hasty Constable and don't

forget we've just heard the most compelling character reference from his old CO."

"But even so. He was caught on film, right there, right at the time."

The link between London and Helmand was broken, but not until after Alfie had tried to convince both officer's that he would see that justice was done.

He did have one last question before they left though.

"Why didn't the Colonel come forward before? After all, he'd seen the photo?"

"He'd shown Keenan and Keean ran before he could be questioned about it. He bummed a lift on an aircraft that was headed back this way. That's all I know."

"That sounds plausible I suppose. Well once again thank you sir and I'll keep you posted. Don't worry, I give you my word that Kev. err Keenan will get a fair hearing. Should we ever catch up with him that is."

The two police officers made their excuses and left. As they walked back to the car Alfie just said. "We need to find Keenan and we need to find him fast."

"Yes sir."

"I know that this might sound like a strange request, son, but could I just ask that you don't mention any of this to anyone else for now?"

"Of course sir, but can I ask why?"

"I just need time to make sure of some facts, especially as the military have a vested interest in our man."

"I see. That kind of makes sense, I suppose." Constable Nixon, in a very unconvinced way.

Chapter 19

She had been instructed to familiarise herself with the facility, so Daisy made arrangements, packed a small bag and departed.

The journey to Rostov on Don took forever, especially in the car that Daisy was provided with. For this reason she decided to split the journey in half and stop for the night at a place called Voronezh. The countryside wasn't much to write home about either, so she couldn't even distract herself with the view. She did find it mildly amusing that the road, which took her all the way from Moscow to Rostov, was the M4.

When she finally arrived at the factory it was a dingy affair, but Daisy wasn't surprised, after all most of what she'd seen in Russia so far, was dingy. However the laboratory space had been spruced up partially and indeed did appear to contain some modern looking equipment.

She was met at the front desk by a rather overly enthusiastic middle aged woman in a white coat that had a slightly torn top pocket and a button missing.

"Anyway, this is where the magic happens." The person responsible for Daisy's tour did her best to sound convincing, but Daisy soon picked up on the fact that this woman knew very little about what went on in the lab. It was almost as if the powers that be had supplied someone who knew nothing, so that questions couldn't be answered.

"Thank you. Do you guys have such a thing as a canteen here?"

"Sure we do. We're not philistines, you know." The tour guide thought that she was amazingly funny, so Daisy just smiled back to keep her happy. She led her through to the staff canteen, which was in just as bad a condition as the rest of the building. The only difference was that there was a slightly more pleasant smell emanating from it and there was even a radio playing somewhere in the background.

As they entered, a man in a white coat came out backwards through the swing doors. He was carrying a coffee and something wrapped in paper. He turned just as he exited and nearly collided with Daisy, so he apologised profusely and as he did so Daisy noted that he was quite young and handsome. He also noticed Daisy, making it even more obvious by stopping dead in his tracks.

"My name is Andreiv." He said while proffering a hand.

"Mine's Daisy." Pleased to meet you.

"Very pleased to meet you, Daisy."

"Put your tongue away Andreiv. I'm a married woman."

"Yes, of course, sorry Mrs Daisy." Andreiv wasn't sure what to say next so he just walked hastily away, but not quick enough that Daisy couldn't see his face reddening.

Daisy couldn't help herself as she laughed out loud. Andreiv just wanted the floor to open up and swallow him. He didn't stop to look back, but he did spill some of his coffee and left a small trail of drips behind him as he scurried off.

What Daisy had noticed, during this minor distraction, was that Andreiv was very polite and he didn't appear to fit the profile of the kind of lab technician that she'd envisaged working here. He looked and sounded very much like a fish out of water. She intended to discover his back story. She started her inquiries by asking her guide what Andreiv was doing here.

"Oh, he's the lead laboratory technician."

"So, he's the one who designed the stuff?"

"I suppose so, but he's no big cheese." Her guide knew immediately that she'd said too much and was busy trying to back track. "He's a nobody."

"Nevertheless, I would like to be introduced to him properly."

"I thought you wanted to go to the canteen?"

"I can do that after our introduction, so please kindly take me back to where that gentleman works."

The guide grudgingly led Daisy back to the laboratory where she saw her man as soon as they entered.

"Andreiv, this is Ms Wilcox."

"Yes I know, we've met. I thought you said that you were married."

"It's a long story Andreiv and now isn't the time."

"That's not a very Russian sounding name you have there either." Andreiv was sounding a lot more confident now that he was on his home turf.

"No, it's English. East End of London to be exact."

"I see,so what brings an East End of London lady to the middle of nowhere, Russia?"

"That's another long story I'm afraid Andreiv, most of which would get the pair of us shot, if I told you."

There was a very polite chuckle from both Andreiv and her guide.

Thinking on her feet, Daisy asked the guide if she would be so kind as to get the three of them a coffee, especially as she hadn't got as far as the canteen yet. She tried to suggest that they should all go to the canteen, but Daisy was adamant and said that it would save her some time if she could drink while on the move.

She knew that she'd have to go because she had been instructed to comply with Daisy's wishes to a point, but she did so very grudgingly, after all another part of her remit was to keep an eye on the English woman. She walked very slowly out of the laboratory, but broke into a run as soon as she thought that it was safe to do so.

Daisy wasted no time. She looked all

around and checked for any cameras or listening devices. She found one of each, neither of which she guessed that Andreiv was aware of, so by using a swift arm movement she gestured for him to follow her.

He didn't realise what she was doing at first, but then it dawned on him, so he did as she instructed. They walked toward a large basin where Daisy turned on the cold water tap and only once she was fairly sure that it was safe, she spoke to Andreiv in a very hushed tone.

"Why have you turned the tap on?" Andreiv asked completely naively.

"Shh Andeiv. Keep your voice down. Someone might be listening."

"Really, who?"

Daisy avoided the question for the sake of saving precious time.

"Andreiv, if there is anything that you would like to tell me please do. I mean anything, if you understand me?"

Andreiv wasn't sure how to handle the question, but he did know that this could be the only opportunity to get his grievances heard. He also felt instinctively that he could trust Daisy. She appeared to be acting very strangely, but only in a defensive way. A way that demonstrated that she really wanted to help.

"Can we meet?" Andreiv asked.

She knew that she was going out on a limb by asking questions that would mean that she would have to sneak out unchaperoned, but felt that it was too important a chance to miss.

"Certainly. Have you got a paper and pen? I'll give you my number."

Andreiv hurriedly found both and passed them to Daisy. She wrote down her number and added, do not call me from here or your home, then passed it back to Andreiv just as the door opened. 'Christ. Were we seen?' Daisy wondered worriedly.

Nothing untoward happened and her guide just handed the two of them their coffees, so hopefully he hadn't seen the passing of the piece of paper. Daisy felt sure that even if the guide had tried to play it down, there would have been a tell tale sign that he had seen something untoward. There was however a pregnant pause in the conversation, until Daisy broke the deadlock.

"Anyway Andreiv, I really must dash. Maybe see you again some time?"

"Maybe." Was all that he said.

Daisy put her unfinished coffee down and left. The guide just followed in her wake.

That night Daisy's phone didn't ring.

Chapter 20

The news came on the TV and although Trevor generally took no notice of it, for some strange reason one article piqued his interest.

"Last night a local girl was shot in the head while she was asleep. So far there doesn't appear to be any motive."

Trevor breathed a small sigh of relief before the newsreader continued.

"Her flat mate, one Katy Weller, said that when she arrived home late last night the crime had already been committed. In fact it was she who phoned the police. She added that it looked like whoever did it wasn't a seasoned criminal because it looked like they had thrown up right outside her door."

Trevor couldn't believe what he was hearing, but if he thought that was bad the next bit was far worse.

"The police have confirmed that they can extract DNA from the vomit, so should either be able to eliminate the person from their enquiries or maybe find the perpetrator."

Trevor didn't know what to do. Not only had he missed his target and not only had he killed an innocent party, but he'd managed to leave a massive clue in doing so. "I'm fucked." Was all that he could come up with.

He packed a bag, jumped into his car and drove. The gun was still on the passenger seat. 'Oh my God. I even left the murder weapon in plain sight while I went to bed.' He started crying. He had to pull over as he couldn't see through his tears. He felt like a child who had done something wrong and knew that he had, but didn't know what to do about it. He felt totally lost and alone.

While he was parked at the side of the road and sobbing his heart out, with his head resting on his hands and both on the steering wheel, an elderly bystander knocked on his side window and enquired as to whether he was alright.

"For fuck sake, you scared the crap out of me." Was his reply to the genuine and heartfelt query.

The lady walked away disgusted, but at least she had managed to bring Trevor out of his stupor.

He knew there would be no point in approaching his dad for support. At times like this his dad would just curse him and probably even punch him. That wasn't exactly what he needed right now. He decided that running wasn't the smartest move either, so he drove back home, removed his bag and the gun from the car, took both upstairs and sat on the edge of his bed. He sat for about an hour and it was only the sound of the doorbell ringing that broke him out of his fug.

Just for a moment Martin King couldn't believe his luck, as he thought that his boy had successfully done away with that witch Katy. Although Trevor hadn't confided in him, he knew what he was planning to do. It was never difficult to figure out what that little dipstick was up to.

That brief spell of euphoria was soon replaced by the usual feeling of disappointment once he'd heard the news. He might have guessed that Trevor would cock it up. Now he'd have to clear up the mess himself. As for Trevor, he couldn't care less if he got arrested, after all it would free up some room in the flat.

Chapter 21

T he planning was complete, down to the tiniest detail. This was going to be the best payday ever.

"I don't know who is at the top, but I don't really care." Claude said to no one in particular.

This question had been asked several times, but it couldn't be answered and at this precise moment, it didn't matter. The fact was that they had been given a tipoff and were about to pull off a massive jewellery heist in the middle of Paris and the planning was immaculate.

They'd left nothing to chance. The shop owner wouldn't even get in the way as he had gone away for the weekend.

"Listen, whoever is at the top is on our side. We've proved that the plan works and we know exactly what there is to be gained, so let's not worry who the informant is, for now."

Claude wasn't convinced, but he did have to agree that the plan appeared to be bulletproof and that within the next twenty four hours they could all be rich, extremely rich.

The time soon arrived and they were all ready, the gemologist, the safe expert, the lock picker, the explosives guy, the getaway driver and the grunts. They were all ready and it was go time. They slipped into their respective rolls like a well oiled machine.

It was as they were about half way into the job and just about to lay their hands on the loot, that blue lights were seen appearing from what seemed to be everywhere. Then there was the screeching noise of multiple vehicles sliding to a halt and finally there was a lot of shouting. Then for the briefest moment, it went quiet. The silence was soon broken by a lone voice that came through a megaphone.

"You have one chance and one chance only to put everything down and come out with your hands up."

The getaway driver thought that he had an opportunity to make a break for it, as he was the only one already on the outside and already waiting in a car. He started the engine and with wheels spinning he accelerated away. He managed to get about a hundred metres, before being blocked by a police vehicle, the passenger of which jumped out with his revolver held at arm's length. He pointed it straight at the driver of the getaway car and shouted at him to get out slowly and lay on the floor. The driver did exactly as he was told.

Everyone else was rounded up, handcuffed and marched to waiting police vehicles. They were driven to different police stations around Paris. No two captivates being near each other and able to communicate.

Once the interrogation began nobody said a word. They couldn't, as no one knew who had given the tip off.

Claude didn't bother congratulating himself for being the only one who smelt a rat at the outset. If he'd have been half as smart as he thought he was, he wouldn't now be sitting in a Parisian jail cell. All that kept going round in his head was. 'Where did that tipoff come from? Was it someone who was no longer a member of the gang?'

Chapter 22

Andreiv appreciated the fact that he may have an ally in Daisy. He was putting all of his trust in her. There was something about her straightforward talking and the fact that she'd offered to listen to him in a sincere sounding way, made him believe in her. Also there was the fact that she was quite possibly the most attractive woman that he'd ever laid eyes on, but that was just a bonus. 'I can only but dream' He dreamed.

There was one small issue and that was the fact that she was once British, before she decided to change sides. 'That may be exactly the reason I shouldn't trust her though. After all, she's turned her back on her own country.' Andreiv was now in two minds, but it was too late to go back. Now that Mikhail was gone, there was no one else that he could trust and he was desperate to talk to somebody.

"Can you talk?"

"That depends.Who is it?" His phone voice was unfamiliar to her as so far, she'd only spoken to him within the confines of the factory.

"Andreiv."

"Where are you calling from?" 'Has he remembered what I told him?'

"I'm outside walking. There's no one around."

"Don't believe it Andreiv." 'I've got to talk to him about his naivety. It will be for his own good and mine.'

Andreiv had another look around, but the street looked empty.

"Keep it brief Andreiv, but I am listening." Daisy wasn't sure whether she was doing the right thing, as this young man with all his innocence could sink her, if she wasn't careful.

"All I wanted to say is that I just need to tell someone that I'm not happy with what I've been asked to do. I do hope that I can trust you."

Daisy didn't respond to the latter statement.

"What do you think you're being asked to

do?"

"Produce synthetic drugs for sale on the open
market."

"All I can say Andreiv, is that you're not wrong, but please keep going for now." Daisy wasn't in any position to reassure him, but she had offered to listen and she knew how badly he was feeling. She wasn't best pleased with what she was being asked to do either, but then hopefully both of them would get their day.

"Okay. If that's what's best. They've already murdered my partner."

"Who was that?"

"His name was Mikhail. He was also my best friend. We made the mistake of discussing work in a park. The next day he was missing and the GU left a note to say that he wouldn't be back."

This statement shook Daisy and served to remind her of just how precarious her position was.

"All the more reason to continue for now. I'll help when I can."

"Will you? Thank you."

"Bye Andreiv."

"Bye Daisy."

'I wonder what her part in this really is? Whatever it is, I have to trust her now.'

Andreiv collected his coat and gloves and left for home. Whilst on his journey he tried to act naturally, but felt as though everyone he saw was watching him; that lone person at the bus stop, the street cleaner, the bus driver, a passing cyclist. It could have been anyone and it may have been no one.

He couldn't even talk to his mother and normally she would have been his sounding board for all things. She understood and would always have a few pearls of wisdom to impart. The stress was starting to get to him, but he had to carry on, somehow.

'That was one worried young man. I guess he's struggling with his conscience and he's scared.' Daisy continued to mull over what she believed must have happened. She came to the conclusion that the two young protege's must have been coerced somehow and only realised what they were being asked to do, at a later stage.

The powers that be obviously decided to scare the crap out of them both and chose Mikhail as the target. That would suggest that Andreiv was the real brain of the operation, as either could have been selected for disposal.

Chapter 23

"That bullet was meant for me wasn't it?" Katy had called Trevor as soon as she'd realised that it was him. It didn't take a lot of figuring out, but she had to admit to herself that he was made of sterner stuff than she ever would have thought.

She already had a plan for Trevor. "Look, before you say anything I just need to say that I don't want to die thankyou, so wouldn't now be a good time for us two to pool our resources."

"You're only saying that because I've got you scared shitless."

"That's partially the reason, yes." 'Well he didn't even try to deny it.' She stopped to think carefully, before continuing. Then she said. "I also think that it would be much better for the pair of us to work together. We both have successful businesses and we both operate over roughly the same patch. It would just save a lot of grief."

"If I take you out, both businesses could be mine and as it was me that got you to where you are, that seems the better bet to me."

"Okay, but that means you've got to be able to take me out before I get to the police. Do you think you can do that?"

Trevor thought about this for a second. He also recalled how he felt immediately after the last debacle. He knew that he wasn't really cut out for murder.

"Listen, I'm not happy about being blackmailed, but at this precise moment I suppose I need you more than you need me."

'Oh you do.' She thought. "Irrespective of who needs who the most, we can be of mutual help to each other. I bet you haven't even got rid of that gun yet have you?"

"How did you know that?"

"Because I know you."

"Well no, I haven't actually. What should I do with it?"

"Bring it over here. The police would never think that you would hide it at the scene of the crime."

"That sounds good. We could have a chat

at the same time."

"Exactly."

"When can I come over?"

"How about this afternoon, say twoish? I've just got to run some errands first. You know the kind."

"Sure do." Trevor felt a bit more like his old self and he could certainly do with a friend right now. "I'll see you later." It did feel a little odd to be chatting like this with someone that he'd tried to kill only a short while ago.

He went straight to the bathroom and had a shower to freshen, for old times sake. Trevor always liked to keep his options open, especially when it came to Katy.

Katy made another call and then went out to run her errands. She had every intention of being back in plenty of time to see that gruesome little shit get what was coming and to make sure that he saw her there. She would even witness him handing over the murder weapon.

The plan went even better than Katy could have hoped because as Trevor pulled up outside the flats another car pulled up just behind him and he was totally unaware of it. He was so wrapped up in he had to do. She watched from her first floor window.

Trevor reached across to the passenger seat and lifted the gun. He slipped it into a brown paper bag and then got out and locked the driver's door. The two gentlemen in the car behind witnessed all of this and then they followed Trevor up the stairs towards Katy's flat. They waited for him to enter and then immediately rang her doorbell. Katy answered the door with Trevor still standing at her side and still holding the gun.

"I think this belongs to you." Katy said to the two officers, while pointing at Trevor. "The murder weapon is in the paper bag. Very original by the way, Trev."

"What's going on?" Trevor squeaked. His voice was even letting him down now.

"You're under arrest Mr King, for the murder of one Ms Wendy Conran." The police officer continued with the caution.

Trevor looked at Katy who just smiled at him, but instead of giving her a mouth full of expletives, he just smiled back. The smile was unlike any that she'd seen Trevor give before. It was demonic and although it emanated from Trevor, it made Katy shiver. She thought that the smile came from a man who had tipped over the edge. Katy no longer felt as smug as she had just a few minutes before.

What was even worse for Katy, was the fact that someone else was making plans for her.

Chapter 24

As usual Alfie was in the office early and was just about to file some paperwork, when he heard a voice that he thought that he recognised. It wasn't a voice from his recent past and to be quite honest it wasn't just the voice itself, it was the intonation. He just had to try and see who it was.

Trevor was being his usual obnoxious self and swearing that next time 'that bitch would get it', even while he was being taken to the interview room.

"Trevor King, is that you?"

Trevor stopped dead in his tracks. "Who wants to know?"

Alfie left his office and came face to face with Trevor.

"It's Alfie, Alfie Edwards or rather Detective Inspector Edwards."

"Oh my God, so you did go over to the dark side then." He sniggered.

Alfie ignored the snide remark. After all this time, Trevor still managed to make his skin crawl. "What have you been pulled in for?"

"They think I murdered someone."

"Did you?"

"Couldn't possibly say. You won't get anything from me until I see my brief."

"Trevor, Trevor. You've been watching too many episodes of The Sweeney."

Trevor thought it best to ignore that remark and just continue to his destination, however before he could continue, a sargeant informed Alfie that Trevor had been found in possession of the murder weapon, from the girl in the flat murder and that his DNA matched that taken from the vomit sample at the murder scene.

Alfie stared at Trevor in disbelief, but there was one more shock that was about to come his way when, just before the latter disappeared into the interview room, he shouted back. "I saw your old mate the other day."

Alfie strode toward the interview room, passed the two accompanying officers and grabbed Trevors arm.

"Who?" He knew he was grasping at straws, but there just might be the outside chance.

"Do a deal with me and I'll talk."

"It doesn't work like that Trevor and until you tell me who it was that you saw, I can't even tell you if it would be worth doing any deal."

"Keenan. I saw Kevin Keenan."

His outside chance had paid off. He had an idea that Trevor might be referring to Kevin, but couldn't believe his luck. He had made no progress with regard to finding Kevin and now, out of the blue, someone could be handing him in on a plate.

"Sergeant. Listen, I know this request is a little unconventional, but do you think I could have a word with your suspect? I promise not to smuggle him out."

Alfie thought that making light of the situation might be the best tactic. He was either correct or the sergeant was going to oblige anyway. "Okay sir. I can give you a few minutes I suppose. We'll be standing right here though."

"That's absolutely fine. I just need a couple of unofficial words with regard to another case that I'm working on."

Trevor was manhandled to a seat and told to sit. He was surprised to see the sergeant and the constable leave.

"Why have they left? Are you going to rough me up or something?"

"Grow up Trevor." Was all that Alfie could be bothered to say. He sat opposite Trevor and wasted no time on niceties.

"Listen Trevor I can't promise you anything officially, but if you can help me locate Kevin, there may be something I can do to help your case. What exactly is your case by the way?"

"I murdered that girl in the flat. I'm sure you know all about it."

Alfie couldn't believe that Trevor had just confessed to the murder, albeit unofficially. "Why did you do that Trevor?"

"Why are you interested?"

"I suppose because I'm just dismayed that a kid that I grew up with could turn out to be a cold blooded killer. I mean I always knew that you had a temper and that your dad gave you a hard time, but murder. Where did that come from?"

Trevor broke down. Suddenly and without ever thinking that he'd feel this way, he felt ashamed. He felt vulnerable and he felt very alone.

"I don't know Alf. My life seems to have continued down a predetermined path of destruction. That's the simplest way that I can explain it."

Even though Trevor appeared to be genuinely remorseful, Alfie knew that this could be a ruse. He remembered that although Trevor was always thick, he was very adept at playing the sympathy card.

"So what led to the murder?"
"Listen, whatever I tell you is off the record, right?"
"Of course."
"I run drugs. It started with running them for my dad, but then I got sick of being his underling, so I started on my own." He sniffed and wiped his nose on his sleeve. "I met this tramp, she was just a young girl really, but she was homeless, so I gave her a bed and food etc."
"I suppose you wanted something in return?"
"Alfie, what do you take me for?" There

was that slight smile. "Well yes, but I never forced myself and it was all done by mutual consent. Anyway, she started working for me, but before long she was outstripping me income wise. Helped by my dear old dad of course, who also found that Katy, the girl, was a sure thing in bed."

"So you tried to kill her because you thought that she was better than you or worse still, you thought that your dad thought that she was better than you?"

"I suppose so, yeah."

Alfie suddenly thought that if Trevor was running drugs, he might know something about the new strain that was coming from Russia.

"Trevor, do you know anything about a synthetic cocaine that's coming from Russia?"

"No." Said in all honesty.

"Let me reword that question. Do you know anything about a supply line change recently? Like where it's coming from or the quality. Anything like that?"

"I do know that there has been a sudden drop in price, from a certain source and it just so happens that it is cocaine."

"Where is it coming from?"

"France, Paris to be exact."

"Would you be willing to lead me to the

source?"

"That depends, doesn't it?"

"Listen, I've said that I'll see what I can do, but this is all very unofficial."

"Okay. I suppose, if that's the best you can offer, it might still help in some way. Anyway before I tell you that, didn't you want to know where that pillock Keenan is?"

"Oh crikey, yes. I'd forgotten about him."

"I saw him coming out of Sainsburys on Romford Road."

"How long ago?"

"Only a couple of weeks. He gave me the slip when I called out to him."

"Well, you can hardly blame him, can you? You used to make his life a misery."

Just for a second, the familiar old smirk appeared on Trevors face and it wasn't missed by Alfie. That, along with the earlier smile, told him all he needed to know about how repentant Trevor truly was.

"Right, I'm going to go and have a word with the sergeant and I'll catch up with you later."

Alfie left the interview room and so as to remain good to his word, he asked the sergeant to go gently with Trevor, for now. He did explain that Trevor could be a valuable informer. His priority for now was to find

Kevin, but he would have to remember to speak to Trevor again about the drugs issue.

Chapter 25

The project was going well so far and already Paris, Milan and Madrid had succumbed to her wishes.

The project concept was relatively simple to conceive and document, but not so to implement. Basically the plan was to dislodge the current leading drug barons from most of the major cities in western europe, introduce their own or rather Russia's own personnel and then bring in the drugs. This would have a two fold advantage. The first being that the mother country would have full control over the supply of cocaine and marajuana and the profits thereof and the second and almost as a bonus really, they could establish a new spy network, mainly made up of criminals admittedly, but a new source of information, nonetheless.

The trickiest part of the project was to manage the removal of the current incumbents in each city. This took an inordinate amount of time as not only did they need to gather an accurate list of names, addresses, responsibilities, current movements etc. they also had to then come up with a fool proof plan that would guarantee that they were neutralised.

The only good news was that crooks being what they are, if you give them a good enough and a 'fool proof' motive, they can be coerced into carrying out most money making schemes. The upshot of this was that Daisy didn't have to invent a drug related crime in order to achieve her goal. She had free reign to come up with whatever scheme she felt necessary. Although this would be based on intelligence provided, which she wasn't sure, could be relied on.

So far so good, but she was running low on resources. Even a country the size of Russia couldn't supply the quantity of criminals or at the very least lowlife, with enough about them, to run each new regime. She would have to go and ask for help.

Daisy arranged a meeting with the men

from the government. She wasn't looking forward to it, but at least her new ally Dimitri would be there to support her request. He was fully on board with regard to her dilemma. That's what he told her anyway. She knew enough to know that she couldn't really rely or trust anyone.

She made her own way this time, by driving her little Trabant. She never enjoyed driving that yellow antiquity, but it did give her a certain amount of freedom and at a dizzying maximum speed of about forty miles an hour as well. She finally arrived, just about in one piece after being shaken remorselessly by the rudimentary suspension. She parked up and made her way to the correct office after meeting Dimitri in the foyer. They climbed the stairs together. Nothing was said.

There were no childish games this time. This was very much a business meeting, however the opening comment from Grigori put her straight on her back foot. She should have known that this wasn't going to be a cake walk.

"So, Ms Wilcox, you have a burner phone." He didn't wait for her to admit or deny the fact. He pressed on. "Why do you feel the need to have such a device, when we have supplied you with a phone?"

Daisy immediately bit. "Why do you have one?" She knew that she was going out on a limb by making this statement and also that this could land her in big trouble, in fact the biggest, but there were certain times when she had to stand her ground and this was one of them. "If you answer me truthfully, I think that your answer would hold true for both of us, don't you?"

"You insolent witch. I'll have you dealt with."

Dimitri stood up and while pointing at the politician in an accusatory manner, said. "Are you denying that you have a burner phone then?"

"I don't need to answer that question. I'm not here to answer to either of you two."

"Maybe not, but you and I both know that you have one and we both know why, so why bother Ms Wilcox with such spiteful and pointless questioning?" Before the now red faced politician could answer, Dimitri continued. "We have come here to ask for your co-operation, in order that we are able to continue to run your project, so you decide that the way to get the best from your project manager is to berate her." There was no immediate answer, so Dimitri pressed home his advantage. "We need manpower. If we are expected to run the drug traffic in whatever major cities you choose, we need the resources to do it."

Now, feeling a little more confident and supported by at least one person at the table, Daisy chipped in.

"We have delivered so far and we want to be able to continue to do so, but even we can't magic up the manpower required."

"Leave it with us. You can go now, but we're watching you. Both of you."

Dimitri wasn't going to let the tall streak of piss politician get away with that comment, especially as he won the last spat, so just as they were about to pass through the large double doors at the end of the room, he turned and said in a very threatening way. "And we are watching you. All of you. Pleasant dreams. Don't forget, we have far less to lose than any of you."

As soon as they got into the corridor Daisy turned to Dimitri and just said. "I owe you big time, thankyou."

"You better hope that I don't collect." Dimitri replied with a sly grin on his face.

As usual Daisy had no idea how to read that statement, but for now at least she was deeply grateful for being able to get out of that room in one piece and with her point made.

She desperately wanted to contact the one person in the world who she could trust and the one person that she wanted to wrap herself around, but she knew that now wasn't the right time.

Chapter 26

"**H**ow could they have known?"

"I know exactly how they knew. It was the unknown informant. We were set up." Claude was the leader of the gang and by far the most shrewd, but not necessarily the smartest.

"But why? What could whoever they are, have gained? They didn't get the jewels either."

"No, but they did get us off the streets didn't they."

"So, do you think that it was the rozzers that set us up?"

"I don't know, but that's not the kind of tactic that they would usually employ. They've never been that clever before."

"Well they have now and we're up to our necks in shite."

"Not necessarily."

"How do you work that out? We were caught in the shop when it was shut. It was obvious even to plod that we weren't shopping. Also, you don't normally shop with drills and explosives."

"Stop panicking will you. It's not good for your blood pressure. We've got lawyers you know."

No one knew who the 'man' at the top was, not even the police. All that anyone did know was that whoever it was, knew how to pull strings with the underworld and also knew how to work the law.

As well as Paris, similar stories had been repeated in two other major European cities. The upper echelons of the local underworld had been suckered into crimes that were destined to fail. The police were informed and the criminals arrested. It didn't really matter how long they were out of action for. It just needed to be long enough for them to be usurped, their circles to be broken and the leadership replaced by the Russian replacements. If they dared to try and make a comeback, they would be dealt with.

Initially, these incidents weren't seen as being linked. In fact the individual cities had no idea that similar scenarios were being played out in other places. However when it happened for a fourth time, this time in Hamburg, someone smelt a rat and that was purely down to the fact that one person with the right knowledge was in the right place at the right time.

The first glaring similarity between all of these events was that these were all major crimes that had gone wrong. The second was that they all happened in major cities within europe. The third and so far the most mysterious, was that all of these crimes took place after a tip off. Likewise the criminals were caught after another tip off.

So far there was no clear motive.

Claude was not going to let this go. "Well I've already put the word out. I'm going to make it my personal mission to find out who has stitched us up. I'm not too bothered why, but if I can find that out as well that would be a bonus."

"That's fine, as long as it doesn't drop us any further in the crap. You don't know who you're dealing with and whoever they are knows how to pull strings."

"I don't give a shit. They're not getting away with it and they're definitely going to rue the day that they messed with me."

"Well good luck." Claude's sidekick was well aware that whatever the outcome was for his comrade, it would be the same for the rest of the team. He prayed that Claude would remain calm and calculated, but he knew his old mucker well enough to know that neither would be the case.

Chapter 27

In the last two weeks Alfie had managed to put on six pounds. This was mainly due to the fact that he was spending a good part of his working day, sitting in his car and outside Sainsburys in the Romford Road.

Finally, the extra weight and wait paid off. He saw Kevin entering the store, dressed in what looked like a bib and brace and checked shirt, with his sleeves rolled up. He was obviously working around here somewhere.

Alfie jumped out of his car. He was alone and although this wasn't the normal protocol, he didn't want to be any more heavy handed with his old friend than he knew he had to be. He walked into the store and stood where he could clearly see all of the checkouts. It only took a couple of minutes for Kevin to appear, armed with a sandwich, a bag of crisps and a banana.

He was just about to leave the store when Alfie quietly sidled up to him.

"Hello old friend."

"Jesus Christ, you scared the shit out of me. What do you want?"

"You don't recognise me do you?"

"I don't have any money."

"Liar. I just witnessed you purchasing that extravagant lunch."

Kevin thought that if this guy was a 'would be' assailant, at least he had a sense of humour. He stopped walking and turned to look the stranger in the eye.

"No it can't be. Alfie Edwards? Is it really you under that ridiculous hat?"

"'Fraid so."

They both laughed and then hugged each other. Kevin's bag of crisps was caught in the crush and split.

"Oh bollocks. There goes the favourite part of my lunch."

"I'll get you another bag. We mustn't have you going hungry must we? Listen Kevin, can we talk, I mean seriously?"

"Of course we can Alf and may I just say that if you are who I think you are I already know what you want to talk to me about and that's fine."

"Who do you think I am then?"

"Well let me see. Stalking, questions, turning up out of the blue and of course, flat feet. You're no milkman are you?"

"That's all down to you, you know."

"What, flat feet? How have I managed to get the blame for that one?"

Alfie smiled warmly, but decided not to rise to the bait. "Do you remember what you said to me all those years ago?"

"I dunno. Get a job? I do remember thinking that you'll never be a fighter."

"You certainly got that last bit right, but you also added, 'use your brain and do good Alfie.' Well I did that but not by following plan A. My wife and I had a baby before I could get to uni, so I joined the police instead."

"Congratulations on both securing a wife and having a child. I'm not so sure about the police bit though. Seriously though, nice one Alfie."

"Thanks. We had a daughter by the way and we called her Daisy."

It was as if Kevin had been put under some kind of spell.

"Kev. Are you okay?"

"You really called your daughter Daisy?"

"Yup. Couldn't call her anything else really could I? Anyway, listen, officially I have to place you under arrest for the murder of Mr Wilcox on the night of September the ninth last year, but I want to talk to you about it rather than do anything hasty. Are you okay with that?"

"As I already stated Alfie, I knew why you wanted to talk to me, so I'm fine and don't worry I'm not going to do a runner. Where shall we meet?"

"You tell me. I'm happy to come over to you and we can have a proper catch up as well as deal with this crap."

Kevin gave Alfie the name of a local pub that did good food and they arranged to meet there that evening.

Chapter 28

The feedback from her punters wasn't good. Some of her customers had dropped by the wayside and others complained that they just weren't feeling right. Initially, Katy shrugged the problem off and justified it by consoling herself with the fact that they were all just addicts and that they were bound to have bad days. The latter part was exactly what she told them as well, but she always tried to do it in a conciliatory way, so as not to offend any of them. If there was one great skill that she'd learned, it was how to keep and where possible, win customers.

Of course what they didn't know was that they were getting coke from a different source and to be fair Katy didn't know where it was coming from either. She just purchased it through her supplier without questioning the source. She did think it a little odd that the price had recently gone down slightly. This was something that had been unheard of before, but because of the recent complaints, she dropped her prices as well. This came at just the right time to pacify some at least.

After a while and with more customers complaining, she felt it necessary to speak to her suppliers about the growing problem. She'd also heard about a cheaper form of the drugs coming through the supply chain, but she hadn't ordered any and her supplier hadn't mentioned any change. Irrespective of the price drop she could no longer manage the drop in trade.

"Listen, something has changed and you're not being upfront about it."

"I don't have to be upfront about anything. As far as I'm aware you are getting the same stuff as everyone else."

"Well I'm losing customers and that will directly impact how much I order from you, so if you don't want a drop in income I suggest you find out what's going on."

The supplier, who'd never been pushed around by a strip of a girl before and didn't appreciate it now, finally came clean with one snippet of information and at least that explained part of what had changed. The dilemma that this left Katy with now, was what to do with this information.

"All I can tell you is that my supply appears to be coming via a different route, so something has changed, but I have no idea what."

"Right, in that case let's just hope that this is a short term glitch." She put the phone down.

The same problem appeared to be impacting other dealers, but Katy had to tread carefully with regard to her probing questions. For obvious reasons dealers didn't really want to communicate with each other. There was never any chance of starting a dealers union.

With business now being directly impacted, Katy decided to take a similar trip to the one that Trevor had taken a month or so earlier. She wanted to find the new source of the cocaine, but more importantly she wanted to try and find fresh suppliers who used a different supply line.

It took a couple of days to organise her business affairs but as soon as that was accomplished she made arrangements to travel to Paris. She was hoping to be there and back within two days. Being away from her patch was always a difficult affair to manage, as it took no time at all for the wrong people to find out that she was absent and then they would attempt to muscle in straight away. Fortunately she had established a relationship with a couple of her heavy's, who she felt that she could trust and who would look after her best interests while she was away. Even so, she felt that two days was as long as she could afford to be away. She knew that she couldn't afford to push the trust.

As cut throat as her business was, most in the trade abided by the unofficially agreed boundaries. That was until someone went missing for a day or two and then their patch would be fair game. It was the same for everyone of course.

Where Katy had to really watch her back was with the King's, especially as it was their patch that she'd muscled into in the first place.

Chapter 29

O nce their drinks had been purchased they sat at a table that was situated in a quiet bay window. They ordered their food, whilst exchanging pleasantries and then ate in near silence. The food was okay, but that wasn't the primary reason for this particular visit to the pub and they both knew it. It was awkward for them both and made much more so because they were old friends.

As soon as the meal was finished however, Kevin decided to open up to Alfie. It actually felt great to be able to tell someone everything, especially someone who he trusted implicitly and someone who he knew would make the right judgement call.

"So Alfie old friend there you have it. All

of it, I promise you."

"So you did attempt to murder Daisy's step father then?"

"Yes I did. It was because many years earlier, I had promised her that I would and I don't let my friends down when I make promises to them."

"I know you well enough to know that's true, but you don't need me to tell you that had you succeeded you would be in a whole lot more trouble than you're in already."

"Of course, but as things stand I'm the number one suspect anyway. Let me ask you one question?"

"Certainly, fire away."

"Who took the photo of me at the scene?"

"We don't know."

"Well in that case I'll ask another. Who just happened to be in the right place at the right time with a fairly powerful camera and then be in a position to send said photo to you guys the moment the case broke?"

Alfie sat and mulled all of this over. He didn't know at this stage that Kevin had already posed the same questions to the army.

"I don't know if I mentioned this earlier, but there was someone working in the garden of a house further down the road. I thought it a little strange at the time because they seemed to be there for ages. Before you ask, I didn't get a clear look at them. I wouldn't even be able to tell you what colour they were."

"Could you take me to the house?"

"I suppose so. What good would that do?"

"I've got no idea, but let's see when we get there."

They wasted no time, so Alfie settled the bill, they left the pub and jumped into his car.

"Thanks for believing me by the way."

"That was never in question Kevin. I just need to find a way to keep you out of jail and also to keep my superiors off my back."

No more was said and it only took ten minutes to arrive at Daisy's road. As soon as Kevin climbed out of the car he recognized the front garden that had held the suspicious looking gardener. It had a Sold sign pinned to the front fence.

Alfie jumped in. "So this place could have been on the market and therefore empty, when you were last here."

"It does seem that way, but I didn't see a for sale sign.

"Maybe they removed it and tucked it behind the fence."

"I'll call the estate agent first thing tomorrow."

They both had a good look around the front garden before leaving, but found nothing.

"Thinking about it, this would have given whoever it was a perfect view of Mrs Wilcox using her spare door key as well."

"What do you mean?"

"Sorry Kev. I never told you that part. Mrs Wilcox told me that she knew that her spare front door key had been moved sometime after she'd gone away for the weekend. We've spent all this time concentrating on your entrance through the french doors when I believe that the murderer just let themself in through the front door."

"Well, that does make a difference doesn't it?"

"At the moment no, because it's just a hypothesis."

"Have you considered whether someone on the other side of the road has a video doorbell?"

"No, I must admit I haven't."

"Let's go and have a shufty."

They walked across the road, split up and began to scour the front doors for the correct type of bell. After only checking a couple Alfie noticed one. He asked Kevin to wait at the gate with his back to the property. He didn't want the person who lived at this property to recognise his accomplice. This was just in case Kevin's face was to ever become public and the mess that could lead to. 'I just hope the camera in that bell hasn't been able to capture his face already.' Alfie thought. "I'll go and knock or ring, in this case."

He approached the door with some trepidation, as the whole house had a look of mild dilapidation about it.
In fact the only modern and vaguely shiny looking item was the video doorbell, which still managed to look slightly jaded.

He pushed the button and heard nothing, but he decided to wait for a few seconds before attempting a second push. The door eventually opened and an elderly gentleman with no teeth was standing there in his pyjamas. He said nothing.

"Good evening sir. My name is Detective Inspector Edwards and I'm from the met. Police."
"Looking for that murderer are you?"
"Well yes, I am actually."
"What do you want from me and who's that dodgy looking bloke at the bottom of my garden?"

Alfie did his best to ignore the second question. "I just wondered if you had any recorded video on this doorbell?" He said clearly pointing to the device.

"Nope. It's just there to make people think that I'm recording them. Never been connected and who is that bloke there?"

Alfie surrendered. He accepted that the elderly gentleman wasn't going to let that particular subject go.

"He's one of my officers. I've just asked him to wait outside because I don't like there to be more than one of us standing on peoples doorsteps. It can look a little overwhelming to some of the public." Alfie knew that this sounded very implausible, but it was the best he could offer on the fly.

"Why is he facing the street? He's not moving."

"He's on look out. We have to make sure that the public are safe at all times, when we can." 'Wow, I'm really going out on a limb here.'

"Do you think the murderer is still here?"

"No we don't, but you can't be too careful can you?"

"I suppose not, no."

Alfie pressed home his slight advantage. "Oh really. That's a shame. Your bell is pointing right at the area of interest."

"Are you interested in those two

gardeners then?"

Alfie was completely taken aback by the last comment, but didn't want to appear so. He managed to say "Yes."

"What do you want to know? All I can really tell you is that two blokes turned up in a car, which is odd anyway for gardeners don't you think? They then got a couple of spades and a bag out of the boot. I don't know what car it was other than it was white and largeish. I can tell you that both of the guys looked foreign but not black. More like Arabs. I can also tell you that one of them left after a couple of hours. He drove away, but I did see the same car, I think it was the same car anyway, parked further up the road, later in the day."

"Did the occupant leave the car?"

"Not while I was watching."

"Did you see what was in the bag?"

"No, I'm afraid not."

"Strange isn't it? Having gardeners come to a house that's empty."

"Oh, so it was empty when they were there was it?"

"It's been empty for six months. The last owner passed away and it's only just gone on the market."

Alfie stepped back as if to go, but in all actuality it was because of the smell that had gently started to waft past the elderly gentleman. 'I do hope that's not coming from the kitchen.'

"Thank you sir. You've been a great help."

"I'm sure I haven't but good luck anyway."

"Before I go, I must just ask, did you tell anyone else this story?"

"No one's asked."

Alfie was fuming. His men hadn't even been thorough enough to question this man. It was inexcusable, as even if he was out on their first visit, someone should have noted the fact and made a plan to return.

He bade the elderly man a good evening and went back down the path.

"Did you hear all that?"

"Certainly did."

"I need to make a call, but I don't want to do it here. Let's go back to the car."

Chapter 30

That one call had triggered several more. These calls had then instigated a meeting, which was held in a house somewhere in Belgravia. Alfie wasn't aware of any of what had transpired after his initial call. He had just been instructed to make the call once Kevin was captive.

During this time Kevin was held in jail, which he didn't find any particular hardship. In fact the only thing that bothered him was not being able to tell his customers that he wouldn't be available. As it was he had only been there for two days when Alfie returned to his cell with news.

"You've been sent for. You lucky lad."
"What's going on Alf?"

"I have no idea, old son. I've just been asked to come and get you."

"Well where are we going? You must know that at least?"

"I'm taking you to a waiting car and that's nearly all I know."

"What do you mean by nearly?"

"You'll find out. Let's just say that of your two current options, option two seems like it should far outweigh option one with regard to, let's just say freedom of movement."

"Thank you Alfie."

"What do you mean thank you. You don't know what's going to happen yet."

"I mean thank you. Whatever happens, had you not stepped in, we both know that I would have had to settle for option one."

"I've got to say that I had very little influence in this matter, but I did get the ball rolling. I wasn't about to see an innocent man go down, now was I. Especially one who I've known and looked up to for nearly all my life."

As unaccustomed as Kevin was, to shows of emotion, he grabbed Alfie, pulling him in close and then hugged him.

"No crisps were hurt during the making of this hug." Kevin joked.

They both laughed and Alfie returned the hug for a few seconds before saying to Kevin that they needed to get going. As soon as they reached the outside Kevin took in a lung full of fresh air and smiled the smile of a free man.

"Your limo awaits." Said Alfie, while pointing to a black cab.

Kevin turned to shake Alfies hand and said that they will catch up with each other sooner rather than later. While there hands were in contact Kevin shoved a note into Alfies hand.

Alfie just responded with a "Get out of here, before I get sacked." He waited until Kevin had got into the car and then took a quick look at the note, which read:

Please contact these customers and let them know that due to unforeseen circumstances I won't be available.

THE LIST OF NAMES AND NUMBERS NEXT.

This was followed by:

My old van is parked behind Sainsburys. Could you please take care of it for me (Key under brick to the left of Sainsburys loading bay door).

Thanks for everything Alf.

K

Alfie smiled to himself and tucked the note into his trouser pocket.

The cab pulled away from the curb and Kevin turned to waive, but Alfie had already ducked back inside. He was never any good at goodbyes, especially those that so closely followed hello's, from old friends.

Kevin sat back in his seat and after a few minutes he gave up trying to guess where he was going, which was just as well because he would never have been able to.

The taxi finally pulled up outside a Belgravia mews house and the cabby said into his rear view mirror: "Number thirty eight, oh and good luck." In a way that suggested to Kevin that the cabby knew a little more than it at first seemed.

Kevin opened the rear door of the cab and looked straight at number thirty eight. It looked just like numbers thirty six on the one side and forty on the other. He walked tentatively up the steps and rang the doorbell. He couldn't hear if it rang inside but within a couple of seconds a smart suited man appeared at the now open door and uttered: "This way sir." He then just turned and walked back inside, so Kevin duly followed.

The two of them finally arrived at an ornately carved door, which was at the far end of the entrance hall. The door was opened by the gentleman in the suit and Kevin went to follow him into what could only be described as a board room that was decorated in a style that wouldn't have looked out of place in the forties. The only concession being the modern looking phones that were situated on the large mahogany desk. However before he could go any further the suit asked Kevin to step back and remain in the hall until he was called for.

Mr. Suit came back to the door and beckoned Kevin in. There was a large leather wing back chair on the far side of the desk and it was facing the wrong way. That was until it slowly rotated revealing its occupant. Kevin thought 'Please don't tell me he's stroking a cat.' He wasn't, but he was wearing a fob watch and chain and there was a hanky in his top pocket. He was obviously dressed to match the room.

The occupant of the wing back chair was a middle aged gentleman of rather large proportions. Not all fat though. There was something about him. Also he had more than just a twinkle in his eye. There was something about his face that suggested a wealth of experience. He exuded a steely grit.

'Obviously ex-military.' He then thought and that was the last thought he had before he was spoken to.

"Well 'K' welcome to our little abode." He gestured for Kevin to take a seat.

This was Kevin's introduction to the SOE (Special Operations Executive), an organisation that he and the rest of the world believed, was disbanded at the end of the war. As far as most of the government was concerned it had, however the military services had all agreed that it would be prudent to continue to run their own secret service, funded by them and totally autonomous to the politically run agencies. A chosen few civil servants in Whitehall also knew about the service, but they were there just in case there was ever a need for some kind of liaison between the SOE and the government.

"Aren't you supposed to be in Baker Street?" Was Kevin's witty retort.

His interviewer ignored the humour and just replied dryly with. "We had to move out." He went on. "We know all about you lad. Including your little sojourn to the house in the east end. We know your history and we know your contacts. We know almost as much about you as you do."

"If you know that much, maybe you can tell me who it was that actually killed Mr W?"

"Funnily enough, we can."

"Oh!" This really took Kevin by surprise.

"We will deal with that case thankyou. What I need you to do for now, is train and that starts with losing your identity. From now on you will be known as K."

"Yes sir." Kevin immediately felt alive. This was more like it, even though he had no idea what 'it' would be in this case.

For the next six months Kevin or 'K' went through intense training. This course would normally take a year, but as Kevin was ex-SAS and martial arts trained, extremely fit and last but not least, now needed on a case, he was put through his paces. It was tough and to his surprise much tougher than his SAS training. This course required mental agility to match his physical prowess.

He had his fingerprints removed, his eyes recoloured and even his teeth straightened. He was removed from all official databases and was issued with a set of false identities along with passports, birth certificates etc. for when the needs arose. He had to learn and be tested on the background stories for his 'other' identities. Dan Smith wasn't one of them unfortunately, as he had already developed a backstory for that guy.

It was during his training that Kevin received news that his mother had passed away. It came through by means of a handwritten note from Alfie and he immediately started to sob, but couldn't understand why, as he hadn't seen or heard from either of his parents in years. As usual and after just a few minutes, he parked his emotions as he always had and proceeded with his training.

He had considered attending the funeral, but when he approached his senior officer about the matter he was told very politely that as he didn't exist it would be unwise to go. He accepted the answer professionally and courteously and that was the end of the matter as far as he was concerned.

Kevin's mother had died of an overdose. She was buried by his father, who other than a couple of officials, was the only attendee at her funeral. His father had then returned home, walked upstairs, sat in the bath and slit his wrists. It was he who had purchased the drugs, but his suicide wasn't so much because he felt deeply guilty, but more because he knew that he couldn't survive without her. She had kept him alive, so now there was no point.

Kevin wasn't informed of any of the

details of his mothers passing. He wasn't even told that his father had also passed. It was felt that managing the one death, especially his mothers, was enough for now.

He was still a little rough around the edges, but the powers that be decided that he was ready. They had a mission for him and he was needed in France straight away.

Chapter 31

Not only to prove to herself that there was nothing wrong with the quality of what she was selling, but also to give herself some dutch courage before setting off, she snorted a line of coke. Initially it seemed fine and appeared to have the desired effect, so she climbed into her car, set the satnav and set off for Dover.

Traffic on the M20 was horrendous, but for a while Katy wasn't at all phased by this. She stayed amazingly chilled until one untimely honk from another driver. Normally this wouldn't have bothered her, but she could feel the hackles rise on her neck. She tried to calm herself, but found that she was feeling quite angry. She started to stare at any unsuspecting driver who happened to look her way. To try and alleviate this currently constant angry emotion, she tried listening to Taylor Swift through her MP3 player and felt that this worked to a degree. Making this last for the remainder of the journey was going to be somewhat of a problem.

She finally arrived at the ferry terminal where she pulled over for a minute to fumble for the ticket in her bag. Once found, she got out of her car and started to make her way to the ticket office. While walking briskly toward her target she became aware of two uniformed police officers looking in her direction. Her heightened senses along with the guilty look that she knew that she was demonstrating, told her that it was she who they were interested in, so rather than wait for the inevitable to happen, she turned and walked rapidly away.

The feeling of anger returned.

She headed back toward her car, but immediately noticed it too was now being inspected by another couple of officers. Everywhere she looked there seemed to be a uniform. Her thought process was now very woolly. She felt as though she was losing control of her mind and the situation.

The red mist had descended again. She

stopped in her tracks, shook her head and focussed. She decided that another tack was necessary, so she walked over to the two officers that were standing by her car and calmly removed a small firearm from her jacket.

She unloaded one shot towards the chest of each unsuspecting policeman and they both slumped to the floor. The sound was magnified by the fact that the shot's took place within a roofed parking area. This immediately brought the other officers running, so she jumped into her now available car, started it, reversed in a sweeping ark, running over the legs of one of the downed officers and then she drove towards some stationary lorries.

A shot rang out and the bullet passed through both her rear then front screens, missing her head by inches. She managed to cling on to enough of her logic to drive out of sight momentarily by manoeuvring between two rows of trucks. Whilst hidden from view she quickly jumped out of the car while it was still rolling and then she leapt in through the unlocked side door of a campervan that was just making its way onto the ferry. Her hope was that her moving car would cause a minor distraction when it impacted with another vehicle, which it surely would and that should give her just enough time to gain access to the ferry.

The occupants of the campervan were given no time at all to react. She held her pistol up and told them to continue with their journey as if nothing had happened. The camper made its way onto the ferry unobstructed. Once there however, Katy told the elderly owners that if she found out that they had grassed her up, she would find them and then kill them. The couple promised that they wouldn't breathe a word. She then jumped out, checked to make sure that she wasn't seen and made for another vehicle. This time she made for an HGV, but rather than approach the driver she just crawled underneath and hid herself among the chassis and associated equipment.

The ferry was held from departing and this caused major disruption. There were people complaining to the police in the terminal and to ferry staff in the terminal and on the ferry. It was pandemonium and all this played into Katy's hands, as it meant that a more thorough search couldn't take place. They didn't find her and eventually the ferry was allowed to sail. She guessed that the police had assumed that she had given them the slip and made her way back to the quayside.

Later and on reflection, she knew that she

wouldn't have shot those two policemen had she not succumbed to snorting some of her own stuff, prior to the trip. It had been a dumb idea and it was very dangerous, irrespective of any side effects or worse still, poisoning. She was now wanted for the murder of two police officers or so she thought.

What she hadn't stopped to consider, during all of the mayhem, was why the police appeared to be interested in her in the first place. However it didn't take too long to realise who may be responsible. 'Of course it was that bastard Trevor King. That would explain the smile that he gave me just prior to his arrest.'

One fact was that the two officers were wearing body armour, so they had survived. However one of them did sustain two broken legs.

The other was that it was the other King who had given the authorities the tip off.

Chapter 32

"I'm telling you it's the Russians." The lawyer said.

"What do you mean, it's the Russians? Russian who? What do they want with our patch? What's going on?"

"To answer your first question and that's about the only one I can answer right now, it's the Russian mafia and we don't really know why they've made a sudden push west. It is worrying though and not just from a drugs point of view."

"It's more than worrying. Even if by some miracle you do manage to get me out of here, I've then got to deal with the Russians. That could prove messy."

Lucas, Claude's lawyer, knew that what he was about to say wouldn't be received well, but he decided that it needed to be said. "My advice to you is to leave well alone. If you must insist on living this kind of lifestyle, do it somewhere else."

"May I remind you that just because I've been a client of yours for many years that doesn't give you the right to advise me on anything outside of your remit. I will ask when I need information or advice."

'I knew it'. Lucas thought. 'I don't know why I bother.'

"Certainly, but it's precisely because I've known you for a long time Claude, that I feel I'm trying to look after your best interests, even at my own cost, might I add."

"Well in that case, I do appreciate your concern Lucas, however I have absolutely no intention of handing Paris to the Russians."

"When you put it like that, I can't say that I disagree. We've got to get you out of here first though."

"How's that going?"

"I'm currently working on bail, but it's not looking good I'm afraid. You've got form, you know."

"Do you have a plan B?"

"There is only one plan B and that's not for me to either know about or be concerned with."

There was a pregnant pause, which to both men signified that they were jointly thinking about the same plan B, albeit from different perspectives.

"Anyway, I'll bid you farewell Claude and I'll be in touch as soon as I hear anything. That's assuming that you're still here of course."

They both smiled at each other as the lawyer made his way to the door. He knocked once and was let out.

Chapter 33

The ferry had been at sea for around half an hour, so Katy decided to release herself from her self imposed incarceration. She ached all over and it took a couple of minutes for the circulation to come back to her hands and feet. It looked like she was now alone on the freight deck and that everyone else had made their way to the decks above, where the food, the comfy seats and the fresh air was. She made a mental note of the location of her ride, as she was going to be using it once again in order to gain entry to France, then she decided it was safe enough for her to make her way upstairs to.

There was a door just to her left and adjacent to the door was the deck number and location. She headed through the door and up the steps, continuing up until she finally came out on the main deck. Once there, her first port of call had to be the toilet, but from there she made straight for the cafe, not only to stock up on the sustenance that she required immediately, but also to purchase some for her onward journey.

Katy still fully intended to reach her original goal, which was her dealer, who was based in Paris. She had nowhere else to go anyway and she certainly couldn't head back home. Of course she didn't have her car now, so would have to ride with the articulated unit until she was close enough to Paris to make a swap. This was assuming that the truck would be heading anywhere near that direction to start with. Either way she needed to get off the ferry and away from the port.

Long before the ferry came into Calais, Katy made her way back to her ride, checking first to make sure that the driver hadn't returned. She needed to be sure that she was unseen by whoever he or she might be.

Just before she hid herself away under the truck, it suddenly dawned on her that the best way to hide would be to ride in the cab. No one was going to search a place that the driver could clearly vouch for as being devoid of passengers. It would also be far more comfortable and offer shelter. Fortunately, for the short time that she'd spent underneath so far, the conditions had been dry. It hadn't dawned on her until now, that she probably wouldn't have been able to hang on in the wet.

The driver's door was unlocked, so she climbed in and hid in the sleeper unit at the rear. If the driver became aware of her prior to leaving the dock, she would just persuade him to keep quiet by pointing her little gun at the back of his head. This could also be used to persuade him to detour to Paris, should he start heading in the wrong direction. She made herself as comfortable as she could and began the long wait.

For what seemed like hours, but what was in reality only about thirty minutes nothing happened, then suddenly the cab door opened and the driver climbed in. After a few minutes the lorry's engine started and this jolted her back to full alertness. She peered around and could just see and hear movement elsewhere.

The deck slowly started to empty and then it was their turn to move. The unit jerked forward and then maintained walking speed until it broke free of the constraints of the ferry. It picked up speed but was still only doing around fifteen miles an hour.

After a couple of minutes the vehicle slowed to a crawl again. It remained this way for a minute or so and then Katy heard voices. Her heart sank. She instinctively knew that something was wrong. The vehicle crawled forward for a few more yards, then stopped. From her limited vantage point it looked like they were surrounded by uniformed border officials.

A short time later the driver climbed out of the unit and started talking to one of the uniformed officials, but she couldn't make out what he was saying. She could just discern that it was English that was being spoken with an English accent, so at least her driver came from her home country. That may or may not be an advantage later. If there was to be a later.

The cab door opened again and the driver climbed back in. The engine started and then they moved off. The vehicle started to gain speed. Katy couldn't believe that they hadn't discovered her, but she thanked her lucky stars. She reached inside a pocket and took out a biscuit. It was all that she could eat given her current situation. The driver heard the packet of biscuits open but ignored the sound. He had already been made aware that he was carrying a passenger.

What Katy had no idea of was that the police and border guards had detected her in the vehicle by using a body heat scanner while they were stationary. They had then been instructed to let her through the port, as she was being tailed by an unmarked police car. This was all done with the cooperation of the French authorities, although they did initially want to get involved. Once it had been explained that this was a matter of state security, they relented, but of course insisted on being kept fully appraised of the situation. They would only be told what the British police via the SOE, wanted them to hear of course.

By the time the Alldays Shipping Ltd wagon had cleared the terminal and made its way onto the autoroute it was getting late, so the driver made for a truck stop where he could spend the night. Katy was oblivious to this plan until she noticed that they were pulling off the road and into a yard that contained many trucks of all different shapes and sizes.

There appeared to be a motel and a petrol station on site, so she now realised what was going to happen and she started to panic. It was obvious that the driver would be climbing into the rear of the cab for his sleep. She had absolutely no idea what she was going to do.

Then, for the second time that day, she had another stroke of luck when as soon as they pulled in the driver, who was desperate for the loo, parked the truck, turned off the engine and almost ran for the toilet block. As soon as the coast was clear Katy took the opportunity to jump out, but as soon as she did so she realised that she had now lost her ride to Paris. She wouldn't have the opportunity to climb back aboard and she did not want to revert to hanging underneath.

As Paris was still some miles away, she decided to doss down for the night. There were ample facilities and she could make a fresh start in the morning. She also decided that she would thumb a lift the rest of the way and a truck stop was as good a place as any to do that.

Her tail watched her check into the motel and then he sent an update through to the office. He then checked into the same motel and asked for an early alarm call.

The following morning Katy woke with a crick in her neck, but otherwise fine. She wasn't in any particular rush, so she took her time over a shower and breakfast, before choosing a likely place to thumb a lift. She stood there for only about five minutes when a car drew up and the driver, who thankfully looked quite dishy and not all like a mad sex fiend, lowered the passenger side window and asked Katy where she was heading. 'He's English too, bonus.'

"Paris please." She thought that she ought to come up with a proper destination. "near The Louvre." It was the only Paris destination that she knew.

"That's fairly close to where I'm going. I can give you a lift if you like."

"That would be great thanks. My last lift only got me this far I'm afraid." She jumped in.

"No baggage?"

"Nope. I'm not staying long enough." She knew that it wasn't a very convincing reason, but she couldn't be bothered to expand.

"Oh, right. Jump in and we'll get going then."

Katy slid into the passenger seat and engaged her seatbelt. "I'm Katy by the way."

"Jim." He said without batting an eyelid. His actual name was Geoff. They shook hands.

This was the car that had been tailing her. Katy wasn't the only one who couldn't believe their luck.

"Visiting friends?"
"Friend."

Katy said no more and Geoff knew enough to know not to push it. Now that he had her he wasn't about to blow it. He would keep the conversation simple and non intrusive.

Chapter 34

'K' picked up his new burner and continued on his way to the cafe. He sat where he usually sat and picked up a menu, which he didn't really read. He already knew what he'd be having. It was what he always had at this particular cafe and at this time of day. No sooner had he ordered his eggs benedict when the phone in his pocket buzzed.

A new message came through and on this occasion it read:

Drugs coming into the UK from Paris. They are contaminated. We are holding a dealer who has given us a name.

The dealer was Trevor, but K didn't know this at the time.

You are to tail that name, one Katy Weller and try to find out why she's in Paris. We believe that drug activity is linked to failed crimes in Paris, Madrid, Milan and almost Hamburg, but we don't know why. We need you to find the source of the drugs and the distribution network. We believe that Russia is manufacturing them, but we don't know who is sponsoring the manufacture i.e. government agency, crime etc. The police are currently following Ms Weller and will update us on her location. You will probably get diverted from the original rendezvous. Be ready.Brother.End.

This was closely followed by a second message:

"toffee.infants.warnings.Charlie.08:00."

While in the field, agents always worked from coded messages, if they were dropping off or collecting. The W3W code would always be thirty squares south and west of the true destination. This gave adequate cover, should any third party get wind. The fourth word would always be the sender's code, the first letter of which would change with each text and go through the alphabet. This confirmed that it was he or she who was sending the remainder of the code. The 08:00 would be 20:00, so he had time to finish his breakfast.

Sometimes on the bigger jobs there

would be two agents, but never more and although they would know that there was another on the case, they would never meet. They wouldn't even know the identity of the other, but they would be made aware of the other's latest mobile number. They would also travel separately and by two different modes of transport. This had a two fold benefit. The first being that there would be cover in case of issues, like being discovered or worse, eliminated. The second was so that most contingencies could be dealt with.

All briefings, updates or future rendezvous, while he was active, would take place via SMS, which he would be expected to delete once he had read and digested the information. His phone would be kept on silent and all phones were changed regularly. K digested the information and deleted the messages.

In this particular case the second 'agent' was actually a police officer who had been briefed on the communications etiquette, but not about the organisation that he was communicating with.

K set off for St. Pancras station, as soon as he'd finished his eggs benedict and latte, where upon arrival he made his way towards the ticket booth. As he walked toward his destination someone bumped into him, slid a newspaper under his arm and blended back into the crowd. All before K could catch a glimpse of whoever it was. K removed the newspaper and discovered a Eurostar ticket in an unmarked envelope.

He smiled and thought that this was all very clichéd, but as it worked in all the best spy movies, he supposed that there was no reason why it shouldn't work here.

The Eurostar sat at the platform looking resplendent in the morning sunshine. He boarded and made for his reserved seat. He had a long journey ahead of him, so he made himself comfortable. As soon as he had done so he started to ponder the current situation.

After a while his mind wandered to Daisy and he considered the irony of her possibly being in Russia and the fact that he could end up there. He also mused over the fact that because of wheels within wheels, he was no longer wanted for murder.

'The powers that be can shape your life whichever way they want and that is scary. In my case, it has worked to my advantage, so far.' He thought. 'I wonder what lies ahead? I wonder where Katy Weller is now? I wonder what France is like?' He smiled to himself. The thought of adventure always made him feel better.

The Eurostar departed on time and K noted just how

smooth it was. It was also very spacious. It was nothing like the London Underground, which was the only train that he could compare it to. The one similarity was the fact that soon he was travelling underground and he noted that one tunnel looked very much like the next.

Once the train exited the tunnel on the far side, he watched the French countryside slide past his window as if seeing it through a fast moving viewfinder. It suddenly dawned on him that he'd never even travelled this fast before. Not on land anyway.

The countryside looked familiar to that in southern England, but somehow different. He tried to spot those differences to use as a distraction and although he did note the more obvious ones, the architecture of the buildings, the odd car on the wrong side of the road and weird shaped street lights etc. these didn't keep him occupied for long.

This was his first mission and he was determined not to screw it up. He tried to think through all possible eventualities, but it didn't take too long to realise that he couldn't. He would just need to be on his 'A' game all the time. As far as his part was concerned he knew exactly what he had to do, so far. He would just have to deal with whatever came next as it arose, but that was what he loved most. It could be dangerous of course and this reminded him of his days and nights in Helmand. This made him feel alive. This was exactly why he had been recruited after all.

Eventually the Eurostar slowed to a halt as it came to rest alongside a platform at Paris Gare du Nord. K was surprised at how quick the whole journey had appeared to be.

He alighted and headed straight for the exit, whereupon he jumped into a waiting taxi and made for the pre-booked three star hotel that was situated near his evening rendezvous.

His appointment had been set for twenty hundred hours, so once he had checked in he had plenty of time to acclimatise himself with his neighbourhood and to pop out to a local cafe where he ordered his first ever cup of French coffee. He decided that he needed to acclimatise himself to the coffee as well. It just wasn't the same as the one that he normally had at his local watering hole.

Once he'd digested the local scenery and

settled the bill he returned to his hotel where, as he collected his room key, the lady on reception also handed him an envelope. He thanked her and decided to get to his room before opening it.

Chapter 35

Things were getting tricky and by tricky read worrying, at the Russian end of the project. Daisy had no spare manpower and manufacturing couldn't maintain output, let alone increase it, as demand was outstripping supply, especially for the coke.

Fortunately for Daisy and the people who worked in the factory they didn't know about the mounting fatality figures. Dimitri was aware, but didn't see the necessity of passing the negative news on to Daisy. His priority was to make sure that the project ran smoothly. They both kept their heads down and just kept pressing on with the project, as their bosses didn't want to know about failure. Anyway, so far the project itself and the profitability had been a resounding success.

Even with all of this success Daisy was now starting to worry for her own safety. The cracks were starting to show and it would only be a matter of time before the same cracks were evident to the powers that be. Also, whilst she accepted that dealing with the criminal fraternity was never going to be a cake walk, it was now about to become even trickier as the supply line started to show signs of slowing and therefore losing profit. It wouldn't be long until her 'team' would revolt. Not something that she wanted to contemplate, let alone be around to witness.

She had become the master of her own possible downfall. The project was so successful that the boffins wanted more and even though she had already requested additional bodies, something that had only been partially dealt with, she now needed many more. She also needed more materials, but this could partially be dealt with once the manpower was increased.

Another issue that she hadn't encountered initially was the fact that there were now so many Russian criminals floating around western europe, just trying to keep them out of the way of the respective police forces, without raising suspicion, was becoming a much more complex problem.

Some of her team members weren't the smartest cookies, but she wasn't about to tell them that. That was Dimitri's department. The trouble with that was that she didn't quite know how to deal with Dimitri either.

Because she was slowly losing control and she knew that it would only be a matter of time before something went drastically wrong, she started to compile a dossier on the project and all of the names associated with it. It was all she could try and do to mitigate the thought that she would be viewed as being a traitor, should she be able to escape back to the west. The dossier was hidden behind a false wall at the back of one of her kitchen cabinets.

As another form of defence and although it was extremely risky she decided to send another message to Kevin. She had no idea whether any of her messages had hit their intended target, but she knew that if anyone could bail her out when the time came, it would be Kevin.

Her next and last message from this phone, read:

This will probably be the last time I message you. Please get to the factory on Ulitsa Shosseynaya, Rostov on Don. Anytime. If you find Andreiv you will find me. X

The message was sent and the phone immediately destroyed.

At the end of another stressful day she let herself into her small flat. 'If I could just get them to accept that the project was a success at this size, my work here would be done or at least it would be manageable.'

Luckily for Daisy, whilst he didn't dare carry his old phone with him any more, Kevin did have a couple of contacts i.e. Alfie and Daisy, forwarded to whichever burner phone he was carrying. Something that his new boss knew nothing about.

Dimitri had also come to a decision, which was that he didn't like projects and he certainly didn't like project meetings or sucking up to arseholes, so he decided to spend more time out in the field making sure that the criminals were all playing nicely. This played into Daisy's hands in a small way as she now didn't have to worry about telling Dimitri to do exactly what he'd now volunteered to. Dimitri's scheme had worked fairly well so far because everyone had been making a decent profit and nearly everyone had managed to stay out of trouble. Not everyone was playing ball though.

One instance that he had to deal with recently was when a couple of men had argued that they didn't feel the need to pass a percentage of their profit back to HQ, however they were soon reminded that they could be removed completely and not necessarily in the conventional way. In the short term that appeared to do the trick.

When he actually took the time to think about it, Dimitri had never been any good at sitting behind a desk, even as a school boy. He knew that he was smart, he just wasn't an academic. That was one of the reasons why he'd chosen the kind of life that he had. That and the lure of making big money in a country where making any kind of decent living legally, was nearly impossible.

He wasn't what you would call a hardened criminal, but more of an entrepreneur who always seemed to find the most favourable kind of business on the wrong side of the law. In the west he would have been known as a lovable rogue. Although this was possibly not what the police would have called him.

Chapter 36

The car was indeed heading toward Paris, so Katy breathed a sigh of relief. She still couldn't believe her luck and she certainly didn't want to have to threaten her driver. That would be a wicked waste. The pair chatted amiably enough throughout the journey. Neither giving away their true motives for the trip. This was quite difficult at times for Katy, as she felt that she could open up to her new knight in shining armour, who sounded like he would somehow care and maybe even help. Something told her not to be so naive though, so she kept the level of conversation detail to a minimum.

As they drove, she noticed the Eurostar train pulling into a station. The station sign read: Paris Gare Du Nord, so at least she now knew that she was somewhere in Paris. They continued to drive and Geoff assured her that he was heading toward her destination. He drove to within a few streets of The Louvre before letting her out. He pointed her in the right direction and wished her well before driving off. He explained that he was tight for time and that he needed to head off in a different direction in order to get to his office. He had already told her that he was a salesman, although Katy never did find out what it was that he sold.

Katy walked toward Le Louvre without really knowing where she was going. She did know where she was to meet her contact though, so she hailed a cab and asked the driver to go to the same road. From there she would look for some accommodation for one night only. She was totally oblivious to the tracker that 'Geoff' had inserted into the side pocket of her shoulder bag.

Mr King was singing like a budgerigar. He couldn't help the police enough. He had put them onto Katy after receiving a visit from Alfie and his side kick.

"So, you see Mr King, we are fully aware of your little side hustle, especially since taking your little boy into custody." Alfie went out on a limb here because Trevor hadn't mentioned a word about his father, let alone what he was up to. The lead had come from investigations into the local drug distribution network and the fact that the King's name cropped up on several occasions.

'That little bastard has grassed me up. I knew he couldn't keep his trap shut.' Martin King wrongly guessed. 'I bet this has got to do with that little slut Katy as well. He never liked the fact that I was bedding her. They're both going to pay.'

"Anyway officer, if there is anything that I can help you with, I'd be only too happy. Especially if it keeps me out of the poky."

"It's Inspector and I'm afraid I can't promise that, Mr King, but for now your input is most welcome and I do appreciate it." Alfie knew that they didn't have any hard evidence on this joker, so he was going to have to play it very carefully. He would be watching King's movements like a hawk from now on though.

He was also aware that his attitude toward King senior was a little less than professional currently, but he hated this particular type of lowlife. They made his skin crawl.

Chapter 37

T he note within read:

New rendezvous
gallons.panics.mule.Now.Droopy.End.

He checked the location and left the hotel immediately, tossing his room key to the receptionist on his way out. He jumped into a waiting taxi. He still couldn't quite get his head round how this was all going to work, but assumed that it was a tried and trusted system. Someone knew where he was and there was a police tail on Ms Weller. 'I wonder if I've got a proper partner that they haven't told me about yet or whether I just keep co-operating with the police?' He wondered.

As he had a short ride in the cab he used the time to shake himself back into the present and prepare himself mentally for what might happen next. He had no idea what Katy Weller looked like and for that matter he had no idea what his contact looked like. He would soon learn that this would be the norm as far as his clandestine activities were concerned. It was kind of comforting to know that he wasn't working alone. It was quite spooky too, because he felt that he was being watched.

It took about twenty minutes to get to his destination, so he hoped that he wasn't too late. Hopefully his partner, wherever he or she might be, would keep him appraised if anything were to change.

He paid the driver and made the remainder of his way on foot. He wasn't sure what he was looking for, but he did know that his contact was Katy, whoever she might be. He kept walking toward the middle of the park and while walking he noted a young lady walking on her own. She appeared to be walking straight through the park, without slowing.

'Do I follow her or wait until someone more dodgy looking arrives? Do I wait for my contact to contact me? What to do?'

He decided to watch her for a few more seconds before moving. While he was watching her he suddenly realised two things. One, that no one had approached him or contacted him in any way since arriving at the park and two, that two other people had wandered into his field of vision. One was female and one male. He took his eyes off his original prey and studied the pair.

Bingo! He knew it had to be Katy by the shifty way that she was looking around and the fact that her contact was doing the same. There appeared to be a lot of hand gesturing and even raised voices, but they were too far away for K to pick up on the speech. He then witnessed the young man looking at his watch and then irritatingly looking around again before he walked away. Katy ran after him.

This was what he had been waiting for. This had to be them. The other girl had vanished now anyway. It wasn't like K to doubt himself, but this kind of surveillance was new to him. Everyone that he'd spied on while he was serving, looked like terrorists, well they looked different to him anyway and generally they were armed. He would have to rely on his gut instinct and right at that moment it was telling him that the pair were Katy and her supplier.

He wanted to be led back to Katy's lair

or better still, her supplier's lair. From there he should be able to find out all sorts of information, like who the other connections were and where they were based. It may take a while, but by adopting this method he could gather all of the information that he might require.

He needed to get a message to his contact. A text message was sent:

Located contact and supplier. Will stay with them until further info gained.Entity.End.

He would use a name beginning with 'F' in his next text, unless one was received first, in which case the sender would use a name beginning with 'F' and so it went on.

A reply came straight back.

Once Ms Weller leaves her contact she will be arrested. Concentrate on supplier.Flipflop.End.

'Makes my job easier I suppose.' K didn't question his orders. He would concentrate on whoever the guy was.

K followed them both out of the park. Katy was still trailing behind and shouting. The supplier looked like he was trying to shake her off.

Chapter 38

He was never going to get bail and he knew he was going to go down for a long stretch. He knew it and his brief knew it, so there was only ever going to be one alternative. Normally he would ride out the storm, take his punishment, serve his time and then walk out a free man, albeit tagged. Not this time. He needed to get out. There wasn't enough time to do the right thing, so he had to make this phone call count.

"You have to spring me from the van."

"I don't know. I mean we've lost a lot of our manpower anyway and if that goes wrong the rest of us are sunk. You do know the Russians are running things don't you?"

"It's precisely because the Russians are running things that I need to get out. Do you want them to run things forever?"

"No, of course not."

"Well nothing's going to change unless we make it change. There is no alternative."

"I suppose not."

"Anyway, listen, I don't have a lot of time. They are transferring me from here to the main court next Tuesday at eleven o'clock. I need you to spring me somewhere on that route. I don't care where. Just make it work. If you can get me out I promise I'll make it my mission to get rid of the Russians."

"Okay. Leave it with me. I promise we'll get you out, so just be ready."

"I'm ready now."

Claude knew that those of his men who weren't in jail,

wouldn't let him down, even if they sounded less than confident. They had obviously let the Russians spook them.

Once he was out he'd soon whip them back into shape. The next thing that he had to do was to arrange a hiding place and some ammo. 'Shouldn't be too much of a problem.' He thought. 'But it will have to wait. I can't push it on this phone.'

The following Tuesday finally rolled around. Nothing like soon enough for Claude. At precisely eleven a.m. he was rudely disturbed.

"Balland! Get up. We're on the move."

"Oh, do we have to. I've got quite comfy here."

"Less of your lip sunshine. Get up."

"Okay, okay. What's the hurry?"

"You've got a big day, so make sure you're looking your best."

"I always look my next, especially when I know you're on duty big boy."

"Shut your mouth. I'd like to….."

"Go on, big feller. You were saying?"

"Just get fucking dressed."

"I knew you couldn't resist. No one can."

"It's going to please me immensely when you go down for a stretch."

"And what if I don't? You have no idea whether I'm going down or not."

"Listen smart arse, if you weren't due in court today, I'd pay you a little visit in the wee small hours. Still I'll have plenty of time for that won't I?"

"I'm sure you will, but just so you know, I'll be waiting and as I've got little to lose, I'll make sure that it's worth my while."

Claude smiled a crooked smile, finished washing and threw his shirt on. He wasn't too bothered about looking his best, after all it wasn't as if his looks were going to affect the outcome.

What Claude hadn't noticed was that his last remark had taken it's toll on the prison officer, who suddenly felt queezy. He felt an icy shiver go down his spine. He'd never felt this way before and it shook him to the core. He wasn't about to let it show though.

"Shut the fuck up and get in that van."

Claude decided that now wasn't the time to try and win a battle. After all, he was about to win the war, he hoped.

Chapter 39

"Listen Dimitri. I think they are baying for blood and that blood is mine."

"What are you talking about? You've done a fantastic job so far."

"You know that and I know that and God knows we've tried to make it the success that they believe it should be, but they want more. I'm not sure if it's actually because they want more or if it's because they want to see me fail. They just keep pushing and pushing and I can't take it anymore."

"What do you intend to do?"

"I've got no idea. Don't get me wrong. It's not that I feel that I can't manage. It's just that I feel that I'm being pushed into a position that will give them an excuse to get rid of me and when I say get rid I mean extinguish."

"I think that you're overreacting."

"Well I don't and I've confided in you because I thought that you could see what was happening and obviously because I thought that I could trust you."

It wasn't in his nature normally, but Dimtri did feel for Daisy, especially as he had been put on the project specifically to keep an eye on her and now he felt torn. If she knew that the burner phone fiasco had been played out so as to make him look like a good guy, she wouldn't be quite so forthcoming. He was now faced with a dilemma that he didn't feel at all comfortable with. To grass or not to grass, that was the question.

When he thought about it, he knew that his loyalties had shifted since working with her and it wasn't that he suddenly felt compelled to do the right thing. It was just that he no longer felt compelled to do the wrong thing. He was no lover of the government after all and up until now they had done all they could to make his life hell. The money had made the difference in the beginning, but now it didn't seem to matter. If he played his cards right he could still take the money without doing any further damage to Daisy.

"I'll help if I can, but my hands are pretty tied. After all, until recently I was a bad guy too, don't forget."

"I know and thank you Dimitri. I'll try and keep a lid on it, but if I get to a point where I genuinely fear for my life, I might need to call on your services."

"That's fine. I'll be here."

"Are you sure? I don't want to make you promise to do anything that you later can't or won't deliver on."

"I mean what I say. I'm not promising that I will be in a position to do exactly as you might ask, but I do promise that I will do whatever I can and I also promise not to speak to anyone else about this. I have to say that I'm still of the opinion that you are overreacting."

"Your word is good enough for me Dimitri, thank you. I too hope that I'm wrong, but I can usually rely on my instincts."

Daisy continued with the project to the best of her ability, but what she hadn't told Dimitri was that she feared for Andreiv's life even more than her own, especially as more and more people had got involved with the manufacturing. Andreiv was gradually making himself redundant and that was exactly what the powers that be planned and hoped for.

Chapter 40

K aty had pursued her supplier back to his apartment and questioned him irritatingly all the way, however that tactic hadn't worked, as she wasn't able to glean any further assurances with regard to the consistency of supply. In fact once he had gained entry to his flat, he just shut the door firmly in her face. For a minute she just stood there fuming. She considered kicking his door, but realised that this would just attract unwanted attention, so she descended the stairs and left the building.

She walked out into the evening air not really paying attention to what was going on outside. However when she did finally let her surroundings register, she was shocked to see the guy who had given her a lift, leaning against his car and looking straight at her.

"Miss Katy Weller."

"No, it's Wendy, remember?" Katy started to feel for her pistol.

A gun appeared as if from nowhere and halted Katy's action. "Please don't do that Miss Weller. Just get into my car, if you would be so kind."

"Who the hell are you?"

"I'm a police officer and I've been following you since you killed two of my colleagues in Dover, so I'm not best pleased with you. Don't give me an excuse to do to you what you did to them, please."

Katy walked toward the car, her hand still resting on the pocket that contained her weapon.

"Before you come any closer, peel your jacket back with your left hand then reach into that inside pocket with the thumb and forefinger of your right hand and very carefully remove the gun. Using the same thumb and forefinger, place said gun on the ground. Once there, kick the gun towards me."

"You expect me to remember that lot?" Katy said, trying to sound nonchalant, but not quite managing it.

"Just do it."

The gun was removed, put down and then kicked, as instructed. It slid across the pavement and Katy just stood still while waiting for the next instruction.

"There, you see you did remember." The detective said without smiling. "I'm afraid that I have to place these on your hands now." Said while producing a pair of handcuffs. "But before I do I have to caution you."

The officer carried out the caution, cuffed Katy and then helped her into the car. He jumped in and started the engine and let the car idle for a minute. 'At least one more killer and drug dealer has been taken off the streets. Whoever the other guy is can pick up the case from here. I better let him know that I've got missy.'

Weller in custody. Good luck with rest. End.

He forgot that he was supposed to add a code word at the end, but guessed that whoever was on the other end of his text would realise that he was the real deal. After all, who else cared whether the scum bag on the back seat was in custody. He settled in for the long drive back.

Just as he was about to pull away, Katy silently slid forward in her seat and hooked her wrists, complete with handcuffs around the driver's neck. She buried her knees into the back of the front seat and pulled with all her might. The officer was given no time to react and after a few seconds struggle and a quick but pointless grab at the handcuffs, he succumbed and shortly afterwards, went limp.

Katy made sure that her task was complete and then wasted no time in searching the body for the handcuff keys. Once secured she quickly freed herself, shoved the dead officer over and then drove the car away from the scene.

The officer had made the rooky error of cuffing his captive with her arms in front. It was to prove a fatal mistake.

Chapter 41

K received the message and had indeed witnessed nearly the whole thing. He'd seen the two get into the car and he'd even heard the car start, so he turned and walked away. At least that meant that he could concentrate on the French connection.

He had ascertained exactly which flat that the dealer lived in, so decided that he would observe from a distance. If this didn't work there was always the threat of violence, but K really didn't want to go down that route. This wasn't because he was averse to beating the crap out of a low life, it was just that he felt that he couldn't justify it. The martial arts teacher, with all that he had imparted all those years ago, still played a major part in Kevins thought process and his emotions, given certain mental criteria.

As it was getting late K headed back to his own hotel. He aimed to be back at this location for seven in the morning, however just as he was about to leave for the night he heard a door close behind him and when he turned he saw that it was the guy that he had been tailing. The man walked swiftly away and headed back toward the park. K had to put any thought of sleep to one side and he duly followed.

It didn't appear that this particular park closed, so was an ideal meeting place, especially as all but the real night owls had departed for the evening. K stood at the entrance and watched his prey walk toward the centre. There was no point in following as, even though it was dusk, he could see clearly as far as the middle of the park. He hoped that the dealer was going to wait there.

Sure enough, the guy came to a stand still and after checking all around, he'd rested on the wall that surrounded the pond at the heart of Le Jardin Du Luxembourg. He looked at his watch, again.

Once he was sure that the dealer wasn't looking in his direction, K moved forward and took up a more advantageous position. He wanted to be able to hear any conversation, if that were to take place. He didn't have to wait long.

There were two men approaching from the east and K's subject was starting to look nervous. As they got to within talking distance, totally out of the blue one of them lurched forward and pushed the dealer into the pond. Once fully in, the other guy grabbed hold of the dealer's hair and held his head under the water. He didn't let the drowning man up for what seemed like an eternity and when he did so the dealer was just gasping for air and coughing. They allowed him to catch his breath and then spoke in broken English.

"You owe us and we told you that you had until yesterday." Said in a heavily Russian accent.

"I know, I know, but I got held up by some silly little English tart, who wanted to know where the stuff was coming from. I couldn't get rid of her." He didn't let on that this particular incident had only taken place earlier that day. He didn't actually have the money the day before.

"So, where is she now?"
"No idea."
"What did you tell her?"
"Nothing because I know nothing, do I."
"No and that's the way it's going to stay."

"Fine by me as long as you can keep up with demand. You've been a bit sluggish lately."

"Sluggish. What is sluggish?"

"Slow. I need the stuff quicker."

His head was pushed back under the water and held again. This time for longer. They finally pulled him out.

"You don't get to speak to us that way and you don't get to complain about service, okay?"

"Okay."

"So, where's our money?"

"It's here. You didn't give me a chance to produce it before you decided to drown me."

A soggy bank roll was produced.

"We can't accept that. It's wet. We can't even count it."

"Well I......" Pierre decided to leave that statement parked.

"Look. You've seen that I have it, so if you give me until this time tomorrow, I'll have it dry by then.

They pushed him back into the pond, but this time they just walked off laughing.

K witnessed the conversation and it bore out the theory that the drugs were being supplied at least via the Russians, if not directly from Russia. He followed them until they left the park.

Once outside they both jumped into the rear of a waiting car. K didn't bother remembering the number plate.
He knew that it would be a waste of time. As he was on foot he decided to head back to his hotel, which he thought would be fine, as hopefully there should be another rendezvous the next night.

The receptionist threw the room keys at him as he walked in, then smiled. He walked over in a mock aggressive way, but then smiled and said thanks. Another skill that he'd learned many years ago, was to always try and keep people on side as, not only did it cost nothing to be friendly, but also you never knew when they might be able to help in some small way.

As soon as he was back in his room he sent an update back to London, then showered and then slept. He needed to be up early, as he wanted to see what else he could learn from the dealer, prior to the meeting that had been scheduled for the following evening.

Chapter 42

There was one outrider and two escort cars, with the van in between the cars. It was only going to be a short journey from the police station to the magistrates court, so Claude wouldn't have long to think about whether his friend was going to come to the rescue.

Within five minutes of the journey starting his prayers were answered, when he was suddenly propelled forward as the vehicle that he was travelling in was brought to a sudden stop. There were two shots fired and then there was a small explosion. This was followed by the smell of cordite. One of the rear doors was then flung open. He dragged himself up off the floor, held a bent arm to his nose to stifle the smell and the smoke and made for the open door.

"Come on Claude. Jump on the back of that bike there."

Claude didn't need telling twice. He cocked his leg over the rear of the BMW F900 and held onto the rider. They and the others all rode off, leaving the other four wheeled vehicles that they had used, on fire and in the middle of the road. This would add to the chaos that was ensuing, as well as act as a roadblock from one direction at least.

Half an hour later everyone arrived at the agreed rendezvous, which was a currently uninhabited ramshackle old farmhouse. They disembarked and as soon as Claude dismounted he ran over to Jaque and hugged him.

"Thank you Jaque. I wasn't sure that you would come."
"As if I'd let you down. What do you take me for?"

"Well, you must admit, you did have doubts didn't you?"
"Only until you made me realise that we could forever be living under Russian rule. That and the fact that I couldn't honestly let you down."
"Thanks again."

"You're welcome. Now what's the plan?"

The rest of the men were all ears at this point.

"Yes, go on Claude. What's the plan?" This was said in all sincerity although it sounded a little sarcastic to Claude.

"The plan is that we get our patch back, by whatever means necessary."

"With all due respect Claude, that's not a plan. That's just a wish."

"It's only a wish at the moment because I haven't had the time to plan and I certainly can't plan on an empty stomach. I hope someone bought food."

They all looked at each other in awkward silence.

"For fuck sake, if you lot hadn't just saved me from the scales of justice, I'd throttle you."

They broke into a nervous laugh. Claude laughed too, although he was genuinely starving. He very much appreciated his merry, but thick, band of men.

Chapter 43

"**A**ndreiv, you do know that they are going to come for you don't you?"

"Do you think so?"

"I wouldn't be risking my neck by coming here to warn you, if I didn't."

"Why would they do that? I'm producing what they've asked aren't I? I'm not causing any trouble."

"It's precisely because you've already produced what they want, that they can now dispose of you. Your job is done and now you are seen as a weak link."

"But no one else knows the whole process."

"Of course they do. Every single person they've sent here has been making notes, taking photos and where necessary recording you and all the while you've noticed nothing."

"Well no. I've always been too busy to notice what other people are doing. I've just shown the others whatever I've needed them to do and then left them to it."

"So now. You've made yourself surplus to requirements."

"How do you know this?"

"I know it because I've been around these people for long enough to know how they operate. Believe me, you are not the only one that they're going to come after."

"Who else do you think they will be after?"

"Me." Daisy said this while looking at the floor. She was pondering that last word and trying to think about how she was going to try and save Andreiv whilst saving herself.

"Oh Daisy. What are we going to do?"

"We're going to get out of here, but first I need to think. If we just run we will be caught." She didn't bother to explain that she was also hanging her hopes on Kevin. 'Did he actually get my messages? Even if he did, could he do anything about it? Maybe I should come up with a plan 'D'. D standing for Dimitri, but can I really trust him that far?'

Daisy felt lost and alone. She tried not to show her despondency to Andreiv, but he immediately picked up on it.

"Daisy, listen, we are both smart cookies

and we can plan a way out of here. Please remain strong, I will need you much more than you need me."

Daisy did her best to perk up, as she knew that Andreiv was relying on her. "I won't let you down Andreiv. I won't let either of us down, I hope." She did wish that she could have sounded a little more positive.

What they both needed was a place to hide. One that was secure and one that they could hole up in for the foreseeable future. 'I have to find one within a week, if possible. No problem.' Daisy thought sarcastically.

She left Andreiv to ponder their situation.

Chapter 44

At seven fifteen the following morning, K slipped out of his room and headed for the dealers flat. He was a little disappointed about over sleeping, but then reminded himself of the previous day and how long it had been. 'Not good enough. Never mind the excuses. This is a tougher gig than I'd envisaged, but I'm going to make sure that I'm ready for anything in future.'

One of the many things that K hadn't considered, along with long days and nights, was the long time waiting for something to happen. He took up his station over the road from the flat and waited. Then he waited some more. He didn't dare move, but now he was dying to relieve himself and he was hungry. The hunger was easier to deal with as, whilst he'd had to bottle it on many occasions while serving, he was now feeling decidedly uncomfortable. He was beginning to lose concentration, when finally his prey emerged. At least this gave K the opportunity to distract himself from his current predicament.

The dealer walked for a few minutes then suddenly broke into a run. He crossed the busy road and almost lost K for a second, but he managed to find a gap in the traffic and keep up. What he wasn't quite sure of was whether he had managed to remain inconspicuous. 'Has he seen me and is now testing me?' K slowed without losing sight and tried to hide behind everything and anyone that he could. Luckily the dealer now slowed too. He didn't keep checking behind, so it looked like he wasn't aware of being followed. K kept his distance.

Still panting, the dealer turned into a shop, so K just loitered outside. He hadn't noticed the dealer checking his watch yet again. That was the reason he'd run. He'd already suffered a near drowning at the hands of these people and wasn't about to suffer a similar or worse fate again.

'I've taken the trouble to follow him, when all he's doing is buying milk, typical. All part of the service I suppose.'

There was an alleyway right next to K's position, so he quickly ducked into it and relieved himself. He only lost sight of the shop doorway for about thirty seconds and came back immediately after he had finished. After waiting about ten minutes K started to wonder whether the dealer had slipped out during the thirty second hiatus. 'Surely not. He'd only just gone in.' He decided to enter the shop.

The till assistant was busy, so K strolled casually by and started to search everywhere. He found no trace of the dealer. 'Shit. Maybe he went straight through the shop and out the back. Maybe he knew I was behind him after all.' K strode back through the store and checked one last time that the man on the till was still busy. He then turned back and entered the stockroom at the rear. He looked all around, but found no unlocked exit. Then he heard voices. They were coming from just to his left, where he saw a closed office door. At least it didn't appear that they'd heard him, so he pressed his ear to the door.

"You know that two of your goons tried to drown me last night don't you?" Spoken in English with a heavy French accent.

"No, I didn't know that, but you know that those that are running the show get very twitchy if you miss a payment. Did you miss a payment?" Spoken in English with a heavy Russian accent.

"I've never missed it before and I only missed it this time because someone showed up." He'd almost convinced himself that was what actually happened.

"Not my problem or theirs. You decided to play this less than friendly game. Nobody twisted your arm up your back. Anyway, what are you doing here?"

"I need more crack. I can live without the spliff for now. I've got punters lined up and I'm losing money. If I don't feed the need soon, I'll have them kicking the shit out of me too."

"I'm telling you I don't have it. Weren't you told that last night? If I had it, I would sell it to you wouldn't I, you moron. I'm losing money too. The difference is that I dare not approach my supplier and complain. If I did those same two goons would be coming for me and I would be propping up some motorway somewhere."

"So what is the problem?"

"The problem is that they can't make it fast enough."

"What do you mean, make it. I thought it was grown somewhere in South America."

"It was, that was until we in Russia figured out a way to make it synthetically."

K stood up and his jaw dropped. He

couldn't believe what he was hearing.

Just then the guy who had been at the till when K rushed through the store, appeared at his side.

"What the hell are you doing in here? I never saw you come in." Said in French, to which K just said "Englaise?"

"Why you here?"

Fortunately, because K wasn't bent at the door just after he'd heard the bombshell, the till minder didn't know he'd been listening. He still had to think on his feet though.

"My dog ran off and I was sure that he ran into this store. I just need to find him."

Just as he finished his weak explanation the two who had been huddled in the meeting came out to see what the fracas was all about.

"What's going on Bendek?" The Russian shouted.

"I think this guy said something about a dog. I found him snooping around out here."

K didn't know what was being said, so interjected:

"Excuse me. I wasn't snooping. I was merely looking for my dog, Pedro. Have either of you two seen him? He's small, brown and fast." K thought that the best form of defence was attack, as indeed it was in most cases.

"Why did you come back here?" This was asked by one of the two who were in the office and it was spoken in broken English. It was the Russian.

"Well I thought I saw him come into this shop and your man Bendek was busy when I came in. I thought that I could just retrieve him and go, but obviously he's not here."

"I think you'd better leave Mr?"

"Okay I'm going. My ruddy dog is probably long gone now." He didn't proffer any name, but just turned and pushed past Bendek. He made it back out onto the pavement.

"Do you think he'd lost a dog Bendek or was he listening at the door?"

"I can definitely say that he wasn't listening at the door. He was just standing."

"He wasn't carrying a lead either, but then the dog could have run off with it still attached I suppose."

"Okay. You better get back to the till. I suggest we all keep our eyes peeled just in case."

K knew that he'd had a lucky escape, however it had been well worth it. He now knew exactly what was going on and he even knew the whereabouts of a Russian link in the chain.

The shop was actually a Polish Deli, which was fronting a Russian distribution network. 'I suppose to the French one Eastern European sounds very much like another. It would work that way at home anyway.'

He could afford to drop his French dealer now and as a bonus he also shouldn't need to be at the meeting in the park that night. He would refrain from getting the French dealer arrested for now as he didn't want to spook anyone in the chain.

He needed to get back to his room and update his control.

Chapter 45

In a small room in a run down farmhouse, a meeting was taking place because this particular organisation had also discovered exactly what K had. Their network, although drastically reduced by the Russians, was still operational, albeit in a much more underground fashion. They had a very different motive for wanting this information.

"Right, we now know that there is at least one Russian operating from the Polish Deli on the Rue De La Glacier. I suggest we capture him and torture the shit out of him. We can get him to squeal."

"No Claude. With all due respect, we shouldn't do that. If he doesn't squeal and he croaks, we are back to square one. I suggest that we follow him until we have enough information to then form a plan."

"Yes, yes. Of course. This is what happens when your heart starts to rule your head. We will establish round the clock surveillance of the shop." Claude hated to be corrected, but he had to accept that his plan was based purely on the fact that he wanted rid of the Russians.

Now that at least one of the Paris hubs appeared to have been discovered, the six men sat round a table at the hideaway and put their heads together in order to come up with a surveillance rota. However there would have to be one caveat.

"I think that Claude shouldn't be included in the rota. He's a very wanted man and we can't afford for him to be seen."

"You are all wanted." Claude now had his feelings hurt for a second time and he didn't like it.

"We may all be wanted, but it's your face that's on every TV station and in every paper at the moment. Christ Claude, you're more famous than Emmanuel Macron."

That at least, bought a laugh from everyone including Claude. He had to admit that the national infamy was satisfying.

"Okay. I'll stay here and formulate a plan for when we can do something about the

Russian bastards."

"Great idea Claude. Stick to what you're good at."

"Don't push it Manny. Just because you have the same forename as our illustrious president doesn't make you the brains of the outfit."

This time there was a more nervous laugh and not from everyone.

Manny took the first shift at the shop, but couldn't really concentrate on the surveillance as he was too busy watching his own back. He knew that he'd trodden on thin ice with Claude and Claude wasn't someone you upset. Not twice anyway.

Chapter 46

"Dimitri, I appreciate that I'm going out on a limb here, but do you think you could get hold of a phone for me?"

"I could yes, but why should I?"

"Because I'm asking."

"Not good enough, I'm afraid."

"Listen, I'm afraid alright. I think my days are numbered as I've already told you. I also think that Andreiv's are too. I also think that yours might be, but hopefully you've got contacts in some very low places, so maybe you will be okay."

Dimitri laughed, then said. "Why do you think this?"

"Because I know how these things work

and because if you think about it, they have managed to pick two of the most expendable people that they could find, to run with this project. They then did exactly the same with the manufacturing scientist. I'm a foreigner and you are a criminal. Poor old Andreiv is just a nobody, a youngster from a backwater."

"I hadn't thought that way. I'm sorry for you Daisy. You must appreciate that I have to be careful too, you know. One man cannot take on the state and hope to come out on top."

"Well I'm sorry Dimitri. I suppose until now, I had thought that you were invincible, but the more I think about it the more I am convinced of the reason why the three of us have been chosen."

Dimitri tried to break the tension slightly. "I must admit, I do like people to think of me as invincible. That's how the people in my trade survive, so at least that worked with you for a while."

Daisy smiled and for the first time she could see that there was a soft side to this otherwise formidable character.

"Your secret is safe with me, don't worry."
"What secret?"
"The fact that you're a pussycat really."
"Please don't start believing that Daisy."
"Don't worry I don't."

"I'll get you your phone, but I don't want to know anything else about it."

"Thank you Dimitri. I promise I'll be out of your hair soon, I hope."

"I will miss you, even though you've been nothing but a major pain on the arse."

"Don't worry, I'm a pain in the arse wherever I am. See you later."

Daisy left for home. She knew that she had Dimitri twisted round her little finger, but she also knew that she would have to be careful.

The next morning just before Daisy left for the office, there was a knock at the door and she froze. 'They will know I haven't left for work and there's absolutely nowhere to hide.' She grabbed her gun, tucked it down the back of her trousers and walked to the door. She looked through the spy hole and could see nothing. 'What are they playing at?' She opened the door very slowly and as the gap got to approximately six inches, she heard an odd noise at the bottom. A small parcel had been propped against the door and it slid down and onto her door mat. She took it back indoors and listened to it. 'Why do we do that? It's not likely to be ticking is it.'

Once in the kitchen, Daisy opened the drawer and retrieved the scissors. She cut open the packaging and the contents were revealed. It was a phone. She sat down at the kitchen table and thought that it was mildly amusing that Dimitri could scare the crap out of her even when he was absent.

She immediately checked the phone's number and texted it to Kevin. She needed to remember to delete any information that came in and also to not keep any data on it, except Kevins number that is.

After hiding the phone behind the panel in her kitchen cupboard and making herself a cup of coffee, she finally left for the office. Once there she would start to consider how she was going to get Andreiv out.

Chapter 47

K had no idea that he wasn't the only one who was watching the Polish Deli. In fact he had no idea that he had already been spotted by Claude's team. The only small advantage that he had going for him was the fact that they had no idea who he was or why he appeared to be reconnoitring the same property as them.

"He could be un flic."

"He's definitely not the police. He's operating on his own. He's not even contacting anyone and he walks everywhere. If he was a un flic, he'd have a change of shifts and he would be driven and dropped off nearby."

"I suppose so, but he's got to be working for someone."

"He could be another supplier and maybe

he's got a beef with one of the Russians."

"Maybe, but he doesn't seem to want to make any moves. He's just watching."

"Why don't we pull him in?"

"Because the moment we do that, he will know that we're watching too. He's not causing us any problem at the moment."

Over the next couple of days K noted the comings and goings at the shop. There were numerous dubious looking people, entering empty handed and leaving with similarly sized packages. Some tried to disguise them in carrier bags or similar, but some just carried small packages wrapped in similar brown paper.

He also noticed a car that seemed to be parked within observational distance of the shop and always occupied, but with different people at different times of the day. The occupant, at any given time, didn't seem to take their eyes off the shop doorway.

On the third day he decided to walk over and chat to whichever occupant just happened to be on shift. As he approached, the guy inside suddenly had the look of a deer caught in the headlights. He just froze and stared unblinking at K.

As the car was a left hand drive and

parked facing the wrong way, on the left hand side of the street, K tapped on the driver's side window. This appeared to break the spell and the window slid down.

"I'm unarmed." Was K's introduction in English.

The occupant just raised both arms in the air as if to say, sorry I don't understand, which was exactly what he was saying.

K had to think quickly. He pointed at the driver and made a drive away motion and then just said "English." He had no idea what he was hoping to achieve, but did feel that whoever the other party was, they could be mutually beneficial. The driver sat for a minute or so, trying to figure out exactly what K was trying to communicate, so in this time K repeated his gestures. It looked like the penny or euro finally dropped, as the driver finally appeared to acknowledge what K was suggesting. He drove away.

All he could do was wait, so he went back to his surveillance position. He only had to wait thirty or so minutes when the same car appeared, but driven by a different man. The original driver was now the passenger. The car came to a halt and the passenger pointed toward K and said something that K couldn't make out. Not that he would have understood it anyway. The driver got out, while the passenger remained in the car and tried to look intimidating.

"My friend seems to think that you speak English and that you wish to speak with us. Is that true?" It was Claude who spoke and this was mainly because he spoke the best English of a bad bunch. It was also because he was the leader and he wasn't about to let someone else negotiate.

"He's correct, yes."

"Well what could we possibly do for you my friend?" Said with a certain amount of menace.

"I'm not sure. It may be a case of us both doing something for each other, especially as we are both casing the same joint."

"Casing the same joint? I'm sorry I don't understand."

"Oh I think you do, but I'll make it clearer. You are looking at the same building as me and you seem to be studying who is coming and going, just like me. Maybe we could help each other with whatever it is that we both want."

"How could you possibly help us? We're doing fine."

"Well maybe you can help me then and in doing so, it may help you. I assume that you operate on the wrong side of the law."

"Are you the police then?"

"No, but I do have the ear of the authorities."

"I think that you and I need to go and have a coffee. What do you say?"

"Sounds good. I'll even buy."

Claude went back to his driver and had a few words. He then walked back to K and pointed to a small cafe just a few metres along from the Deli. They walked in silence.

Chapter 48

K aty had driven an unmarked English police car that still contained its original occupant, around a strange city and on the wrong side of the road, for what seemed like hours. She was trying to find somewhere safe and unobserved, so that she could dispose of both the car and its other occupant.

After a while she found her way out of the city and on to more rural roads. She just needed a deserted farm track that would take her away from prying eyes. She was so consumed with her quest that she didn't notice the car that had been following her all the way from Paris. The occupants of which had even witnessed the untimely death of the police officer.

Eventually she found what she'd been looking for. It was a rarely used track that looked like it wended its way away from the road and more importantly, towards the middle of nowhere. The last thing she needed was for there to be a house at the end of the drive.

She turned into the lane and followed it for around three hundred metres. She exited the car and had a final scout around. She was alone, nearly. The next dilemma was that of setting light to the car. She tried putting a flame to the soft furnishing, but this was coated with some kind of fire proofing.

It was almost impossible to get the car to ignite when all that she was armed with was a lighter, something that she was never without. Eventually she considered the engine compartment as possibly the best place to start. 'There should be something flammable under there.' She thought while trying to find the bonnet catch. She realised just how much she didn't know about cars in general.

There was a trigger like device in the passenger footwell, so she pulled it and was surprised to hear a reassuring thud from the direction of the bonnet. It had popped up a small amount, but when she tried to lift it she found that it wouldn't come up any further.

"Fuck it. What's wrong with this pile of shit?" She said out loud.

"There's nothing wrong with it." A foreign sounding voice said from behind her.

She nearly jumped out of her skin. "Who the fuck are you?" She couldn't believe that she'd been rumbled and at that precise moment she didn't know who by.

"Just run your hand along under the front edge of the bonnet and then you will find the secondary trigger." Said very calmly by the observer, who didn't appear to be at all shocked by the fact that she was obviously trying to set light to a car.

Katy nervously ran her hand along as requested. She never took her eyes from the man who seemed to be helping her. She found the latch and fiddled with it until she felt the bonnet lift.

Her admirer just stood and watched as she reached in with her lighter. She tried several places that looked likely, until a small fire finally started. It grew rapidly, so Katy stood back, still with one eye on the man.

"I guess you're in need of a lift now?"
"Piss off."

"That's not a nice way to thank the person who just helped you is it. Especially as I know that there is a person in that car."

"Who the fuck are you?"

"I'm your saviour. Are you coming?"

She had no idea why, but she followed her 'saviour' back down the track where, once they'd reached the road, there was a black car waiting with someone sat behind the wheel.

"Please sit in the back."

Katy said nothing and just as she was about to slide into the car there was an explosion from back up the track. She briefly looked over her shoulder and witnessed a large black plume of smoke billowing out from the area of the car. She opened the rear door of the car and jumped in, as requested.

"We're the Russians." Was the introduction finally offered.

Chapter 49

"It is time that we make changes." Bogdan said in a hushed tone. He was referring to ramping up production at the new factory, so wasn't quite expecting the response that he received.

"I believe it is. We need to remove a couple of objects, possibly three, that all surplus to requirements." Grigori replied while smiling.

Bogdan smiled back, but wasn't quite sure why, although the thought of removing objects always brought about a certain sense of excitement. Their sense of immaturity never failed them even though the combined age of the two Russian gentlemen was one hundred and forty five.

"The objects need to be removed at the

same time. We don't want to run the risk of any of them disappearing if they find out that someone else is missing or worse still eliminated."

The penny finally dropped with Bogdan, as to who the three were that Grigori was referring to. He would have to wait until this thorny subject had been dealt with, before discussing the changes that he was referring to.

"Are you sure that Dimitri has to go? He is our link to the underworld."

"We don't need that link anymore and he is dangerous. Everyone else knows their role and at the end of the day their prime motivator is making money, so as long as they continue to do that, they will do as we tell them."

"When shall we do it?"

"I think as soon as possible. There is no good reason for a delay. In fact, certain of them could be seen as becoming a liability, so the sooner they are removed the better."

The conversation had taken place away from everyone else, even their own team. No one else could be trusted with this kind of information. In fact Grigori didn't really like entrusting his old friend with such information either, but on this occasion he felt that he needed him.

He made a call. "Dimitri, can you talk?"

"Yes of course Grigori. Please continue." He put his finger to his mouth to illustrate to Daisy that now was not a good time to make a noise.

"We need you to perform an additional task. Of course you will be paid handsomely for it."

"Okay. What is it that you wish me to do?"

"We need you to make our project manager and the scientist disappear. It doesn't matter how. It just needs to look like an accident. Do you think that you can manage that?"

"It will take a little preparation, but yes of course. Leave it with me."

"We need it carried out as soon as possible and certainly before anyone else gets wind of what's occurring."

"Leave it with me. It will be done within the next few days."

"Good, good." Grigori ended the call. He then dialled again. This time to another number.

"Can you talk?"

"Yes. Go ahead."

"Target to be eliminated no sooner than Friday, but as soon as possible after that. Not concerned how you do it."

"No problem."

"So, my old friend, by the end of the week we should be rid of all three of them. Dimitri is just a bonus really. At least the state won't be paying for him to be incarcerated once again."

"Did you hear the conversation Daisy?"

"I heard enough."

"So, you have to vanish as of now. I don't want to know where you go, that way my conscience can be clear when they interrogate me, which they will."

"Can I contact you when this is all over so at least you will know that I'm safe?" Daisy's heart still belonged very firmly to Kevin, but she did have a deep admiration for Dimitri and she knew that if it weren't for him she would probably already be dead.

"You can, but by text only and not for a while please."

Chapter 50

"So, who are you and why are you so interested in the Polish Deli?"

"I think that it is I who should ask you the same, as it's you who is interested in having this conversation, not me."

"Okay. All I can tell you is that my name is K, spelt Kay."

Claude interjected with: "Of course it is." After all, he wasn't about to give his name away either.

K continued. "I am currently working for a government organisation. We are interested in the possible Russian involvement in drug trafficking in Paris."

"So you are English but you're interested in French drug trafficking?"

"Well not quite. The French operation has spilled over into the UK."

"How do you think I can help?"

"Because, my guess is that you were the French drug trafficker and now you've been ousted by the Russians."

"If I were and I'm definitely not saying that I am, I repeat, how can I help?"

"Because, for now at least, we are on the same side believe it or not. We both want rid of the Russians and I think that if we pool resources we can make that happen. Of course once we've accomplished that, we would be on opposite sides of the law again, but you have my word that unless we bump into each other at some future time, I won't tell anyone about you or any of your men."

"I will need to speak to my men of course, but in principle I think that neither of us has anything to lose currently. Of course I will need to see what you can do for us, but we could take some small steps first."

"Yes of course. Listen, for now I will maintain my station opposite the Deli, so when you are ready you will find me there."

Both coffees had gone cold, but neither party bothered to reorder and there was no shaking of hands. Claude got up from the table and immediately crossed the road, heading back to the car. K sat for a while longer and watched. He decided to make a highly risky call.

The phone at the other end picked up after only two rings. "Alfie, don't talk. Can you call me when you are away from work? I'm fine, I just need to offload some info and not through the normal channels." He ended the call.

K left the cafe and went back to his station. The car had gone.

Later that day he felt his phone vibrate in his pocket, so he quickly retrieved it.

"Hi Alfie, thanks for calling back. Are you sure that it's safe to talk?"
"Of course I'm sure. I've been a police officer for long enough to know."
"Yes, sorry. Anyway I have news from France and I'm operating on very dodgy ground, which is why I'm telling you and no one else."

He relayed all of the story so far, including the part where he may well now be in collusion with the French underworld.

"Do you really know what you're doing?"
"Nope."
"Should you really be having this conversation with a British police officer?"
"Nope."

"What do you expect me to do with this information?"

"Keep it under your hat until the time's right."

"What do you mean, until the time's right? When will be the right time?"

"I guess when I'm really in shit street and I need a friend."

"Oh, that time, so just like the last time then?"

"You got it, thanks Alf."

"Don't thank me yet. I'm not sure that I'm fully on board with this."

"Listen. I would not be in cahoots with these lowlife if I didn't need to be. It's just that I am one man, possibly against the Russian Mafia as it stands, so I'm just maximising my chance of success by utilising the local resources."

"Wow, I didn't know you had that sort of speech in you. You have come a long way since juniors."

"Cheek."

"Okay. You have my word that I'll keep quiet, but you must try and keep me in the loop. I will need to know if anything goes pear shaped before anyone else does."

"You have a deal. Anyway, how's the wife and kids?"

"Kid, K, kid. Let's get one up and running first."

The banter continued for a couple of minutes more and then they said their goodbyes.

K hadn't noticed another message had come through while he'd been talking:

Have had to go into hiding near rendezvous. My no. is +7 9402 0796778. X

K was working as fast as he could and he still had to get to the bottom of the drug manufacture and distribution problem, but there was now a real sense of urgency. He had to get to Russia to try and save Daisy, but he had to do it in such a way as to achieve the aim of the project. He would try and let any leads in the drug enquiry lead him to both Daisy and the people behind the Russian operation.

Chapter 51

Daisy had been preparing for this for sometime, so when she had to move she was ready. She had her phone, her notes, some money and a few warm clothes. She had managed to sneak her clothes out of her flat, one at a time and then hide them under the rear seat of her car. Preparing in this way meant that when the final day came all she had to do was pick up her attaché case, which now contained her phone and the dossier that she'd been keeping, lock the door behind her and calmly walk to her car. All done just as if it were a normal working day. This was just in case she was being watched.

She drove away from her flat and turned right at the end of the road, exactly as she would when she was heading for her office.

Instead of carrying on this route, she then took the next left, left twice more and then right. She was now heading for the factory, but hoped that she had done this in a way that would throw off any would-be spies. Daisy had texted Andreiv and told him to make himself ready. She just hoped that he'd received the message and fully appreciated what it meant.

A month or so prior to this day and shortly after Daisy had warned him of the fact that they could both be targets of the Russian government, Andreiv had discovered a secret bunker. He hadn't been purposely looking for a possible hiding place, but he'd stumbled across it while generally poking around at the rear of the factory. On further inspection it looked like no one had entered it since at least the last war, when it would have possibly been utilised as a bomb shelter.

Hopefully it was one that had long since been forgotten about. It was located directly under one of the buildings associated with the factory, but not under the main factory building itself. The entrance was also obscure. This made it easy to forget and hopefully also easy to miss, if a search were to take place. He likewise had texted Daisy and informed her of his discovery.

Guards were now placed at the front entrance of the factory because of the importance of the work being carried out inside, but fortunately the powers that be didn't deem it necessary to place them all round the perimeter as yet, even though there was only a partial fence surrounding the compound.

Knowing this, Daisy arrived at the rear of the factory and made for the department that she knew Andreiv to be working in. He wasn't there. 'Of all days to go AWOL, it has to be today. Where can he be?' She made herself scarce, so as to not arouse any suspicions.

After waiting outside for around fifteen minutes, Daisy could wait no longer, so she went back over to the factory and peered through the window. Andreiv was standing by some equipment and looking completely calm. He was blissfully unaware of the panic that he had caused. She walked in and hissed at Andreiv.

"Andreiv, what do you think you're doing?"

"Hello Daisy. I thought it best to carry on with my normal duties until you arrived. Was I wrong?"

Daisy said nothing, but gestured for

Andreiv to follow her outside, whereupon she just said. "You are naive beyond belief. After all that I've told you, you decide to advertise my name as soon as I walk in."

"I'm very sorry Daisy. I totally forgot. I'm just not used to living my life this way."

"Well you are going to have to get used to it right now. They're coming for us today."

"How do you know this?"

"Because I was at the other end of a phone call that I shouldn't have been, so I heard it first hand."

"What are we going to do?"

"We're going to get out of here, get some supplies and pray that our hidey-hole isn't found until the cavalry arrive. Do you have all of your clothes ready?"

"Of course I do. What do you take me for?"

"Do you really want to know?"

"Possibly not."

Daisy drove them both away from the site and went in search of some supplies. They purchased a microwave and a small fridge from a small electrical retailer, who for some strange reason had a smirk on his face that suggested that he thought that they were shacking up together in a less than conventional way. They then went to another couple of shops to get the longlife versions of whatever food and drink that they could find.

As long as there was power to the factory, there was power to the bunker. At least that was what Andreiv believed to be true. He had seen a light switch inside the door to the bunker, but hadn't ventured further.

As soon as they arrived back at the factory she let Andreiv lead her to the bunker and then asked him to start to set up their new home, while she ran an errand. Now that she had learned the bunker's location she had to drive away again, but this time to ditch the car.

The local canal ran along the rear perimeter of the factory complex and because of it's proximity to the factory on one side and the fact that it was open countryside on the other, Daisy could see that there was no one else around.

She didn't have too far to go to find a suitable place and because the car was small, it was easy to push in and equally easy to lose in the water, even though it took an inordinate amount of time to sink. She tried to enjoy the walk back as she knew that it could be a while before she enjoyed any freedom of movement again.

On her return, Andreiv tried his best to appease Daisy for his earlier indiscretion. He made her a cup of tea with their newly acquired long life milk. It didn't work, but she knew that they were about to spend a protracted length of time together, so she just smiled and drank her tea.

Chapter 52

Alfie sat on the eurostar alone. He had taken some long overdue leave and so decided that a sojourn to France would be a great idea. Of course the fact that his oldest friend might be in trouble had absolutely nothing to do with this holiday.

He told his wife that he was going away on police business, which of course in a way he was, but if she'd known why he was actually going and who might be at the other end to greet him, there was a good chance that she would have refused his leave of absence. He couldn't risk that. This was the first time in his marriage that he had told Mary a lie or at least withheld the truth. He didn't feel good about it, but he knew that it was for the greater good. At least that's what he'd convinced himself.

As soon as he arrived in Paris he texted Kevin or K as he must be known. He immediately received a reply: 'Hi Alfie. Why?'

Alfie responded: 'That's nice. I thought you could do with a hand and knowing you, you don't speak French.'

The reply was: 'You're right. Get to pond in centre of Le Jardin Du Luxembourg. I'll meet you.'

Finally from Alfie: 'Will do.'

Alfie jumped into the next available cab and gave the requisite instructions.

K decided that he now needed a car and this would give him his first chance at trying out a fake ID. He looked up the nearest car hire company and thought that he had time to get there before he had to meet Alfie. That idea was quashed as soon as it had made its entrance into his head however.

"Kay!" Came a shout from a parked car.

K turned to see the car that contained the other surveillance team, parked near its usual spot. He walked over. Claude was behind the wheel. This time he was alone.

"We have agreed that for now at least, it wouldn't be in the best interest of either party to refuse any help, so we're in."

"Excellent. Listen err, I didn't catch your name?"

"That's because I didn't give it. Let's just say that my name is C. That's spelt See." They both smiled as K immediately understood the irony in the joke.

"Okay See. Can I meet you back here in about an hour? I've just got to run an errand and meet a friend. Don't worry he's on his own and he's on my side."

"I suppose so. It's my turn to sit here anyway." Which it wasn't because Claude wasn't supposed to be visible to humankind, but he didn't want to miss the chance of checking the shop out for himself.

"What do you do for a toilet here by the way?"

"Just round the back of those shops. There's a small alleyway."

"Thanks."

As soon as K was out of sight of the car, he ran. He didn't want to make Alfie wait too long in strange surroundings, but he needed to try and get the car first.

He arrived at the car hire office about twenty minutes later, so just before he entered he texted Alfie to say that he was running late but that he would still be there.

The documents worked a treat and he was now in possession of a small Renault. 'This'll save some legwork.' He thought as he jumped in.

As he started to move toward the exit of the underground car park, he was suddenly reminded to drive on the right. A car came in and K found that they were both in a face off, so he swiftly changed lanes. 'This isn't going to be easy and it didn't come up in training.' He gingerly drove out into the daylight and turned right. It was by far the easiest way to go.

After driving around the back streets for a short while K started to become accustomed to the right hand side of the road. He reminded himself that it wasn't the first time that he'd driven on the right, but the only other time was in Afghanistan and there the roads were no more than dirt tracks and there was no traffic. Now that he felt a little more confident he set his satnav so as to get him to the park. He had no idea where he was in relation to it, but fortunately he'd actually been working his way in that direction. It only took five minutes to arrive at one of the entrances.

Rather than leave the car in a parking place that he probably wouldn't be able to find again, he just pulled over to the curb, outside the park and phoned Alfie.

"Hi friend, K here. If you are standing at the pond look toward the eastern entrance. I am parked in a small yellow Renault directly outside that gate."

Alfie had to think about where east was. He tried to work it out by looking for the sun and then his watch and then gave up on that approach, so he just looked at each exit until his eyes finally alighted on what he believed to be a yellow Renault with a man standing by it. He half heartedly waved at the man and luckily the wave was returned.

As soon as they met, K shook his friend's hand.

"Get in, get in. We've got to go and meet some friends."

"Are these the dubious ones?"

"Oh yes. They're the best kind. Until you turned up that was."

"You smooth talker you." Alfie joked as he slid into the car.

They drove back to the Deli and K brought Alfie right up to date. He informed him about his training and of his total identity transformation. He even showed him his fingertips with the now missing printlines.

"So. I'm K now and you must promise me that you won't let my true identity slip. If you do, the game's up and I will probably be heading back to jail."

"Message received and understood, K." Alfie couldn't help smiling, but noticed that his friend wasn't, so quickly wiped the smile from his face.

Once parked, K asked Alfie to remain in the car until he'd had a word with C, just to make sure that everything was still okay. C was still where K had left him, so he sidled into the car alongside his French counterpart.

"Seen anything interesting?"

"I've seen enough to know that there is something extremely dodgy going on in that shop. I've also seen a couple of trucks drive around to the rear."

"Might I make a suggestion in that case?"

"Go ahead."

"Why don't we take it in turns to monitor both the front and rear of the shop and then swap notes at the end of the day?"

"I like it. Twice the area covered in the same amount of time."

"Precisely and if we do this for the next few days we should know exactly who is coming and going. We can then widen our search to find out where they are going to and where they are coming from."

"In that case we need to agree on what information is gathered so that we have a standard format to follow. This way when we swap notes, we'll both understand each others."

"Great idea."

Chapter 53

A meeting had been set up between the two of them. No one else, including dear old Bogdan, had any idea about this part of the plan and that was exactly the way Grigori wanted it kept.

"What do you mean you haven't been able to accomplish your task? It was easy enough."

"It would only be easy if they were still there, but they are not."

"Well in that case someone had to have tipped them off, didn't they Dimitri?"

"Don't you go accusing me. I have done nothing to deserve this distrust. In fact I've been your eyes and ears until now. You would know nothing of what's gone on."

"So tell me how they just happened to choose now to elope?"

"I think that young Daisy is much smarter than we gave her credit for. I think she worked out for herself that her time would come and that because you haven't been supplying her with the additional resource that she requested lately or the correct resource for the factory, she would cut and run. After all she is just another westerner without any particular loyalties, least of all to us."

"That's what you think, is it Dimitri? You've obviously given this a great deal of thought. Why would that be, unless you were trying to cover your tracks?"

"I'll tell you why. Because ever since I was sent on the mission to find and remove them, but couldn't do either, I've had plenty of time to think. I knew exactly what your stance would be and I even think that might be considering doing the same to me. That's why I'm afraid, I've had to do what I've done."

"What have you done?" For the first time that Dimitri could ever remember.

"I've spiked your drink." Dimitri said while smiling broadly.

"You've done what?"

"Yes. I'm afraid that's what you get for entrusting me with pouring you a coffee when I arrived. You have approximately two minutes, probably less now. Is there anything you'd like to say, while we wait?"

"You won't get away with this."

"Maybe not, but then you definitely won't."

For the past couple of years Dimitri had become used to carrying a little capsule around with him. He thought that he would be the one who was going to have to use it, but fortunately it came in very handy at this crucial time.

He waited until the inevitable happened. He watched the old bastard squirm and writhe around in agony, for a few seconds and then almost comically protrude his tongue. That was the last movement that Grigori made.

Carefully and deliberately he set about removing all traces of his visit, including the incriminating cup. He also removed Grigoris' phone from his inner pocket. There was some cash in a wallet, so he thought 'waste not want not' and took that as well. He even remembered to brush the carpet as he left, so that there would be no trace of tread marks.

He knew that with Grigori removed, Bogdan wouldn't have the stomach to continue hounding him. He wasn't sure if
it would mean the end of the project however. In fact he doubted it, as Grigori would have made sure that once it had been proven successful the right people would have been informed. He also couldn't vouch for the safety

of Daisy and possibly Andreiv, as the wheels may already have been set in motion to take over should he fail.

He walked out through the front door and nodded to the security guard as he did so. No one knew who he had been visiting and there was no immediate reason to suspect him once the body was found. Of course the penny would eventually drop, but by then he would be long gone.

What Dimitri didn't know was that within the next few days he too would become a target, irrespective of any murder investigation, but he did know how Grigori worked and for that reason alone he made plans to go into hiding straight away. He had plenty of places to choose from and he could even slip over the border if necessary. This would mean that all of those colleagues who had become reliant on him for support with the project, were now on their own and most were marooned in foreign lands.

Chapter 54

Four of them were sitting in the car opposite the Deli and so far all had gone well with regard to co-operation. K now felt that he could introduce Alfie without fear of recrimination, especially as he was sat next to him.

"So, anyway C, this is my friend and colleague Alfie."

Claude said nothing, so K continued. "He is here to help me and he too has a position that may be of benefit to you in the long term, so please play nicely."

"What could he possibly do that could help me or us I should say?" Claude had to be careful with his choice of words as he was also sitting next to one of his men.

"Let's just say that through your co-operation with this matter of international importance, some leniency might well be shown should you currently be in or even get into any trouble once normal service is resumed."

"I see, so you have obviously decided that we do operate on the wrong side of the law have you, even though I did not agree that this was necessarily the case?"

"Please C. Do we really have to go through this? You know why we're here and we of course, know why you're here. I thought that we had got past this already?"

"I just don't like being judged by someone who doesn't know me, but I suppose for the sake of diplomatic relations, I can overlook your indiscretion on this occasion."

'Blimey, talk about over egging your part' Both Alfie and K thought simultaneously.

"Okay, then let's press on and swap notes."

They exchanged paperwork and the patterns soon became apparent. Basically the dealers came in the front the day after the trucks, which swapped their number plates every day, arrived at the rear. All present agreed that this kind of pattern was occurring at other sites around Paris.

For now K and Alfie only needed to concentrate on this one shop as they had a possible route to Russia via the delivery vans. Claude and his men were going to concentrate on giving the dealers as much grief as they could. They hoped that by intimidating and where possible interrogating the local branch, word might spread that the French were trying to muscle back in and this might cause some kind of backlash.

All of this started to happen just at a point when co-operation from the motherland was starting to collapse. There was no sign of Dimitri and production was slowing to a stand still. Word had it that both the project manager and the main scientist had gone into hiding.

"Thank God I got the car when I did Alfie."

"I guess we're going to follow a van are we?"

"We are. According to our records one is due back the day after tomorrow, so we'll be here waiting."

They headed back to the hotel. K had managed to get Alfie booked in, however he was on the next floor down.

"Hi Celeste, are you going to throw the keys at me today or can I collect them like everyone else seems to be able to do?"

"You can collect them, but only because you have your charming friend with you."

"Well Alfie, it would appear that you have to be with me every time I check in, otherwise I get treated abysmally by this woman."

They all laughed and the two men carried on up to K's room.

"Make yourself comfortable Alfie. Do you need to call home?"

"I suppose so yes."

"Please be careful what you say."

Alfie just smiled ruefully. He was sure that Kevin sometimes forgot exactly what it was that he did for a living.

K continued. "While you're doing that I'll go into the bedroom and send my daily report."

K re-emerged to find Alfie still on the phone, so he made them both a cup of coffee and took his back into the bedroom. A few minutes later, Alfie knocked and stuck his head round the door.

"I'll come out Alfie and then we need to talk about what might happen next."

"That sounds ominous."

"Well I fear it may be."

K came out and sat down by the window.

Alfie made himself comfortable at the small writing table.

"If we are successful at following the supply truck, it will lead us back to wherever they are loading it. That is not going to be a pleasant environment. There will be armed guards and all kinds of ugly low life. They will be making sure that none of their precious cargo goes anywhere but on the back of the vans."

"I'm dying to find out where this stuff is coming from aren't you Kev?"

"What's my name?"

"Sorry, K." 'Maybe I do need reminding, every now and then.'

"This is why we work alone. It's a good job I like you."

"I'm sorry K. I thought you could do with a hand. I had no idea what had happened to you once I'd handed you over, you see."

"I do appreciate that Alfie and I do very much appreciate you wanting to help me, but we have to be very careful otherwise there will be no future for me. I know that It's my fault anyway, for keeping yours and Daisy's numbers in my phone. If my boss ever found out that I'd done that I'd be for the high jump."

K decided to change the subject as he could see that Alfie looked very despondent and somewhat confused.

"Do you carry a firearm?"

"Of course not."

"It's a good job that I've got two then isn't it."

"I can't carry one K."

"You must Alfie. It's called self preservation. Don't forget you are here without permission anyway, so you could be in loads of trouble even without a gun."

"I suppose so."

"I presume you have a firearm certificate and that you've done the police training?"

"Yes. I am familiar with all kinds of firearm."

"Good. Let's hope that neither of us need them."

The following day they decided to go sightseeing. Neither had visited Paris before and there wasn't anything they could do until the day after, when the truck was due in.

Chapter 55

The bunker wasn't comfortable, but it did have running water, cold only, bunk beds, electricity and a working toilet. It even had natural daylight provided via a grill. This was the bunker's achilles heel however, as noise could carry through it. Also, if anyone nosing around at the rear of the bunker found the grill at night, they may see light emitting from it and therefore they would work out that there was a subterranean room that couldn't be seen from the front of the building. Hopefully, certainly during the day, it would look like a drain and therefore be ignored. They would have to cover it somehow, at night.

Because word had reached Bogdan and his colleagues that Daisy and the boy had gone missing and because his old friend had been murdered, he had put two and two together and decided that Daisy must be the killer. He therefore put out a search party and that search party started at the factory.

The grill, disguised as a drain theory, was about to be tested.

"How's your chess Daisy?" Enquired Andreiv.

"I've never played." Daisy lied. She lied because she hadn't played since she was a youngster and even then she had no real idea of the concept. It would be easier if she just started all over again.

"Well as it happens, I've bought a board along with me. I'll teach you, if you like?"

"I think I'll be rubbish at it Andreiv."

"I promise that I will teach you well and that I'll even teach you some of the moves that I used to beat my friend Mikhail with." He looked reflective for a fleeting second and in that second Daisy decided to ask about Andreiv's young life. Chess could wait.

"I promise I'll play chess with you Andreiv, but first, tell me about life at home and your friendship with Mikhail."

Andreiv looked sad at first, but then relished in reliving his early days. No one had asked him about this before and it made him recollect a lot of things that he thought that he'd long since forgotten.

He was well into his story when Daisy thought that she heard voices.

"Shh Andreiv. I heard something. Turn off the light."

They both listened and it was completely quiet. Then suddenly a shadow was cast over the grill. Someone was either looking in or they were standing directly over it and blocking the light. A voice could now clearly be heard.

"They're not likely to be hiding right on top of their last known position are they?" Said voice number one.

"We have been instructed to search everywhere, so that's what we're doing." Came voice number two.

"I can't believe that there's only four of us to cover this whole site."

"I think that's because everyone else is in France or Spain or wherever else they've all been posted."

Suddenly there was a small tinkling noise.

"Shit, I've just dropped some change down the drain."

"That's what you get for playing pocket

billiards isn't it. Try taking your hands out of your pockets and looking for missing persons instead of loose change."

"Shut up you bastard." Voice number two lowered himself toward the drain. He peered in, but luckily there was no background light in the bunker, so it appeared completely black. "I've lost that then."

"Come on. This site is huge, let's catch up with the others."

Footsteps on gravel could be heard moving away.

"We've got no idea how long they're going to be here for, so I suggest we keep the noise to a minimum and make sure that our light stays off for now. We'll have to flush the loo carefully with a bucket of water as well, otherwise the cistern will be heard."

"Wow Daisy. You've got it all worked out haven't you."

"No, unfortunately, but when you are on the front line you do kind of pick up on the little things that can make the difference between life and death."

They sat in silence and played chess.

Chapter 56

K and Alfie watched the next truck roll into the alley at the rear of the shop. They waited for about fifteen minutes and then K told Alfie to stay put. Before Alfie could ask why, K left their hiding place and made his way over the road. He returned five minutes later, with a beaming smile on his face.

"I've managed to install a tracker and I've tucked it up on top of the fuel tank, so it can't be seen."

"Where the hell did you get a tracker from?"

"Standard spy tool kit. Surely you knew that?"

"Do you really get a tool kit?"

"No, but we do get a couple of trackers

because working alone means that there are times when we need to be in two places at once, so they come in very handy. On this occasion it will mean that we won't have to be obvious to the truck driver. We can do it from a mile back, if we want."

"Nice."

"Are you ready to go Alf? I've no idea how long we might be gone for."

"Yup. I've left most of my luggage at the hotel, but I have enough in the holdall that's in the boot."

"Things still okay at home?"

"Yup. Let's go."

"I want to involve Claude as well, so when his lads turn up I'm going to ask them to get hold of him. I just hope they get here before the truck disappears."

"We've got a tracker, so why do we need to involve criminals anymore than we have already?"

"For two reasons. One, it helps to build trust and we may need their help later and two, we may need a second car so that we can pull off for fuel, food etc. after all, we have no idea how far we're going. We might have a tracker, but we need to keep an eye on them when we can."

Just as K finished his speech the other car pulled up, so he went over directly. He always forgot that none of Claude's men spoke English, so yet again he was reduced to sign language. This time it was easy, as all he had to do was say Claude's name as C and make the sign of a phone call. The call was made and the phone was handed to K.

"Good morning C, how would you like to help us stake out the truck?"

"I would, but I'm not supposed to show my face in public."

"I wondered why we hadn't seen you on the stake out, but we really do need a second car. I've installed a tracker on the truck, but I'd rather we had backup in case we need to pull off for any reason."

"I'll do it, but my men aren't going to like it."

"Can you get past that? We're going to need to move as soon as that truck pulls out of the alley."

"Of course. Listen, you two get on the road and contact me when you're on the way. I'll catch up."

"I can't contact you I'm afraid."

"Why not? How's this going to work, if we don't keep in touch?"

"Because, I don't have your number."

"Oh yes, I forgot. Well it should be on the display of the phone that's in your hand."

K relayed the number to Alfie. "Got it.

Right, got to go, the truck's just leaving. See you later."

K ran back to his car, where Alfie was already ensconced behind the wheel.

"Have you driven on the right before?"
"Of course not, but how hard can it be?"

They pulled out into the traffic. The oncoming traffic. Alfie swerved to the right and swore that he wouldn't make that mistake again. Lesson learned. They had lost sight of the truck, but it was showing clearly on K's phone, so they settled in behind.

"Luckily when I made that mistake I was still in a carpark." K admitted to Alfie.
"Ah, so what happened to all that spy training?"
"We didn't cover driving on the right, funnily enough."

Chapter 57

Although Dimitri had the choice of several places in which he could hide, he seemed to be drawn toward Rostov-on-Don, which was where the factory was situated.

He didn't want to admit it, even to himself, but he wanted to see Daisy. He thanked his lucky stars that he'd noted her burner phone number, prior to handing it over.

After travelling for a couple of hours he pulled off the road and ducked into a cafe. He ordered a coffee and some food and once he'd eaten he plucked up the courage to phone Daisy. As he picked up his phone he could hear a siren approaching. He held his breath and looked intently out of the cafe window. The police car was pulling into the cafe car park.

'What do I do? Sit and play it cool or try and get out?'

It was too late for the latter, so Dimitri tried to just play it cool. He reached for his gun, just in case.

The two officers came into the cafe and immediately started to survey the patrons. They continued to the counter.

'What the hell are they playing at?'

The officers ordered breakfasts and drinks and sat at a table in the corner. They continued to look shifty and spoke to each other in hushed tones. Neither appeared to be paying any attention to Dimitri in particular. They thought it was fun to make everyone feel equally guilty. This was typical.

As the officers were now tucking into their food, Dimitri decided it was a good time to leave. He collected his hat and coat, both of which had been hanging on the collective rack just inside the door and pulled the door open. He could feel himself shaking and not because of the cold. He hated being made to feel this way and even though the two policemen weren't taking any notice of him, he hated them, just for making him feel insecure.

He got into his car and while he was in the carpark he took the time to text Daisy. He was going to call, but found that he didn't have the courage to do that. He was having a bad day as far as being his usual alpha male self was concerned.

'Hi Daisy - Dimitri here. Where are you?' For a second he considered putting a kiss at the end of the message, but that thought was immediately quashed. That was not his style and Daisy would know that. He waited a few minutes before moving off, just in case an answer came back. It didn't, so he drove away from the cafe. Thankfully the police car stayed put.

'So all that siren playing bullshit, was just for show, typical.'

This irritated him further and at times like this he couldn't help himself, so he parked round the back of the cafe and walked back round to the front. Once he felt sure that no one could see him, he crouched down beside the police car and jabbed his stiletto into the rear tyre. He couldn't help laughing as he crept away. 'Maybe today isn't so bad after all'.

While climbing back into his car, he took one last look back toward the cafe. There was no movement in the car park. He drove away feeling much better, until he remembered that Daisy hadn't replied. He consoled himself with the thought: 'It could be for any number of reasons, I suppose.'

Chapter 58

They were on their way out of Paris and onto the A10, which was heading toward the south west. They had no idea where they were going, but they did know that in order to gain the information required, they needed to stay out of sight, but behind that truck.

K contacted Claude by text and explained the route taken so far. He received a reply almost immediately: 'I should be with you within about half an hour.' He added: 'What car are you driving?' So K replied: 'yellow Renault Clio'. Claude came back with: 'nice colour.' K just ignored the last remark. He could picture Claude tittering at his own childish remark.

They swung south and stayed on this

road until, after about an hour, they exited at the Artenay turning as according to the tracker the truck had pulled off here too. They found a service stop here and sure enough, after a quick look around the car park they found the truck parked and devoid of any occupants. Just as they exited their car, another pulled up right next to them. It was Claude.

"I picked you up on the L'Aquitaine, about a quarter of an hour ago and just stayed a few cars back."

'I need to improve my observational skills.' K thought.

"Good. If we pop in and grab a bite etc. could you keep an eye on the truck. We'll only be ten minutes and then we'll swap with you." He didn't let slip that he hadn't noticed Claude behind them. After all, he had a truck to look out for.

"Could I go first, I'm busting for the loo." Claude felt a little like a school boy, but where need must.

"Yes of course. Just go."

The two men who belonged with the truck came out of the restaurant while Claude was otherwise indisposed. Fortunately Alfie had taken the car off for fuel and returned before they drove away. They moved off with a full tank but empty bellies. K was driving now, so he passed his phone to Alfie and asked him to text Claude with the update.

Both vehicles continued down the A10 until it forked on to the A71. They took the A71 turn and continued south.

"How far down do you think we're going?"

"I've got no idea, but it does look like the drugs are coming in across the med."

"That's a bit of a stretch theory wise, don't you think?"

"Maybe, but I can't think of another reason why the truck would be heading this far south. It would kind of make sense too, as there is a route straight from Russia to the south of France, via the med. It cuts out all of the dodgy road routes."

"Wow, you have been doing your homework haven't you."

They drove on in silence, both starving by now. K noticed Claude in the rear view mirror. He wasn't about to let lack of observation be a weakness in the future.

After an hour's drive the truck finally pulled off of the main road just to the north of Vierson. It pulled into a small trading estate and then into a car park adjacent to a warehouse. The two men jumped out, locked up, walked away and jumped into a nearby car.

Claude had pulled in behind K and Alfie, so K ran over to him and asked if he wouldn't mind following the car, especially as he was the only one of the three who'd had a comfort break. He agreed.

K and Alfie drove away to find food and fuel, but they returned to the warehouse as soon as they could, in order to have a good look around. Alfie stayed with the car as instructed, while K approached the building.

The problem with this arrangement was that Alfie wasn't very good at just sitting still while his friend did all the hard work, so he got out of the car and went over to the truck instead. He walked around the back and tried the rear shutter. It opened, so he slid it up a fraction and peered inside. Initially he couldn't see much, as it was now pitch black, except for the lighting in the car park. What he eventually did see shook him. He looked again and it only confirmed what he'd seen the first time.

He ran over and tapped K on the shoulder. K nearly jumped out of his skin.

"What the hell are you doing Arch?"
"Sorry K. Come and have a look at this."

They both ran across the car park and towards the rear of the truck.

"Look in there and tell me that I'm not going crazy."

K peered inside and then lifted the shutter some more, allowing enough room to climb in. Alfie moved forward so that he could witness what it was that K was about to uncover.

Chapter 59

Dimitri pulled into the factory car park, which was outside the perimeter of the secure factory complex. It was getting late and already dark. The factory lights were off, but what Dimitri didn't know was that the factory was now guarded, albeit with just the two guards at the main gate. They watched his car pull into the now nearly empty car park. The headlights were extinguished and the engine shut off. All went quiet and the two guards strained their eyes to see what was going on.

There were no cameras in the car park, as when it was daylight, it was in plain sight of the guards hut. This was not so at night, so one of the guards decided that he would cautiously approach the car. He drew his gun, removed a torch from its charger and set off across the car park.

Fifteen minutes passed and the other guard was starting to inwardly panic. There was no sign of either his colleague or the driver of the car. He decided that he needed to call for reinforcements, so he reached for his mobile, but just as his finger pressed the first button, the door to the hut opened. He put the phone back down, thinking that his partner had returned, however it wasn't him. It was a stranger with a stiletto in one hand and a torch in the other. Before he could take any evasive action the stiletto was swiftly thrust into his neck and held there until he dropped silently to the floor.

Now that both guards had been dealt with, Dimitri could start to look for Daisy. He had no idea where she was, but starting at the last place that he knew her to be, seemed like the logical thing to do. He set off around the site, starting with checking all the doors to the factory itself. 'This is nonsense.' He thought to himself. 'Daisy is smarter than this.' He decided that if she were still here, she would find somewhere far less obvious to hide. The one big doubt that he had about the fact that Daisy was hiding nearby was that her car was missing, but he knew that could be a ruse. He knew Daisy well enough to know that she was very capable of hiding her tracks by setting up a bluff. Her car could be at the bottom of the nearest river.

He soon covered the front of the factory and it didn't take long to work out that there was nowhere that could be used as a hiding place. It was well surveyed by both cameras and guards anyway. He walked round to the rear of the building, only to be faced with a series of other buildings that he'd never seen before. The whole of the area was surrounded by a high barbed wire fence. 'No wonder they've only bothered to guard the front so far.'

He proceeded along the fence until he found a break, which he lifted until there was enough of an arch to drag himself through. He pulled himself back onto his feet and continued his quest. Just as he started to walk around the third building and back toward the main factory, he thought he saw a dim light. He stood perfectly still and looked in the direction of the light. He had seen it and it was coming up through a grill that looked like a drain. He tiptoed up to the grill and put his ear to it.

Because they were oblivious to Dimitris' silent approach neither Daisy nor Andreiv noticed that someone's head was pressed to the grill, so they innocently continued talking.

Dimitri clearly heard the conversation and recognised Daisy's voice immediately. She was talking in Russian to a male. 'It must be the young scientist. She had hinted that she would look out for him, silly girl.'

There had to be a door, so Dimitri set about looking for it. It was getting very late and he was tired, but he wasn't about to give up now that he'd found his quarry.

Chapter 60

"**W**e've got to contact the French Police."

"No Alf."

"But we have to. There's a body in this van."

"I know that, but with all due respect you shouldn't even be here and I've been tasked with finding out where the drugs are coming from."

Just then they both heard a vehicle approaching.

"Get that shutter down, quick."

"But we're on the inside."

"Do it Alf. We can hide up there." K said while pointing to the part of the cargo hold that sat over the cab. We can put that blanket in front of us as a shield."

Alfie slammed the shutter down and just as he did so the engine of the other vehicle was shut off. The two of them climbed up onto the overhang and pushed themselves as far as possible toward the front of the vehicle. They covered themselves with the blanket and waited.

A couple of minutes passed and during that time they heard glass break and then a large whooshing noise. Then the shutter rolled up and someone climbed in. There was an eerie flickering orange glow reaching into the truck and through a gap in the blanket. A short conversation in Russian took place and then they heard a soft noise, like that of a body being dragged along the truck floor. This of course was exactly what was happening. The two mystery visitors jumped down and the dragging noise started again and then immediately ceased. The shutter remained up.

Another few minutes passed until another noise was heard by the two hiding men. It was the noise of something being slid into the back of the truck. The shutter was finally pulled down and then a short while later an engine was heard starting. The vehicle was heard moving off and only then did K finally suggest that they get out.

"I recognised that body by the way."

"You what?"

"I recognised the body. It was the dealer that Katy met in Paris. He must have made one to many demands or neglected to settle his tab. They weren't happy with him when they last met."

Alfie was stunned. Now he really didn't know what to do or say. He finally asked a question that he knew K wouldn't have the answer to.

"On a totally different subject, but kind of the same, have you heard anything from the police officer who took that girl in? I don't know why, but I'm getting a bad feeling about everything to do with this case."

"I haven't Alf, but what made you bring that up now?"

"I don't know, it's just that these Russians seem to be everywhere and they are dangerous. Have you heard from the police officer? Do we even know if he made it as far as the ferry?"

"No I haven't, but then I wouldn't expect to. He's with your lot, not mine. Why don't you make some discreet enquiries if you're concerned."

They removed the blanket and climbed down in silence. After a rudimentary check it was obvious that the boxes contained drugs and by the weight it was mainly coke. They rolled up the shutter, jumped down and walked around the side of the truck, where they were met by a still fiercely burning Renault hire car.

"Shit." They said in unison.

K phoned Claude, who didn't pick up immediately, so he left a voicemail: "Can you come and collect us from the car park. Our car has been torched. K."

"Why do you think they torched our car?" Alfie asked quite innocently.

The moment he asked he realised that he'd slipped straight back into schoolboy mode. K had that effect on him. He found that he still looked to him for reassurance.

"I have no idea. They probably did it for the hell of it. They were probably high on their own stuff."

They both walked away from the car park just in case the authorities turned up. No one came, but then no return phone call came either. K was just starting to think that they were going to have to sort this mess out on their own when his phone finally rang. It was Claude.

"I'm following a black Peugeot south. I

saw it leaving your car park. I also saw a car on fire, but had no idea that it was yours. I don't want to lose the van, so can you make your own way for now?"

"Okay C. Good man. We will try and continue south somehow and we'll catch up with you tomorrow."

K put the phone down and said to Alfie that they should try and get a few hours sleep and recharge their batteries, as well as the phone batteries. They walked towards town, which fortunately was only five minutes away. While on the way they came across a petrol station that was still open. They found the attendant and after a very difficult conversation they managed to find a room. It was in fact his spare room and it was at the rear of the petrol station. They paid way too much for the accommodation, but they were desperate and it was now very late. The bonus was that the attendant stated that he could find them a car in the morning.

At precisely eight o'clock the following morning they were back on the road in what could only be described as a veteran French jalopy. It was a Citroen de chevaux of nineteen eighty four vintage to be precise, with a top speed of about sixty miles an hour and that was when it was going down hill with the wind behind it.

K phoned Claude as Alfie was once more behind the wheel. He clearly woke the Frenchman up.

While he was doing that, Alfies phone rang.

Chapter 61

On closer inspection there appeared to be a door behind a door. Dimitri could have easily missed it and it almost looked like it had been designed that way. He pulled the exterior door shut and listened at the interior one. There was no sign of life, so he tried the handle, which gave but didn't allow access to whatever was behind. There was no sign of a lock, but the door must have been able to be locked from the inside. He decided that it was time for another message.

'Daisy, I'm standing outside your door. Please open it. I am alone and you know me well enough to know that I wouldn't lie about such a thing.'

Of course Dimitri didn't really know

whether he was at the correct door or not, but he did know that they were here somewhere. There was a sound of movement behind the door. Feet shuffling and latches being unlocked. The door swung open and there stood both Daisy and Andreiv, with guns poised.

"Dimitri. Are you honestly on your own?"

"I am, but I have to warn you both that we've got to move away from here now." He went on. "I'll explain while you grab your stuff. Just grab what you absolutely need and come with me."

They did exactly as they were told as they could tell from Dimitri's tone that there was genuine panic in what was usually a calm and cool voice. Dimitri told them both about the fate of the two guards and that was all they needed to hear to realise that the place would be crawling with all sorts of uniformed and plain clothed enforcement officers, at day break.

Daisy was actually quietly fuming at Dimitri, as she felt that had he not killed the guards they could have sat out the immediate dilemma and then taken their leave in a much more relaxed manner and at a convenient time. She never said anything though as she knew that Dimitri was now doing his level best to keep them alive. As it was, they now had to rush with virtually no belongings, not that they had many anyway. The two precious items that she had to make sure to grab were her phone and the dossier that she'd been keeping.

Dimitri led them to his car, but they had no idea where they were going.

"I have a place near the coast and we should be safe there until we can get away."

"Oh hang on Dimitri. I just have to do something."

"What are you up to?" Both men stood and watched Daisy as she ran over to the main building.

She moved into the shadows and neither of the men could see what she was up to. After a couple of minutes Daisy ran back out of the gloom smiling like a child and swinging a set of keys from her right hand. She shouted to the two of them to hit the ground face down and as they watched her do the same, they instinctively followed her instruction.

A split second later there was a huge explosion followed by the sound of thousands of shards of glass smashing to the ground as the factory windows blew out. The glass landed all around them and a few pieces hit them. They were all frozen to the spot for what seemed like ages, but eventually two of them started to move. Daisy and Dimitri slowly stood up, but Andreiv remained firmly planted to the ground.

Daisy approached him slowly and very softly said: "Andreiv, you can get up now, it's safe."

He didn't move, so Daisy bent to touch his hand. As she did so, she noticed the blood trickling out from underneath his torso. She took a closer look and then she saw what looked like a huge shard of glass embedded in his upper rib cage.

She turned to Dimitri, who was watching all that was going on.

"Can you check his vital signs please Dimitri. I'm shaking too much?"

"Of course. Go and sit in the car Daisy."

"I'll do that when you tell me whether he's alive or dead."

Dimitri knelt down and put his head to Andreiv's back. He listened for a heartbeat and while he did this he held Andreiv's left wrist to feel for a pulse. He could sense neither, so he turned to Daisy and just shook his head.

Daisy sobbed uncontrollably, so Dimitri got up and walked over to her. He took her in his arms and pulled her close. She didn't resist, as right at this moment she really needed to be held and fortunately for Dimitri, he was in the right place at the right time. Daisy didn't want to tell him, but she would have accepted a cuddle from the devil himself at this precise moment.

"We can't leave him here. We have to do something for him."

"Daisy, there is nothing we can do for Andreiv and we certainly can't take him with us."

"I promised him that I'd look after him and what I've done is kill him."

Dimitri couldn't answer immediately, as he was still a little bemused as to what she had just been up to, prior to the explosion. He eventually spoke and he tried to choose his words carefully.

"Listen, he wouldn't want us to get captured and you have done your level best to protect him. That glass shard could have hit any of us and you obviously had your reasons for blowing the factory up."

Daisy took the last comment to mean, 'I don't know why you did it.'

"I had to blow that place of poison up. You might just see it as a business, but I see it as a place of misery. It ruins lives and kills people. It had to go."

"You're right Daisy." Dimitri wasn't sure whether he meant it or not, but he did know that it was the right thing to say. "How did you do it by the way?"

"We can discuss that on the way. We need to go." Daisy had quickly come to her senses and knew that they needed to get far away from there and as quickly as possible.

The factory was now well alight and the roof of part of it had already collapsed. It was an old building and consequently there was no sprinkler system. It was also remote, so no one would know about the fire until the morning, or at least that's what Daisy thought and hoped.

They pulled out of the car park and sped down the narrow and winding road, through the woods. As they got to about a mile from the factory they noticed a set of headlamps coming the other way, so Dimitri immediately killed his own headlights and pulled off the road. As it was a heavily wooded area he slowly picked his way through the trees until he felt that they were far enough from the road so as not to be seen. He then turned off the engine and they sat and waited.

The vehicle coming the other way slowed

to a walking pace as it approached the point at which they left the road. It was an army personnel carrier, but the occupants of the car couldn't see if it was full of troops or contained just a driver. The carrier continued past the point of entry by about twenty yards and then stopped. Daisy's heart was in her mouth.

Dimitri kept his cool and suggested to his two comrades that the driver of the troop carrier had misjudged where he thought that they had left the road. This would hopefully mean that their tyre marks wouldn't be seen. Daisy grabbed Dimitri's hand and gripped it tightly.

"I'm so sorry Dimitri. I'm not used to this kind of lifestyle. It might be better if I just get out, walk to the nearest village and give myself up."

"Please do." Said Dimitri sarcastically. "Come on Daisy, pull yourself together. This doesn't sound like you."

"No, I Know. I think that Andreiv has really got to me. He was so young and he didn't deserve any of this."

"He didn't, I know, but then he wouldn't want you to give yourself up either. Wherever you or either of us go, we are as good as dead. They will not show you any mercy just because you've handed yourself in."

Luckily it looked like the rear of the carrier was unoccupied and there was only the driver and one passenger who, after a brief look around the wrong area, walked back to the truck and then climbed in. After the engine started, there was a grinding of gears and then it drove away.

Dimitri drove back to the road with his lights off.

Chapter 62

The black Peugeot pulled into a car park that was alongside a hotel that had definitely seen better days. Only half of the neon sign was still illuminated and several shutters of the once rather grand building were now hanging by just one hinge. Paint had obviously gone out of fashion as well, as what was left was busy trying to disassociate itself with the building. The two occupants spilled from the car. They grabbed a couple of overnight bags from the back and walked toward the building.

Claude kept watch until he was fairly sure that they were not coming back out and then he left a short text message for K. Once sent, he bedded down for the night, on his own rear seat. He set his phone alarm for six a.m.

The following morning at around eight he was rudely awakened by a phone call. It was K, who fortunately had woken him after he had slept through his own alarm.

Now that he knew that his comrades in arms were back on the road, he set off to see what he could find in the way of food, hopefully before the two adversaries left the hotel. As it was, he needn't have worried as they didn't appear until around ten that morning. They weren't in any hurry, it seemed, even though they had a decomposing passenger in the boot of the car.

As Claude had been up for nearly two hours he was more than ready for them. In fact, to while away the time he made a note of the Peugeots registration plate and then contacted a certain member of his clan. This particular member was the 'mechanic' and as such one of his particular skills was to be able to find out where vehicles were registered and who the owners were. Claude didn't expect to be able to find an owner, but he did think that he might be able to find out where the car had come from. This may or may not be valuable information.

K and Alfie were still some way behind Claude, but because of the late start of the

Peugeot occupants, they had at least gained some ground.

The two Russian crooks came out of the hotel, laughing and generally larking about. Claude guessed that they had already partaken of a small amount of their usual cargo. They set off at a sedate pace and continued south. Claude placed his croissant on the passenger seat, started his car and set off behind them.

His phone pinged and this meant that a message had come through. It would have to wait for now as he needed to keep a close eye on the car in front. Also, he was more concerned about finishing his croissant than grappling with his phone. 'What a mess. Why would I choose this when I knew that I'd have to eat in the car?' He brushed half of the pastry onto the floor and tried not to be so disappointed.

Breakfast finished, he finally checked his screen and the message read: 'Car registered in Marseille.'

'Well that's not exactly proof of where we're headed, but we are travelling in that direction. Does that mean that the coke is coming in through one of our southern ports?' He called K as it was marginally safer than texting while driving.

"The car is registered in Marseilles."

"What, your car? Why would I want to know that C?"

"No, you fool. The van that I'm following. It's on hire from a company based in Marseilles."

"Oh sorry. I forgot that you're now following a car, how embarrassing."

"Never mind that. The car is registered in Marseilles and we're all heading south. I just thought you ought to know. I wonder if the stuff is coming through a southern port?"

"Good work C. You could be right. Where are you exactly?"

"I'm just passing a place called Aspiran and that's not a mistake."

"Right. We are near the junction with the A750, so I guess we are about half an hour behind you."

"How's your Russian?"

"What an obtuse question."

"How is it?"

"Very rudimentary. They did cover some basics with me, but I haven't used it since. Why do you ask?"

"Because if we ever do catch up with these two, someone is going to have to talk to them."

"I hadn't thought of that. Anyway, let's wait and see what happens."

"They're speeding up. I need to concentrate." The phone went dead.

Alfies phone went dead at the same time. He'd been having his own conversation.

"What's up Alf?" K asked.

"They didn't make it to the ferry."

"Oh shit." K said.

Chapter 63

The project manager had gone missing. The scientist had gone missing and now the man who was sent to get rid of the former two, had gone missing. On top of this two of the factory guards had been murdered, possibly by the man who had been sent to kill Daisy and Andreiv and the old factory had been destroyed.

To compound the problem even further the whole European operation was in danger of collapsing and as much as Bogdan didn't want to admit it, this appeared to be all because of the lack of resources that the project manager had warned them about.

Once upon a time Bogdan could have relied on his old friend and colleague Grigori, to lead them out of a mess such as this, however it was he who had very definitely got them into it, by not taking Daisy's requests seriously and of course he wasn't around now to see the outcome of his refusal to help. It was now solely down to Bogdan to get them out of the current situation, but he was at a total loss.

Even the fact that they'd established a second factory didn't help as there was now no liaison at the distribution level. He could live without Daisy and Andreiv now, but he needed Dimitri as he was the only one who had the ear of the underworld. The order to take out Dimitri was another of Grigori's decisions that Bogdan couldn't understand, but as the crook had gone to ground, it didn't matter for now. He just hoped that he could prevent Dimitri from being assassinated should he ever surface. The problem was that he didn't know who it was that Grigori had contacted the day that he'd given the order to have him eliminated.

Bogdan decided to call a meeting. Hopefully someone would come up with an idea to move the project forward or at least someone might know who had been given the contract to kill Dimitri. He didn't dare tell them the whole truth.

"So, you old bastard, you thought that by

getting us together now it would solve all of the problems that you and that other old misfit created."

"That's not exactly how I see it, but if you could help?"

"Listen, you have excluded all of us from your secret meetings and this has already brought about the demise of our beloved leader. Next you'll be telling us that the project isn't really running as smoothly as you've led us to believe."

There was a titter throughout the group who were sitting around the table. The titter soon turned to something that sounded a little more threatening after Bogdan's next statement however.

"Well actually, that's why I've called this meeting. The project is collapsing as I speak."

"I thought that we had a second factory and we were about to expand?"

"The first part of your statement is correct, however the second part relied heavily on our friend Dimitri and it would appear that he has now gone to ground."

"And why would that be?"

"I don't really know, but my guess is that he thinks that he's a marked man." Bogdan had to lie at this point because he knew that his own life would be in danger if he didn't play his cards right.

"Why would he think that Bogdan?"

"I think that Grigori got to him."

"And he didn't talk to you about it?"

The questions were very loaded and Bogdan could feel himself squirming. He just hoped that it wasn't outwardly visible.

"No, he didn't. There were many things that he didn't talk to me about. He often thought of me as an oaf."

"Well he got one thing right didn't he." The brevity of the statement demonstrated that the team weren't afraid of Bogdan now that he was without his old comrade.

Bogdan ignored the insult and fortunately his answer seemed to do the trick. Equally fortunately, no one asked where the project manager and the scientist were. It was assumed that they were both still hard at work.

"So, what do you want from us?"

"I want you to concentrate on establishing the new factory and I also want you all to keep your ear to the ground with regard to any possible hit on Dimitri. We need him."

"Consider it done. What are you going to do?"

"I'm going to look after the old factory and make sure that manufacturing is kept up at that end. I'll also be trying to find Dimitri."

"Now that Grigori has gone, can you please promise to keep us in the loop from now on."

"Of course, of course."

As soon as the meeting finished Bogdan went home and packed his bags. He then planned his escape. It would only be a matter of time before the rest of the team found out that both Daisy and Andreiv were missing and that the first factory didn't even exist any more. His would be the next head that rolled.

Chapter 64

They were heading for the coast, but Dimitri wouldn't say where. He felt, rather stupidly, that the less Daisy knew, the safer she would be. Of course he had no idea that his old comrades believed that it was her who killed Grigori.

Fortunately for Daisy the GU weren't involved in the search for her. Unfortunately the police were as there was no way, even in Russia, that a blatant murder of a high profile figure, could be brushed under the carpet. The police loved the fact that the GU weren't involved, so were only too happy to oblige when they were asked to investigate the murder on their own.

The reason for not involving the GU was

simple. The project didn't have the blessing of the entire Russian government and therefore the project team didn't want the GU poking their noses into their business. That would lead to serious trouble for all of the team members.

The car continued south and the one thing that Daisy was sure of was that they were heading for the coast.

"You have a boat on standby don't you?"

Dimitri was wrong footed by this statement, especially as it was correct.

"What makes you say that?" He was trying to buy a little time.

"Simple. We're heading for the coast and we're on the run. I certainly hope you have a boat anyway."

"I do as it happens and yes we are heading to it."

"So you might as well tell me where it is then?"

Dimitri knew that it was a falsehood to keep the information from Daisy. It wouldn't hurt either of them if she knew. This another first for him though, as he'd never told anyone where his secret hideout or boat was.

"The boat is moored in a little place called Mys Zhelenznyy Rog. It's only thirty minutes from here, but of course we are still relatively close to the factory so we must expect trouble at some stage between here and the boat."

"Don't worry about me. I'm used to trouble. Trouble is what got me here after all."

"Well at least you sound more like your old self now. How did you get here anyway?"

"I did something stupid in Afghanistan and then before I knew it, I was being invited to join the GU."

"I don't see you as a traitor."

"I'm definitely not a traitor. I was naive and I didn't know what to do. What I haven't done is betray my country." She had no intention of telling Dimitri about her dossier. That would have to keep until she was back home.

"Good. Good." Dimitri wasn't sure what to say, as he now knew exactly where her loyalties lay. He didn't blame her and in fact it was that loyalty that might help them out of this mess, after all it would appear that they were both heading west.

"I know what you're thinking Dimitri. You now don't know whether to trust me or not."

"The truth is that you are right Daisy, but I also am not stupid. I think we both know that we have to head toward Europe and I will rely on you to get me in."

"You can rely on me Dimitri. It's the very least I can do."

He smiled at her and started to feel a little more at ease. They drove on in silence for another fifteen minutes, before finally slowing as they entered the village of Volna.

Daisy broke the silence. "Are we putting to sea tonight?"

"No. We will get our heads down tonight and leave on the tide tomorrow evening."

"Where will we stay?"

"Don't worry. I've planned for just an occasion such as this, for years. I have a fully stocked bolt hole."

They drove through the village and just as they were exiting the far side, Dimtri turned into an unadopted lane between two high banks. After a couple of hundred metres he stopped the car as the lane came to an end or so Daisy thought. He got out of the car and walked toward the hedge that was blocking their path. He reached into the hedge, lifted it slightly at one end and pulled it toward the car. The whole thing swung out and opened up to show a continuation of the lane.

Once the car had been moved forward

a few metres, Dimitri jumped back out and pulled the hedge back to the closed position. He climbed back in.

"That hedge looks so real. How did you do that?"

"It is real. I've trained it to grow along a trellis that now can't be seen. It's effective no?"

"It certainly is."

"Do you think we should do something about the tyre marks on the far side?"

"Already taken care of. A friend of mine will move a scrap car into the entrance of the lane and it will look like it's been dumped there."

"I'm impressed."

"Thank you. It's taken a long time to achieve, but I had to make this place as hidden and impenetrable as I could. Part of the price to pay when you do what I do for a living."

They continued up the lane until another small hill blocked their path.

"Don't tell me, you're going to move that hill as well?"

"No, but we are going inside it."

Chapter 65

The lead vehicle swung on to the D613, so the other two duly followed, with K and Archie still a few minutes behind Claude. They were all now heading toward Mèze.

K couldn't be sure, but he had a feeling that their small convoy had increased to four vehicles, as a red citroen DS4 that had been maintaining a steady speed and distance from his own car, had now taken the same exit. He couldn't make out whether the occupants were male or female, but it did appear to have two as it looked like there was a smaller occupant in the rear.

"I think we have a tail Alf. It's the red DS4 that's four cars back."

"I wonder who they're tailing though? Could be the same car that we're tailing."

"Could be. Who the hell are they? We have the good guys, the bad guys and the ones in between, in our existing convoy. I can't think of any other interested parties."

"It could be a disgruntled customer, I suppose?"

"I'm sure we're going to find out soon enough. We just need to make sure that we keep an eye on them. I'll tell Claude to concentrate on the lead car."

K was about to make yet another call when a text message came in. It was Daisy.

'If we make it out alive, we're heading for Greece. Will keep you posted. X'

'What the hell is going on with Daisy and who is the 'we' she's referring to?'

K parked that thought for long enough to make the call that he needed to. He passed the phone to Alfie and dictated.

"Claude, don't worry about answering. Just listen. We have a tail and we don't know if it's to do with the car that you are pursuing, so you concentrate on the car in front. We are going to try and check out the car behind." He ended the call.

"We need to peel off Alf and see if the car behind stays with us."

"Okay, well you're driving, so just choose a sensible place. Try not to run us into a cul de sac. That's a dead end in English."

"Oh ha ha. That's probably the only French I do know. Well that and mangetout and that's only because of Del Boy."

They both laughed - in English.

K swung off the main road at the last minute and without indicating. This nearly caught the tail off guard, but not quite.

"Well, we have confirmation that they are tailing us, so now we just need to find out if they are with the others and the only way we're going to do that is by interrogating one of them."

"I'm afraid I'm going to have to follow your lead on this one K. I'm only used to working within the realms of the law."

"You're going to have to turn a massive blind eye then Alf. I can guarantee that this is going to get messy."

"What are you going to do?"

"First things first. We need to get them to stop the car and we need to do that in such a way as to not impede our exit, so no cul de sacs, as you've said already. I'm going to aim for an industrial area that hopefully should be empty by now. Could you try and find me one on the maps app? And make sure that it has more than one way in and out."

"Okay. Give me a second."

A few seconds later Alfie said. "Right according to this, we have just such a place coming up on our right. I'll tell you when to turn."

They continued for a few hundred metres and were already passing some industrial buildings when Alfie told K to turn.

The plan was to drive into the area, then pull up somewhere on the right and in plain sight of the following car. The hope being that the other car would drive past so as to not look obvious. While it did so, K would jump out and hide somewhere leaving Alfie in the car. The other vehicle should then go round the block and pull up some way behind. K would sneak out from his hiding place, go round behind the car and jump the occupants.

The plan, up to this point, ran like clockwork. K was now standing with his gun pulled and aimed straight at the driver's head. It was then that he noticed that he'd seen the driver before. It was the girl from the drug dealers flat in Paris.

The few seconds that it took to dawn on him was all that she needed to slam her door out and into his knees. He doubled up and fell backwards, but didn't let go of his gun. His left knee felt like it was on fire. Alfie watched helplessly from the car in front. He knew that there was another gun in the glove compartment, but he froze.

Katy jumped out and just as she raised her weapon K fired a single shot. She folded over the door and just hung there.

There was a second shot and when K looked up he saw the passenger stagger forward and then also drop. Alfie stood next to their car with a gun now hanging from his hand.

K checked Katy's pulse. She was alive, just. He then went round the car to check on the state of the passenger. He was also alive and in a slightly better condition than Katy. Fortunately for him, Alfies shot was from a distance, so his accuracy was affected. The bullet had hit the man in the stomach. K wasted no time, he grabbed Katy by the hair, pulled her round the car and stood her or rather held her upright, in front of the passenger.

"So my friend and I do know that you

can hear me." K had to hope that the man could understand some English at least, but then suddenly thought that the guy might understand French. "Alf. Get over here, now."

Alfie, who was already walking shakily over toward his friend, broke into a run and as soon as he arrived, K made his request.

"Can you say what I tell you, to this guy, in French? Please don't alter my narrative."
"Sure. Of course. Please go ahead."

K sat Katy in the passenger seat, but facing out. She was clearly unconscious and bleeding profusely. He then grabbed the man and shook him until he was looking straight into his own eyes.

"See her? She is dying." Alfie started to translate. "She will die if you don't talk quickly. Do you understand?"

There was no immediate movement until after a few seconds, when he nodded his head very weakly.

"Are you with the Russians?"

He nodded.

"Are you with the black Peugeot?"

He nodded again.

"Where are they going?"

There was another short delay, then. "Sète."

"Are you meeting a boat?"

He nodded.

"Do you know about the body in their boot?"

He nodded.

"Alf, we need to get going, so call for an ambulance and then let's go."

Alfie reached inside his pocket and just as he drew his phone out from his inside pocket a further shot rang out. Katy had come around just long enough and was still in possession of her gun. Something that neither K nor Alfie had noticed. Alfie dropped to his knees. He just stared at K, unblinking and as he sat back on his haunches he died.

K kicked the gun from Katy's hand and aimed his own gun at her forehead. She didn't move, but she was still conscious.

K withdrew the gun and just turned and walked away. There would be no ambulance.

'That bitch must have killed her arresting officer. I know that now. She must have sweet talked the Russians into helping her dispose of the body. Well now she can die slowly and rot in hell.'

"Rest in peace my old friend." He said out loud, while facing Alfie, who was still eerily sat on his haunches and staring blankly.

K shed no tears over his old friend. There was no time for that now. He needed to get to Claude. What he did do was walk back over to Alfie, lay him down and close his eyes.

Chapter 66

Daisy and Dimitri slept fitfully and awoke early the following morning. They had made love the night before, but Daisy had almost immediately regretted it. It wouldn't happen again. She realised that she had done it more out of a sense of gratitude than any strong feeling for Dimitri.

"Today we prepare and tonight we go."

"Yes boss." Daisy was smiling when she said this, so Dimitri took it for the sarcasm that was meant.

"We have a lot to do Daisy. We have no idea how long we may be at sea or what we may encounter along the way."

"I understand, so what do we do first?"

"We make sure that the coast is clear and by the coast, I mean the coast. My boat is hidden just like my shelter, so we need to know that we can get to it." Dimitri thought for a second. "I suggest that you start stacking the supplies outside and I go and take a look. What we don't need is for nosey neighbours to become curious just because there's a new person in the village."

"Okay. Exactly what would you like me to pack?"

"Just anything and everything that you can find and that you think might come in handy. Please make sure it's not too big or too heavy, whatever it is."

Daisy gave him a quizzical look, but decided to leave that conversation right there.

"I shouldn't be too long." With that Dimitri pulled the door to one side and left the den. He pulled it back from the other side. Shortly afterward Daisy heard the engine of the truck start up and then fade as it was driven down the track.

She thought to herself that he'd seemed a little cool this morning. Maybe he had thought last night was a mistake as well or maybe he just had other things on his mind.

Dimitri drove to the coast and checked that no one had been anywhere near his hideout. There was a fisherman on the beach, but hopefully he would be long gone by the time the two of them came back later that night. Dimitri stayed out of sight in order to reconnoitre the remainder of the beach and surrounding coast. All seemed to be exactly as it was when he last visited.

What Dimitri hadn't told Daisy was that the 'real' boat was actually moored at a nearby marina, hidden in full sight. He had no real reason for her not to know. It was his feeble attempt at making light of a dire situation. He just wanted to see the look on her face when she saw the size of the boat that was currently hiding in his man made cave. They would use this boat to get to the main one.

Chapter 67

The Russian plan had collapsed in Madrid and Milan, it hadn't even got off the ground in Hamburg and things were rapidly disintegrating in Paris.

"We have to get the new factory into full production as soon as possible and we have to re-establish our distribution network. As it is, we are going to have to start afresh from Paris, as it's the only city remaining that we have any influence over. The good news is that we now have additional resources as the personnel from the other cities have pulled back and are available."

"Why don't we just chuck the towel in before someone exaggerates our failure to those who are above us?" This was said by a project member who hadn't spoken a word throughout the entire affair so far, but now felt compelled to as he feared for his life.

"Because those who are above us will crucify us for not running this whole project past them anyway, regardless of any exaggeration, so if we can make a go of the new factory we may be able to get back into profit and therefore save our skins."

"I don't like this. I think I'm out."

"I'm afraid you're not out my friend. The moment you agreed to back this project you signed your death warrant, should you back out at any point."

"You can't do that."

"Oh I can and what's more you know I can."

"I thought Grigori was the killer, but you are just as bad."

"Grigori and I went to the same school in our adolescence and then went on to learn the same skills in our adulthood. When you speak of my friend you speak of me."

The other project member shut up. He knew that he was on very dicey ground as he could equally be assassinated by one of the government's people or by one of Bogdans. Neither way held any appeal. 'I have grossly underestimated Bogdan. I thought that he was just Grigori's puppet, but obviously not.'

"Who is going to communicate with our people in Paris?" Bogdan asked while looking straight into the eyes of the member who had just tried to duck out of the project.

Another member was about to step in and volunteer when Bogdan waved his arm as if to say, be quiet. He then patiently waited for his chosen 'volunteer' to actually speak up.

"I'll do it Bogdan, but I will need guidance."

"You don't need any guidance. Just make sure that the Paris links are in place to accept orders from the new factory, simple."

"But I don't even know who we have in Paris."

"Then you should have been paying attention during the project meetings shouldn't you."

Bogdan laughed as he knew that he had this particular member on the ropes, which is exactly where he wanted him. He also knew that this person would fail and therefore was now expendable. He would deal with the matter later. For now he would have to make arrangements with someone who could actually get things moving again. Unfortunately the person required was already on the hunt for Dimitri. That too would have to wait for now as getting the project back on track was far more urgent.

'Oh Grigori, what have you done?'

Chapter 68

A s soon as the sun was seen to slip below the horizon somewhere on the Black Sea and at the end of a flat calm but cold day.

"It's time. We have to leave now in order to give ourselves the maximum amount of darkness as cover."

"This was all that I could find that was either not too heavy, not too big and that I thought might be necessary. It doesn't amount to much."

"That will be fine."

"Do we have enough fuel?"

"We have enough to get us well into international waters. We'll have to wing it from there."

As they left the den there didn't appear to be anyone else around, although Dimitri was well aware that their drive through the village wouldn't go unnoticed. There were always curtain twitchers and in Russia a curtain twitcher could prove fatal. They drove as quietly and sensibly as they could until they were on the far side of the village. Dimitri then wound the old four by four up for the remaining half a mile as time was of the essence.

They finally pulled off the main road and onto a track that looked like it passed between a couple of deserted huts and then just vanished into the darkness. It actually led to the cliff edge, so they continued at a slightly more sedate pace until they reached its end where Dimitri instructed Daisy to get out. 'I wish I knew what was going on. Does he intend to kill me and push me over the edge or what?'

Before Daisy had time to convince herself that was what was going to happen, Dimitri snapped her out of it by telling her to grab whatever she could from the four by four.

"Just to your left are steps down to the beach. We need to get down there now."
"Yes, I see them." Daisy headed quickly for the steps. 'I hate this feeling of being controlled

by someone I hardly know'. She realised that she had not only spent last night with a man whose loyalties she still couldn't reconcile, but not for the first time she was entrusting her life to him. While she was thinking this she also recollected that this just about summed up how her life had been for the past six months or more.

Dimitri led her along the back of the beach a further hundred metres. As they approached their destination Dimitri suddenly veered toward the cliff and on first inspection it looked like he was going to walk straight into it, however as he approached he slipped behind what looked like a fold in the rock face. A few seconds later a two metre section of fake rock swung out to reveal the cave behind.

Just as much thought and ingenuity had gone into the design and making of the boat cave and it's contents as had the den that they spent last night in. From the sea it was impossible to make out the entrance and there was even a slipway that was concealed under the gravel of the beach, until it was needed.

Daisy walked up the shingle beach and then stopped at the cave entrance. She looked at the boat and her jaw dropped.

"Is that it? Are we expected to escape in

that thing? No wonder you didn't want too many supplies, we'd never fit in with them. How are we going to get anywhere in that dinghy?"

"So many questions. Where would you like me to start with the answers?"

"By telling me that we're not going to put to sea in that."

"Oh, but we are."

"We'll never get further than a kilometre before we sink or worse."

"Well that's okay then."

"What do you mean by, well that's okay then? How can that be okay?"

"Well in all honesty I think we've got to do closer to two kilometres, but the old girl should be good for that."

"What are you talking about Dimitri?"

"Come on. I haven't got time to explain now. Help me pull the boat out will you?"

The tide was high, so the boat wouldn't have far to run down the slip before it entered the sea. It would then remain tethered until they covered their tracks by re-covering the slipway with shingle and closing the rock faced door to the hideout. The hope was that the authorities wouldn't find any evidence of the hideout until the boat was long gone.

They stood either side of the hull and heaved. The boat was already sitting on the landward end of the slipway, which although relatively level at this end, soon pitched onto a downward slope toward the sea. They found that it almost slid under its own weight for the last few metres, before splashing into the small waves and coming to an abrupt halt as it took up the slack in the rope that held it back.

"Can you try and cover the slipway with some shingle while I go and shut up shop? Don't worry about being too tidy. Someone is bound to find it sooner or later."

They both set too with their tasks and then met back at the boat.

"Okay, here we go. Jump in Daisy and I'll untie us."

Dimitri untied the boat and jumped in. The electric motor hummed into action.

"I wish I knew what was going on Dimitri." Daisy sounded sincerely pathetic.

"You will soon enough. Just wait and see."

Chapter 69

K jumped into the car and set off toward the coast. He needed to catch up with Claude before he too became another statistic. While K stopped for fuel at Poussan he texted Claude. For some strange reason intuition told him that now might not be a good time to call.

The reply came back immediately.

'I have just witnessed them disposing of the body. They are now heading south on D2 to Sète.'

K responded with. 'Will catch up with you as soon as possible.'

'I wish he'd said where he saw the body being disposed of. Never mind, I'll find out when I catch up with him, hopefully. I wonder who he really is? Who is C?' It was starting to bug K now. Everything was. He felt lost without his old buddy.

He walked to the small shop and settled his petrol bill, never quite knowing what he was doing with regard to speaking the language, using their pumps and paying in Euros. All very confusing and still very new to him. At least the pump attendant smiled when he handed over the money, so he either paid the correct amount or over the odds, either way he needed to get out of there and back on the road. He climbed back into the car and set the satnav for Sète.

Half an hour later he guessed that he was passing the place where Claude had replied to his text from. He spent exactly two seconds wondering where the body was now, before returning to concentrating on the task at hand. He needed to keep his mind occupied, so paid particular attention to all the road signs and advertising, especially as he couldn't shake that last image of his old friend from his mind. He also couldn't allow himself to grieve right now because he knew that if he started he wasn't likely to stop.

On approaching Sète, K realised that he had no idea where to head, so he decided that for now at least he would make for the quayside, while keeping an eye open for Claude's car . Along there somewhere appeared to be the logical termination of this long drive.

Not really knowing where he was going he stayed on the D2 and from there drove straight on to the Route de Cayenne. The scenery was becoming quite industrial.

While driving slowly along the coastal road he thought that he caught sight of Claude's car, parked up on the pavement outside a warehouse, but he couldn't be sure. He drove on until it was safe to turn around and go back. The road wasn't busy so he allowed himself to crawl past the same spot and sure enough it was the car that Claude had been driving. Parked a few cars further along was the black Peugeot. Neither car was occupied, but both were adjacent to a small warehouse that had its sliding door slightly ajar.

K parked up and quickly returned to Claude's car. He felt the bonnet, which was still just warm. He then tried the driver's door and it was open. There was a smear of blood on the seat and the key was still in the ignition. 'Someone must have come up behind Claude as soon as he parked. They must have dragged him out of the car.'

K drew his gun, screwed on the silencer and tiptoed toward the open door. It was quite dark inside, as this door and the one that K had just noticed, on the other side of the building, provided the only natural light. The fact that it was now approaching dusk outside didn't help. By studying the building's whereabouts with regard to its proximity to the sea, K guessed that the other door must lead directly on to the quayside.

He moved inside and stood, letting his eyes acclimatise to the dark within. Once he could see further than a few yards he looked all around. The building appeared to be empty except for a few crates and pallets. There was a forklift truck over to the left and that looked like it was connected to a charger. Over to the right were a couple of offices, but these were unlit and therefore he believed them to be unoccupied.

K continued through the warehouse, but did so by walking around its perimeter, that way if someone opened one of the doors he wouldn't immediately appear as a silhouette in the middle of the floor. He almost reached the far side when that particular door slid open. He froze and luckily as he did so he was hidden from direct view by the forklift. Someone entered, slid the door back behind them and then they too stopped for a few seconds.

K watched the person walk forward and stop again as if spooked by something. He could clearly see the outline of a gun in the person's hand and this made his next move easier to decide upon. He fired his silenced gun. There was a small flash and a thudding noise as the bullet parted ways with the end of the nozzle. The person dropped and their gun clattered to the ground.

K stood exactly where he was, waiting to see if the noise had attracted some attention. After waiting for a minute or two K took some tentative steps forward, knowing that he had just taken a huge risk with regard to the fact that the person who he'd just shot could have been totally innocent. That was except for the fact that they were carrying a gun of course.

The body wasn't moving and no one came, so K took the opportunity to remove the gun and tuck it into his waistband. He then searched the pockets just to find out what he could. All he found of any consequence was a packet of Russian cigarettes and a spare magazine for the gun.

He then dragged the body into the shadows, behind the forklift truck. Once done, he crossed the floor to the door that was adjacent to the quayside, not forgetting that Claude was probably being held captive. He put one eye to the gap that remained between the door and its frame and scoured what part of the quayside that he could see. There was a very expensive looking boat moored directly in front of the warehouse and several others of a less elegant design moored to its left and right.

The boat that was moored immediately to the left of the expensive boat looked quite industrial and old. It was rusty but quite large and looked more like a trawler but without all of the prerequisite superstructure. It did look to have a large hold that was forward of the bridge. This was distinguishable by virtue of the fact that there was a derrick, which is a type of crane, mounted on the deck.

There appeared to be movement onboard, as K could just make out the shapes of people passing port holes that were in the hull. As there was no movement at all on the prestigious boat in front, K guessed that the people he was looking for were on the indistinguishable rust bucket to the left. That was exactly the kind of boat that wouldn't attract unwanted attention.

Now was a good time to send a message back to base. Just in case.

'In Sète at quayside. Found boat that I believe brings the drugs into France. Boat name is Mirabelle. Require small naval assist to standby Malta. May need a sea rescue of British citizen with Russian asylum seekers. Request comms with naval assist. K.'

He then sent a second message:

'Get to Malta if you can. Naval assist should be there. K. X'

K decided to wait until it was fully dark before attempting to rescue Claude and maybe find out what was going on. If Claude was in any immediate danger he would have already been killed, which of course he might have. Either way, waiting increased K's chance of mounting a rescue attempt.

No one else left the boat before night time fell and this confused K, as he was sure that someone would have come looking for the missing comrade. 'Maybe he was leaving the boat to go somewhere?' K was counting on that, as it meant that he could take out another one or possibly two on his terms. 'Maybe they know that someone else is casing the boat and therefore maybe they're laying in wait for an attempt at a rescue.' These and other thoughts rushed through K's head. 'There was just no way to know.'

About an hour after darkness fell, K climbed stealthily onto the boat and took up station in the wheelhouse, which was unlit. He squatted in the corner with his silenced gun poised. The next action that he took was to purposely make a small noise. One that might just draw the attention of a passing crew member without causing action stations.

He tapped once on the deck with the butt of his gun and then waited. Nothing happened, so he waited for a few minutes and then tried again. Again nothing happened. He tapped once more and this time almost immediately a head appeared at the hatch that led to the stairs down to the deck below. K froze as the head continued to rise through the hatch. He quietly took aim and as soon as he felt that there was enough of a target to aim at, he fired.

The bullet passed through the head and then through the timber panelling of the bridge, so fortunately it made little noise. The body slumped forward and stayed leaning over the top of the steps. K listened for any further movement from below, but there wasn't any.

'Perfect' K thought. As he could now drag the body over the top step and into the bridge before anyone below noticed the unmoving feet at the top of the steps. He accomplished this in a minute or so and there still wasn't any movement from below.

K moved swiftly onto the steps. He assumed that there would only be between four and six crew and maybe a couple of visitors in total and therefore there should only be somewhere between two and four now that he had eliminated two of them. The odds had improved but were still stacked against him. He climbed down until his first foot touched the deck and as soon as it did so he took a few seconds to look all around.

The steps brought him down roughly mid way between fore and aft of the boat and there were doors off the to the port and starboard, in both directions. He had to think quickly, as it wouldn't be long before someone else walked into the passageway. He decided to tiptoe towards the stern and then stop to listen at each door. The first one was almost immediately on his right, so he pressed his ear to the door and he could hear a voice quite clearly.

"He will be here anytime. He told me that he was half an hour behind." This was said in English, but with a heavy French accent.

Chapter 70

The small boat slid quietly along the coast until a marina could just be seen coming up on their starboard bow.

"We're heading for another boat. Thank God for that."

"Well done, but could you keep your voice down please. We're supposed to be sneaking in undetected."

"Sorry."

They moved past the first two sets of moorings and then Dimitri turned in alongside the third.

"We have basically sailed back past the lair that we spent last night in. Why didn't we just drive to the boat?"

"Because there's a coast guard station

at the entrance to the marina, so by slipping in this way we've avoided any unwanted attention. When you've been in my business for as long as I have, you automatically avoid everyone with a uniform on."

"I suppose you would."

They eventually moored up alongside a large craft that looked much more seaworthy.

The main boat itself was large enough to put to sea in and to survive in. It was about sixty feet long, had two large turbo diesel engines and an electric motor for such times as when silent running was needed. Putting to sea from the marina launch would be one of those times. It had a large cabin that boasted the latest in navigation, sonar, radar and radio equipment and a hold for food, fuel, tools etc. The living accommodation was fairly rudimentary because it was much more important to carry all of the required supplies, as they could be at sea for several weeks. There were two single bunks.

Dimitri told Daisy the boat had a name, which was Lizabeta. Daisy had noticed this, but was surprised as she didn't see Dimitri as being sentimental. She also didn't think that he would want it to be recognised, but he explained that it was needed as part of the registration process and that registration took place when the boat was commissioned. It was all because Lizabeta was over a certain size.

Dimitri had convinced someone else to register the boat in their name, so that he could remain anonymous, but at least the craft was legitimate. When asked why he had called it Lizabeta he initially went quiet, but then told Daisy that he'd named it after a daughter that he'd lost. He didn't elaborate.

"I'm very sorry for your loss Dimitri."

He went straight to the bridge and whispered to Daisy to go forward and let go of the line. After doing what he needed to do he then went aft and let go of that line. The boat drifted lazily away from the pontoon, before Dimitri went back into the cabin that was the bridge and engaged the electric motor. Noiselessly they crept toward the marina exit.

Daisy thought that now might be a good time to tell Dimitri of her and Kevin's plan.

"Can we head for Malta?"

"Malta, why Malta. You do know that's about twelve hundred miles away?"

"Because the British Navy are waiting for us there."

"My, you have been a busy girl haven't you." This was said with a certain amount of distaste as Dimitri never appreciated being kept out of anybody's loop, let alone that of someone he was busy saving.

"I have a contact in the British Services. I was bound to ask for help, don't you think?"

"I suppose so. I just wish you told me."

"Ah, but that would mean trusting you wouldn't it."

"Touché."

Dimitri steered the craft away from its mooring and around to the starboard once it was clear of the end of the pontoon. By taking this course he could keep it away from any prying eyes that may be near or in the coastguard centre.

It was a moonless night and because the boat was currently sailing with all lights off and under electric power, they made it to the open sea without being seen. The water became a little choppy as soon as they'd left the extremities of the marina.

"Can you hold this course Daisy, while I start to plot a new one."

"Where are we heading?"

"Don't worry. If we can get to Malta, we will. After all that would be best for me as well. I'll not be welcome anywhere east of Ukraine."

"Okay, but we won't be going straight there I assume?"

"No, no. We're aiming for Istanbul. There

is a straight there that will take us into the Med. In principle, once we're in international waters we're safe, however the Russian Navy being what it is, we won't really be safe until we can take shelter somewhere neutral. Either that or the British Navy find us before the Russian Navy."

"We're a long way from being out of the woods yet then?"

"Probably, but as I don't understand what you just said, I can't really say."

Daisy laughed and explained what she meant when she used the term 'out of the woods.'

Dimitri just nodded and looked back at his charts, which were illuminated by the light of a small overhead lamp.

Chapter 71

The French authorities had found a burnt out car at one industrial location and at another they found an abandoned car, one male corpse and one female corpse. Both as yet unidentified. They also found a barely alive male who they believed was of Russian nationality.

An ambulance was called for the Russian and a doctor called in order to sign to the effect that the bodies were indeed dead. Two black vans arrived shortly afterward. A Russian translator was sent to the hospital and instructed to wait there until the man had regained consciousness. A list of questions would be supplied shortly.

Meanwhile back at the industrial estate

the police started to ask questions locally and within half an hour had found that someone who was cleaning the offices of one of the businesses on the estate, had seen a small car heading south from the car park. She couldn't say what make the car was, but she did say that it was grey. When the police spoke to a petrol attendant at a small station in Poussan, he had told them that an English man had come through earlier that day. He was driving a 2CV. He neglected to say that it was he who had arranged the car.

Three unmarked cars arrived on the scene and the occupants immediately took charge of the investigation. They quizzed the police and those locals who had come forward. They also obtained copies of the forensic photo's and took several of their own. They had driven all the way from the scene of another crime whereby a corpse had been found in a completely burnt out BMW.

The police were instructed to continue with their local investigation and the three unmarked cars left the scene, heading south. No sirens or lights. They were from the DGSI, which is the French equivalent of MI5.

They had no way of knowing exactly where they were heading, but like K earlier, they did assume that they were aiming for the coast.

They would have to wait for new intelligence to come in.

Chapter 72

'T hat's Claude and he doesn't sound like he's being tortured.'

K was shocked, but inevitably not surprised. When all was said and done Claude was a crook. It was just that K also thought that he was a patriot. Obviously not.

'I wonder if Claude's comrades know of his liaison with the Russians? I wouldn't mind betting that they don't.'

K checked which way the cabin door opened and then stationed himself behind the hinge side. He noticed that all the doors opened into the cabins, which made sense, so his thought was that when the cabin occupants exit, they would initially be looking toward the handle side as the gap would widen from there.

As his head was pressed firmly to the door they wouldn't see him straight away. He continued to try and listen.

"We've got to get the drugs back on track by any means, we're struggling back in Paris you know."

"We are all struggling, Claude. We can't get the stuff from the mother country either."

"Right, well let's start by getting past our immediate problem."

"Which is?"

"Which is our friend in the car that was behind me."

K decided not to wait for someone to exit the cabin. Claude had clearly identified exactly where his loyalties lie.

K grabbed the cabin handle in his left hand and took a couple of deep breaths. He visibly checked that his gun was in his right hand, stupid though that was, he just wanted the visual reassurance. He brought the gun up to waist height and pushed the door open simultaneously. He just caught sight of two men rising together from behind a desk, the look of total surprise on both faces. Before either could reach for any kind of firearm, K let off two shots. One straight at the chest of the first recipient of his two small but lethal gifts and the other at the stomach of the second.

This was done on purpose, as he wanted Claude alive.

Although the whole event had only taken around five seconds, he had managed to identify each victim and aim accordingly.

Claude watched in utter disbelief as the man who he was talking to just moments earlier, sat back down and then continued to fall forward until his face hit the desk.

"Why C? Why get into bed with the Russians and what is your bloody name by the way?"

"Money my friend, money. The root of all evil I'm afraid. As for my name, you'll have to find out for yourself."

"You have sold your patriotism to the highest bidder."

"I sold it to make a better life for me and my men. It has nothing to do with patriotism."

"Do your men know that your dealing with their adversaries?"

"No. They wouldn't understand, if I were to try and explain."

"I think you were flying solo weren't you Claude?"

"How?" Claude didn't bother asking the remainder of the question.

K couldn't be bothered to continue with

this line of questions. He wasn't in the mood. "Why did you kill a British police officer just to help out a druggy?" K went out on a limb here, but he trusted his instinct.

"Because she was in trouble and we just happened to be in the same part of Paris as you at that time. We just didn't show ourselves until you noticed us outside the shop."

"What you don't know is that your little friend has killed my best friend and that displeases me greatly."

"I'm sorry for that, but I didn't control her. She is a free agent."

"Was."

"Pardon?"

"I said was. She's dead."

For the first time Claude was visibly shaken. He obviously had a soft spot for the little British tramp.

"Never mind. She had it coming I suppose."

"So do you Claude."

"You work for the British government. You have to play by the rules." Claude was now worried and he wasn't doing a very good job of hiding it as his voice croaked slightly.

K fired another shot. This time he aimed for Claude's left leg. He wanted to see the look of agony on the man's face. He had no idea that he could be this cruel, but he did find that he was taking some small pleasure at avenging his friend's death. He knew that it would only be a short term gain, but it was still worth it and he certainly didn't regret the outcome.

"That was for the officer that you killed."

Claude spun to the left and tried not to cry out but a small whimpering noise did escape from between closed lips.

K fired again. This time at the exposed right arm. He found that he was even taking care to aim for the centre of a tattoo, but he had no real idea why. 'Maybe accuracy.' He briefly thought.

Claude was sobbing. He tried to stop but the agony was clearly too much for him to bear. He sank to his knees. "My men will hunt you down and kill you in the worst possible way." It sounded more like a gently whispered gesture than a threat.

"I don't think so. Not once word gets round that you were working for the opposition."

K fired again and this time there was no reply.

Chapter 73

They were now a couple of miles off the coast and heading west. Dimitri felt that it would now be safe to start the diesel engines, as long as they kept the throttle down. He took over from Daisy for the start procedure as it wasn't as straightforward as just turning a key. He started by winding down the electric motor and then switching it off and isolating it. Then he switched the battery charging circuit over so that the twin alternators charged both the engine batteries and the electric motor batteries. He then switched on the fuel pumps, waited until they had primed and then he turned on the glow plugs, waited for about ten seconds and finally he turned the key. He turned the glowplugs off. Both engines purred into life with a reassuring burble. He let them do that for about thirty seconds and then he gradually opened the throttles until they were running at about a third.

They kept the cabin lights off, which complicated matters with regard to steering a set course, but Dimitri manoeuvred the boat into a heading of 260 degrees and then handed the wheel back to Daisy.

"Just hold her on that course and don't let her wander."

"What do I do if it does wander?"

"First, it's a she not an it. Second, don't let it wander. You can go two degrees either side of that number there." He said while pointing to the compass. "But no more. I'll watch for a few minutes and then I'm going to get some sleep. I'll relieve you in four hours."

"Why don't you steer first and let me watch you?"

"Because if we're going to have any trouble, it will first arrive at dawn and I want to be here if we have a problem."

Daisy kept Lizabeta on course. Fortunately the weather was good, so the swell was small. This meant that the craft was easier to steer. The problem that she did have was one of staying awake. They had a long day the day before and for Daisy it wasn't over yet. She made herself stare at the needle on the compass and set herself a challenge to not let the setting drift by more than the allowed two degrees port or starboard. In fact she spent so much time looking at the compass that she didn't notice the small lights that were twinkling on the horizon, just over her right shoulder.

The four hours seemed to go on forever, but Daisy was happy with her navigation. She felt sure that Dimitri would be pleased with her when he checked to see whether they were still on course.

He appeared on the bridge, shortly after Daisy had patted herself mentally on the back.

"So, how do you think you've done?"

"I think I've done pretty well actually. I'm sure that I was helped by the fact that it's a calm night though."

"Oh you were. It is almost impossible to hold a straight course when this old tub starts to roll with the tide. You can end up facing the way that you came, if you're not careful."

Daisy smiled and wasn't sure what else to say. It had been an uneventful shift at the wheel, so there was nothing else to report. She let go of the wheel and was just about to head off for her bunk.

"So you didn't notice the Russian Frigate

that's tailing us then?"

"What are you talking about Dimitri. Look for yourself. The sea is devoid of all human life, except for us."

Daisy was now facing toward the port side as she had started to make her way to the stairs that led below.

"Look over your left shoulder and toward the stern, if you would. Take a good long look and tell me what you see."

Daisy knew that Dimitri wasn't joking, so she did as he requested. She scoured the horizon to the rear starboard of Lizabeta. It took a couple of minutes to truly focus, but then she saw them. Twinkling navigation lights against a black backdrop.

"How can you tell that's a Russian Frigate from here?"

"Because I know these waters and I know the configuration of the lights. Also the speed of the vessel helps. If that had been a Destroyer it would have been approaching us already."

"I'm sorry I didn't see it. I was concentrating so hard on keeping us on course, I barely looked in front let alone behind."

"That's okay. I may have missed it as well. That's exactly why boats of this size have a radar. See that dot just there?" He said while pointing to a device on the dash that Daisy was not familiar with.

"I should have warned you to take notice of this, so it's my fault really."

"Never mind who's fault it is, what are we going to do?"

"Nothing."

"Won't that ship catch up with us?"

"It will if we let it, but I don't intend to let it. We just mustn't do anything rash. We will watch them watching us, for
a while. I want to assess whether they do intend to try and catch up. Don't forget, hopefully they don't know who we are."

"And if they do?" Daisy was doing her best to hide her fear, but Dimitri could hear that her voice wasn't its usual confident and sexy self.

"We will outrun them of course. This old girl was built for speed and on a good day can exceed thirty five knots. That old rust bucket of theirs is good for about twenty eight and that's with the wind behind it."

"You sound very confident."

"I am. The very reason that I purchased LIzabeta was because of her potential. Of course I've further improved her since then and that includes her engines. Go and get some sleep. We're already eating into your rest time."

Daisy left the bridge, but knew that she wouldn't be getting a lot of sleep. Not while the Russians were a few miles behind.

Chapter 74

T he DGSI arrived at the port approximately thirty minutes after K had departed in the old tub that had been the drug running boat. They still had to find the warehouse and then the body, so K would be safely clear of the harbour by then and of course the DGSI had no idea what vessel they were looking for or even that they were looking for a vessel at all.

K had spent a precious few minutes going over the boat's controls and luckily because of its age and purpose, they were fairly rudimentary. The hardest part about putting to sea on his own was managing to drop the mooring lines and then steer away from the dock. This didn't go entirely to plan as he did actually nudge the multi million dollar super yacht that was moored just to his stern, but then that's what insurance is for surely? As far as he could see there was only a small area of black paint where white once was and no one came running.

It was now completely dark and this also played into K's hands as the details of the boat would be less easy to distinguish: The name of the boat, the shape, the quantity of crew, the face of the person behind the wheel would all be very difficult for an eye witness to be certain of.

K did remember to put his running lights on as he had seen the switch while looking around the pilothouse. This at least would help to make him blend in with any other craft that were leaving or arriving.

He could just make out a wall that was looming up directly in front of him, so he steered sharply to the starboard and as soon as he did so he could see a flashing beacon of light that looked like it was about half a mile away. He proceeded to follow the wall, towards the light. It felt as though the wall was never ending, but then he was only proceeding at a snail's pace. Eventually he saw the termination of the wall, which had been running along his port side, with the navigation beacon flashing on the top. He turned to the port and headed south.

He was just about to open the throttle when another wall appeared directly in front of him. This time however, he could see that it ended just to his port side, so he made a small correction to his current heading and avoided a collision. 'Surely this is the open sea?' He queried to himself.

There were no more walls and there didn't appear to be any other traffic. He had nothing to guide him but his compass, so for now at least he just maintained a steady southerly course, increasing his speed steadily and so as not to arouse too much attention from any stray onlookers who might still be on the dock. Within the next few minutes he would be out of earshot anyway and a few miles further on he would be in international waters.

Fuel was the next big issue. K had no idea how much he had, so he started to look more closely at the console.

'What was that?' he heard a noise coming from below, just as he was studying the dials. The good news was that the boat appeared to have just over half a tank of diesel. The bad was that he assumed that all of his passengers were dead and obviously that wasn't the case. He either had someone down there who he hadn't accounted for or one of his previous victims had sprung back to life. He was hoping that it was the latter as they should be easier to deal with. At least the boat was in open water so he could take his hands from the wheel for a while.

The noise happened again. It was a scraping noise, but not repetitive. K moved to the top of the steps, flung open the hatch and immediately stepped to one side. As he did so a shot rang out and a bullet ricocheted off the roof just behind him. He tried to peer into the gloom below, but couldn't make anything out. Someone had extinguished all of the lights.

Instinctively K slammed the hatch shut and then slid the bolt. He leaned back on the console and took a few seconds to ponder his situation. 'I've got to eliminate whoever is down there. I've got no idea how much damage they can do from that part of the boat.' K thought and then he remembered seeing the hatch that was forward of the bridge. If he could get that back far enough, he could gain access to the hold and maybe then gain access to the remainder of the deck below.

Chapter 75

It was evident that the frigate had increased speed, so Dimitri did exactly the same. He was managing to keep them at arms length. He knew that he'd specified Lizabetas performance to be better than the pursuant, but he still felt uncomfortable. It probably meant that the Russian Navy knew who they were following, although he didn't know how.

The other problem that he now had was one of fuel. He'd calculated that they would have enough to get to Istanbul at a cruising speed of fifteen knots, in fair weather, but now that they were being forced to hold nearer twenty knots, they wouldn't have the range. Maybe the Russians knew that as well.

As dawn approached it became harder to see the following vessel. Dimitri counted on the same being the case, the other way round, so for a short time he decided to increase their speed further and change course for Turkey. There was a small town called Sinop and it had a marina. They could refuel and hopefully shake off the Frigate.

Daisy came back to the bridge just as the new course was being plotted.

"Good morning Dimitri. I've brought you some coffee."

Dimitri considered whether or not to tell Daisy about the course change, but decided that she would need to know sooner or later. He still found it extremely difficult to share his plans with anyone, even when they were on the run with him. He'd worked on his own nearly all of his adult life and even when he was forced to work as part of a team he kept his cards very close to his chest.

"I've had to change course I'm afraid."
"Oh?"
"We have only just been able to shake off our Naval friends and the only way to do that was to increase speed. They're not even on our radar now, look."
"So why the change of course?"

"Because speed affects fuel consumption and so we wouldn't have enough to get to Istanbul if we maintain this speed."

"Right and of course, we have to maintain this speed in order to stay out of site of that ship."

"Exactly."

"So where are we headed?"

"Turkey. A little place called Sinop actually. I've found that they have a marina there and the marina has fuel."

"Can we just pull up to a pump and refuel?"

"No, but as long as you stay out of sight, I should be able to use my false papers and my charm to get what we need. That's generally been what's happened in the past anyway." He said this as he winked at Daisy, which oddly made her feel uncomfortable for the second time since they had been thrown together. He continued. "We can then turn back to our original course."

"Okay. Sounds good."

"Have you heard anymore from your boyfriend?"

"Wow, Dimitri. I never thought that I'd hear jealousy in your voice." Daisy had never mentioned Kevin in that vein and had never given a thought to the fact that Dimtri would think that.

"I'm not jealous. I just wanted to test your

feelings for the other guy and now I know."

"You no nothing Dimitri." She felt that by using his name just at that point, it would somehow soften the blow. "He and I have a very long history and we have shared things that I wouldn't want to revisit."

"You mean that he has harmed you."

"Oh God no. Just the opposite. Let's just say that someone else harmed me and when they did Kevin promised that he would never forget and that he would do something about it when he could."

"And has he?"

"Yes."

"I have to ask Daisy and only because as I'm sure that you know already, I have feelings for you too. Do you love him?"

"Yes." Daisy started to weep. She tried to control her tears, but found that they gently came of their own accord so she succumbed and just let them flow.

Dimitri now felt powerless to help. He knew that he couldn't comfort her in the way that he wanted too.

"I won't press anymore and I know that you have been more than fair with me. I'll make sure that you get home."

"Thank you Dimitri and for what it's worth I do love you too, but not in the way that you would wish. Under all that bravado there is a very decent human being." She smiled warmly.

Dimitri had to look away as he was choking up and the last thing that Daisy needed to see was him acting like a wimp.

They continued toward Turkey in silence, so to prevent any prolonged awkwardness, Daisy went below and prepared some food.

Chapter 76

A quick visual check of his surroundings confirmed that he was in open water with no known obstructions in front of him. The swell was small and so if he throttled back for a while and tethered the wheel, he should remain on course.

K left the wheelhouse and it was only now that he noticed just how narrow the walkway was between there and the hatch. Luckily there was a relatively tall gunwale to prevent him from falling over the edge, so this made him feel a little more confident about making progress.

He mused on the fact that he really was a landlubber and that he didn't feel his usual confident self whilst negotiating a boat, even in relatively calm waters. As he approached the hatch the deck widened to around two metres in depth and it stretched across the foredeck. He knelt and tried to slide the hatch, but it didn't budge. He looked across the full width to see if there was some kind of locking mechanism, but there wasn't one, so he stood back up and took another look but this time all around the hatch. It suddenly dawned on him that it actually slid toward the stern and he had been trying to push it in the opposite direction.

He knelt again, but this time forward of the hatch. There was a locking pin, so he slid it back by wiggling it as he pushed. This hopefully would prevent it from squeaking. Once fully disengaged he started to slide the hatch back. It rolled easily, but again he tried to roll it slowly so as to avoid making any noise. He slid it back approximately thirty centimetres and then put his head down into the opening. It was pitch black and there was no ladder, however it did look like some boxes were stacked near the hatch. The height of these brought them to within a couple of metres of the hatch.

The hatch was very carefully opened to its full capacity and K could see that he might just be able to drop onto the top of some of the stacked boxes, but it was going to be tricky as they weren't directly below him. He would have to swing slightly in order to catch the top box.

He checked that he had his arsenal with him and proceeded to lower himself. He could just touch the edge of one the boxes by reaching out with his foot, so he started to swing gently toward it. He tried to swing enough so as to alight on to the centre of the top of the box. One more swing forward and he let go of the lip that ran around the edge of the hatch. He landed but one foot slipped off the edge and the box started to wobble. He leant forward and steadied himself. The box stopped wobbling. He was in.

After letting a couple of minutes go by, so as to accustom his sight to the darkness of the hold, he began to climb down until he could feel something more substantial beneath his feet. He stood upright and looked up through the hole in the deck, to a starlit night. There was no time for sentiment, especially as the moment that crept in he couldn't help thinking about Alfie. The thought that kept nagging at him was that he needed to get a message to Alfies wife as soon as possible. Something he should have done while he was back on the dock side.

He illuminated the hold with the torch on his phone and soon found a bulkhead with a door that looked like it would lead in the right direction. The big problem for K was that there were numerous latches around the door and he would have to swing each one of them noiselessly, before he could get out. It was a big ask.

Chapter 77

"It was an Englishman and he was tall and dark haired. That's all I know." This was said while he was reclining on a hospital bed and it was through a Russian interpreter.

"So you are telling me that you don't know anymore?"

"That's correct. Oh, he was relatively young. Possibly late twenties or early thirties, I'd say."

"How was the English girl involved?"

"We were told to take her along. I just followed orders."

"Oh right, so she was with you then. We weren't sure where she fitted in. Whose orders were you following?"

"The people above. I don't know any

names. We never see who gives the orders. We just follow them."

"Why are you in France?"

"Business."

"What kind of business?"

"Oh you know. This and that."

"This and that doesn't get people killed."

The Russian said nothing.

"I can tell you that the Englishman was ex-military."

"Really. How do you know that?"

"Because I am and you can tell instantly. The way he held himself. The way he spoke and certainly the ease of which he used his gun."

"Anything else?"

"No."

"Okay thank you."

The officer left the ward and told the interpreter to stay nearby, just in case the hospital case decided to talk, even in his sleep.

As soon as he was outside he made a call.

"All I can tell you with any certainty is that he's English. He may be ex-military."

"Do you know where he was headed?"

"No idea."

"We need to know. We are at the coast but have no idea where to be. We assume that there's a boat involved but there is a lot of coastline here." Before the man from the DGSI could say anymore, he was interrupted by a colleague who was either extremely unfit or who had just run a marathon.

"We've found a car."

"Whose?"

"I don't know, but it fits the description of one that was spotted at the industrial estate and it's parked outside a warehouse that's adjacent to the quayside."

"I'm on my way."

He dismissed the officer who had been patiently waiting on the phone and ran with his colleague, to the small Citroen 2CV. After an extensive search nothing came to light, but at least the proximity to the quay might lead to something tangible.

A thorough search of the surrounding area took place and during this another body was found. This time it had been pulled behind a forklift truck, presumably to hide it.

It didn't take long to identify the corpse as a known lowlife. He was linked to the Russian drug gang.

"No great loss but I suppose we should do the right thing and get the boys down here."

"Yes boss."

"Can you make sure that you recover the bullet before the police turn up? We need a head start on them."

"Will do."

"Do we know what boat is normally moored here?"

"Not yet. It doesn't appear that there was only one."

"Okay, stay on that as well please?"

"Will do. Anything else boss?"

"I'm sure there will be, but for now a bullet and a boat would be good."

They parted ways and both went about their respective duties.

Chapter 78

"**W**e are losing a hold on the project. Those of our people who are still in place are now working with the low life from those respective countries. They have learned that they cannot rely on our supply."

"What are we going to do Bogdan?"

"Why is it always me who has to come up with the plan?"

"Because you are the boss and we are here to serve." The speaker knew that the only way to survive in this environment was to suck up. Sometimes however, sucking up back fired.

"You cretin. I don't need sycophants on this project. I need thinkers. People who aren't afraid to speak up and suggest things."

"With all due respect Bogdan, the last

man who spoke up hasn't been seen since. Is he just off sick?"

"Shut up. I need positive suggestions."

There was total silence.

"Luckily I do have some good news. The man who was sent to find Dimitri has found that he was at the old factory, only a few days ago, so because the project is going nowhere currently I have tasked him with continuing his search."

"Dare we ask what you intend to do once you find him?"

"No." That was the end of that particular conversation.

"We still have the new factory ready and waiting and in fact because of the current lack of demand, we are actually producing a stockpile, so that when we are back on stream we will have plenty to go around."

"What are we going to do about the manpower, Bogdan?" This question was asked very nervously.

"We are going to root out the traitors who have deserted us and make them serve us again, but on a reduced commission. If they don't wish to co-operate, we will make them wish that they had and then their colleagues will play ball willingly. You know, the usual Russian way."

Bogdan had his smile back and it was the kind of smile that made everyone else nervous. The best thing to do at a time like this was to smile back. Preferably with your back against a wall.

A few days later Bogdan received further good news.

"I have been informed that Dimitri was seen with a woman in tow. They were near the coast in a small place called Volna. My guess is that they are now at sea."

"Yes, thanks for that. I think that I could have worked that out for myself."

"Sorry for stating the obvious Bogdan. I am used to working for clowns."

"Right. I need you to find out what boat they are using. It will give us an idea of range etc."

"I'll get on to it first thing in the morning."

"You'll get on to it now."

"I'll get on to it now."

As usual there were no goodbyes from Bogdan, so the line just went dead. At least there was no misunderstanding as to when a call would be ending.

Chapter 79

The first handle swung away from it's locked position with virtually no noise. K found that if he gently tapped it, rather than just tugging on it, it moved without noise. Just the other five to go.

He stopped and listened each time he successfully unlocked a handle. The problem was that even though he was managing to disengage them all silently, they could be seen from the other side, so anyone who had posted themselves in the gangway outside the hold, would see that someone was trying to emerge. They would even see what order the handles were being thrown in, so they would know when the door was ready to open.

K continued until he had got to the sixth

and final handle. He took a deep breath and started to tap it round until it was clear of the door. There was a noise. He stopped and listened. It fell silent. 'Shit. How do I know who or what, is the other side of that door?' There was only one thing for it. The door would have to be opened very slowly. At least the door was made of steel and would offer cover until he was ready to emerge.

The gangway was unlit, but K could see enough as there was a light at the far end. He continued to pull the door back. It too swung silently, until it was almost fully open and then it squealed like a pig. He stopped and stood back against the wall. Once again a shot rang out and the bullet hit something at the back of the hold, with a thud. K flung himself onto his stomach and fired. He heard nothing! He rolled over and took a quick look. There was someone laying against the steps at the far end of the gangway. Initially they didn't appear to be moving, but then an arm was raised. K fired again and this time there was the sound of a heavy sigh. The body fell from the steps and lay prostrate at the foot. K walked very gingerly toward whoever it was and when he was within an arm's length he kicked the would be assailants gun along the floor.

It was Claude.

K decided that he needed to make a swift but thorough search of the remainder of the vessel, before he could resume his post at the helm.

The weather had started to change for the worse and K was being made to walk in a drunken manner by the movement of the boat. He could also hear rain. He completed his search, noting that the only other passengers appeared to be the two Russians who he'd killed while still in dock. He kicked Claude hard as he passed, but there was no movement this time.

"Stay dead this time." He said to the unlistening body.

As soon as he reached the wheelhouse he was met with a totally different scene to the one that he'd seen when he left. Visibility was now quite poor and the horizon was moving in a wallowing way. The boat was both rolling and pitching and though not hugely, it did make him feel slightly queasy. He steadied himself at the helm and concentrated on the horizon.

He noticed that the compass had swung to the south east, but he didn't know how long the boat had been on that heading. Not that he knew where he was heading anyway. Of the many skills that had been taught both during and post military service, unfortunately ship navigation wasn't one of them. He could read a compass and he knew roughly where in the world he was, at least he did a few hours earlier. He could be anywhere now.

Chapter 80

The sea had started to pick up and Daisy felt sick. She stepped into the cockpit and pulled the door close behind her.

"How long until we get to that port?" She enquired, trying to sound as brave as she could without throwing up.

Dimitri smiled. "We should make landfall in the next few hours."

"Oh God. I could be dead by then."

"Stop being a pansy. Come on Daisy, you're made of sterner stuff than that surely?"

"You're going to see what stuff I'm made of shortly."

Dimitri decided that distraction was the best cure, so he told her a story.

"I haven't told you how I managed to keep my boat a secret for so long, have I?"

"No you haven't. Is this your idea of trying to distract me?"

"Yes. Is it working?"

"Kind of. Keep going."

"Well, during the planning stage I was already aware that if I were to purchase a large vessel and then keep it moored somewhere, sooner or later someone would become curious. That was something that I couldn't afford to happen of course. I always knew that the Lizabeta was going to be my ticket out of some sticky situation or the other."

"So what did you do?"

"I bribed a businessman."

"How did that work?"

"I made him take ownership of the Lizabeta. I obviously made sure that he was a man of certain means and therefore wouldn't arouse any suspicion when purchasing a boat."

"And how did you make sure that he would remain on board. If you pardon the pun?"

"By setting him up in such a way as to make it impossible for him to break his promise without knowing that he would suffer in a very dangerous way and I don't mean by threat of physical violence. I can be subtle sometimes, you know."

"I am intrigued now. What did you do exactly?"

"Let's just say that I convinced him to take part in a nefarious deal and should it ever emerge that he was involved, he would be finished in the Moscow business world."

"Very clever."

"Where needs must and all that. You have a similar saying in English I believe?"

"The same actually."

Daisy found that oddly, she did feel better by the time that Dimitri had finished his story. Distraction obviously worked, right up to the point when she started thinking about being sick again. She headed for the gunwale and leaned over the side. Dimitri laughed. He knew that he shouldn't and he knew that Daisy would take a very dim view of the fact that he had, but now that he was aware that there wouldn't be any romantic involvement, he felt that he had nothing to lose.

"You bastard."

"That's me." He said. Not bothering to hide the smirk on his face. "In all seriousness are you going to be able to take your turn at the wheel?"

"Is that all you care about?"

"Of course. It should be all you care

about as well. We need to get to Turkey and we need to get there while we have fuel in the tanks."

Daisy noticed a certain frostiness had now crept into Dimitris' voice. She thought 'And they say that hell hath no fury like a woman scorned. Well he takes some beating.'

"I'm ready for my turn at the wheel."

"Are you sure? I was only joking with you before."

"No you weren't Dimitri and yes I'm sure." Daisy really just wanted this journey to end now. Things were starting to get decidedly uncomfortable between them. 'Why did he have to ruin this by asking that immature question?'

Daisy headed for the cockpit, but not before Dimitri said: "They weren't racking us by the way."

"What do you mean? Why do you think they were not after us?"

"Because it suddenly dawned on me that they were actually hugging the coast. We just happened to be going the same way initially. They are obviously involved in the war with Ukraine. I'd forgotten that we were nearly travelling through a war zone."

"I did as well. Even from here it's hard

to imagine what's going on just a few miles to the north of us. Do you still want to head for Turkey?"

"Yes. We have to because we still need fuel."

Chapter 81

Mary was up to her elbows in soap suds, when the front door bell rang. She wasn't expecting anyone, but even so she removed her marigolds, placed them on the draining board and went to the door. There were two very young but business like people, standing on the step. One man and one woman. As she opened the door they both stepped back on to the path and then looked awkwardly at each other, as if one was expecting the other to speak.

"May we come in please Mrs Edwards. We are from your husbands office." It was the young lady who had drawn the short straw.

Mary's heart sank and she could already feel herself welling up. She knew that this was not going to be good news.

"Of course. Please go through. First on the right."

"Thank you." The man now spoke for the first time.

"Would you both like a cup of tea?" This was the last thing that Mary really wanted to say, but protocol kicked in, even at a time such as this.

"We're fine thankyou Mrs Edwards."
"Mary please."
"We're fine thank you Mary."
"Please take a seat."

They sat side by side on the sofa. They had looked like a pair of siamese twins since they arrived.

The young lady introduced herself and then started to relay the story.

"But I didn't even know that he'd gone to France, let alone what he was doing there. He just told me that he was going away on police business."

Alfie wasn't the only one who didn't tell her the truth. The two visitors hadn't told her the truth mainly because they didn't know it either, but also because the actual case was ongoing and was still top secret.

"The work of a police officer is sometimes confidential and when it comes to matters of state that confidentiality stretches to his wife, I'm afraid." The speech had been rehearsed meticulously by the officials from the home office.

They had been given the names of all of Alfies family, their relationship to him and then a copy of exactly what to say.

"Can you tell me how he died at least?"

"All we can tell you Mary, is that he died in the line of duty and that you can be very proud of him. He will receive a full police funeral with honours. As long as that is your wish of course."

"When can I see him?"

"He should be here in a couple of days. We'll be back in touch as soon as we can, I promise."

"I've got to think of how to tell the children. Can you please go now?"

"Yes, of course." The man reached inside his jacket and pulled out a business card. He handed it to Mary.

"Please call anytime day or night, if there's anything we can do." This wasn't part of the script, but he didn't know what else to say. He genuinely felt sorry for Mary and hated this part of his job.

They walked back down the path saying nothing, but each knowing what the other was thinking. They didn't look back. The front door clicked shut.

Chapter 82

He had totally forgotten about the open hatch and the boat was now pitching so badly that water was pouring over the side and into the hold. He had to get back to the hold and close it before the boat sank.

Once the wheel was lashed so that it couldn't move off course anymore, K made his way very tentatively out of the pilot house and back along the deck. He was concentrating on every step as one false move and he would be pitched over the side with no way of ever coming back.

He considered lashing himself to the gunwale, but soon put that idea to bed when he couldn't see any spare rope. Time of the essence as water was now pouring in with nearly every roll of the boat.

A wave slammed into the side and sent a shudder through the vessel. K lost his grip for a split second, but managed to reach out and clasp back onto the rail. He decided that the best way forward from now on was on his hands and knees. He continued to crawl until he was at the aft end of the hatch. From here he grabbed the side rail of the hatch lid and started to drag it with him. All the while the sea was becoming more angry and the wind was picking up. A storm was approaching.

The hatch lid was finally pulled shut, but each time the boat rose at the bow the hatch tried to slide back and K had to hold on with all his might. He held it firm until he managed to slide the locking mechanism back into place.

He crawled all the way back to the pilot house and only stood once he could hold the pilot house door. By now he was absolutely soaking wet, so while the wheel was still lashed to the bulkhead he decided to go in search of some dry clothes. He knew where some weren't needed anymore, but they might be rather stained.

The old diesel engine kept chugging away without

missing a beat, but K had absolutely no idea where he was headed. For now dry clothes and maybe even a cup of tea were the order of the day.

'I hope this weather doesn't get much worse. I don't want to spill tea down my dry clothes, do I?' He thought to himself as he descended the steps to the deck below.

Chapter 83

The coast line started to appear on their starboard bow. The weather was foul, but at least they were heading for shelter. Daisy decided that given the choice she would happily give herself up to the Russians if it meant that she never had to go to sea again. Dimitri on the other hand was in his element and that didn't help with Daisy's mood either.

"We should make landfall in about an hour. We have to go around the headland because the harbour is on the far side"

Daisy just went back below and laid down. She stayed in that position until Dimitri briefly came down to join her.

"We're entering the harbour so just stay put and I'll try and persuade the authorities that I'm alone and just making my way back to Greece. I won't mention Malta because I think that might raise a red flag because of the distance."

"Whatever Dimitri. My life as usual these days, is in your hands. Not something that I'm comfortable with."

"I know, but remember, once we get clear of here and hopefully make it to Malta, my life will most definitely be in your hands."

Dimitri headed back up top and guided Lizabeta skillfully into a mooring that was adjacent to the fuel tanks.

Someone came over and helped with tying the boat off. Dimitri thanked them in English, but received no reply. The other man just waved his hands as if to say no problem or it might have been a gesture that said 'sorry, I don't understand a word you're saying.' Either way, he just walked off.

Dimitri thought that his best course of action would be to head straight for the harbour masters office, rather than wait for the harbour master to come to him. He went below, grabbed his paperwork and then went in search of the office.

Daisy looked at the clock on the bulkhead and saw that Dimitri had been gone for about three quarters of an hour. She started to worry. 'What if he's been arrested? I can't just stay here. I'll have to sneak out after dark, unless I'm found beforehand, that is.'

A few minutes later he appeared, grinning like a Cheshire cat.

"Where the hell have you been? I've been worried sick and planning my escape after dark."

"Sorry Daisy. I got chatting. It would appear that the harbour manager, as he likes to call himself, once visited Ukraine, which is where I told him that I'm from. Luckily I have been there, so I was able to give him some details that sounded convincing. He has total sympathy with the Ukraine people and therefore gave me no trouble at all."

Daisy felt foolish. She hadn't stopped to consider that Dimitri was going to great lengths to try and get them safely to Malta and that making background stories up, on the fly, were going to form part of that process.

"There's no need to apologise, Dimitri. I should apologise to you. You're the one sticking his neck out on our behalf."

Although Daisy always spoke to Dimitri in his mother tongue, she had the habit of adding English nuances like 'sticking your neck out'. Dimitri had kind of got used to these, but every now and again he was flummoxed. There appeared to be no correlation between what they were talking about and sticking your neck out.

"What has sticking my neck out got to do with what we're doing?"

Daisy chuckled and explained. Dimitri looked just as non plussed as he did before, but continued with his story anyway.

"So we can refuel, as long as we pay the harbour manager directly of course."

"But we don't have any Ruples or whatever they take here."

"He'll accept American dollars. Everyone accepts American dollars, that's why I carry them."

Daisy just smiled. This time it was in awe, as she couldn't believe the level of thought that her compatriot had put into this trip or whichever journey was going to be the one that he used as his escape from Russia.

They set off again, at dusk. This time with a full tank of diesel.

Chapter 84

"We know that the boat was called 'The Corsica'. We also know that it was registered in Liberia, but then aren't they all and we also know that it's only been on the scene for about six months. We know nothing about the crew or what the shipments were. Nothing ever got registered. Don't ask."

"Where is it now and who's on it?"

"We don't know the answer to either of those questions sir. I can tell you that she put to sea last night and it would appear that it was at about twenty one hundred hours. This has been verified by the crew of the large yacht that was moored behind the old tug. Evidently it knocked into them when it was leaving."

"Did they not try and take some details?"

No. They were all below at the time and they just felt the knock. By the time any of them came up top. That's on to the deck you know. The old boat was chugging down the channel."

"Cretin."

"What sir?"

"I know what 'up top' means you fool."

"Sorry sir. Anyway the boat is long gone and evidently the weather out there is foul at the moment, so there's no point in trying to follow it. Not that we'd know where to look anyway."

The senior officer scratched his chin in a 'I'm thinking' sort of way.

"Right. I think we need to concentrate on the landward side of this investigation for now. Whoever is on that boat will surface at some stage."

"Yes sir."

"Have we been in touch with the British authorities yet?"

"Oh yes, we have and we now know that the girl was a miss Katy Weller. A known drug addict and the British gentleman was Inspector Alf Edwards of Scotland Yard. His wife has been informed."

"What was he doing here and more importantly, what was he doing here without us knowing about it?"

"Not sure sir, other than the fact that it all ties in with this Russian Mafia scenario.

"Maybe he was tracking Ms Weller. They both came across the channel after all."

"Yes, but the odd thing is that his wife didn't know where he was. According to the British anyway."

"They may have their own agenda, but it would appear they too are interested in our Russian Mafia case. I wonder why that would be?"

"Katy Weller was a drug addict and we suspect that the Russians are here to deal with drugs. Maybe they were shipping those drugs to England."

"Can you get in touch with Scotland Yard and see if you can find out what cases Mr Edwards was working on?"

"Will do."

The senior officer continued thinking.

Chapter 85

Bogdan and the team had met for the penultimate time. A new goal had been set and it was agreed that this revised ambition was much more achievable. It also meant that no one needed to worry about losing their credibility or worse.

Now the project was deemed complete and as such a success. It had been saved by the fact that the new factory was in full production and the revised distribution method meant that there was very little need for the Russian underworld to be involved. The drugs were shipped straight to the dealers much as they had been prior to Russians taking over.

The one big concession was that there

would be no information gathering. This was no great loss however as asking the underworld to supply decent and relevant information was tantamount to asking them to get a job.

The team melted away and each member went back to whatever day job they had. The only one who didn't was Bogdan as he had been summoned to Moscow. He wasn't overly bothered as he was sure that it was now safe to discuss what had been going on and what a success it was.

He was very wrong. He had been called to Moscow, not to visit with like minded politicians, but to be interviewed by the GU. They weren't at all happy with the amount of interest that his project had garnered from the west. Bogdan was instructed to either close the project down or find out what Siberia was like at that time of year.

He left for home, trying to guess which one of his team had grassed him up. They would pay and if it meant that each of them received a visit, so be it.

First things first. He had to demolish the factory and he was going to make it look like someone else did it. Preferably that English woman.

Chapter 86

At last the sea was calming, but K had absolutely no idea where he was. With the wheel still lashed he had decided to get some sleep and so the old boat had just chugged on through the night.

When he woke he immediately noticed that the Corsica was listing quite heavily to the starboard. It had taken on more water than he at first thought.

K tried to find the bilge pump control, but gave up, so he decided not to worry about that for now. He needed food, so he went in search of the instead. He had more luck with this as the galley was quite well stocked.

The Corsica chugged on.

By the time that K was actually ready to face the day and enter the pilot house the sea was once again flat calm. He scanned the horizon and had to take a second look when he thought that he noticed land ahead. It was a way off, but it was definitely there. Wherever 'there' was, he was going to head for it, especially as his fuel was now extremely low.

Another hour passed and K was now following a partially rocky coastline. He needed to find a harbour or at least a jetty. He kept heading south with the coastline on his port side. He needed to send a message to the navy and to Daisy, but there was little point until he knew where he was.

Finally a harbour wall appeared just ahead, so K slowed to a crawl and steered a course for the entrance. He hadn't noted that the tide was out and the harbour was really shallow. As he turned in he noticed the seabed, which only looked like it was a couple of feet from the surface. He immediately threw the boat into reverse, but a vessel this size wasn't going to stop straight away. It drifted inexorably toward the sand and only stopped once it had wedged itself firmly into it.

He was now blocking the harbour entrance so it didn't take long for him to attract interest from several different parties. Mainly boat owners who were waiting to take their craft out.

K decided that acting slightly coy with a dose of friendliness would help the situation along.

"Good morning everybody. Does anyone speak English."

After a few seconds passed with everyone looking at each other, one hand rose.

"Oh hello. My name is K and I'm lost. My boat is out of fuel and I kind of drifted here." A couple of little white lies, but nothing that K felt wasn't justified in the circumstances.

"Hi K. My name's Mike. I'm here on holiday. This is Buggerru by the way."
"Bugger you to mate."
"No. This is Buggerru. That is the name of this town."
"Oh sorry. What country is that?"
"Wow, you are in a bad way aren't you. It's Sardinia."
"Sardinia? Is that in the Med?"

A couple of horns were now being honked and other people were shouting for K to move. At least that is what he assumed they were shouting. There were a few internationally recognised hand signs made, which K found extremely difficult not to replicate. However for the sake of diplomacy he resisted.

"Nearly. It's in the Tyrrhenian, which leads into the med."

"Do you know where I can get fuel?"

"You can get it here, but you're going to have to wait for the tide. That's why no one can get past you."

"Sorry to be a pain, but once I leave here which way is Malta?"

"Turn left and keep the coast line on your port side until you come across a gap. Turn hard a starboard at the gap and then continue to follow the coastline. You will pass another gap and then go on until you see a small island. It doesn't matter which side of you the island ends up, but as soon as you get to it you need to head west south west and that should put you roughly in a line with Malta."

"Thanks Mike. Do you think I should try and alert someone here about my plight?"

"I wouldn't worry. They'll come to you when they're ready."

"Okay and thanks again. I'm sorry that I've ruined your day."

"Well at least I can understand why you have. Most of these people don't speak English, so good luck with them."

Mike reversed his boat and manoeuvred it

back to the jetty. Fortunately most of the others had watched him and decided to do the same. They obviously thought that he knew what was going on and therefore what he did was the thing to do.

Within half an hour, a small craft approached the Corsica and it looked like it had a couple of uniformed officials onboard.

K suddenly remembered that he had three bodies reclining in various positions and at various locations around his vessel, so he made a great effort to try and keep the coastguards or whatever they were occupied, without inviting them onboard. This worked, mainly because they were so bemused by his story that they both felt totally sympathetic toward him. He told them that had loaned the boat from a friend who was a businessman in Marseilles. It was because his girlfriend was stuck on Malta with no way to get off. He elaborated by saying that he'd got lost in a storm last night and that he'd run out of fuel, all of which was true.

At this point his new friend Mike came forward and vouched for K's story. This further distracted the two Italian Coastguards and leant weight to K's story.

The outcome was that he was kindly

requested to remove the Corsica as soon as was practicably possible, to refuel with their blessing and to leave. They obviously wanted to pretend that none of this had officially happened and therefore no official paperwork would need to be generated.

The two officials spoke to the few disgruntled tourists who remained, in their native tongue and this did the trick with regard to finally dispersing them. K, in the meantime went back below, hid the bodies as best he could, made a cup of tea, sent two messages and waited for the tide to turn.

There was a knock on the pilothouse door. It was Mike.

"I'm going to come with you. I think you could do with some help."

"You really don't have to and any way, how are you going to get back?"

"That's easy. The missus will come and get me from wherever we end up. We love a good old mystery tour and we're not in any hurry."

"Well as long as you're sure. I suppose I could use the help and the navigation."

"Let's go Captain."

'I do hope this is going to be alright.' K thought while smiling benignly at his new ship mate.

"Anyway, I told her that you worked for the Secret Service and that sold her completely."

K had to stop himself from going weak at the knees.

Chapter 87

Night time had fallen once again as they approached the Yavuz Sultan Selim Bridge. Dimitri once again turned most of the lights off and switched over to electric power. They were hoping to slide through unseen. This was until Daisy had a brainwave.

"Why don't we go through in broad daylight and when everyone else is going through?"

"I must admit I hadn't thought of that. Okay we'll wait."

"Let's go through mid morning. Hopefully it will be at it's busiest then"

"That's fine by me."

Fortunately there was a marina on the port side prior to the bridge, so they crept into there instead. There didn't seem to be anyone around so they moored up and settled down for the night.

"I do very much appreciate what you are doing for me Dimitri. I'm well aware of your feelings for me and I'm also aware that it can't be easy."

"I'm absolutely fine, thank you. I've had my fill of women over the years, so missing out on one, who I have already bedded anyway, is no problem to me."

"That's not nice Dimitri and I know that it's not what you truly want to say. That's just your male bravado speaking. Please, if you can't be nice, don't speak at all. It hurts when you are horrible."

"I'm sorry Daisy and you are right. It is difficult and although in the eyes of the law, I'm seen as a lowlife, I would like to think that is not how you view me."

"Not at all and you know that. If I truly believed that of you, I wouldn't have gone to bed with you at all."

"I suppose not. Anyway we need to sleep. I'll see you bright and early in the morning."

They made for their respective bunks, but neither of them slept right away. Each thinking of the other and how this escape from Russia was truly going to play out.

The following morning they both ate a light breakfast and took some time to look around before leaving. They realised that they hadn't had the time to appreciate anything of the countries that they'd recently frequented, until now. Even so, they couldn't afford to hang around for too long as they didn't want or need a visit from any official.

"Come on, let's go. We've got plenty of time for sightseeing once we're free."

"I must admit that since I've felt ill, being on the boat doesn't fill me with the joys of spring, especially as we still have a long way to go."

"Maybe not Daisy, but we still have to do it, so let's go."

"You can be a real slave driver, do you know that?" She continued before Dimitri could react. "But I do know that you're looking after our best interests."

"Good. I'm glad to hear it."

"I wonder if anyone has found Andreiv yet? That poor young man didn't deserve any of this."

Dimitri said nothing as there was nothing too say. They'd been over this before and they needed to concentrate on the way forward.

It was a beautiful morning and the sea was perfectly calm. Daisy felt that it was going to be a good day and even the short walk had done her a power of good. She needed to try and keep Dimitri in a good mood as he could make or break her bid for freedom.

They sailed under the Yavuz Sultan Selim Bridge and did their best to blend in with the other watercraft. Unfortunately, this also meant that they had to slow down. Not something that either wanted, but in order to blend, that would be the order of the day.

Chapter 88

The French authorities were briefed by Scotland Yard and they were also told that one British agent was currently involved in trying to extradite another.

It was explained that the Yard had indeed been investigating an international drugs case and that the case had become complicated when it was found that a British Secret Service agent had been kidnapped and taken to Russia. They didn't expand.

The French were not happy with this vague synopsis, but did agree that because of the delicate nature of the investigation, that they would co-operate in anyway that they could and indeed they would cease any further investigation of their own. Of course they wouldn't stop their own investigation and that was mainly due to the fact that the British had fed them a load of baloney.

Either way, K was free from being hounded across international waters and as long as he could steer a straight course was able to continue on his course for Malta, with impunity.

The French had no idea that he was carrying three corpses with him and that one of them was a French citizen. Actually the British didn't either.

He hadn't heard anymore from Daisy, so assumed that she was also on course for their rendezvous.

They rounded the island that Mike had told K to head for and then set a course of west south west.

As it would remain that way for the remainder of the journey Mike decided to take himself off on a tour of the boat, while K remained on watch. He hadn't counted on bumping into three dead people while doing so. K never gave a thought to the fact that MIke would be so thorough with his investigation of the Corsica.

"Hey K or whatever your real name is. Did you know that there are three bodies down here?" Mike shouted excitedly.

'There'll be four if you carry on.' K thought. "Yes I did know. I put them there." K thought that would shut Mike up.

Mike ran back up the steps and asked about a million questions at once, so K just let him rant on until he finally ran out of breath.

Just as he was about to speak he noticed what looked like a Frigate, approaching from dead ahead. He just pointed and said to Mike: "Here comes my ride, hopefully."

Mikes jaw dropped as all the pennies started to drop simultaneously.

"Are you the real James Bond?" Was all that he could whisper.

"Yes." K said with authority. "And you would be doing His Majesty a personal favour if you skuttle this hunk of junk, once your wife has arrived to collect you that is."

"I'll try. If that's really what you want me to do?"

"It is Mike."

The frigate stopped about half a mile from K's boat and a small tender was sent over to him.

He made sure that Mike had contacted his wife and that she knew where she was going and then climbed down on to the small craft. He saluted Mike who instinctively saluted back and the craft turned back to the mothership.

'I've met a real life secret agent. You wait 'til my missus hear's about this.' He then thought, 'She'll never believe me.' He felt quite demoralised. 'Still, I know it's true and I've got a task to complete on behalf of His Majesty's Government.' That thought boyd him up again.

He went in search of the drain plug.

Chapter 89

The Frigate turned about and headed for a position just south of Kythira, Greece.

On board was a suit and that suit contained a rather portly gentleman who, upon his suit wore a fob watch and chain. He also had a hanky that was sitting pertly in his top pocket.

"Well K, what have you got to say for yourself?"

"Hopefully I can explain everything sir."

K proceeded to tell his story, including the part where Alfie volunteered to travel to Paris and help. Something that K announced was invaluable, especially with the language.

He explained that at many times he had to think on his feet and that he felt that he'd done that very well so far.

"So, how do you know where Ms Wilcox is?"

K had no idea what to say to this. He knew that the rules were clear with regard phone usage.

"I'm sorry sir, but I've looked out for Daisy ever since we were children. I won't bore you with her story, but let's just say that she was abused and I did what I could to help."

"Rules are there for a reason K. You could have compromised National security."

"I know sir. All I can say is that if I am given a second chance, I won't let you down again. I love this work and I know that I'm good at it, barring the odd indiscretion of course."

"Well lets just see shall we? You may be able to redeem yourself if your Daisy has some useful intelligence."

"Thank you sir. In that case may I communicate with her? I've lost track of her exact position."

"Do it."

K sent a message, explaining that he'd been picked up by the Navy and where they were headed. Initially he heard nothing.

Chapter 90

Unfortunately, just as K's message came through, it was not Daisy, but Dimitri who read it. He then proceeded to hide the phone under a cushion in the lounge, before making his way back up to the bridge.

Unfortunately for Dimitri, this had all been witnessed by Daisy who unbeknown to him was in the head (the toilet) and had a small but invaluable vantage point. Although he had scanned the room he hadn't realised that a section of the lounge was visible through a gap between the door and frame.

'Now what do I do? Is he just jealous or is he planning something? I need to see that message.'

"Are you alright in there?"

"I'm fine thankyou."

"Are you being sick again?"

"No I'm not. I don't need to be sick to use the toilet, you know. Can I have some space please?"

"Yes, sorry."

Daisy wasted no time in grabbing her phone and reading the last message. She quickly sent one back and then replaced the phone. Her message read:

'Held captive. Dimitri up to something. Last known position passed under Yavuz Sultan Selim Bridge about an hour ago, heading west. Try and track my phone. X'

She went up top to join Dimitri, but couldn't bring herself to speak.

"Are you okay Daisy? You seem distant."

"Oh, I'm just wondering what comes next?" Which, of course she was.

"We get off this boat and start a new life. That's what."

'But where?' Daisy thought worriedly. She tried to smile, but that didn't quite work. Luckily Dimitri didn't notice.

A new message came in, but this time it was to Dimitri. His phone was on silent but it vibrated in his pocket, so he made his way below in order to read it. He asked Daisy to take the wheel for a minute while he went to the head.

The message read:

'Make way to Marmaritsa Beach. Will collect package from there. B.'

Bogdan knew that if he were to rescue his reputation, he had to make this work. He had to take that British spy back to Moscow and make her stand trial for the murder of his old friend.

Dimitri now had to come up with some kind of ruse in order to land his captive on the beach.

'I'll make it sound like the boat has a mechanical problem and that we need to get to an unscheduled landing point.'

Chapter 91

Twenty four hours had passed since the last messages were passed between K and Daisy. The Frigate was at full steam ahead and was weaving it's way through the many Greek Islands. They were in the Aegean Sea and tracking Daisy's phone.

"Sir. They appear to be heading North."

"Where will that take them?"

"On their current course it will be somewhere on the eastern Greek seaboard."

'What's he up to?' K wondered.

"Can we intercept them?"

"We can if we can catch them. They are a little ahead of us."

"Please push."

"Yes sir."

K had never wielded this kind of authority before. It felt good, but it also made him nervous. He couldn't afford to get anything wrong, especially as he was on thin ice personally.

They were now passing Skiros, but it was getting late. The day had flashed past as far as K was concerned, but at least they were able to track Daisy.

***

Dimitri and his almost unsuspecting passenger were approaching Marmaritsa. Daisy had no idea that they had veered off course. She just knew that all was not well. Dimitri had a new sense of purpose about him and he was saying

very little. If Daisy didn't know better she'd say that he was heading on a very distinct course. If only she knew what was

going on. She did not dare ask, as she didn't want him to suspect that she was on to him. She certainly didn't want him to move her phone.

While Dimitri was concentrating she decided send another message:

'Not sure wh...............' The message

ended.

"So, you found your phone. Why didn't you say that you thought it was missing?"

"I just thought that I'd misplaced it and so I looked for it."

"Really? You saw me place it there didn't you?"

"Yes. What's going on Dimitri?"

"There's been a slight change of plan. That's all I can say."

"Why?"

"Let's just say that I've had a better offer."

"How does that affect me?"

"You're my guarantee of safe passage."

"So, I'm not going home then?"

"I'm afraid not, no."

Daisy had to think and fast, but she felt as if her body was slowly turning lead. 'What's happening? Why can't I move?'

"Oh, by the way, I put a little something in your coffee."

"You bastard. Is this all because I love someone else?" Her words were starting to slur.

"You think too highly of yourself Daisy. Just rest and let me take care of you."

"Are you going to kill me?"

"Only if you play up."

Daisy slowly felt herself slumping to the floor. There was nothing that she could do. She was falling asleep. It wasn't an unpleasant feeling.

Dimitri slowed the boat so that he could prepare Daisy for disembarkation. He tied her up and gagged her. He then pressed on toward the bay.

Once again night was falling and Dimitri needed to get ashore before that happened. He didn't know what to expect once they landed as this was going to be a place that he'd never visited before.

***

The other craft was too far ahead for K's comfort.

"Do we have a fast launch that I could take, to try and make up some time?" The question was aimed at the officer who was standing next to K, on the bridge.

"As it happens we do, but I'm afraid I can't let you take it?"
"Who can?"
"We have a launch crew. You're more than welcome to go with them."

"Okay. Can we get going please?"

The loud speaker system crackled into action immediately.

"Launch crew to action stations. Launch crew to action stations."

K asked for directions and then ran to the meeting point.

The first question he asked one of the crew members was how fast the launch could go.

"Forty knots at a push sir."

"Right. In that case can we do forty knots please. I'll navigate."

"With all due respect sir, I think we should let the navigation system navigate. You can just point us in the right direction."

"Okay, let's go."

K was guessing, but he thought that Daisy had approximately one hour on them. The fact that night was fast approaching wasn't helping. He wasn't aware that Dimitri had slowed almost to a crawl for most of the day and the data on the tracker wasn't quite real time.

In reality they were thirty minutes behind.

***

Lizabeta was beached and Dimitri grabbed all the necessary, before slinging Daisy unceremoniously over his shoulder. He then climbed down onto the shingle beach and made his way toward a lane that he'd already noted on his maps app. It was hard going and not just because he had an unconscious woman over his shoulder. He stumbled a couple of times but luckily he didn't drop his cargo.

Eventually the lane hove into view and in the low light Dimitri made his way onto the tarmac.

There was a very indistinct low hum coming from somewhere out at sea, but Dimitri was too busy to pay attention to it.

**

They slowed as they started to turn toward the beach.

"There. Just there. I can see a boat. It looks like it's beached."

They turned the twin engines off for the last few yards and came in alongside the darkened and seemingly abandoned boat. K slipped silently onto the beached craft and started to investigate. After a cursory scout around the bridge, he descended into the darkness of the lounge where he almost immediately found evidence of Daisy. He smelt her perfume first, but then saw her hair brush. Something that she would never have been seen without. The boat was devoid of either of it's occupants.

It was now completely dark outside, so K made his way topside and gestured to the other four to climb ovr the boat and then follow him onto the beach.

***

"Where are you? I am at the rendezvous."

"We're on our way. Getting across the border into Bulgaria wasn't as straightforward as we were hoping."

"Any idea how long you'll be? I'm not sure how long my friend will be unconscious for."

"I'm sure you can keep her amused until we arrive."

"Not funny Bogdan. How long?"

"Listen Dimitri. You are not calling the shots now, do you understand?" Bogdan knew that Dimitri's need of him was reciprocal because he needed to get them both back to Russia in one piece in order for him to save his own skin, but he wasn't about to weaken now.

"I do Bogdan, but you need me just as

much. I need to get away from here as fast as possible."

'I suppose I was asking for that. Dimitri is nobody's fool.'

"We're about thirty minutes away. I am accompanying your rescuers personally, so I'll also be with you soon."

Dimitri thought how it wasn't like that old dinosaur to put himself out there, like this. But then he probably wasn't all that welcome at home either. He didn't say that though.

"Good."
"Will you be easy to find?"

"I've just found a small fishing hut, just off the track at the back of the beach. Assuming that I can get the door open, we'll be in there."
"Okay."

Dimitri dropped Daisy onto the bank that was adjacent to the hut and she let out a small groan.

'Shit, she's coming round.'

He tried the door and fortunately it was unlocked. He quickly grabbed Daisy before she was again fully conscious and slung her inside.

'Now we wait.'

***

"K. Over here."

K approached with his torch.

"There are fresh footprints leading onto this track."

"I see them. They look like male size prints. Where are the female one's?"

"There's definitely only a single set."

K's heart sank. 'What's he done with Daisy? I didn't come this far to take a corpse home.'

"Listen everyone, we have no idea where they are, but they're not too far ahead of us. I'm still counting on there being two of them and therefore I can only guess that Daisy err the woman is being carried. Let's keep it very quiet please."

They carried on up the track and were just about to turn a corner when they heard a vehicle coming from the opposite direction.

They instinctively split into two groups and dive behind the dunes that are on either side of the road. They all watch in silence, but prepare their weapons.

The rather large SUV slid to a halt and in the glow from the headlights the group of three, which included K, on the left hand side of the road could clearly see a small hut. As they watched, the door opened and a man came out. Three men exited the car and stood in a row. The man in the middle spoke. Clearly he was Russian.

"Dimitri old friend. We have arrived to whisk you away. I take it your friend is ready?"

One of K's compatriots translates: "He said that they've arrived to take Dimitri and his friend away."

"Daisy." K couldn't help saying below his breath. 'She's alive.'

"Only the British woman needs to survive, but if we can capture any Russians alive that will just be a bonus."

The lieutenant in charge of the naval group slipped across the road and gave an order for the two on the other side of the road to creep round behind the hut and then to show themselves when the group of three do. He came back to join K and the one other naval recruit on the far side of the track.

"I'm going with the team that are going round the back." K said to the lieutenant.

"That's a very risky thing to do sir."

"Lieutenant, with all due respect, this whole thing is risky and I've come a long way to rescue that young lady."

He tiptoed over the road and joined the other men just as they were about to set off.

The Russian conversation appeared to have ended.

***

Dimitri had gone back inside to try to rouse Daisy and just as he did so Bogdan decided to join them. There were now two Russian sidekicks standing by the car and looking completely bored with whole affair as two shots rang out and two of the SUV's tyres were deflated instantly.

The two would be bodyguards took up positions at either end of the car, facing the direction of fire. They were immediately taken out by the group on the other side of the road who had a clear shot at their backs. This left Bogdan and an as yet unknown number of others inside the cabin.

Because there were no windows, Bogdan decided to very cautiously stick his head out of the door and as he scanned around through the small crack that he'd opened he could see nothing. He couldn't even see the two felled comrades, so he wrongly thought that it was they who had carried out some kind os assassination. He ventured out a little further and as soon as he did, one of the marksmen took aim and fired. He was shot in the head. He dropped immediately and was dragged back into the hut.

K decided that now was a good time to play good cop, so he called out.

"If you walk out now Dimitri, with your hands up, you will be spared."

An answer came back immediately. "And if you come in here Daisy will die. I take it I'm talking to K?"

There was no answer. K had to rethink. He crept forward and took up station just outside the door. He was trying to listen to anything that might give him a clue as to what was going on inside.

"Dimitri. You have lost your ticket home. Why don't you come back to the west with me?"

"Shut up. I need to think."

"About what exactly. You have only one decent choice to make."

K heard movement, then he heard a slap.

"I told you to......"

As he was half way through his speech

K yanked the door open and with the small amount of light available, made a split second decision.

From outside a shot was heard to ricochet.

Chapter 92

The agent stepped through the front door of the Belgravia mews house and straight into the sunlight of a beautiful spring morning. It was a little chilly, but otherwise perfect.

Considering this was the centre of London, the UK's largest sprawling metropolis, it was blissfully quiet, almost. Just the sweet sound of birds singing in the gardens opposite, the gentle woosh of a passing aircraft and the distant hum of traffic.

'D' started every day by thinking about Kevin and the way that he'd died in pursuit of her freedom. Only once since that day had she stopped to consider the fact that he must have loved her as much as she loved him. She would not allow that sentiment to cloud her judgement ever again.

The bullet that had ricocheted off the wall of that stone hut, took both him and Dimitri simultaneously. The fact that without both of them, she wouldn't be where she was today were also thoughts that haunted her. The thought of Dimitri and his reason for rescuing her, could always be dismissed easily, although it was because of him that she relished the thought of taking on this new mission.

As for Kevin the least that she could do was continue to live as she had always promised she would, in his image.

***

Although the GU had officially requested the closure of the 'new' factory (this was for the benefit of the west), they could it's potential worth, so it was kept open.

A rumour about the factory had leaked to the west, but this wasn't known by the GU. Someone from the west would have to investigate the truth behind the rumour.

With her fluent Russian and her knowledge of what had gone on before, she was the perfect candidate to seek out the truth and if possible destroy whatever is found.

'D' had names and places. The fact that they'd stopped to collect her dossier from the Lizabeta, would help immensely, in her quest.

THE END
(Probably)

Epilogue

Mike never did manage to find the bung and skuttle the old tug, but after giving it some serious thought, his wife did rescue him.

If you see a rusty old boat by the name of Mirabelle floating around the med somewhere, could you finish the job?

Don't worry about the passengers as they flatly refuse to get off.

Printed in Great Britain
by Amazon

37246568R00381